THE SONG AND THE SWORD

29th sept 2022

Dear
Kathryn

T. Chevalier

THE SONG AND THE SWORD

ISABELLE CHEVALLOT

Published by Fetterlock Publishing England

Isabelle Chevallot has asserted her right under
the Copyright, Designs and Patents Act 1988
to be identified as the author of this work

Author's website www.isabellechevallot.com

ISBN 978-1-9995910-9-0

A catalogue record for this book is available from the
British Library and the American Library of Congress

Cover design Alejandro Colucci

Typeset in Palatino by
Palimpsest Book Production Ltd, Falkirk, Stirlingshire

For Tabby, Alex and Basty

1.

Eleanor

The wind tore at her clothes and hair, a salt spray lashed her face and the oceans of her heart and mind churned the reality that Hugh was lost to her forever.

'Let me hold back your hair, Lady Eleanor,' said Matilda.

She brushed Matilda away with her arm. Much as she loved her maid, she hated people fussing over her. She leaned over the side of the ship and retched into the sea below. There was nothing but bile left in her stomach. When at long last the dreadful feeling of sickness had abated, she lifted her weary head to a dismal grey dawn breaking on the horizon. The rain was coming down in torrents. Never had she been out on a more evil-looking morning. A tainted day.

Shivering under the shelter of the awning, she clung onto the wooden rail in a white-knuckled grip. Her head swam again as she stared down at the agitated mass of froth and murky sea below and nausea roiled in the pit of her stomach. She did not know what was making her feel worse: the undulating sea or the terror of her impending marriage.

She and her father had endured a tumultuous four days at sea, their ship buffeted by relentless moaning winds and lashed by angry waves.

Her father kept his sharp blue eyes fixed on the horizon. A baron of Normandy, he had a cap of dark-brown hair, greying a little at the temples. Tall and broad-shouldered, he had once been an attractive man, but now he was running to fat.

Her heart missed a beat at her first glimpse of the white cliffs of Dover looming in the distance through the grey gloom as the ship drew nearer. Sheer chalk cliffs towered fearfully high and a huge castle with soaring battlements and turrets perched on its precipice.

Her father issued directions to the captain. 'We are already a week overdue because of stormy weather. We will make straight for the shore so that the wedding need not be further delayed.'

The captain helped Eleanor and her father down a rope ladder into a waiting rowing boat. She didn't want his help but she retched as she glanced down at the swirling water that threatened to swallow her up should she slip on the rungs. When they were safely seated in the boat, the coffers containing her dowry were lowered carefully onto the bench beside them. Several sailors pulled away from the side of the ship.

She cast a last look over her shoulder at the great hull of the *Lady Anneis* with its castles at the bow and stern, its tangle of complicated rigging and its two masts with the flags of Normandy flapping in the wind. Matilda waved down at her from the deck; a small figure bundled up in a cloak. Eleanor waved back then turned away abruptly, a lump in her throat.

They passed the journey in a sodden silence. She stared intently at the foaming cataracts created by the oars pulling against the sea. It seemed her father had nothing to say to her, not even a few words of comfort or reassurance. And, for her part, she was too angry and upset to attempt conversation. She drew her woollen cloak around her, attempting to keep out the damp and the chill but she still felt horribly cold. After so many days at sea, she couldn't wait to feel solid ground beneath her feet.

Presently, they found themselves in a busy harbour teeming with life. On the wharves, sailors unloaded cargo from small boats, a stream of filthy oaths floating in the air around them. This was her first glimpse of the English port of Dover. The sailors and the fishy stench of the harbour failed to endear her to the town.

She thought of the life she had left behind in Normandy. She would have given anything to be back on her beloved horse, Golda, roaming her father's lands. Only the previous week she had been hunting with her cousins in the dappled sunlight of the ancient oak forest. High up in the soaring boughs of the trees, the birds had sung out with the promise of spring. She ached to be back there with her favourite hound, Fulk, breathing in the sweet smell of damp earth and wood, listening out for the shudder of foliage in the tangled undergrowth, the only sound that betrayed the noiseless deer. More than anything, she longed to be engrossed in a thrilling tale of adventure in her father's library, for reading was her other great passion.

All too quickly, the boat drew close to the wharf. The waves slapped against the mussel-studded walls of the harbour. An alarming thud as the boat docked winded her. One of the sailors leapt out and onto the wharf and secured the vessel. Another offered a calloused hand to help her out of the boat. She accepted reluctantly. Finally, she stood on the jetty on weak, uncertain legs and with the unpleasant sensation that the earth was still undulating beneath her.

The baron turned his attention to the captain and barked out instructions about the precious cargo in the coffers: her dowry, which consisted of vast quantities of gold and diamonds.

A short, thick-set man walked towards them with a self-important gait, his dripping hair plastered to his forehead. He had a pale, heavy face. Somehow, she took an immediate dislike to the man. A long woollen cloak hung about his shoulders. Behind him a flock of men awaited his orders. They all had the same pallid, unhealthy look about them.

'Welcome, Lord Adelard,' said the short man with a gracious bow. 'Allow me to introduce myself. I am Baron Rolf's steward, Arthur. He has tasked me with escorting you to the castle.'

There was a clip-clop of approaching horses. A horse litter, pulled by a team of four white palfreys drew up beside the wharf. It had red velvet seats and a velvet brocade canopy and curtains.

'Your litter to the citadel is ready,' said the steward. 'Lord Rolf awaits your arrival with impatience.'

The man scarcely acknowledged her. She glared at him, but he didn't even notice. Feeling as insignificant as a serving girl, she trailed behind her father and the steward.

'I should like the coffers to travel in our litter,' said her father. 'That way I can keep an eye on them.'

'Very good, my lord,' said the steward with a bow.

Once installed in the litter, out of the rain and the cold, Eleanor threw off her sodden cloak. 'The heavens themselves have opened!'

Her father didn't look up, but merely snorted. 'I'm reliably informed this is quite normal for England.'

She was filled with longing for the warm spring in Normandy that she had been obliged to leave behind. She peered out through a gap in the drapes. Outside, it still rained heavily, giving the sprawling thatched wattle and daub houses a forlorn look. It didn't help that the houses had been built very close together and blocked out what little natural light there was. The sky above the roofs was gloomy with menace. The narrow streets were awash with a swill of dirty water. People scurried about in the deluge, ankle deep, sheltering where they could under the overhanging eaves.

The horses slackened their pace on the approach to what looked like the main gate of the town, where they queued for a while behind a pair of carts. As they passed under the arch, she looked up at skeletal wretches hanging in cages, crouching against the weather. She shivered at their witless shrieks. High above them, atop spikes, sat two putrid heads. Their swollen sightless eyes seem to bore into her. It could only be an ill omen. She shuddered involuntarily.

As though noticing her for the first time, her father cocked one grey eyebrow at her and shook his head in disapproval. 'Good God, you'd better smarten up before you meet Rolf. No man could want to marry such a pitiful creature!'

She glared at him but sat up straight all the same and smoothed out her crumpled dress as best she could.

Her father's expression was stern until a smile softened his face. 'Come now, you knew this day would come. You are a woman now and ripe for marriage. This is an excellent match for you, for the family. Baron Rolf is one of King Richard's favourites after all.'

It was no news to her that she was expected to

marry advantageously. It was her duty to do so. But it didn't make being forced to marry and spend the rest of her life with a stranger any easier. 'But I love Hugh and he loves me,' she countered. 'And he comes from a good family!' She and Hugh had fallen in love after he had come to squire in her father's castle.

Her father sighed. 'Now you know that is just childish thinking. You understand nothing about the real world!'

More like he didn't understand her! Angry tears pricked her eyes. Hugh was the only man she had ever met who had properly listened to her and displayed curiosity and interest in what she thought and how she felt. To keep herself from crying she turned away from her father and concentrated on the passing landscape. They travelled across an unwelcoming stretch of land strewn with torn tree stumps where nothing grew but ragged grass. The horses gathered pace up a steep incline. Her heart was in her mouth; before long she would be in her new home.

The stark grey walls of an imposing fortress came into view. It was perched on the summit of a precipice and looked to be a dismal place. The sky above it had an evil look about it. A sense of foreboding chilled her.

Minutes later, the horses stopped on the edge of a wide murky moat that surrounded the castle. The steward exchanged a few words with the gatekeeper, and the drawbridge lowered with the screech of rusted metal chains. The horses thundered across it, then through a narrow passageway. Above were the narrow slits of a fighting gallery over the gatehouse and she thought she saw the glint of steel arrowheads in the gloom. Then they passed under another archway into an open courtyard surrounded by fishponds and pigpens. The horse litter rattled through a second gate, then trundled to a halt outside a heavily buttressed rectangular keep with turrets that seemed to stretch up to the very heavens.

A servant helped her and her father down from the litter and the coffers were offloaded. The steward ushered them up a staircase on the outside of the keep to the first floor. Here, they were kept waiting in the driving rain for a guard to open the massive iron-bound door.

'Lady Beatrice instructs that the lady be shown up to her quarters to wash and change her clothes after her long journey,' said the steward. He waved at a tall graceful woman who appeared in the doorway. 'If the lady would follow Lady Cecily.'

Cecily surveyed her with huge almond-shaped green eyes. Her long pale-gold hair glistened. She was dressed becomingly in a cobalt-blue silk kirtle, tight-fitting to her hips. She swept a disdainful glance over Eleanor's crumpled dress.

Eleanor was painfully conscious of her dishevelled appearance. She couldn't help feeling envious of the other woman's beauty and poise.

'I trust you have had a good journey,' said Cecily. 'If you will follow me.' Her face broke into a wide smile that revealed a perfect set of teeth and lit up her beautiful eyes.

She followed Cecily through a labyrinth of torchlit stone passageways and up a steep spiral staircase to the third floor of the keep.

'This is your chamber,' said Cecily. 'Lady Beatrice requests your presence after you have washed and changed.' She turned on her heel and disappeared down the passageway leaving Eleanor alone.

Eleanor found herself in a large, draughty room. It was sparsely furnished, with a huge fireplace facing the bed. Instinctively, she moved towards the fire to warm her cold, damp hands and face. The warmth of the flames comforted her skin. She looked around, taking in every inch of her surroundings. It was an austere room with bare walls that appeared to close in on her, as dreary and claustrophobic as a prison cell. Her heart sank. Back home, bright wall hangings decorated her bedchamber, which was south-facing and flooded with sunlight. In contrast this room was cheerless and would have been cold if not for the fire blazing in the hearth. It gave her some reassurance to see that the trunks containing her clothes, shoes and familiar trinkets from home had been brought up and now stood under the window.

A sharp knock at the door made her jump. It was Lady Cecily, come to inform her that a bath was ready for her in the adjoining chamber.

Eleanor spent the next hour languishing in a warm bath filled with fresh herbs. A serving girl washed her with a soft sponge and rinsed her skin and hair with rosewater. It was wonderful to be clean again, to wash the tang of the sea out of her hair and escape the rank smell of her own vomit.

Presently Cecily returned and, reluctantly, Eleanor climbed out of the bath. Cecily dried her with a towel and dragged a comb through her knotty hair. She brought her a fresh chemise with tight sleeves from her trunk. Eleanor dressed quickly, conscious of her naked, childlike body.

Cecily brought Eleanor's green silk bliaut from the chest and helped her into the voluminous gown, which was cut in one piece from the neck to the hem with wide sleeves at the wrists. Lacing Eleanor up tight at the sides to accentuate her slender figure, she knotted a golden girdle that glistened with precious gems about her hips. Eleanor slipped on a pair of golden silk slippers.

Eleanor sat shivering with her back to the fire to better dry her hair. Meanwhile Cecily attended to Eleanor's face and applied a fine powder of lily root to whiten her complexion and dried flowers of the saffron plant as a rouge. She finished off with a smudge of red paint on her lips. Looking at herself in the mirror, Eleanor had never felt so grown up.

When her hair was dry, Cecily divided the tresses and wove them into two fat plaits interwoven with golden thread. Finally, she arranged a gossamer-thin veil over Eleanor's head and set her diamond-studded diadem over the top to secure it in place.

'If you will follow me, I shall take you to Lady Beatrice's apartments.' Cecily favoured her with another of her dazzling smiles.

They entered a lavish room hung with bright wall hangings depicting the story of Paris and Helen of Troy. Lady Beatrice sat on a high-backed chair at the far end of the chamber, deep in conversation with one of her ladies-in-waiting. Eleanor knew it was her, because of her resemblance to the portrait of Rolf she had been sent ahead of her betrothal. Beatrice was a small neat woman, dressed in a magnificent gown of scarlet brocade that was turned down at the sleeves revealing a rich fur lining. Her long dark tresses, streaked here and there with grey, were parted in the centre and plaited, and a golden coronet adorned her head. Still an attractive woman despite her advancing years, she surveyed Eleanor with vivid blue eyes. Eleanor was not usually shy but now a crippling wave of bashfulness swept over her.

'Welcome to England, Lady Eleanor,' said Lady Beatrice in a silky voice. 'May I introduce you to Lady Millicent.' She gestured to the woman beside her. 'I trust that Lady Cecily has seen to your comfort and your chamber is to your liking.' Smiling broadly, Lady Beatrice revealed a good set of pearly white teeth, but Eleanor discerned no warmth in her eyes.

'Thank you, Lady Beatrice.' Remembering her manners, Eleanor curtseyed hurriedly, painfully conscious that her colour was rising. She looked from one woman to the other. Both women seemed to sense her unease. Lady Millicent, who could not have been more than a few years older than her, was tall and attractive in a proud, haughty sort of way, with even features and pouting lips. She had the air of one who had been born bored. She shot Eleanor a faintly supercilious smile.

'Indeed, it is a beautiful room and Lady Cecily has been very kind,' said Eleanor. She found it harder and harder to think of something to say. Lingering awkwardly in the doorway, she wrung her hands.

'Very good,' said Beatrice. 'We will now join Baron Rolf and your father for dinner.'

Eleanor followed the women through the passageways and down the spiral staircase, passing a myriad of smaller rooms.

The Great Hall was a vast elongated chamber with a vaulted arched ceiling. Huge fires blazed in the hearths at either end and the walls were covered with tapestries of silver and gold silk. On one wall, the tapestry represented the Twenty-Four Elders of the Apocalypse being serenaded by musicians with lutes, lyres and rebecs. On another was depicted a hunting scene with centaurs, lions and hounds.

The silverware on the long tables glinted in the candlelight. The air was rich with the scent of sweet cherry wood burning in the hearths. Beatrice indicated that she should sit beside her husband-to-be, Baron Rolf. Her breath caught in her throat. It was the first time she had set eyes on Lord Rolf. She knew he was five years older than her, but he looked older than she had expected and had the build of a man. He wore his tawny hair in long ringlets, with a fringe plastered down on his forehead in an arrangement of curls, emphasising his heavy brow and beak of a nose. She made to greet her prospective husband, but he looked up with cold blue eyes, gave her the merest nod, and then turned away, resuming his conversation with the nobleman sitting beside him.

'I have petitioned his majesty the king to declare jousts two or three times a year,' said Rolf. He took a long draught from his goblet of wine. 'So that every knight might come to the lists and tourney against each other. He welcomed the suggestion and indeed we shall be hosting a joust here at Dover Castle in a couple of months.'

'A joust?' Eleanor finally summoned the courage to speak. 'How exciting! Will you be competing?' Her words hung in the air for a moment but her future husband and the lord beside him paid her no heed. She wanted to shake them, to make them look at her, but of course she didn't, only a passive role had ever been expected of her – or indeed been allowed her.

At that moment, the delicious smell of roasting meat wafted in from the open door. The squires and pages brought in the feast: a great platter with a boar's head garlanded with bay leaves and with a glazed apple in its mouth, accompanied by platters of various roasted vegetables.

'Once upon a time, the honourable deeds of

England's knights were legendary throughout Christendom.' The lord next to Rolf fingered his long white beard thoughtfully. 'The burning question is, when will the king lead the charge to win back Jerusalem from the infidels.'

Rolf brought down his goblet onto the table with a crash. 'It is about time something was done! What do the knights of England but squander their lives and talent playing at dice? We must give them something to aspire to. If we abandon them to idleness, they shall be open to seditious thoughts – which inevitably translate to rebellious deeds. After all, what are words but bellows that kindle the sparks.'

The lord nodded his white head. 'You speak the truth. Loose talk in the taverns fosters an interest in state affairs, fanning the aspirations of the lowborn and encouraging conspiracy.'

Eleanor turned to the withered little man with wiry-white hair who occupied the seat on the other side of her. He had a grey haggard face. 'What a splendid banquet we have set before us!' she said, forcing herself to stay cheerful.

The man blinked back at her with rheumy blue eyes, crumpling up his wrinkled face in an effort to hear what she was saying.

She tried again. 'Delicious food.' She gestured at the platter of roast boar and vegetables set before them.

The man gave a slow nod.

She gave up, weary of the effort, and held her silence

for the duration of the meal and occupied herself with studying the hunting scene hanging on the opposite wall to prevent the tears welling in her eyes. Try as she might, she could barely bring herself to eat a morsel. She had lost her appetite despite her great hunger and the lavish banquet set before her.

Beatrice shot a critical glance in her direction. 'Pray eat, my dear. You look wan after your journey. We would not have you sickening for something.' She smiled broadly.

'Alas, she is not a good traveller, I fear,' said her father. He shot Eleanor a reproachful look.

There was a momentary lull in the conversation around them. It was as though everybody had heard Beatrice's remarks, and it seemed as if the entire table turned their heads to look at her. Under their gaze she felt the heat rise to her cheeks and she forced herself to swallow her embarrassment.

'We are at the mercy of the whims of our children,' said Beatrice. 'My Rolf is headstrong, overly fond of swordplay, feasting and hunting. If his father were still alive, he would have brought him in hand. I try my best, of course.'

Rolf's face darkened, but he continued his conversation with his neighbour.

Eleanor's father nodded. 'Much as they are everything to us, children can be such a thorn in one's side.'

'Rolf is a trial to me, I confess. His father was a great man, the kind of man one could entrust with anything. Indeed, the late King Henry entrusted him with this castle and now King Richard has bestowed that honour upon Rolf.'

The rich food stuck in Eleanor's throat and her tender stomach gurgled disconcertingly. The bitter English wine was barely palatable and made her eyes water.

She struggled to follow the conversation around the table. As the wine flowed, the babel of voices and laughter in the Great Hall grew louder and the songs coming from the musicians' gallery became increasingly raucous.

'Rolf, you neglect Lady Eleanor.' Beatrice cut into her son's conversation. 'It is a sorry welcome you offer her.'

Eleanor cringed. There was a strained silence. Rolf's hand, which was resting on the table, stiffened suddenly and his lip lifted like a dog about to bare his teeth, but then he subsided with a snort and laughed instead. A captivating smile gave to his face all that it lacked before, but the smile was not directed to her.

Suddenly, she was stricken by a desolate weeping in a lonely place deep down inside her. The thought of a lifetime separated from her beloved Hugh and being this man's wife was intolerable. A page set her pudding before her, but the spiced ginger cake stuck in her throat and she had to wash it down with a draught of wine.

After supper was finished, Cecily escorted her back to her chamber and helped her undress.

When Cecily had finally gone, she rummaged in her trunk until eventually she found the locket that contained a lock of Hugh's hair. Having prised it open, she flung herself down full length across the bed and wept inconsolably into the pillows with Hugh's soft lock of hair twisted around her fingers.

2.

Hugh

Embers burned low in the hearth and candlelight flickered and danced along the walls of his mother's chamber. He knelt beside her prostrate body, his thick head of dark hair bowed in prayer. Her limp hand lay motionless in his. Her skin felt as dry and lifeless as parchment. Her face had sunken in recent months as a result of her prolonged illness and she was no more than a shell of her former self. The kernel that had been his beloved mother had withered away. The sparkle in her eyes had died and she stared up blankly at the painted ceiling with unseeing eyes.

It seemed to him that he was cursed to remain in this moment, forever bearing witness to his mother's suffering. Ever since she had first fallen ill, some six months before, his world had been crumbling. He came daily for his vigil. It was his wish that his mother should not be alone. She let out a small cry of agony and a tear trickled down his face. Ashamed, he rubbed at his eyes with his sleeve.

Barking hounds outside in the courtyard encroached on the silence of his mother's chamber and summoned him back to everyday life in the castle. He got to his feet and kissed his mother's forehead in tender farewell, but she didn't stir.

'Where is that wretched boy?' his father bellowed down in the courtyard. 'Must we be forever waiting for him?'

He hurried down the stone staircase, anxious to avoid another scolding from his father.

'For heaven's sake, boy, stop snivelling!' His father was a tall, athletic man with a pinched, severe face and iron-grey locks.

Hugh felt himself flush to the roots of his hair, but he wiped his eyes and bit his tongue. If he retorted, he would be in for a lashing.

'When will you grow up to be a man? You were always tied to your mother's apron strings!'

'I cannot fathom why Hugh spends so much time moping about in our mother's chamber,' pitched in William. William was his older brother, a tall youth with sullen blue eyes, a thatch of blond straw-like hair and a crop of manly bristles on his jaw.

Hugh glared at his brother, doing his best to suppress the anger that surged in his blood.

'Hugh has always been sentimental,' scoffed his father. 'He is no spawn of mine. He is his mother's child. She indulged such nonsense. Whereas you, Will, have grown to be a fine young man any father would be proud of.' He gave William an affectionate slap on the shoulder.

Hugh's stomach clenched involuntarily. For as long as he could remember he had been on the sharp end of his father's tongue. Over the years, it had chipped away at him like a stonemason's chisel.

'Make haste, boy!' said his father.

Hugh swallowed his anger, tossed a heavy woollen cloak about his shoulders and harnessed his horse.

Though it was mid-morning, it was almost as dark as night outside and the skies wept. But the dogs were not deterred. Frantic with excitement, they pulled at their leashes.

The procession passed through the gatehouse and across the drawbridge. Once they had crossed the moat, his father's steward, Henry, a grizzled giant with a thick head of black hair, blew the horn and they were off. The dogs darted into the undergrowth with the horses in hot pursuit.

～

Later that afternoon, he was in the stable when William came to find him. His brother looked very pleased with himself. 'Father summons you to the Great Hall,' he said with a smirk. 'You are to attend upon the beauty, Lady Bethany, and her estimable father.'

Hugh scowled at his brother, hung up the saddle he had been cleaning and made his way to the Great Hall, a dismal sense of doom settling in his stomach.

He found Bethany and her father seated in the high-backed chairs in front of the fire. His own father was seated beside them.

'At last! There you are, my boy!' Sir Clarenbald scratched his bald scalp with a great hairy paw of a hand.

As was the custom, Hugh lowered his head in greeting to his prospective father-in-law. Then he kissed the clammy little hand Bethany proffered him with as much enthusiasm as he could muster and smiled weakly.

Bethany was a tall girl with a pointed face, wide at the temples and narrow at the chin. Her eyes were sharp and on the small side and her narrow mouth was shut into a hard, hot line. She wore her dark brown hair in two thick plaits. Given to plumpness, she was prinked out in the latest fashion for long pendulous sleeves.

Hugh brought the guests a jug of water for them to wash their hands then filled their goblets with wine.

'We were just saying how we would set a date for the marriage next year when Bethany comes of age,' said Sir Clarenbald, stiff as a corpse on a gibbet.

'Lady Bethany will live here after the marriage, on that we are agreed,' said Hugh's father.

'I cannot impress upon you enough the need to cosset my darling daughter,' Sir Clarenbald said to Hugh. 'She has been used to getting things the way she likes them. Life would be very ill should her wants be frustrated.'

As if to emphasise this point, Lady Bethany pouted and let out a petulant sigh. 'I do get out of sorts,' she conceded. She stroked the long ears of the silky little dog that lay sleeping on her lap. 'But Father is careful not to upset me.'

'Quite right, my darling,' crowed her besotted father. 'If you should become ill, I shall hold Hugh entirely responsible!'

Hugh watched his own father lift a languid eyebrow. His father would have never allowed himself to be put upon by any woman, but he seemed happy enough for his son to wait on Bethany. Hugh had no illusions: all that interested his father was the considerable dowry Sir Clarenbald was offering as part of the marriage settlement. No matter that he had no desire to marry Bethany – this was irrelevant as far as his father was concerned. His mother would have understood his feelings. Having someone on his side of the tilt rail at that moment would have meant the world to him, but he was without an ally and condemned to listen to them prattling away about his future without him having the slightest say.

As Hugh refilled Bethany's goblet, a miniscule drop of wine splashed on her hand. Bethany let out a little cough, showing her displeasure and flashed her tiny eyes at him. He cringed. William would take great pleasure in seeing him manipulated by this harpy. Life would not be worth living if he had to marry her.

~

That evening, fires blazed in both the hearths of the smoky Great Hall at Eynsford Castle. Minstrels entertained the company with bawdy, rollicking songs on the drums and harp. Hugh's father was drunk almost every night. He surrounded himself with hard-drinking men and tonight was no exception. The hall rang with coarse laughter and foul-mouthed cursing. The frivolity of the occasion left a bitter taste in Hugh's mouth. Reluctantly, he took his place with the rest of the squires and stable boys next to the fire. His heart lurched when he thought of his mother suffering on her deathbed upstairs in the turret of the castle.

At the high table, his father pulled a beautiful young widow onto his knee and she let out a giggle. The men around him shouted with drunken cheers and laughter.

'My father has already lined up a replacement for my mother,' said Hugh under his breath to Bardolf, the fair-haired stable boy with ruddy freckled cheeks, sat beside him.

Bardolf nodded sympathetically, his blue eyes bright in the firelight. 'And with the poor mistress on her sick bed too!'

A page ladled broth into Hugh's bowl and heaped

a pudding of pork and eggs flavoured with sage onto his plate.

When Hugh had eaten his fill, he downed the cup of wine set before him and then drained the next one just as quickly when the steward refilled it. He drank greedily, willing the rich tangy liquid to take away his pain as he stared mesmerised by a faggot blazing in the hearth.

Dogs slunk about the tables on the lookout for scraps. His hound, Orry, rested his muzzle in the crook of his arm and gave him a baleful look. He reached under the table and fed Orry some pork rind and tousled his matted fur.

Half an hour later, he began to feel pleasantly exhilarated. He toasted enthusiastically with the stable boys and laughed heartily at their bawdy jokes. He was just beginning to think that the evening might not be so bad after all, when his father approached the table shaking his grey head and William swaggered over behind him, a malicious smile upon his lips.

Hugh sensed danger and braced himself for the onslaught; his father had always been a mean-tempered drunk. His eyes were as black as thunder. 'When will you make something of yourself, whelp? You were sobbing into your sleeve earlier, like a small child and now you are in your cups with wine running out of your mouth. You disgust me!'

Indignation rose in Hugh's belly like nausea, threatening to explode. He struggled to his feet.

'I'm not drunk, Father.' He made a concerted effort to steady his voice. 'I am merely enjoying the evening like everybody else.'

'I don't know whether you heard, little brother,' said William with slow venom. 'Lady Eleanor will marry Baron Rolf in two days' time. And we have been invited to attend the wedding.'

With a great effort Hugh controlled himself. 'Is that so.'

William made it his mission in life to sting. 'You were always dangling after her, weren't you?'

Hugh's fingers closed around the edges of the trestle table like a vice and he clenched his teeth. After a minute, he succeeded in gulping down his wrath and said very sweetly, 'At least dear Eleanor was spared the indignity of marrying a fatuous cretin like you, brother.'

William coloured and seemed disappointed he would not get a rise out of Hugh. But then he rallied and grinned stupidly, enjoying wholeheartedly the discomfort he had caused. 'Thank the heavens Father has arranged a match with Lady Bethany for you. Such a pretty, kind girl!' He stood back a moment, his eyes gleaming with perverse amusement.

His father undulated towards him. 'You're an ungrateful bastard, aren't you?' His voice had a mocking quality. 'Why, son, I did it all for you! I thought you'd like Bethany . . . You're spoiled, self-indulgent . . .'

Anger took over Hugh. 'I told you I loved Eleanor

and I wanted to marry her, and you laughed in my face!'

His father stared at him in disbelief. His eyes narrowed and his voice became hard. 'You're deluded. Why would Eleanor's father want his daughter to marry you? You forget that he knew you well after you had spent two years under his roof. He can't have failed to notice that you will never amount to anything! You're a disgrace to our family!'

Hugh's anger had him close to tears. 'You fondle a widow upon your knee while Mother is upstairs dying and I'm a disgrace!'

His father's eyes dripped contempt. 'Be careful . . . You're always on at me when I'm having a good time, just like your simpering bitch of a mother.'

Hugh sprang to his feet, oversetting his goblet and leaving the wine to drip unheeded onto the rushes on the floor. 'Don't talk about her like that . . . I'll rip you to pieces . . .'

'You aren't man enough . . . you haven't got the guts . . .' weighed in William, beside himself with glee.

His father waggled a finger at him. 'Now you watch yourself! You haven't the guts to make any man proud of you!' Then he broke down in ridiculing laughter. He mimicked Hugh's voice. *'I'll rip you to pieces!'* He waved his hand in a gesture of derision. 'I'd like to see you try!'

His father's cronies at the high table fell about laughing.

The Song and the Sword

Bardolf put a warning hand on Hugh's arm.

It took all Hugh's self-control to sit down again.

His father returned to his seat at the high table and resumed his wooing of the rich widow. William followed him, looking highly pleased with himself.

A disagreeable rasping voice broke into song somewhere at the high table. The singer was clearly the worse for drink, for sometimes he forgot the words, but whenever this happened the men around him applauded and pounded the table appreciatively with their fists. Some of the men were so overcome by the moment they pushed back their chairs and rose to their feet, lurching and swaying and clutching at each other to keep their balance, their faces flushed crimson with wine.

Hugh cradled his head in his hands, full of self-pity. 'I cannot bring myself to think of Eleanor marrying a man like Rolf,' he said to Bardolf. 'And my father insists that I marry that loathsome Lady Bethany.'

Bardolf put a comforting arm about Hugh's shoulder, but he was beyond consolation. He took another swig of wine from his goblet. Toying with his knife, he carved a notch on the edge of the wooden table. 'You must excuse me. I am growing maudlin. I love Lady Eleanor and I would have given the world to marry her. The moment I laid eyes upon her when I went to squire for her father, I knew at once I would never love another. What is more, she felt the same about me. The thought of her father forcing her to marry Rolf sinks me into the lowest of spirits.'

A page brought more wine, but he put his palm across the top of his goblet. His head was spinning. 'I better go and sleep off the wine.'

He pulled himself to his feet and wove his way out of the Great Hall through the shouting and lurching throng. As he passed the high table, William put out an outstretched leg on the sly, calculated to trip him.

Hugh stumbled but didn't fall. He cursed under his breath but refused to snap at the bait. Instead, he made for the spiral staircase and the gloomy quarters he shared with his brother where he collapsed into his bunk. Sleep eluded him. And he spent a wakeful night blazing with hatred for his father and brother and grieving the loss of his dying mother. The last of his boyhood gone, he felt sure he was doomed. Sick as he was with his heart's longing for Eleanor, he tossed and turned and grappled with the horror of her forthcoming marriage to Baron Rolf and the melancholy prospect of his marriage to Lady Bethany.

3.
The Wedding

At the first light of dawn coming in through the gaps in the curtains, Eleanor rose to bathe her eyes so that no one would know she had spent yet another night in weeping. Hands shaking, she carefully stowed Hugh's precious lock of hair away in the golden locket she had brought from Normandy specifically for the purpose.

'Lady Eleanor . . .' Cecily walked into the chamber. 'Lady Beatrice has bid me help you prepare for the wedding ceremony.'

Eleanor turned her head away to hide her grief. It was an unwelcome reminder of what was to come: she was to be married this very day to Baron Rolf. The thought of it filled her with an icy dread.

Cecily brought Eleanor's salmon-pink silk gown from the chest. She helped her into the garment, which was tight-fitting to the hips in the latest fashion and then fell in a profusion of folds to the ground. The sleeves were tight to the elbows where they expanded into cuffs so long they brushed the floor. They were decorated with bands of embroidery heavy with precious stones. Eleanor slipped a pair of salmon-pink silk slippers over her stockinged feet.

Cecily attended to Eleanor's face and braided her hair. Placing a veil over her head, she secured it with a golden diadem studded with gems.

Eleanor thought of the coffers of gold and diamonds her father would have to part with to seal the marriage deal. He was probably regretting relinquishing his precious metal and stones more than parting with her, she reflected with a sudden stab of pain.

She followed Cecily down the spiral staircase and into the chapel. It was a lofty and spacious chamber with soaring arches, groined vaults and richly decorated wall arcades. But she barely noticed her surroundings. She walked down the aisle towards her father and her future husband as if she were in a dream – a nightmare.

A congregation of forty or so nobles were in attendance. The voices of the crowd fell away as they craned their necks to catch their first glimpse of the woman who was to marry the baron. For a fleeting moment she discerned Hugh's face stricken with sadness where he stood towards the back of the congregation. Her heart lurched with unbearable longing for what could never be.

It was then she caught sight of Baron Rolf who stood by the altar. It was the first time she had seen him standing and she perceived at once that he was tall and of immensely powerful build. As she was brought to stand beside him, she noticed she was positively dwarfed by him. She felt puny by his side – like a child. Indeed, at fifteen, she was barely more than a child. His blue eyes lingered on her for a moment, his face unreadable, and then he turned abruptly away. Her heart sank to her stomach. Dressed in polished chain mail, befitting the formality of the occasion, Rolf stood proud with his crested helmet in the crook of his arm. A flowing scarlet cloak of fine samite hung about his shoulders emblazoned with a black eagle with wings outstretched on a silver shield. She followed his gaze and noticed with dismay that he was smiling at Lady Cecily.

The priest, a short bald man with a wizened face, officiated over the ceremony and murmured the prerequisite words. But she heard nothing save the sound of her own blood pounding in her ears.

Then suddenly her father pulled at her arm and nudged her to speak. She stammered out her consent in a small voice that seemed not to belong to her. 'B-behold my oath that I d-do take thee to wed.'

Rolf forced a ring onto her finger. She wanted him to like her, but she got a sickening feeling that he didn't. She hazarded a smile in his direction, but he did not return it. Dropping her eyes hurriedly to her feet, she felt the blood drain from her cheeks.

A harpist took up a psalm and the congregation rose to their feet to sing, but she found that her mouth was dry and the words stuck in her throat.

At last, a fanfare of trumpets declared the ceremony over and the herald announced the start of the wedding feast. There was a steady hum of voices behind her as the lords and ladies of the congregation rose and each came in turn to wish the couple joy before processing to the Great Hall to take their seats. Hollow inside, she tried to make her face a façade of gladness. But when Hugh approached and his lips gently brushed her cheek, she thought her heart would break. And her return words of thanks strangled in her throat and she could hardly speak. In desperate need of comfort, she scanned the room for her father, but he was deep in conversation with one of the nobles.

She followed her husband, who strode on ahead without thinking to wait for her. And then she found herself alone on the threshold of the Great Hall.

Long tables were laid with damask cloths and gleaming silver plates, knives and wine-cups. The air was fragrant with the mouth-watering smell of roast meat mingled with sweet cherry wood burning in the hearths. Dishes heaped with roast venison, capons, pheasants, trout and carp adorned the tables, together with dishes of vegetables and flagons of wine. Up in the musicians' gallery a harp, vielle and lute came together in glorious harmony.

She took her allotted seat to the left of her husband. But again, she might as well have not been there, for he didn't take the least notice of her and continued conversing with Lord Frederick on his other side. Their conversation set her teeth on edge.

'With Lady Cateline, it is definitely a case of the fruit turned rotten at the instant it turned ripe,' said Frederick. His shoulders and head of blond curls shook at his own wit. 'There was talk she had an assignation with a Cistercian scribe. Apparently, he groped her so passionately a pot of ink was spilled and made a horrendous mess. And there was also that time when she was riding pillion behind Sir Geoffrey with her hand on his . . .' He trailed off and flashed an eyebrow.

Rolf let out a bark of laughter.

'That Sir Gosse got the wench with child and married her afterward,' said Rolf. He shook his head. 'It is as if a knight should defecate in his helm and then afterward clap it on his head.'

'Perchance he loves her,' said Eleanor through gritted teeth.

Rolf let out a sharp laugh in the back of his throat but made no sign of having heard what she said. The two men exchanged meaningful glances.

'A man should drink as he brews,' said the red-faced abbot who sat opposite them.

Frederick put his hand on Rolf's shoulder and said in confidential tones, 'Truly, the only way to safely navigate the rocks and sandbanks of marriage is to take a string of mistresses.'

'What think you of John's schemes?' The abbot changed the subject hastily. 'Surely he is a threat to King Richard's authority?'

Rolf burst out laughing. 'A threat? John Lackland and his like are never right hearty for the cause unless merry over a flagon of wine or barrel of ale. They do not care to gamble their carcasses further than the tavern. Besides, the king will hold him to his promise not to land upon our shores.'

'And what of the rebels in the north?' persisted the abbot.

'Let them swing.' Rolf gave a dismissive wave. 'The only way to tar independent thought is with the brush of treason.'

Eleanor's thoughts were preoccupied with what would come later: the bedding. The very thought of lying with the baron made her skin crawl. Sitting rigid in her chair, her hand clenched around the stem of her goblet, she scanned the room. At length, she found Hugh seated with the squires on the lower tables of the hall. He must have felt her eyes upon him, for he looked up at that instant and their eyes met. There was such sadness in the depth of his gaze that her own heart wept with misery and she wanted to die.

The servants served the pudding of stewed apple and dumplings. She forced it down to keep her mother-in-law happy. When the feast ended, Rolf and her father proposed various toasts.

Having dispensed with the feast, the squires set back the tables to make the hall ready for dancing.

'The bride and groom must lead the first dance together,' said Beatrice.

Eleanor stood up as Rolf grasped her hand and pulled her forward to open the dance. As she moved across the floor, she felt wooden and clumsy and her hands were ice-cold in his iron grip.

All the guests stood up to dance. For a fleeting instant, Hugh held her hand gently in his and their eyes met in a moment of yearning, but then Rolf pulled her roughly away and she was brought to stand in front of another nobleman.

All too quickly the evening wore to an end and the dreaded moment came. The last dregs of wine were drained from the guests' goblets and the minstrels departed. A horde of excited lords and ladies escorted the bride and groom to their wedding chamber at the top of the keep. Her legs were leaden as she climbed the spiral staircase as though she were walking to her own funeral.

The matrimonial chamber was full of dancing lights from the candles that burned in the sconces beside the vast canopied bed and from the fire that roared in the hearth. When all the company that had brought them there had finally departed and their laughter sank away, Rolf threw his cloak upon the cushioned chair beside the hearth and the draught from the movement forced the candle flames sideways. She lingered back in the doorway, her eyes drawn irresistibly to the fire burning in the hearth. She racked her brains for something to say to put things on a more friendly footing between them, but words escaped her. Rolf stared at her for a moment. Sick with misery, she felt positively undressed by his relentless blue eyes.

'I had no inclination to marry you, you know,' he said at last.

Nor I you, she thought. She said, 'Parents make the business of matrimony theirs.'

'Did you desire our marriage?'

'Of course.' She hated her cowardice, but to risk his wrath would be stupid. She had heard the stories about him, the violence and brutality.

'It is not a question of you being ugly, but you must know you hold no candle to the other ladies in this castle. But, of course, it is not just a question of looks – pray don't mistake me as shallow. Nothing on earth could bring me to love a shamefully cringing woman like you! Don't expect me to feign affection for you.'

She stared at him in disbelief.

'You think me cruel? But at least you cannot accuse me of deceit or false chivalry. Fear not, I shall do what is required of me.'

With a sweep of his arm, he gestured that she should go to the bed. The instant she turned her back on him, he pounced on her. There was the sound of shredding silk as he ripped the bodice of her dress with one violent tug. Shocked, she turned to face him clutching her tattered dress about her to cover her nakedness. Shameful tears welled in her eyes.

～

'Farewell, my dearest Eleanor!'

Please take me home with you, Father, she wanted to beg, but she was too proud, and she knew there was no use.

She watched in dismay as her father disappeared off into the distance on a white palfrey accompanied by his guards. A painful ache took root in her heart. She was utterly alone. Her father had been the last link with home. Much as she longed for him to look back over his shoulder at her, he didn't. She waved and smiled but inside she raged at his unkindness and her own desperate longing for his love.

'Come now . . .' Lady Beatrice stood beside her and jangled the keys hanging from her girdle like a gaoler. 'There is no time to be lost. We must get you to embroidery with the other ladies.'

Eleanor dabbed at her eyes with a silk handkerchief. She turned away reluctantly and followed her mother-in-law over the drawbridge through the gatehouse into Dover Castle, her new home. There was a loud clanking of chains as the drawbridge was drawn up behind them, sealing the entrance to the castle. As they passed under the archway, the shadowy figures of archers observed them through the arrow slits high in the wall. In the courtyard ahead there was a clatter of horses slipping about on the wet cobbles.

'This castle is known as the Key to England, you know,' said Lady Beatrice in her silky voice. 'It shall never fall, mark you.'

Eleanor didn't doubt it. She glanced up at the stark

grey curtain walls of the castle with their battlements and turrets and their massive ramparts where grim-faced sentries gazed down on them from the breast-high parapets.

The sea wind grew wilder. It had blown away the grey rain clouds, but it snatched the very words from her lips when she tried to speak.

Three blue-jowled sentries gave them a brusque nod as they hurried through the courtyard.

The courtyard itself was filled with the skeins of battery: mangonels, siege towers and trebuchets. They passed through the second curtain wall and second gatehouse with a huge iron portcullis and hurried past the stinking latrines and garbage piles until they found themselves in front of the square tower of the keep. The high steps up to the massive ironbound door on the first floor proved awkward for them in their trailing dresses.

Once inside, Eleanor followed her mother-in-law up the steep spiral staircase. At the great oak door of the second floor of the keep a sudden scuffling and giggling could be heard on the other side of the door.

Beatrice pursed her lips and flung the door open, revealing Cecily and Rolf looking shifty and embarrassed. Eleanor attempted to conceal her dismay. Beatrice's eyes flew to her son and flicked at him with a disdainful glance. For a minute Cecily's large green eyes looked anxious, but Rolf was as suave as ever and bowed to his mother in greeting. Beatrice advanced with hand outstretched and he stooped to kiss it. But something made Eleanor think that this peace was false, and that what lay beneath was somewhat different.

'Dear Cecily, would you be good enough to escort Lady Eleanor to join the other ladies in embroidery?' said Beatrice with a thin-lipped smile.

Eleanor couldn't help thinking that a touch of asperity lurked behind her mother-in-law's polite words. She followed Cecily into the day room where the ladies of the castle were engaged in their embroidery. It was a pleasant chamber with large windows and plenty of natural light, decorated with bright wall hangings and furnished with couches heaped with richly embroidered cushions. She stood a while at the threshold admiring the chamber. The women fell silent as she entered and stared at her.

'Pray go in, Eleanor,' said Beatrice in a coaxing tone. She had followed them into the chamber.

Beatrice beckoned to Cecily with a bejewelled hand. 'Please give Eleanor everything she needs.' With a swish of her velvet gown she was gone.

Cecily made a face at Eleanor and handed her a piece of silk cloth and needle and a silver tray heaped with colourful threads. Then she, too, turned on her heels and left the chamber.

Eleanor took an empty couch at the back of the room by the door and settled down to her embroidery. Already, she had a design in mind. She was keen to show people that she was good at something. Using a stick of charcoal, she lightly sketched out a design for a walled rectangular garden on the silk cloth, with closely grown shrubs forming a complicated arabesque pattern. It had low hedges of hyssop, lavender, germander and thyme enclosing raised beds of daffodils, narcissi, tulips and wallflowers.

Presently she heard Lady Matilda, a woman with a fair but rather foolish face, whisper something to Lady Millicent beside her and she flung up her head with a crow of laughter.

'I am surprised she hasn't noticed,' remarked Millicent airily.

'She must be blind,' said Matilda in a conspiratorial tone. 'I should have thought that it would be obvious that she was his favourite.'

'Frankly, it is not surprising, given her beauty,' said Millicent with a giggle. 'I doubt there is a man alive who would spurn her.'

'I should hate her, if I were in her shoes, but then she is so shrinking.' Matilda glanced at Eleanor with a faint smile.

Eleanor drove the needle through the tulip she was embroidering deep into her finger and a drop of blood sprang out and stained her embroidery. With a little gasp of pain, she looked up from her work and glared at them. She blinked back the tears that stung her eyes and resolved not to remain a moment longer and endure such remarks or allow them to see they had upset her. The day before she had noticed a library in one of the other rooms adjacent to the day room and she was determined to explore it. She put her embroidery carefully to one side and stole from the chamber.

After a week, she was beginning to get her bearings in the deceptively large keep. In addition to all the staterooms and chapel, there were a multitude of smaller chambers built into the twenty-foot-wide walls. She found the library again easily enough, drew aside the heavy tapestry door and slipped inside.

To her relief, the room was empty. It was wonderful to be alone, away from the other ladies. The library consisted of eight rows of bookshelves packed tight with huge chained volumes. She browsed the shelves for a title that would interest her. Back at home, left to her own devices, she was a voracious reader, devouring classical works by Aristotle, Plato, Ovid and Juvenal. One of her favourite authors was Chrétien de Troyes, an author who wrote tales of love and chivalry. She had fallen in love with his dashing, loyal heroes, particularly Sir Lancelot. And she was keen to find out whether this library held any volumes by this author. But she was disappointed to find no books about chivalric love, the code that prescribed the behaviour of ladies and their lovers.

The next instant, she was conscious of not being alone. Was someone hiding behind the heavy tapestries depicting Chaos, the Creation, the Fall, the Death of Abel and the Deluge? All the candles in the chamber flickered in a sudden draught. She froze, rooted to the spot, but the intruder didn't reveal himself. She waited for a few minutes longer but, hearing nothing, became engrossed in looking through the books once more.

Sometime later, she experienced a rush of panic when a stormy-faced Beatrice swept aside the curtain and stood in the doorway, glaring at her with unyielding blue eyes.

'And what, pray, are you doing in the library?' All the silkiness was gone from her mother-in-law's voice and she spoke in harsh, clipped tones.

'I . . . I was looking for something to read,' gabbled Eleanor. 'I have always loved reading.'

'Such unseemly behaviour in a lady,' said Beatrice. 'I wonder that your father did not beat it out of you!'

Eleanor felt the room go cold. She bit her lip until the blood ran.

'The notion of filling your head with poisonous ideas! There is certainly nothing for you here! You must strive to hold yourself in leash. If you must read, I will see to it that you are supplied with fitting reading material.'

Eleanor scuttled back to the day room like a dog with its tail between its legs, still smarting after her mother-in-law's sharp words.

~

That evening, they took their supper in the Great Hall. There was a moment's hush when Eleanor entered with Beatrice. The only sounds were the crackling of the flames in the hearths and the low growls of two hounds fighting over a bone in the corner. She took her place between her husband and her mother-in-law at the supper table on a raised platform at the far end of the hall. Opposite her sat Cecily, looking rather pleased with herself with glittering eyes and a mocking smile.

Eleanor shot her one of her dirty looks.

Presently the voices resumed their clamour and a harper began to make music up in the gallery. The aroma of roasting meat filled the hall as the covers were lifted off the platters set before them. Conscious of the ever-watchful eye of Beatrice, Eleanor did her best to eat the plate of capon and vegetables set before her, but her appetite had left her. The food was too stodgy for her liking and she could only pick at it. There was some discussion about a planned crusade to the Holy Land, but she wasn't listening.

Fearful thoughts preoccupied her mind. The prospect of being alone again with her husband that night filled her with dread. It was as though his mother had specifically trained him from birth to ride roughshod over people, just as her parents had trained her from birth to be passive and docile. She had been ill prepared for her wedding night; her mother had failed to tell her what to expect. Her mother had reassured her that their physical relationship would come later, after they had had a chance to get to know each other, but Rolf had broken her in straight away.

Her thoughts drifted back to what the priest in Normandy had said about carnal desires being evil, justified only by offspring. The priest made it clear he considered desire not as a sin but as a punishment, viewing a man's passionate love of his own wife as adultery. But she didn't want to believe this. She had read Ovid's work, *Ars Amatoria*, which depicted the lover as a slave to passion. Inspired by his writing, she had entertained some flight of imagination about her first night with her husband and revelled in the anticipated sensations. Chrétien de Troyes' tales had nurtured within her a notion of a faithful, devoted knight who would willingly risk his life and suffer any shame to protect and worship his lover. But how far these ideals were from her experience of marriage!

Millicent helped her into her nightclothes that evening and brushed out her long hair. Much as Eleanor disliked the woman, she was loath to see her go and to be left alone. She awaited Rolf in the candle-light of the austere matrimonial chamber, which was decorated with only the most sombre tapestries, hardly able to breathe for the thumping of her heart. As she heard the thud of his footsteps outside the door, she sat on the edge of the bed, her body taut for what would come next.

The door creaked open and he stood on the threshold, blocking out the light in the passage beyond with his huge frame. He surveyed her for an instant and she felt there was something diabolical in his gaze. He rounded on her and snarled. 'My mother informs me that she found you in the library today.' His voice cut sharper than steel. 'I'll not have women, especially not my wife, frisking through the volumes in the library.'

Her heart sank. 'Err . . . yes, my lord. If you please, I was just looking for something to read.' Despite her best efforts to remain composed, her voice sounded shrill and panic-stricken.

'You were filling your head with romantic nonsense, no doubt. Perhaps you imagined me to be a chivalrous hero who would indulge your every whim. In that case, what a disappointment I must be for you.'

She was at a loss for words. 'Err . . . not a disappointment . . .' Momentarily, she turned away from him and brushed a stray hair from her face.

A blow to the back of her head caught her by surprise and she shrieked in pain. She reeled onto the floor, cowering. Paralysed and struck dumb with fear, she was unable to shout or fight back. Up until now Rolf had not struck her, but there was no mistaking the fact that he meant to hurt her. A shuddering horror seized her by the roots of her hair. Her heart raced and she began to sweat and tremble. With her father gone, she had nobody to protect her. Bile rose up in her throat. Trapped in Dover Castle, the most heavily guarded fortress in England, she had no prospect of escape and was sentenced to living with this brute of a man for the rest of her life. Rolf prodded a toe into her stomach, and she let out a yelp, like a dog in pain.

4.

The Art of Fighting

The night after the wedding, Hugh thrashed about in the tent for hours, unable to sleep. Beside him, his brother slept on, blissfully untouched by anguish. At the wedding feast he had striven to get himself horribly drunk to deaden the pain of his broken heart, but the wine served to do little except give him a splitting headache. When he allowed his eyes to close, his addled mind conjured up skin-crawling visions of Rolf with Eleanor. It was enough to make him vomit. And what made it more unbearable still was the thought that poor Eleanor despised the baron as much as he did. The agony she felt at the prospect of her marriage had been all too evident in her eyes and it would haunt him forever.

Eventually, he realised any attempt to sleep was futile

and he pulled himself to his feet and slunk out of the tent. Just outside, he stepped over Orry, who was asleep outstretched on the grass. A full moon and a clear sky with hundreds of glistening stars greeted him. The sight of Orry who had roused himself and bounded towards him with a wagging tail brought him a sense of solace.

In the eerie shadows of the night, the encampment was like a forest. They threaded their way through the lines of tents from which emanated the disconcerting sounds of snores and heavy breathing.

The unyielding curtain walls of Dover Castle loomed ominous over the camp across the black waters of the moat. In some chamber on the other side of those impenetrable walls lay Eleanor, defiled by her brute of her husband. It made his heart lurch to think of the horror of it. Cold fury bubbled up from his stomach like spew and his fists clenched by his side. With a concerted effort, he summoned strength from deep within himself to resist the urge to smash at the rock wall with his bare hands.

If he allowed his despondency to get the better of him, he might as well be dead. And the last thing he was going to do was to serve up victory on a plate to Rolf. No, the only one other way out of this deplorable situation was to fight.

Now that he had resolved upon a course of action, his mood lifted a little. With a long stretch, he retired to his tent to snatch a few hours' sleep before dawn.

∼

A day later, back home at Eynsford Castle, he was roused at sunrise by the urgent calls of the cockerel. In the bunk beside him, William snored like an old man. He had woken in possession of a sharp clarity. Now he knew what he must do. One way or another, he must leave his father's castle.

His page, Serle, a cheerful little imp of eight with big brown eyes and a head of dense tight curls, brought him his clothes. Moving purposefully, Hugh pulled on his under-garments and braies, fastened his tunic and strapped on his sword.

Down the spiral staircase he went and out into the courtyard, narrowing his eyes into the morning sunlight. Thankfully, the rains of recent weeks had finally abated, but the air struck cold with a chilly tang. He drew a wooden pitcher from the well and immersed his head in the freezing water, shrugging off the grogginess of the preceding night. He shook off the excess water like a dog.

He hurried back to the Great Hall and he took his place next to Bardolf on the long bench beside the crackling fire.

'I have set my heart on training to be a knight,' he told his friend through a mouthful of fresh bread.

'There was talk of you joining the church, I recall,' said Bardolf.

'Much as I love books, that was my father's plan and I have served as page and five years as a squire already – I am ready to be a knight. My mind is full of jousts and tournaments and dreams of chivalry.'

'Aye, it would be glorious to fight in a tourney,' said Bardolf, a wistful look in his eye.

'Eleanor's marriage and my mother's illness have brought things to a head. And I would rather die than marry Lady Bethany.'

Bardolf nodded.

'I'll throw myself into my training in earnest and become a brave, honourable knight and seek service in the household of some great lord.' He shovelled a spoonful of eggs into his mouth. 'Besides, the longing for adventure is in my blood and it has been stirring in me these past few months. Perhaps I will seek my fortune overseas on a crusade.'

He bolted the rest of his breakfast and washed it down with some ale. Anxious to start a new chapter of his life, he hastened to the courtyard where he found Sir Roger by the flint-rubble curtain wall of the castle, polishing his sword.

Sir Roger was a beast of a man who towered over most men with a shaggy head of brown curls, fierce black eyes, a hooked nose and a scraggy beard. One of his father's finest knights, he was a brute but a worthy adversary.

'I would like you to train me to be a knight,' said Hugh, without preamble.

'Is that so, pup?' said the giant in his gruff voice. His hairy lip quivered in amusement. He caressed the blade in his hand as though it were a sentient being.

This response rather took the wind out of Hugh's sails. He abhorred being a figure of ridicule. One day, when he was trained as a knight and experienced in battle, he would come back and teach this man a lesson, he promised himself. 'It is my wish to earn my spurs.'

'Such a feat is easier said than done,' growled the knight, a cool note of laughter in his voice. 'But I'm willing to try, if only for the amusement it will provide me.' He handed Hugh a sword.

This was not the response Hugh had hoped for. Why must his father's men continually mock him? It was enough to raise his neck hair. But there was nothing for it: Sir Roger was the most skilled swordsman in his father's household.

The sword felt cold and heavy in his hands. He envied Sir Roger his blade. It was a formidable sword that Sir Roger bragged had never yet failed him in a fight.

Hugh lunged forward, pressing his attack, but it seemed that his blade couldn't bite the dexterous knight. Their blades kissed and the courtyard rang with the sound of steel. He stumbled beneath the older man's onslaught. There was immense strength in the knight that he couldn't overcome. They fought in silence save for Hugh's gasping breaths. With all his strength, he pitted himself against Sir Roger and fought off his blows, but he knew that he was beaten and eventually sank down onto the dirt of the courtyard, sobbing for breath.

A roar of laughter beat up from the door to the keep.

Hugh turned to see William had surfaced from his bed. His brother's blue eyes glittered and he wore a mocking smile.

Refusing to give his brother satisfaction, Hugh scrambled to his feet and resumed sparring with Sir Roger.

William jeered at him from the doorway. When Hugh missed a strike or received a blow, his brother erupted into fierce laughter.

Panting from the struggle and taking a moment to catch his breath, Hugh turned and was discouraged to see that quite a crowd had congregated in the courtyard to watch the sport and laugh at his discomfort.

Although the effort of holding up the heavy long sword pained him greatly, he forced himself on. Sir Roger might have the mastery of the fight, but he was resolved to persevere no matter how much the others mocked him.

Sir Roger baited him without mercy. 'Come on, you can do better than that! Put your back into it . . . What the hell was that? You fight like a woman!'

A ball of anger seethed in the pit of Hugh's stomach. He channelled it into a sudden sword thrust and caught the knight square on the shoulder.

Sir Roger bellowed in outrage and elbowed him in the stomach. 'Enough fun for today, milksop! Off you go now, run up to your mother's chamber.'

Bent double, Hugh drew in air in great gasps like a runner at the end of a gruelling race.

The audience dispersed and resumed their respective duties in the castle, many of them still laughing heartily. He hung back, his arms and legs aching and bruised. The sickening aftertaste of humiliation lingered in his mouth.

When they had all gone, he made a concerted effort to pull himself up to his full height, and dusted down his tunic and hose.

Sir Roger seemed to have recovered his humour for he smiled affably at him. 'Before you get on with your morning's chores, I have a number of errands I'd like you to run. It is a fair exchange, for I have undertaken to train you in the art of sword fighting and jousting.'

Hugh nodded.

'Here . . .' He slung his chain mail to Hugh. 'To start with, my hauberk needs a good polish – and my sword is blunt.'

Hugh took the heavy steel garment to the barrel in the armoury and began to clean it in the sand.

Sir Roger followed him and watched him closely. 'See that you do a good job, mind. I want that mail to gleam.'

Hugh rubbed at the rust on the mail until his hands were red raw.

'That'll do I suppose. Now get on with my sword.'

Hugh couldn't suppress a gasp as Sir Roger passed him the sword. This was the first time he had ever handled such a fine blade and he relished the weight of it in his hands. He glanced up at the knight.

Sir Roger's face softened. 'It is a beautiful sword

right enough. My father gave it to me on the eve of my knighthood. See that you take care of it.'

Hugh wiped down the blade with a rag and laid it on the armoury table. As he had seen the armourer do, he poured a drop of oil onto the whetstone. Then he ran the sword back and forth on the stone at an angle.

Sir Roger cuffed his ear. 'No, no, idiot! You need to count the strokes on each side to ensure the edge will be even and sharp!'

Hugh reeled back, his ear on fire. He put himself to counting the strokes and honed the blade until the edge was sharp and free of nicks.

Sir Roger took the blade and inspected it. 'That's better. Now test it on this block of wood.'

He brought down the blade and to his satisfaction it sliced through the wood as if it had no more resistance than water.

Just then his father bellowed his name.

He handed the sword back to the knight and hurried out into the courtyard, his hand over his eyes to block out the sun.

'Yet again I find you dodging your duties!' His father grabbed him by his damaged ear.

Hugh cried out, unable to suppress his agony.

'Cease your whimpering. One would think you a child the racket you make! Explain yourself! The steward tells me that he hasn't seen you all morning.'

'I've been assisting Sir Roger.' He wheeled round at the knight who had come out to join them. Sir Roger wore an expression of mild amusement. Hugh soon realised he would get no help from him.

'That is something you'll have to do on your own time!' He relinquished his grip on Hugh's ear.

Hugh darted off into the keep.

In the Great Hall he came face to face with the steward, who glared at him with piercing blue eyes. 'At long last, what kept you?'

Hugh opened his mouth to speak.

'I don't need to hear your excuses. There is far too much to do. These rushes are dirty. Replenish them.'

Hugh swept the Great Hall and shovelled up the detritus of reeds, bones and discarded food. From the hayloft, he brought armfuls of fresh reeds and grasses to lay upon the floor.

For the next couple of hours, he was kept busy in the kitchens. Down in the cellars he topped up the amphoras with wine from the barrels. Then he returned to the kitchen, for the boar roasting on the spit had to be carved. He took pains to slice the meat from the joint and arrange it on a silver platter. To his father and his guests at the high table he brought water to wash their hands. And then he and the other pages served lunch.

After he'd waited at table, he went for a hurried meal with the pages. That afternoon he would be overseeing their education, training them in the courtly arts of singing and dancing. There would be time, he hoped, after that to attend his mother's bedside before his own lessons with the priest and his lessons in heraldry.

Hardly had he finished his lesson with the herald when Sir Roger stopped him with a hairy arm. 'My destrier needs currying and the stable must be mucked out. And my hawk needs exercising.'

Hugh clenched his teeth as he swept the stables in silent fury, all too aware that in approaching Sir Roger for training he had put himself in the man's hands. The knight would exploit him at every opportunity, but he determined to put up with it for he had his sights set on higher purposes. It would all be worth it when he was a knight, or so he hoped.

Sir Roger's destrier snorted. He was a magnificent stallion, black as sin. Before he brushed down the warhorse, he paused and stroked its noble arched neck.

After he'd finished in the stables he headed for the mews. The knight's hawk, a spirited saker, was as troublesome as his master and fought savagely on the glove and left him with a nasty scratch on the arm.

'Hasn't anyone ever taught you how to handle a hawk?' Sir Roger lounged on the grass as Hugh let the bird loose to soar across the sky.

He swallowed down a retort and coaxed the bird back to his glove with a morsel of meat.

'When you've done that, there is my bed to be made and my clothes to be got ready. And tonight, you will bring me my sleeping draught before I turn in.'

'When exactly will my training begin?'

'On the morrow. You shall start by fighting on foot and without chain mail to accustom you to handling the great lances and heavy swords.'

Late that night, Hugh carried a steaming goblet of sleeping draught to the knight's chamber.

Sir Roger took it without a word. Hugh waited while he drank it down.

At that instant, an idea seemed to occur to Sir Roger, and he smiled. 'Tonight, you shall sleep here on the floor just outside my chamber.'

Hugh was about to protest but then remained silent. How else would he get away from this confounded castle and be a man?

That night as he curled up on the cold flagstones with his cloak as a pillow, Hugh wondered if he'd made an error of judgement. When, if ever, would his training begin? How could he possibly fit it in with all the duties he had to fulfil?

Exhausted by all the activity of the day, his eyelids were just beginning to droop when the steel tip of a chain-mailed foot plunged savagely into his stomach.

With a gasp of pain, he rolled into a ball and fought for breath.

'What in hell possessed you to sleep there?' said a familiar voice.

He glanced up at his brother looking down on him with a lopsided smirk. A wave of hatred rose up within him and vied for supremacy over his pain. Before he could scramble to his feet, William disappeared down the passageway leaving a trail of mocking laughter in his wake.

~

The Song and the Sword

As spring's torrential rains gave way to warm summer days, Hugh put in as much sword practice as he could. When he was accustomed to handling the great lances and heavy swords, the knight ordered him to practise hitting targets with his lance as he ran. After this he was able to move on to practising with weapons while wearing armour. A suit of chain mail weighed as much as forty pounds. The weight pulled down on his shoulders and made it hard to move. But, bit by bit, he became stronger and able to bear the weight for longer. And then he was ready to move on to practise fighting and jousting on horseback.

Before long, he was beginning to show promise as a swordsman. Furthermore, he grew in confidence. No longer was he a figure of mockery in the castle. He was learning to harness his strength. Loath as he was to admit it, day after day of being meted out humiliating treatment at the hands of Sir Roger was making him stronger and turning him gradually into a worthy opponent.

'I think Hugh might be ready to compete in the mêlée in next month's tournament at Dover Castle,' said Sir Roger, one evening at dinner.

Hugh's heart leapt with pleasure.

'I have no objection,' said his father, through a mouthful of meat. 'Providing he does not show up the family with his simpering!' He grinned at William and the steward. They sniggered appreciatively.

Hugh exhaled heavily. Familiar hot anger welled in his breast, despite himself. 'Now that's not fair!'

'What's the matter, little brother?' pitched in William. 'Still pining after Lady Eleanor, are you? She's in need of a proper man, not some spineless runt like you.'

'I could spit you like a pig,' muttered Hugh under his breath. If only he had the honour of fighting in single combat like William. He imagined lopping off his older brother's smirking head with his long sword. What pleasure he would derive from throwing Baron Rolf from his horse and spilling his blood! But he would have to be satisfied with fighting in the mêlée, a mock battle, for now.

'I have to hand it to you, Hugh,' allowed Sir Roger, in a rare moment of camaraderie, 'I never thought you'd make a swordsman. But you've been nothing but determined and I respect you for that.' But this fellowship was short-lived, for the next moment he bellowed, 'Now what have you done with my hauberk, fool!'

That night Hugh barely slept. While part of him was almost giddy with excitement at the thought of competing in the tournament, another part of him couldn't stop thinking about the possibility of seeing Eleanor again. The last time he had seen her, at her wedding to Baron Rolf, it had felt as though someone had wrenched out his heart by its very root.

5.
The Crucible

The following day, Eleanor woke with tears in her eyes and a leaden heart. Yet again she had slept badly, and her head ached. She had only been married for two months but already it felt like an eternity. At least she had been spared a nocturnal visit from her husband, though she had been so fearful that he would appear in her chamber and demand his conjugal rights that she had scarcely slept a wink. Through the gap in the drapes was a glimpse of a dismal, grey morning. Desperate for some comfort in the face of such bleakness she reached for her locket, snapped open the clasp and teased Hugh's soft lock of hair with the tips of her fingers.

'Good morning, Lady Eleanor!' Millicent burst into

her chamber unexpectedly. A weight of horror settled upon Eleanor for she had no time to conceal the precious lock and it was too dark to pass off as Rolf's. Millicent's eyes lit up at the sight of it. 'Is that a keepsake of some lost lover?' Her voice invited confidences and she bestowed a smile intended to reassure.

Eleanor admired the lady's skill at being able to turn on such sweetness at will, but knew her to be conniving. 'No. It is a lock of my mother's hair. It brings me comfort to hold it when I am far from home.'

The corner of Millicent's mouth tightened on one side and she broke into a disdainful laugh. 'To be sure.'

With care, Eleanor stowed the tendril of hair safely back in the locket and clipped it shut.

A maid brought a tray with breakfast. Eleanor pushed a boiled egg about her plate; she was not inclined to eat.

At length, she could put off getting out of bed no longer, and she rose. Millicent pulled a fresh chemise over her head and helped her into a jade gown, which she secured with a girdle of golden yarn around her hips. Then, Millicent brushed out and arranged her hair and applied a light dusting of lily root to her face.

Eleanor followed Millicent along the passage, down the spiral staircase and into the day room where they found a group of ladies huddled in the corner deep in discussion.

'Pray do not tell her . . .' said one of the ladies in

a hushed voice. 'But I thought her gown ghastly at the banquet. Previously, I believed she had a good instinct for selecting garments, but I was shocked by her appearance last night.'

'I quite agree it was a monstrosity!' said Cecily with a little giggle as an afterthought. 'Do you suppose they all wear their hair in that unappealing manner in Normandy?'

Millicent let out a small cough. Abruptly the women drew apart and exchanged meaningful glances. Suddenly, Cecily giggled insanely, and then subsided.

A knot formed in Eleanor's belly and she longed to be back in Normandy.

Beside the hearth a harpist began to pluck his instrument.

Cecily's eyes blazed with a sudden passion. 'Do let us sing a song of courtly love. Why, we could each sing a verse!'

'What an inspired notion!' said Millicent.

Eleanor rallied. At last, something she could excel at; she had a remarkable voice, if all her admirers in Normandy were to be believed.

Cecily took up her verse in a confident voice. All the ladies gazed upon her with expressions of awe upon their faces.

Each of the ladies took their turn, Eleanor last of all.

Cecily raised an eyebrow and pouted her lips as Eleanor stood up to sing.

The harpist took up the introduction. Scarcely had

she opened her mouth when Cecily turned away to converse in earnest with Millicent in a loud whisper that drowned out Eleanor's voice and did not desist until she had finished her verse.

'Cecily, you are fortunate to sing so sweetly,' said Millicent afterwards. 'I tip you to be a great favourite!'

'Indeed, you have an exquisite voice!' said another of the ladies.

'Sublime!' said another.

Eleanor had listened carefully to each of the ladies as they sang their verse, but for the life of her she couldn't understand why the women heaped praise upon Cecily, for her voice was not particularly remarkable. Not one of them had complimented her. Then she experienced a pang of doubt – perhaps they were right, and it was she who was guilty of envy.

Cecily beamed a dazzling smile at her adoring crowd. 'I am one of the lucky few who have a talent for song.' She gathered up her loose hair in a ponytail.

Eleanor's heart missed a beat as she glimpsed the diamond pendant that adorned Cecily's slender neck. It was unmistakeably one of the diamonds from her dowry!

'What a beautiful necklace, Cecily!' said Millicent. 'Where did you get it?'

Cecily's white hand flew to her neck. 'It was a gift from an admirer. Do you like it?'

'It was wrought by a master jeweller, no doubt,' said Beatrice, who had come to join the ladies. 'Good heavens, Eleanor, try to muster a smile! If only you troubled yourself to look more agreeable . . . I fear you are apt to look peevish.'

~

That afternoon, a crowd gathered in the windy courtyard to watch the summary execution of four criminals, miscreants and other unfortunate wretches who had deigned to incur Baron Rolf's displeasure.

She would have gladly missed the abhorrent spectacle, but her husband insisted that all attend without exception. She pulled her cloak close about her shoulders for warmth and comfort against the gloom of the cloud-filled sky.

Rolf walked along the line of the condemned, his face a mask of stone. At last he halted in front of the skeletal ruin of a man who had his mouth stuffed with hay. 'This man has displayed his vile designs,' said Rolf in a harsh voice that filled the courtyard. 'Do not be taken in by his polite exterior. Why, this man is devoted to every art that could administer to his pleasure. Lewd without attachment and debauched without gratitude, he has no regard for woman or child. His crimes are unpardonable and shall be punished without remorse.'

The executioner, a brute of a man with sinewy arms, stepped forward with an axe. The prisoner was made to put their neck on the block. Skilled and deadly, the executioner swept down his axe and severed the man's head with a shower of crimson spray.

Despite herself she recoiled, her hand over her mouth, sickened by the sight of blood. Around her, the crowd cheered as the executioner bore the head aloft for all to see.

The next condemned man had black, swollen eyes and his hair was matted with blood. The guards supported him because his spine had been so twisted on the rack that he could no longer stand unaided. The wind carried his putrid stench into the crowd and the ladies held their noses. Unable to bring herself to look upon the poor wretch, Eleanor looked hastily away.

'Behold this man with moral deformity . . .' said Rolf. 'So livid in complexion and brutal in countenance. He would be the instrument of your destruction if we allowed him. I am disgusted by the sight of him!'

The guard shoved the man savagely forward and placed his head on the block. The bloodstained axe swung down, but this time it took several blows to sever head from body. The executioner brandished the dripping head. The knights and ladies around her craned their necks to see it and beat up a shout of approval at the sight of it. The taste of bile rose in her throat and she suppressed a retch. Surely she wasn't the only one who was disgusted by this brutal display?

Rolf smiled, gratified by their appreciation and moved on to his next victim. He held the prisoner's scrawny arm aloft. 'This creature of malignant appearance is pregnant with evil. He may be puny in body and negligent in dress but as a sodomite he is our inveterate foe!'

The crowd hissed and booed as the man was dragged kicking and screaming to the block. The axe swung down and severed his head with one clean blow. The shrill roar of the crowd filled her ears. She felt so lightheaded she thought she would faint, and she shuffled her feet apart to steady herself.

Rolf moved on to his final victim. 'Once this man was a knight, but he has shown himself to be no better than the common robbers of the woods and forests. He first took the lives of respectable people that he might afterwards despoil his victims!'

The former knight met his end on the blood-soaked block. The crowd cheered, their intemperate thirst for more sacrifice apparently sated. Sick to the stomach, she felt besmirched by the horror of what she had witnessed.

~

Later she waited frozen in her chamber, her hands damp with perspiration, her eyes assaulted by a sudden gust of stinging smoke from the fire. Rolf pushed the door open. Her heart hammered.

Rolf's eyes challenged her. 'Did you enjoy the spectacle this afternoon?'

'No doubt . . . those men deserved to be punished,' was all that she could think to say, and her voice was filled with a false heartiness.

'Doling out punishment is one of my pleasures as Constable of Dover. You might say I revel in the brutality. Your father must be extraordinarily fond of you to marry you off to me. Surely he must know my reputation. I have never troubled to hide my baser nature from the world.'

She spoke between gritted teeth. 'He knows nothing of how you treat me.'

'Nor shall he ever know of it, rest assured of that. All messages out of this castle are examined – nothing comes in or out without my knowledge. However, your father cannot fail to have heard rumours of my Dover beauties. Indeed, when he visited, I flaunted them under his nose. And yet he settled his beloved daughter upon me. It is puzzling. One can only conclude he was fonder of power than he was of you.'

'My father loves me . . .'

'If you say so . . . But with a dowry such as yours you could have had any number of suitors.'

After a pause she spoke. 'My dowry . . .'

'Is mine – as are you – to do with as I please.' He rubbed his hands together. 'And I am free to torment you at my pleasure. It is a meagre recompense for the inconvenience of being married to you.' He shot her a withering, one-sided smile. 'What is your opinion of the necklace I had made for Lady Cecily from the diamonds of your dowry? I commissioned it with the express purpose of wounding you.'

She forced herself to smile and tried to make light of it. 'It is a necklace of exquisite workmanship.'

'And there you go again with your infuriating slavish grimaces. You cannot imagine how much you disgust me! Why, I have more fondness for my hunting dog than you!' His eyes narrowed and his voice became harsh. 'Yes, there's an idea . . . I'll teach you to lick and whimper.'

'I beg pardon, my lord. I misunderstand you . . .'

'Do not fawn and entreaty with me. You must know I despise such weakness of character. I know a woman with a broken back when I see one.' He burst into scornful laughter. 'I am told you pine away with a lock of hair of some lost love wrapped around your finger.'

Panic rose in her chest. 'It is my mother's hair. It does not belong to a past lover.'

He grabbed her hair and pulled her head back so savagely it made her eyes water. 'Don't insult me with your tawdry lies! Who is he?'

'No . . .' she sobbed. 'I speak the truth . . . It is a lock of my mother's hair!'

He slapped her across the face with his free hand. 'Don't lie to me, slut! You realise I shall have my men find him and bring him up before the judge on some trumped-up charge . . .'

Her blood ran cold. The thought of her beloved Hugh suffering such a fate was unbearable.

Rolf's eyes filled with glee. 'I have it! I shall induce you to sentence him to a public flogging or perhaps trial by ordeal! Just imagine his pain at being forced to pick up a red-hot iron bar with his bare hands – he certainly would not want to touch you ever again after that. Underestimate me at your peril – I am the chess master and you and he are nothing but wooden pieces to be dropped on my whim. You are a pitiful slut who shames me, and sluts get punished.'

Tears ran down her face.

'It's no use blubbering for I am no friend to pity . . . The more you weep, the more grinding the punishment I will inflict upon you! But then I think you are partial to my brutality – for mark how you cajole and provoke me . . .'

At that moment there was a loud knock on the door and Rolf released his grip on her hair.

Her hand flew to soothe her burning scalp.

'There is an urgent dispatch from London, my lord,' said a voice from behind the door.

'Very well, I shall come into my council chamber directly!'

The sound of footsteps disappeared down the passage. Rolf shot her one last contemptuous glance. 'I shall deal with you later!' Then he left the chamber, leaving the door to bang closed behind him.

With a pounding heart, she sank onto the floor, defeated. Hunched up with her head resting on her knees, she was unable to stop weeping or trembling. Just how much more of this cruelty could she bear? She simply had to escape from her monster of a husband. Even death would be preferable to this hellish marriage!

6.

The Tournament

On the morning of the day of the tournament, Hugh formed part of a procession of knights and squires from his father's household. After several hours of hard riding, they emerged from the dappled sunlight of the forest paths into a clearing. From here, they had a magnificent view of Dover Castle perched imposingly up on the cliff in the distance with the town sprawling below.

He was proud to carry a shield bearing a chalice of gold in each quarter, supported by two wrestling lions, with the inscription *God Is Love*, the insignia of his father's house.

They brought their horses to a standstill outside the main gate of Dover. Here he gazed up in awe at the splendid statue of King Henry that adorned its façade. Above the statue, gnarled hands reached out in supplication from the barred windows of a prison cell. Dover Gate was a massive arched gateway with a drawbridge, moat and portcullis, through which all traffic had to pass.

Eventually, they emerged into the square on the other side of the walls. The streets had been railed off for the procession of knights arriving in town for the tournament and they heaved with a puzzling variety of people from merchants to men of the cloth and peasants and beggars. The local gentry, dressed in their finest furs and with their jewellery sparkling in the sun, were mounted on their best steeds, ready to greet the visiting knights. Citizens of the town, dressed in their finery, bowed their heads in reverence. The procession passed grand new houses with lush gardens and orchards and the impressive stone dwellings of merchants and other citizens of consequence.

The road led them through less salubrious areas of the town, where butchers cleaned their carcasses in the river. Hair and blood ran into the water and gave off an unwholesome stench. Worse still was the stink of tanned hides, which made him retch. If that were not enough, there were the clouds of noxious fumes from the blacksmiths and the deafening blows of the sledgehammers. Frequently, the road became narrow because of dangerously overhanging buildings and the procession had to pass through in single file. Finally, they arrived in the main square. Blinking in the sunshine, Hugh found himself in front of the church, an impressive building with huge stone columns.

The tournament was to take place on the hill below the castle, overlooking the town of Dover. The horses slowed as they laboured up a steep incline to the camp.

A sea of brightly coloured tents was pitched at the summit of the slope. From the shields that decorated the tents and banners flapping in the wind, he recognised many of the armorial bearings. Among others, there was the golden hare rearing up, denoting speed, of the house of Toucy, the silver badgers, denoting endurance, of the house of Ambroise and the cockatrice d'or – a cross between a cockerel and a dragon, supposedly hatched from a cock's egg – of the house of Marbot.

The courtly songs of troubadours carried on the wind, as did the sweet aroma of roast game turning on spits on smoking campfires. The prevailing atmosphere of excited anticipation was intoxicating. The camp resounded with animated chatter, spontaneous bursts of song and raucous laughter.

When they found a suitable place to set up camp by the moat of the castle, the company dismounted, tethered the horses and raised the tents. As a squire, he was expected to prepare the horses for battle. Already the sun was at the highest point in the sky so there was no time to lose. Horses had to be fed, saddles prepared and girths tightened. There was barely time to snatch a light lunch of hunks of bread and cheese before he pulled on his chain mail and put on his helmet.

The main event of the tournament was the jousting. Thousands of townspeople, peasants and labourers, men, women and children had gathered around the tournament arena and jostled for the best view of the fighting. In the ranks of the spectators, he saw eager, greedy faces, their tongues hanging out for blood. The crowd grew thicker at every moment. High on a canopied platform, overlooking the action, grand ladies and lords filed into the galleries to take their seats for the entertainment.

He looked up, searching out Eleanor from among the crowd of ladies decked out in their finest red velvet tunics and red hoods. At last, he located her, and his heart lurched with painful desire. She was even more beautiful than he remembered, as a light sea breeze tousled her soft hair. But on closer inspection, she was pale and anxious-looking and a sad smile quivered at the corners of her mouth. And at once he was assailed by a keen bite of concern. He grabbed the hilt of his sword, ready to spring into action and fight to the death to protect his dearest Eleanor.

Trumpets rang out from the castle battlements and were answered by the blowing of horns in the arena below. The tournament was about to start. Fighting down his longing, he wrenched his eyes away from Eleanor and forced himself to turn to the matter in hand.

Another fanfare of trumpets silenced the excited crowd.

'Lords and ladies,' shouted the herald. 'We welcome you to today's tournament!' He gave the gallery a deferential bow. 'Will the knights in the lists come forward!'

A wave of cheering and applause beat up from the crowd as the first knights rode onto the field.

Hugh groaned as his brother rode forward upon one of his father's prize destriers, playing to the crowd with an ostentatious bow and blowing kisses to the fairest maidens. One of the ladies in the gallery threw William her silk scarf. He cringed as his brother made a point of pressing it to his lips and then tying it round his wrist as though he were some legendary champion. The ladies lapped it all up, believing William to be the epitome of chivalry, but Hugh knew his brother all too well. He was always bragging about his conquests with the ladies. It was a sore point for Hugh. Their father had no plans yet for William to marry. His older brother was the prodigal son. Furthermore, God had seen fit to bestow him with bright blue eyes and a handsome jaw and an excellent height and build. With a flourish of his lance, William sat straight on his horse with an air of entitlement and favoured Hugh with an arrogant smile when he caught sight of him in the crowd. Their father had gifted William the splendid chain mail he had worn years before when he had fought in the lists. It had been polished to a shine and dazzled in the afternoon sun. He wore a magnificent ermine cloak about his shoulders, adorned with the family crest: a chalice of gold in each quarter, supported by two wrestling lions emblazoned in gold. Hugh's chain mail and plain grey cloak paled in comparison and he could not help a rush of jealousy.

William's opponent was a slender knight with a thin face and a hooked nose who had the fearful air of a novice, casting furtive glances at his adversary. Modestly attired in well-worn chain mail and only the most rudimentary helmet and a cloak, as plain as Hugh's, he did not give the impression of being in the least formidable a foe.

William took one look at him and gave a derisory snort and a jut of his jaw. Pulling sharply on the reins, he moved his horse into position with his lance couched. A drum rolled and he set off at a gallop and dealt the poor knight an almighty thwack on the chest with his wooden lance, which exploded into hundreds of splinters on impact with his chain mail. The knight toppled from his horse and lay gasping and fighting for breath. The audience went wild and the townspeople whooped and cheered. The lords and ladies in the gallery even got to their feet and applauded in a wave of appreciation for the sport. William rode along the length of the arena basking in his moment of glory.

William's next opponent was another fledgling knight who came off even worse. William charged at him and struck him a blow of such unnecessary force with his lance that the man flew off his saddle into churned-up earth – only, his foot was still trapped in the stirrup. The crowd was whipped up into a frenzy by the ensuing furore as the horse bolted, dragging the young knight several hundred yards around the arena. The less than sympathetic crowd guffawed and hooted, and William louder than the rest, as they watched the spectacle. It was some time before attendants were able to calm the horse and disentangle the knight's foot. By that time, the knight's ankle was badly broken and his face a grazed mess of crimson under his half helm. If he hadn't been wearing a sturdy suit of chain mail, he would have come off worse. Hugh felt for the man at the shame of it all.

Several jousts later, having unhorsed most of the younger knights, William was drawn to face Baron Rolf.

Lords and ladies in the gallery and the common people in the crowd craned forward for a better view as Rolf rode out on a magnificent destrier. Hugh looked out for Eleanor, but another lady led Rolf's horse onto the field.

Ecstatic shouts and cheers greeted the appearance of Rolf, but it gave Hugh no pleasure that Rolf was more popular with the crowd than his brother. He despised the man. The baron looked resplendent in his chain mail and flowing gold cloak as he acknowledged the crowd with a regal wave of his left arm. A formidable giant on his splendid steed, he rode out onto the square, his lance at the ready. The drum rolled and he sprang forward with a thunder of hooves. William didn't have a chance to shift his position against the brute strength and speed of his charge and was thrown hard from the horse. Fortunately for him, he sustained no more than a few bruises and soon managed to stand, consoled by the maidens who threw flowers at his feet.

Next, Sir Roger rode out onto the field. Compared to some of the younger, handsomer knights competing, Sir Roger had a rough edge. A great hulk of a man, at least six feet, he was almost double the size of most of the men and rode a huge destrier. What he lacked in nimbleness he more than made up for in experience and strength. As Hugh well knew, Sir Roger didn't wash with pomp and gaudiness and instead preferred serviceability, wearing little ornament on his largely plain surcoat, apart from a small badge with the Eynsford insignia, and an old brown cloak that flapped in the rising breeze. At the edge of his side of the lists, Hugh stood by to supply him fresh lances.

Sir Roger's opponent, a shabby young knight errant with long curly hair, rode his swift-footed courser onto the field. Within minutes he fell to the full brunt of Sir Roger's attack, his head thrown back at an unnatural angle, and dented his helmet when he hit the ground. The ladies in the crowd gasped and cried out. Fortunately, he was spared a broken neck, but his head lolled from one side to another and he couldn't keep it upright. The poor youth had to be borne off the field on a litter.

It proved to be an excellent day for Sir Roger as he went on to unhorse another four knights in subsequent jousts. But he met his match when he came to tilt with the crowd's favourite, Baron Rolf, on the final joust of the day.

As Baron Rolf rode into position, the crowd roared and he couched his lance. Sir Roger took up his shield and lance and mounted the horse that Hugh had brought him. The combatants rode away from each other the proper distance and then turned and spurred their horses to a gallop. They thundered down the lists and met in a terrific crash, each taking the other in the centre of their shield and their lances splintered into fragments. Again, they charged their horses and once more their lances exploded. The third time they spurred together, Sir Roger's lance splintered yet again but this time Rolf's took him so hard on the right of his shield that both he and his horse were brought crashing down onto the trampled grass and mud. The crowd shouted and screamed and stamped their feet with appreciation. His fist in the air, Baron Rolf rode a victory circuit while the lords and ladies applauded, the common people cheered and young maidens showered him in flowers.

After a brief interval, the sound of trumpets rang out and it was time for the mêlée. Excitement and its partner, fear, built in the pit of Hugh's stomach. From a rough count, fifty riders were to take part in the mock battle. The herald divided them into two teams of knights and squires, about a score of each. The crowd cheered as the riders paraded into position on horseback for the mêlée. Riding tall, Hugh looked around him at the other riders' shields and saddles emblazoned with heraldic ordinaries and animal charges and devices of their respective houses. The field was a mass of vivid azures, verts, sables and gules. Burning with pride to be part of such a spectacle, he urged his horse into position alongside the other squires of his father's house and pulled on his helm.

'Now remember!' yelled Sir Roger, standing at the edge of the lists. 'Inexperienced knights are frequently slain during the mêlée. You must keep your wits about you!'

At the signal from the horn, there was a thunder of hooves as the main charge began. The air was filled with the shrill cries of war that made the hairs on the back of Hugh's neck stand on end. An intoxicating rush of exhilaration took hold of him as he sprang away and charged at the opposing group of knights and squires with his couched lance. This was what it was like to fight in a battle! There were so many riders that he had to wheel and swerve his horse this way and that to avoid hitting his teammates. The line of horsemen clashed with their opponents with a terrific smash that sent splinters of wood flying everywhere.

To his delight, he unhorsed one of his foes at his first tilt, meeting his opponent's attack and replying with a thrust of his lance that tipped him over the tail of his steed. Many other riders were also unhorsed after the initial charge and were cast down into the churned-up earth, many having sustained injuries from flying shards of broken lances. There were shrieks of pain as some of the fallen men were trampled by their fleeing steeds. Hugh clung onto the reins for dear life, knowing that all depended on him staying in the saddle.

Time passed. The arena became a heaving, chaotic mass of activity. It was difficult to distinguish between friend and foe in the tumult. The air reeked of sweat and leather. The torn-up earth and trampled grass was littered with broken lances. Fallen knights scrambled up onto their feet and, armed with fresh lances, leapt back on their horses. A massive horse writhed on the ground beside Hugh, its legs flailing and lethal hooves lashing in the air as it struggled to get back on its feet. He felt sorry for the beast. It was impossible to think above the battle din, the cheers and boos of the crowd and the war cries of the knights. Directly in front of him, a horse trampled an unseated knight. The unfortunate fellow screamed in pain, grovelling on the ground. Shortly afterwards he was dragged off the field crying out in agony and clutching his injured leg, which hung askew.

Many of the riders were weary and some even wounded. For although they fought with blunted weapons it was impossible to avoid bloody noses, cuts and bruises and more extensive injuries like cracked ribs and broken bones when falling from the saddle. But doggedly the remaining squires and knights errant fought on, determined to show their prowess in the battlefield.

Without warning, one of the opposing knights dealt Hugh's horse such a thumping blow on the muzzle with his lance that the poor animal shook back his head, screaming, and backed up several feet before Hugh could get him under control again. Drawing his sword as he approached his foe, he kept his horse as steady as he could with his left hand. Trumpets rang and drums rolled, and the crowd roared with excitement. With a swing of his sword, Hugh unhorsed another opponent with a rush of pleasure and turned about to tackle the next. Intent as he was pressing forward with his attack, he didn't notice a foe at his left flank who almost took him off guard. Only by a hair's breadth was he able to shift upon his saddle and avoid a lance, after that he lost his grip on the saddle and floundered around trying to hoist himself back up into position. Heart pounding and with almost Herculean effort, he managed to pull himself up and sat up straight. The incident left him shaken and after that he was wary.

As the afternoon wore on, the rising breeze became a chill wind and brought with it grey rain clouds. A heavy shower drenched the riders, their chain mail dripping and the horses damp and forlorn, but still the battle went on. Hooves slipped in the mud. Somehow his steed stayed surefooted and he in turn managed to cling on and stay in his saddle.

At long last, daylight faded. With a fanfare of

trumpets, the Abbot of Dover declared the mêlée over and announced Hugh's team to be the winning side. There was an appreciative roar from what was left of the audience. Many had run off seeking shelter from the downpour. Drums rolled and he joined his triumphant kinsfolk as they took a bow, which earned them wild applause from the crowd. His heart swelled with pleasure. Looking up, he sought out his father among the gentry seated upon the platform, but he was deep in conversation with the portly, raven-haired man beside him. Apparently, his father had missed his moment of glory. A wave of disappointment washed over him until he became aware of Eleanor's beautiful hazel eyes upon him and something in him reached out to her. Did she still love him as he loved her?

⁓

The feast that evening was a grand affair. The Great Hall of Dover Castle dwarfed his father's Great Hall and was packed with over a hundred guests. Fires blazed in the hearths, a silver-bearded bard woke the music of his harp and a roar of laughter broke across the hall. Hugh's mouth watered at the delicious smell of roasting meat. His father and brother took their seats at the high table with the other barons while an attendant ushered Hugh and the other squires to the lower refectory tables, where room was made for them on the crowded benches.

'What a fantastic tourney!' A buck-toothed squire

smashed his goblet down on the table. 'Did you see Baron Rolf make Sir Roger eat the dust?'

Hugh nodded and took a long draught of wine.

The other squires were in high spirits too. The banqueting hall was becoming progressively noisier. The squires around him had their fill of wine and continued to drink still more. Their faces grew red, and they shouted to make themselves heard over the din. He gave in to his hunger and was splendidly feasted and mopped up the puddle of delicious gravy on his plate with a hunk of bread. The servants cleared the remnants of roast boar, chicken, mutton, pheasant and quail from the table. Platters of fruit, steaming pudding, oat-cakes, cheeses and other delicacies were served next.

Hugh had a clear view of the platform. Eleanor sat at the far end of the long table. She looked terribly lonely, but she was still every bit as beautiful as he remembered, dressed in a mauve gown. For some reason, she was not seated beside her husband. The seat on Baron Rolf's left hand had been usurped by a haughty-looking blonde lady with far-apart eyes, who was pretty in a sulky sort of way. He supposed she was Rolf's kept mistress. She showed off with theatrical airs and graces without one touch of real elegance or refinement.

At long last Eleanor met his eye. He saw naked shock on her face the instant she recognised him. Under his gaze, something seemed to move behind her eyes, and he had the distinct impression she was pleading for him to help her. His heart drummed in his throat. Without hesitation, he got to his feet and moved through the crowded hall towards her. A powerful longing to rescue her burned like a flame in his heart. But then she cast a frightened glance at her husband. All at once she appeared fearful of his approach. He nearly stopped in his tracks. Eleanor was shrinking before his very eyes, drooping like a flower in need of water. Cowed and submissive under the watchful eye of her husband, she was as a startled fawn in the power of a huntsman.

He was almost level with the high table when his path was blocked by a surly, broken-nosed attendant built like an ox. 'Return to your place, boy. You have no business here. These men are your betters.' He shoved Hugh back with a huge hand.

Hugh was not about to be deterred and pushed on. 'I only wish to speak to the lady yonder.' He gestured at Eleanor.

The attendant struck him a crashing blow in the belly that almost toppled him over. He doubled up in pain, gasping. A lull had descended on the conversation at the high table at the commotion. He had an overwhelming sense of someone watching him. He turned. Baron Rolf's icy blue eyes bored into him, surveying him with an insufferable air of superiority. Out of the corner of his eye, his father flashed him a warning look. He had been resolved to stand his ground, but he felt himself wilt. He retraced his steps, subdued and impotent.

On the walk back to his bench, he cringed at his own cowardliness. Why had he given up so easily? Hanging his head, he picked at the sweetmeats on his plate; his appetite had left him. The next time he looked in Eleanor's direction he was dismayed to find her seat empty and she was nowhere to be seen.

7.

New Hope for Eleanor

In the middle of the night, Eleanor woke with a shriek, drenched in sweat and with the vile taste of a nightmare in her mouth. The dream was still vivid in her mind. Shrouded in pitch darkness, she had been trapped in a small underground cell of stone, which felt as smooth as polished granite. With no room to either sit up, because the ceiling was so low, or lie flat, as there was a steep ridge across the stone floor, it had been impossible even to extend her legs. Heart racing, she had braced herself against the cold stone, exerting her will to force back the walls and floor, fighting an evil sense of suffocation. But it had been all in vain. She had screamed and screamed. But no one had come to help her.

Now she stretched out her legs. For a moment she relished the relief she had so craved in her nightmare. However, it was a fleeting respite for the grim reality of her situation flooded back to her. Her hands flew to her smarting neck where Rolf's hands had attempted to extinguish the very life from her body.

By the light of the dancing flames in the hearth, she examined the purple bruises that were developing on her wrists where he had held her fast.

Her husband slept on beside her. He stank of sweat. Rolf's heavy frame and muscular arms and legs sprawled out across the mattress. His face was turned towards her, his long greasy fringe was a tangled mess. His breath came in deep rasping snorts. In the eerie light of the fire, his thin lips were twisted in an ugly grimace, as though he smelled something bad under his nose.

A rush of nausea overwhelmed her. She took in deep gulps of air, attempting to steady herself, but the queasiness refused to recede. Beads of sweat formed on her upper lip and at her hairline. The heavy coverlet was excruciatingly hot and she kicked it off, but the effort of doing so only precipitated another wave of nausea. Commanding herself to breathe deeply again, she somehow managed to resist the urge to vomit.

All was quiet in the castle. No light illuminated the windows behind the heavy drapes. Her thoughts returned to the banquet the night before – and Hugh. Her beloved Hugh! How close he had been and yet they had not had the chance even to exchange so much as a word. Her heart whimpered after him and her body ached with bittersweet yearning. It dawned on her that she could no longer hide from the agonising reality that their love was impossible.

Bit by bit, the uninvited guest, despair, overwhelmed her. She was its prey. It had her in its fangs. The hairs on her face and arms stood on end as it shrouded her in its cold veil. She wept. Once she started, she felt as though she would never stop. Her whole body shook with sobs. Despair gripped her aching heart and whispered insistently in her ears, her constant companion in her unhappy marriage.

Another wave of nausea overtook her. She just managed to get to the chamber pot in time and retched several times and then vomited up the contents of her belly. When the nausea finally abated, she lay back spent on the pillow. After her body's sudden purge and her bout of crying, she experienced a dreadful sense of emptiness.

Beside her Rolf slept on, his breath rasping as heavily as before, oblivious to her, thank God. She lay very still on her side with her back to him, hardly daring even to breathe until the bells of the Priory of St Mary rang out for Prime and her husband roused himself with a grunt. He got up without a word and left the chamber.

Soon after, she must have fallen asleep. Sometime later, she crashed awake in alarm, shaken from her groggy slumber by someone entering the chamber.

Thankfully, it was only the maid bringing more logs for the fire and come to light the bedside lamp. A pretty slip of a girl with a lot of soft brown hair, she was dressed in a modest woollen gown. Eleanor watched her prod the fire. The girl brushed away the ashes and added logs to the embers, coaxing the flames with smaller twigs until they produced a splendid, strong blaze. It was only by an accident of birth that Eleanor was married to the baron and lay in this grand bedchamber surrounded by luxury while the other girl was a servant waiting on her. The innocent chit could have no idea of how much she envied her.

One of the ladies-in-waiting bustled into the chamber and the girl scurried off. She was dismayed to see it was Cecily. She sat up in bed and drew her gown up to her neck, covering the bruises that still throbbed painfully.

Cecily scowled down at her and narrowed her huge eyes.

She would be obliged to submit to Cecily's attentions. With a gasp of pain, she pulled herself to her feet and permitted the woman to remove her gown. Cecily did no more than pause momentarily at the sight of her bruised and manhandled body. Her lips twisted into a thin, cruel smile.

At that moment, the periphery of Eleanor's vision became swathed in shadows and an awful rush of nausea took hold of her. Her knees gave way and she fell into darkness.

She came to lying on the reeds on the flagstone floor. A group of ladies fussed around her.

'Get her back onto the bed,' said Millicent.

Servants hoisted her onto the bed where she proceeded to be violently sick all over the covers. She was mortified to find herself in such a predicament; there was nothing she hated more than being the cause of a commotion. She tried to get to her feet, but her head spun.

'Let me look at her,' said Beatrice as she barged into the chamber, her red velvet kirtle rustling against the tapestry hanging. Her dark hair was scraped back harshly from her face and secured with a silk ribbon.

Eleanor suppressed a groan. Beatrice was the last person she wanted to see.

'Have you bled recently?' Her mother-in-law surveyed her with a look of undisguised disgust.

With dawning comprehension, she shook her head. It had been many weeks since she had last bled.

'Perhaps you are with child,' said Beatrice. 'It is certainly about time.'

Beatrice swept out of the room, slammed the door behind her and left her alone.

Lifting her chemise, she glanced down at her naked body. Her breasts did seem more prominent than usual, and perhaps her belly was rounder. And there was something peculiar about the way she felt now.

Without warning, another curtain of nausea swooped down on her. It left her bent double. She retched into the chamber pot. When the wave passed, she rang for the servant and lay back in bed, exhausted and lightheaded from the exertion.

Presently, the servant appeared, and dutifully removed the stinking pot and replaced it with a fresh one. Eleanor requested a cup of wine and some oat-cakes. Perhaps a dry biscuit would ease the sickness.

Momentarily, she knew some respite from nausea. She gazed out of the window at the azure sky. A new spring dawned in her heart.

After a short while, the servant returned with wine and oat-cakes. She sipped the wine and nibbled a biscuit. Presently, she felt more like her usual self. She would take the opportunity to languish in bed for the morning and forgo embroidery with the other women. Perhaps, this afternoon, she would take a walk on the ramparts.

The thought of becoming a mother filled her with feelings of delight. How sweetly her heart ached at the prospect of gazing into her new-born's eyes! She could almost conjure up the milky smell of infants from her childhood.

Presently, Martha, a middle-aged servant woman with a pale face and hollow eyes and a mop of scraggly brown hair, entered the chamber bearing a tray of lunch.

Even the smell of the food made her stomach lurch horribly. Summoning all her strength, she took a few mouthfuls of the bread and shin of beef.

She had hoped to spend all day resting in her chamber, but her mother-in-law had other plans.

Beatrice burst into her room again that afternoon. 'Eleanor . . . you are to accompany me to my chamber where my physician will examine you.'

She cringed. She had no desire to be poked and prodded by a physician.

'Now, Eleanor.' Beatrice arched her brows. 'The physician must examine you.'

At a gesture from Beatrice, Millicent offered her arm. They walked slowly out of the chamber along the corridor leading to her mother-in-law's bower. All the while, she steeled herself, desperate not to be sick.

The physician was already in attendance. A stringy man bent double with age, he squinted at them as they entered the chamber. He shuffled over, unsteady on his arthritic legs.

'Pray lie down, Lady Eleanor.' He gestured to a couch heaped with embroidered cushions.

She moved uncertainly to the couch, sat down and then swung her legs up so that she lay flat, her face upturned to the physician and Beatrice.

The physician moved awkwardly towards her. It appeared his lower back caused him some pain. As he moved closer, she recoiled. The old man stank. It took all her presence of mind to hold back a vomiting fit. The physician leaned over and touched her forehead with the back of his hand, presumably to check for a fever. Then she got a sickening whiff of his rancid breath. She nearly gagged. With a sinewy hand, he took her pulse at the wrist. Apparently satisfied, he moved and lifted her skirts. Every instinct in her body screamed to run. With gritted teeth she braced herself for what was to come. He prodded her abdomen.

'Part your legs,' he said.

She complied, although every nerve in her body was protesting about the intrusion. Frozen, she watched appalled. He rolled up the woollen sleeves of his robe and felt around her opening with his grasping bony fingers. When at last she felt she couldn't endure the invasion a moment longer, he pulled his hand away and straightened, rubbing his back. 'There can be no doubt. Lady Eleanor is with child.'

A curious surge of pleasure danced in her belly.

Even Beatrice seemed momentarily appeased by this news. 'When can we expect her to be confined?'

'Lady Eleanor is already two months past,' said the physician. 'God willing, the child will be born in April.'

'Baron Rolf has gone to London,' said Beatrice. 'I will send him word directly. Summon the messenger.'

Eleanor's heart leapt. A mere seven months and then she would have a baby of her own! But how would her husband react to the news? Thoughts of Rolf brought fresh vomit to her throat. And she retched into her hands. The physician hurried forward with a ceramic bowl outstretched. She brought up her entire lunch. Beatrice turned away, wrinkling her nose and curling her lip.

'I should like to return to my chamber,' said Eleanor. She fought down the treacherous sobs that accompanied her bouts of vomiting.

～

Early that evening, Martha brought her a tray of food. Once again, she was sickened by the smell. A thick vegetable soup with cream and roast partridge was set before her. Forcing herself to eat because she knew she should, she picked at it.

After she had eaten as much as she could stomach, she summoned the servant and announced her intention to go outside to watch the sunset. Dover was a defensive fortress with only a small herb garden within its walls, an extension of Beatrice's bower. She had no wish to linger there! Therefore, the only other safe place to walk undisturbed was the castle terrace, known as the allure, or rampart walk. Beatrice and the other ladies-in-waiting were at supper in the dining-hall, so a servant girl accompanied her.

Her legs were weak after a day in bed. She walked slowly along the torchlit passageways, supported by the servant. Fearful of falling, she was careful of her footing down the two steep flights of spiral staircase to the great gate of the donjon. At the foot of the staircase, the men-at-arms lowered their eyes and bowed in deference to her.

As the portcullis of the donjon was closed, one of the men-at-arms showed them an alternative way out of the keep through a supply passage. Eventually they emerged into the courtyard. She blinked in the natural light. The warmth of the summer air on her skin surprised her. The thick stone walls kept the keep cool, even in summer. It was wonderful to be outside. However, in her delicate state she had the nose of a bloodhound and she caught all sorts of fearful odours in the air: the stink of the fowl-pens and fishponds on the left of the castle as well as the foul stench of the latrines several yards away. As fast as she could, she hurried away, past the outhouses that housed the kitchens, from which wafted the smell of roasting meat, past the chapel and the barracks, towards the stairs that led up to the terrace on the ramparts on the outer curtain walls of the castle.

The high stone steps were awkward in her trailing gown, so she gathered up her skirts in her arms. Given that the walls were at least eight feet thick, the allure was wide enough for her to walk along without fear of falling. In front of her was the protection of the embattled parapet and, to the rear, a lower, lighter wall.

She gazed out towards the north at the world beyond. The red globe of the sun lay low in the sky to the west. The evening sky was bleached of colour after the heat of the day. The salty tang of the sea was in the air and she tasted it on her lips. On the other side of the castle, the sea crashed against the rocks far below.

At the foot of the outer rampart walls was a murky moat, which also served as a fishpond stocked with roach, bream and carp. On the other side of the moat, to the left, was the castle's orchard planted with at least a thousand apple and pear trees, already heavy with green fruit, and to the right was a vineyard. Beyond that was a barren shoulder of hillside where nothing grew but grass, maintained so there was no cover for an approaching enemy. Further still down the valley was the walled town of Dover, a mass of steeples and a sprawl of gold, red and black reed-thatched roofs glinting in the last sun of the day and from which rose the curling plumes of grey smoke from cooking fires. The austere grey-walled Priory of St Mary perched on the hill on the other side of Dover.

The plaintive cries of a young hawk caught her unawares. A falconer was training one of his birds on the open tower to her right. It was a peregrine falcon. Fascinated, she watched as the falcon struggled from the man's gloved fist, either through fright or for liberty. The falconer's apprentice stood down below in the orchard calling off the bird, luring it down for exercise and a hunk of red flesh. The falcon soared aloft and then suddenly struck at a sparrow mid-air. Then it descended with its quarry to claim its pound of flesh.

How she envied that hawk its freedom. To be able to fly away at a moment's notice to some paradise – now, that would be something. If she were a bird, she would return to the gardens of her parents' castle in Normandy where she had spent most of her child-hood. They were a haven of serenity: resonant with birdsong, resplendent with colourful flower sprays and verdant tendrils and filled with a delicate, bitter-sweet scent. As a child, she had liked nothing better than winding in and out among the shrubbery and around and about the statues of nymphs and satyrs and the gushing fountains that spilled into ponds bubbling with ancient carp. During the long summers, she had delighted in lying for hours on a blanket of pink blossom in the dappled sunlight under the gnarled apple trees, listening to the cicadas' incessant hum, gorging on bunches of sweet red grapes that weighed down the withered vines in the vineyard. Though she was leagues away, she could almost hear the birdsong and smell the sweet scent of jasmine.

Down in the orchard beyond the moat, a woman she recognised emerged, basket in hand, from a hut. It was Martha, the middle-aged servant woman who attended to her in her chamber. She was collecting the fallen apples from the orchard. This was a revelation. She hadn't realised there was a way out of the castle apart from the main drawbridge entrance. Like her father's castle, Rolf's had a concealed entrance to be used to bring supplies into the castle in times of siege. At last there was the real possibility of escape from her hell of a marriage – if only she could obtain a key.

As her thoughts turned to her husband she shuddered. How she despised him. Her skin crawled even to think of him. How would he react to the news that she was having a baby? Surely things would be different now. They had to be. He couldn't go on knocking her about anymore, could he?

A lead weight settled upon her and another wave of nausea bubbled up. Right away, the servant was at her side with a bowl. The bitterness of her thoughts seemed to give rise to a great quantity of vomit. Empty and wretched, she clung to the parapet.

8.

Hugh Returns Home

The sky grew overcast on their journey home the morning after the tournament. Ill-omened black clouds hung low in the sky. The shrouded sun cast a gloomy light over the countryside and swathed the surrounding forest in ominous shadow. Hugh rode with a heavy heart. He had half a mind to fall back behind the others and return to the castle to rescue Eleanor. Over and over, he ran rescue plans through his mind, each more outlandish than the one before. But it was useless. He was powerless and a cloak of depression enveloped him.

Towards evening, he recognised familiar land-marks, but this brought him no consolation. Try as he might, he couldn't shake off a feeling of foreboding as they neared the castle. Something was wrong – he was sure of it. By the time they approached the castle gates, darkness was closing in at the last light of the day. His heart pounded when he caught sight of one of his mother's handmaidens who had run out into the courtyard to greet them. The woman's expression was grim.

'I am sorry to inform you that the mistress died in the early hours of this morning.' The woman's homely face was pale and her eyes downcast.

'Pray prepare her body for the funeral.' His father did not betray the slightest hint of emotion.

The shock of the news struck Hugh numb. He had never foreseen that his beloved mother would die so quickly. A knot tightened like a vice in his belly. She had faced death alone. A splinter of guilt embedded itself in his heart.

The horses filed through the gate. The stable hands hurried forward, assisting the knights to dismount. He swung his legs off his horse, his limbs stiff after hours of riding. Everything was unreal, as though he were living another man's life. An overwhelming urge to rush up to his mother's chamber, to reassure himself that she wasn't dead after all, took hold of him.

He walked towards the keep, but his father stopped him. 'Where are you going? You have your duties to attend to. The horses need stabling and the armour has to be cleaned and hung up.'

White hot anger burning in his throat, Hugh led the horses into the stables. Working as fast as he could, he unloaded the saddle bags from the horses, hung up the harnesses and saddles and brushed the horses down. Afterwards he hurried to the armoury and polished his chain mail in a barrel of sand until it gleamed and then did the same for Sir Roger's mail. Accomplishing these routine tasks made him feel a little better.

After he finished his chores in the stables, he had hoped he might have time to slip up to his mother's chamber, but he was sent to serve food and wine in the hall. He knelt at his father's side with a dish of water to wash his hands and a wave of resentment overcame him. He stifled it. Custom, drummed into him after years of training as a page, dictated that he must attend to his elders dutifully.

When, at last, he sat down to eat his stew, Sir Roger interrupted his meal. The knight had lost a garment of clothing and he demanded that Hugh find it for him immediately. By the time he got back to his dish, it was stone cold. He had to take it back to the kitchens and get it reheated. The food was tasteless but he forced it down. A goblet of wine did nothing to raise his spirits.

After his meal, he took Sir Roger's draught of sleeping-wine up to his chamber and waited for the knight to gulp it down. Only then did he have the opportunity to visit his mother's body. His heart hammered as he crept up the spiral staircase to her turret room.

A single candle illuminated his mother's chamber.

No fire burned in the hearth. The room was sombre and cold and smelled faintly of rosewater. His mother's handmaidens had laid out her body on the bed and dressed her in her finest robes. Her white face had taken on an air of unearthly piety. The hair strewn across her pillow had lost its vivid red tint. Her eyes were closed, her arms crossed over her chest and her beloved rosary interlaced her fingers. Instinctively, he reached out and touched her. But his heart missed a beat when he found that her skin was as cold as marble.

He couldn't bear to be in the room a moment longer and so he hurried towards the door. A sting of shame accompanied the relief that washed over him as he closed the door of the chamber. His mother's suffering was finally over.

That night he fell into bed, spent. Yet sleep brought him no rest, filled with bittersweet dreams chronicling the key moments of his life with his mother. She smiled at him radiant with love, his ears resounded with peals of her rich laughter and she caressed his face. She looked at him with concern in her eyes as she had when she had watched over him at his sickbed through various childhood illnesses. Mixed in with these dreams about his mother was Eleanor's unhappy, strained face in the Great Hall of Dover Castle. The full strength of the unbearable longing he felt for both women who were now lost to him tugged at his heart.

∼

He woke, still weary, with the crowing cockerel but could not bring himself to get up and drifted irresistibly back into groggy sleep.

Sometime later, Sir Roger roused him roughly from his slumber with a cuff around his ear. 'Why are you still sleeping?' yelled the knight in Hugh's smarting earhole. 'Did I give you leave to sleep in and shirk your duties? Wait until your father hears about this!'

Hugh dragged himself out of bed. He pulled on his tunic and hose. He wolfed down a breakfast of hot buttered toast and eggs, then applied himself to his usual household tasks. Engaged in humdrum activities, he was surprised to find that he felt reasonably happy, and then experienced a pang of shame that he had forgotten his mother so easily and a painful fissure splintered his heart.

In the afternoon, while exercising the falcons and watching the birds soar into the sky after their prey, he almost forgot his mother and took solace in the pleasure of the distraction. But it only made it worse again when her death came flooding back and guilt seared his heart like a branding iron.

Though he knew that the Eynsford Castle, his home, had not changed, it seemed that its stark flint walls looked more oppressive than usual. The Great Hall appeared more austere than he ever remembered. And the knights and squires in his father's household wore grim expressions on their sallow faces.

Try as he might that day, he struggled to muster

enthusiasm for tasks he previously relished, like fighting and tending the horses.

That night, after his evening meal, he crawled into his bunk exhausted. But even there, he knew no consolation as he slipped into a bleak dream world.

~

Four days later, on the morning of his mother's funeral, he woke with a heavy heart. A solemn Serle helped him dress in his finest tunic and breeches. As a squire, Hugh had important duties to fulfil, for many guests were expected at the castle for the funeral. That morning, he prepared platters of food for the guests, carved thick slices of roast boar and capon and arranged them on silver trays and poured wine into flagons. He and the other squires disposed of the old reeds from the floor of the Great Hall and replenished them with fresh.

His aunt on his mother's side and her husband and son, Guy, had sent word they would be attending the funeral and his heart gladdened at the thought of seeing them.

Guests began to appear towards mid-afternoon and he waited at the castle gates to welcome them. Lords and ladies of high rank arrived, their long trains and hoods made of expensive black wool with black linen and fur trim trailing them. Bardolf, his only friend at the castle, stood beside him, ready to take care of the guests' horses. Hugh ushered the guests into the Great

Hall for refreshments ahead of the funeral that was due to take place in the castle chapel.

At last, his mother's sister, Lady Rosamunde, arrived, a slender woman dressed in an ermine cloak. She had his mother's calm hazel eyes. 'Dearest Hugh . . .' She embraced him warmly. 'You are the image of your sweet mother!'

His cousin, Guy, a tall, well-proportioned youth with blue eyes that sparkled and blond curly hair, pushed past his mother. 'Hugh!' Guy hugged him and slapped him on the back.

Hugh's spirits rose. It was wonderful to see Guy. It seemed only yesterday they had played at being knights in the woods with wooden swords.

The great bell tolled and summoned the guests to the funeral service in the castle chapel. They filed into the high-vaulted chamber, which was filled with the fragrant odour of incense. The chapel heaved with people. All his father's tenants had come to pay their respects to his mother and, as all the seats in the pews were occupied, women with babes in arms were obliged to sit on the rush-strewn floor.

With his heart in his mouth, Hugh left his cousin's side and joined his father and brother in the family pew at the front of the chapel. He bowed his head and murmured prayers at the sight of his mother's casket.

In front of the altar, the priest, a bald man with a grey haggard face dressed in a brown woollen robe cleared his throat. The steady hum of voices in the chapel fell silent.

'Dearly beloved,' began the priest. 'We are gathered here to celebrate dear Lady Joan's life.' He spoke in a low sepulchral tone. 'Let us pray for her soul.'

After the prayers, a harp struck up his mother's favourite psalm and the congregation began to sing. Their voices resounded through the chapel. A chill ran up Hugh's spine and the hairs on his arms stood on end.

Later, tears welled in his eyes as the casket containing his mother's body was lowered into the ground beside the tombs of his ancestors and buried under shovelfuls of earth.

All the guests were invited to the banquet after the funeral. He served the dignitaries seated at the high table and had little time to eat or talk to the guests, but Guy pulled him aside.

'The herald informed us that you fought well in Dover.' A radiant smile lit up his cousin's handsome features.

Hugh was astonished that the herald had spoken well of him. He couldn't help feeling envious of his cousin. Surely Guy had grown more good-looking of late.

'Nothing like a good sword fight to give a man some thirst.' And Guy took a great gulp of wine.

Hugh toasted his goblet against Guy's.

'It is good to get away from Father's watchful eye and have some fun,' said Guy. They both turned and looked at their fathers, who were engaged in conversation with the important guests.

'Yes, and from all thought of impending marriage,' said Hugh.

'You too? My father has been insisting that we entertain all the eligible ladies in the district and that I pick one to marry.'

'At least you have some choice in the matter. My future has been already decided for me. I am to marry a frightful woman.'

'No, who?' Guy smiled sympathetically.

'Lady Bethany.'

'Lord no, not her. She's dreadful! Much given to pouting, I recall – and not even pretty!' Guy laughed.

'It isn't a laughing matter!'

'Of course not.' The smile vanished from Guy's face. 'Let's have another drink to take your mind off it.'

For a while they said nothing until Guy broke the silence. 'Something has to be done about it. A lifetime of Lady Bethany is a fate worse than death!'

'Exactly so! But what can I do? Once my father makes up his mind about something there is no going back.'

'The king has tasked my father with recruiting knights to go on the next crusade. I am to join up. We leave next month.'

'A crusade! How exciting!'

'Why don't you join us?'

Hugh's heart lifted at the prospect of escaping his miserable life. But was he ready for a real battle? 'My father would never agree. You see, I am not yet a knight.'

'Oh pish!' Guy put his arm around Hugh's shoulders. 'I am just fresh from my knighting ceremony – I've not yet seen a real battle. There will be plenty of squires seeking to earn their spurs. You could win your knighthood out in the Holy Land – there can be no greater honour! I could ask my father to put in a word with your father, if you like?'

'Oh yes, thank you.'

'Then it is settled. What adventures we will have together!'

～

At supper that evening, he was surprised to find he had support from many quarters when he broached the possibility of his accompanying Guy and his father on a crusade.

'Hugh proved his prowess in the mêlée, my lord,' said the herald, a man with straight black hair, which hung in heavy locks about his thin face. 'He unseated no fewer than three knights and five squires. Your son strains at the leash. Surely it is time for him to discover the world.'

Hugh grew warm with pleasure.

'That was child's play,' said his father. 'He will be out in the real world – a world of real swords that swish off a man's head.' He regarded Hugh with cold eyes. 'He will never make anything of himself.'

Hugh's face burned with shame.

'What greater honour is there than to fight in God's

army,' pitched in the priest. The eyes under his haggard brow were unexpectedly kindly. 'Surely you can see the boy is eager to prove himself. He was always so conscientious in his study of the ancient texts.'

In the end, it was the steward, gesticulating with his huge hands, who won his father around. 'The king has decreed that each baron of consequence supplies at least thirty men, my lord. Why not let Hugh be one of their number?'

'I suppose it will make a man of him,' his father conceded. He paused to wash his hands in the water Hugh had brought him. He wiped his hands fastidiously on a linen cloth. 'And I would sooner lose him than some of my finer knights. I need good men by my side to keep out marauders and deter my more predatory neighbours.'

The burgeoning pleasure in Hugh's heart at the prospect of going on crusade was rather dampened by his father's slights.

'The time is right to un-boy him,' said Sir Roger. 'He'll have to get used to wearing his mail and accustomed to bearing its weight in addition to the weight of the long sword and lances for battle. This is no child's game. His survival depends on his skill.'

'I dearly wish I was going as a knight, like my cousin,' said Hugh. He turned to Sir Roger. 'Couldn't you dub me?'

There was a stony glare in his father's humourless eyes. 'You will have to win your spurs in battle.'

'But William never saw battle,' argued Hugh. William had been knighted in a huge ceremony in London Temple, where tents were raised to accommodate a crowd of over two hundred young squires. The late King Henry himself had knighted William. Hugh had to admit he was still green with envy about it. But he might as well have been talking to a stone wall for his father turned the conversation abruptly to other matters.

That night, when all the guests had gone, Hugh sat on the wooden bench in the moonlit courtyard with Bardolf. The muffled sound of men's voices could be heard from the Great Hall where his father and his entourage still feasted. A faint smell of smoke hung in the air.

'I have but a month to prepare,' Hugh fretted. 'I doubt that I can reach my peak fitness. Will I be up to wearing my heavy mail hauberk for hours on end? Will I be able to endure weeks of being in the saddle? And yet, what else is there for me to do? To remain in the castle as a drudge for my father and brother is simply beyond contemplation. And to marry Bethany would be a fate worse than death!'

'Don't forget you will have the thrill of adventure and the glory of battle on crusade,' said Bardolf. He gazed up misty-eyed at the crescent moon.

'What do I know of battle? The unbelievers in the east are reputed to be fearsome warriors who employ the devil's tricks. And yet, I yearn to see the Holy Land for myself. I am eager to walk barefoot in the desert and feel the heat of the sun on my skin, and to eat strange, exotic delicacies. Above all, I want to make pilgrimage to Jerusalem, to pay my respects at the birthplace of the Son of God.'

'Would that I could come,' said Bardolf with a wistful smile.

9.
Rolf

In the weeks that followed, Eleanor's nausea receded somewhat. However, she couldn't overcome a creeping sense of dread at the prospect of her husband's home-coming.

On the morning Rolf was due to return, she woke drenched in sweat and with a fearful headache. All night long, she had hardly slept a wink. She had tossed and turned, envisaging his reaction to the news that she was having a baby. Dared she hope that he might be a changed man? In her worst imaginings, she relived the terrifying violence to which he had subjected her time and time again. If her waking terrors were bad, her dreams were worse. At one point she dreamed that she struggled to feed her child with a silver spoon, but then she realised that the babe was already dead; icy and grey, it had been garrotted with a thin silver chain. Weak with lack of sleep and stricken with anxiety, she hoped she might feel better after eating something. She rang for the servant to bring her some food.

The servant brought a platter of fresh bread, cheese, hardboiled eggs and cake. She nibbled at the bread and moist cake and drank some wine. Bit by bit, she felt more herself.

Perhaps she had exaggerated her fears about Rolf. After all, she had achieved what was expected of her and was pregnant with his child. Surely he would be pleased. Yes, in the darkness of the night, she had blown everything out of proportion.

Presently, the servant entered and removed the remains of her meal. Beatrice certainly kept her stuffed to the gills with food. In recent weeks, her belly had swelled noticeably and her breasts had almost doubled in size, giving her a most comely figure. Her hair had grown thick and her skin had lost the pallid tinge it had at the beginning of her pregnancy.

She rang a bell for a lady-in-waiting and Lady Millicent arrived promptly in her chamber.

'Lady Beatrice has bid me come to dress you for chapel this morning,' the young woman drawled in a bored voice. She pursed her haughty lips.

Eleanor suppressed a groan. Chapel services were so tedious. She had been looking forward to being left to her own devices. And there was always the risk she might vomit during the service. It would be mortifying to be sick in front of Beatrice and the other ladies.

The castle seamstress had made new gowns for her expanding belly, and Millicent brought one of their creations from the chest. It was a floor-length, loose green gown with ample room for a baby bump. Millicent helped Eleanor into the gown and secured a loose girdle of golden thread above her belly. She turned her attention first to Eleanor's face, applying rouge to her cheeks, and then to her hair, dividing it into four thick plaits interwoven with gold ribbons stitched with tiny rubies. Afterwards, she fixed a gossamer veil over her head with her golden coronet. She fastened a necklace of rubies about Eleanor's neck.

Eleanor slipped soft calf-hide shoes on her feet. She admired her reflection in the mirror. Already, she was feeling a little better.

Millicent proffered her an arm and they made their way through the passageways and down the staircase to the chapel, which was situated on the first floor of the keep. Eleanor shivered involuntarily. It felt cold out of bed, despite it being summer. At the foot of the spiral staircase, they encountered a gaggle of high-spirited lords and ladies dressed in their finest silks and furs. Her heart sank at the sight of them. They all turned and stared at her, craning their necks to catch a glimpse of Rolf's pregnant wife. They exchanged whispers sotto voce. She concentrated all her efforts on not retching. Whiffs of ripe body odour stopped her in her tracks.

At last, the throng arrived in the chapel and took their pews. The late king had built a splendid chapel with space for forty or more people. It had a vaulted ceiling and tapestries depicting the Last Supper and the Resurrection of Christ hung from the walls.

Millicent pulled her into the seat beside Beatrice. And she sat down with a thud.

The tide of chatter ebbed. The congregation rose to their feet, heads bowed, as the priest moved slowly along the aisle carrying the blessed sacrament from the sacristy to the altar. Tiny twinkling lamps illuminated a golden statue of the Holy Mother and her Infant. The priest chanted in a low voice and swung a thurible of burning incense. It filled the chapel with such a pervasive smell that Eleanor was suffused with nausea.

A harpist played a gentle melody and the congregation lined up to receive the sacrament. Even the body and blood of Christ tasted peculiar. When all had partaken, they returned to their seats for the priest's address. He spoke in a strong eloquent voice.

'On this day, I would like us to think of the holy sacrament of Marriage. It is the women I address today. I bid you be careful of your clacking tongues. Your scolding and prattling of your good husbands is abhorrent and contrary to God's will. Better a devil in red-hot scales and forked tail than a devil in a silk gown! Must I remind you that God instructs you to love, honour and obey your husband in all matters. You will be answerable to any infractions of God's will on Judgement Day. Husbands, I counsel you to keep a firm hand on your wives. It is better to beat them in the early days than to have a lifetime of a scolding tongue, or to have them fly off with another man who turns their foolish head. And if that does not work, threaten them with the cucking stool – that should be deterrent enough. Here ends today's lesson.'

She stole a sideways glance at her mother-in-law. Beatrice's face bore the hallmarks of boredom. As a widow, she had privileged status; she had no husband to answer to, or to punish her scolding tongue – more was the pity.

'Please kneel for prayer,' said the priest. 'Let us pray for the souls of those fallen women who have been taken in by the estimable sisters of St Mary's Priory, and for the souls of their unborn children!'

Finally, the congregation stood to receive their blessing from the priest and to sing the final psalm. The first resounding line of the familiar chant awoke echoes throughout the chamber. The congregation's voices joined in rich unison.

～

At the feast that evening, all eyes were on Rolf. A deep murmur ran from man to man up and down the crowded Great Hall as he made his entrance. The baron looked exceedingly well. His muscular physique was visible through his close-fitting tunic adorned by a splendid jewelled girdle. His outer tunic was a rich pelisson of rabbit fur.

He took his seat in his great, carved chair, leaned forward and addressed the room. 'Let us not tarry a moment longer. Pray, eat!'

The company needed no second invitation. The squires set a fragrant venison stew before them.

In vain, Eleanor sought some sign of recognition or acknowledgement from her husband. With a sinking heart, she stared down at her plate, all her hopes dashed that the pregnancy would change things between them. Despite her great hunger and the delicious stew set before her, she had lost her appetite.

Beatrice was monitoring her closely and piped up with her usual refrain with a thin-lipped smile. 'If you do not eat, Eleanor, how do you expect to nurture a fine strong boy? This is an excellent venison stew that must surely have come from the royal deer!'

For her baby's sake, she did her best to eat the stew.

After the company had eaten their fill, the squires set bowls of plum pudding with lashings of fresh whipped cream before the guests. The pudding was too sweet, but she forced herself to eat it even though she would burst if she ate another morsel. Her belly felt enormous and she longed to leave the table and lie down. However, she was obliged to remain seated until Rolf dismissed the company. This didn't appear at all likely to be soon since he was flushed with wine and in the mood for regaling the other knights with tales of his adventures and boasting of his triumphs on the battlefield.

The ranks of the minstrels were swelled that night so their songs could be heard over the hubbub of raised voices. A group of knights broke into song and precipitated catcalls and jeers from the male nobles.

Her head hurt and she felt dreadfully tired. Perhaps she could discreetly slip away. It was unlikely that Rolf would notice her absence; he had not so much as looked at her all evening. Beatrice was deep in conversation with the lord beside her. She was loath to incur her mother-in-law's wrath on such an occasion. But that evening she enjoyed the advantage of being further away from Beatrice, so she risked rising and making an excuse of pregnancy sickness to the lady who sat beside her. However, she could not even slink away alone. A servant appeared, seemingly from nowhere, to accompany her to her chamber.

The servant attended to her disrobing, helped her into a soft nightgown and then left the chamber. Alone at last, she couldn't hold back her tears. The anxiety of the preceding days combined with the abject fear at the prospect of being alone with her husband.

～

She must have dozed off for she was shaken roughly awake some hours later. She opened her eyes and her heart quickened at the sight of her husband towering over her, red-faced and the worse for drink.

'I did not dismiss you,' he slurred. His breath stank of wine and meat.

'I beg your pardon, my lord,' she said. 'I felt sick from being with child and I had to lie down.'

'You do nothing, say nothing, without my say-so!' Her husband's voice rose dangerously and he moved his hand. She froze, rigid. She glanced up at him, bracing herself for a blow. His fist came down on her cheek and caught the tip of her nose. The pain was blinding. Blood trickled down her face.

'I am sorry,' she gasped.

And again, his fist crashed down on the other side of her face. This time it caught her brow and her eye. Another surge of pain. Her face was on fire.

'Please. Please, don't!' she wept.

Rolf threw his fist towards her body. Alarmed, she brought up her legs and arms to protect the baby in her belly. Her arm took the full impact of the blow. It felt as though it had shattered her very bone. Yet again, he struck her. This time, he caught her square on the breast.

This was fast becoming a fight for survival, not only for her but also for her unborn child. How long could she ward off his attacks? She groped around wildly for some object with which to defend herself but found only an earthenware goblet that slipped from her fingers and smashed on the floor.

Rolf was wilder and more savage than she had

ever known him to be. Another blow aimed at her belly caught her on the side of her hip as she rolled to avoid it.

'Not the baby!' she shrieked.

At once his hands closed around her throat. From that moment on, time itself seemed to elongate. His fingers squeezed and squeezed at a sluggish speed. Her hands inched towards her throat impossibly slowly. It was no use. She couldn't prise his hands away. His fingers grasped her neck in an iron grip. Appalled, she screamed, but no noise came from her throat. She struggled to breathe. A certainty dawned on her that she was going to die. Then she lost consciousness.

10.

Hugh Departs on Crusade

Earlier that same morning, a glorious sun heralded the day of Hugh's departure. The cloudless sky was a magnificent azure. Doing his best to fight down the ache in his heart, he passed under the gatehouse of his childhood home in the company of some thirty knights and squires that comprised his father's contribution to the king's crusade. They joined forces with fifty knights and squires known as the Order of Our Lady, led by Guy's father, Sir Mordaunt. The knights rode upon magnificent destriers, the squires on swift-footed coursers or palfreys loaded up with the baggage and provisions for the journey. Sir Mordaunt had permitted Hugh to ride one of his precious destriers.

What a pleasure it was to ride such a splendid animal and he sat tall in the saddle.

The company travelled in battle dress, complete with the hooded mail hauberk and leggings. He experienced a pang of envy at Guy's impressive golden cloak. His cousin looked like the dashing champion of a tourney. The knights bore their respective coat of arms on their shields and helmets. Two panthers supported a shield of swords on his cousin's shield, and Hugh's shield depicted two wrestling lions supporting a shield decorated with the golden chalices of Eynsford house. The knights and squires carried their weapons of war with pride: heavy swords and lances, small thin swords (for close combat), battle axes, poleaxes, maces, and flails with spiked iron balls at the end capable of smashing through armour and shattering bones.

The procession wound its way through acres of green meadows dotted with colourful wildflowers and fields glinting gold with ripening corn. The road led them through dense woodland alive with the cacophony of birdsong. It was wonderful to be on an adventure, far away from the austere castle and his father. As they rode, he basked in the dappled sunlight under the canopy of trees.

'Nothing like the open road, is there?' said Sir Mordaunt, with an affable smile. He surveyed Hugh with jewel-bright blue eyes. Tall and athletic, he still had a full head of blond curls, though his hair was greying a little at the temples.

'I don't think I've been more content,' said Hugh.

'After everything that has happened, it is good for you to get away,' said his uncle. 'Your mother would have been proud that you are seeking your life's adventure. You were the apple of her eye, you know. She always spoke of you with pride. She adored you. You were always your mother's son. William has taken after your father, I think.'

Hugh drew comfort from the company of his uncle and cousin. Until his mother had fallen gravely ill, he had no notion of how much she had given shape to his world. Never before had he had to quantify her love – only to expect it. It was not just the love she offered him without condition; it was the light and love she brought to the world. Now she was gone, the world felt poorer for her loss.

'She was a wonderful woman,' said Sir Mordaunt. He favoured Hugh with a soft smile. 'We must not let your father sully her memory. He always treated her so insensitively, and with such cruelty.'

Hugh nodded. 'It is wonderful to talk of Mother with someone who took the trouble to know and love her.'

He studied his uncle. Sir Mordaunt was a pleasant, jovial man who always seemed to be in good humour. How he envied Guy his father! How different his own life might have been!

Relaxing into his saddle, he dismissed sour thoughts of his father from his mind. All that was behind him. Finally, he was at liberty to enjoy the world around him. And he revelled in the sun's warmth on his face.

They followed the old Roman road to Dover and passed columns of barefoot pilgrims heading for Canterbury. Once, he had entertained dreams of going there on pilgrimage, but now he was headed to the Holy Land itself. The very idea made him sit up straight and proud on his powerful destrier, and he smiled down at the pilgrims.

By the riverbank, they found a pleasant grassy clearing and stopped for a cold repast of bread and cheese and took great gulps of sweet wine, quenching their thirst.

'Even sitting on horseback for hours is tiring,' said Hugh. He lay back on a bed of daisies and gazed up at the cloudless sky. It was wonderfully quiet, the grasshoppers' incessant chirp the only sound.

'We've made good time,' said Sir Mordaunt. He got up and stretched. 'If the weather holds, we'll reach the port of Dover this afternoon.'

An hour or so later, they found themselves at the port, which heaved with people. The fishy stench turned Hugh's stomach. Lewd-looking women sheltered in doorways and offered themselves out for pennies. Foul-mouthed men swaggered about the dock, their fists clenched, primed for a scuffle. Shamefully dirty and bedraggled children begged for money and pulled at his surcoat. Rough-looking sailors and dockworkers barged past them, staggering under heavy loads.

The Song and the Sword

Sir Mordaunt's Order of Our Lady was only one of the many orders of knights who were off to join the king's forces in Normandy. The wharves were a mass of colour splashed with the vivid azures, yellows and reds of the heraldic symbols and coats of arms emblazoned on the knights' shields and banners.

Moored out to sea was the vessel that would convey them to Normandy. It was a large galley with a great hull built up with castles that seem to reach into the heavens. It made him giddy watching the ship's boys scaling the rigging.

'Surely the vessel belongs to Eleanor's father,' said Hugh.

'Indeed,' said Sir Mordaunt. 'He is one of the wealthiest nobles in the Angevin Kingdom. His fleet of ships trade between the shores of Normandy and England, shipping wool from England to Flanders via the port of Boulogne.'

At the wharf they queued for a place in the rowing boats that would take them out to their ship. When their turn came, Hugh stepped down into the rowing boat and took a seat on the bench beside his cousin. High up on the white cliff, Dover Castle overshadowed them with its stark stone walls.

'Formidable, is it not,' said Guy. Their rowing boat pulled away from the shore.

'In truth it is a stronghold,' said Sir Mordaunt. 'Built to keep the heathen hordes from our shores. They say it is impregnable. The king has left it in the care of Baron Rolf, more's the pity.'

'I can't stop thinking about poor Eleanor,' said Hugh. 'Her father forced her to marry the brute.'

'Dear Eleanor,' said Guy. 'It was a bad business, her father selling her off to the highest bidder like that. I don't envy her at all having to make a life with Rolf's Dover beauties.'

'Dover beauties?' asked Hugh.

'Have you not heard about Rolf's set of kept mistresses? Painted, tawdry women by all accounts.'

'Poor Eleanor.'

'You were always fond of her, weren't you?'

Hugh was unable to speak for a minute, his gaze fixed on the floor. And then at last he spoke up. 'I had hoped to marry her. I love her.'

'You will soon be consoled, cousin,' said Guy. 'What better remedy is there for a broken heart than the warmth of a new woman?' He touched Hugh lightly on the shoulder. 'And where we are going you will feast your eyes on some magnificent ladies. The beauty of the eastern women is well known. To be sure, you will find comfort and know happiness in the soft arms of a woman.'

Hugh could not believe that some eastern strumpet would mend his heart.

'Baron Rolf is widely regarded to have ambitions to extend his territory,' said Sir Mordaunt. 'He has already appropriated at least five castles in Kent, burning villages and crops and displacing people in his grab for land.'

'And yet the king awarded him the honour of being

the Constable of England,' said Hugh in a low, shaking voice. 'Is there no villainy to which he will not descend? He abides by no code of chivalry.'

To wrench his heart from agonising thoughts of Eleanor, he turned away from land and surveyed the great expanse of the sea. It stretched out for as far as the eye could see into the unknown. The placid sea was a murky green colour. If he allowed himself to admit it, he was apprehensive about the crossing. He remembered the priest's tales of terrible storms that had wrecked ships, of sailors drowning in the salty depths and treasure lost forever down on the seabed. But he shrugged off these unwelcome thoughts.

～

For the next two hours the crusaders stripped down to their linen shirts and sweated under the savage glare of the sun. The ship drifted helplessly in a fickle wind as the sea undulated gently beneath its broad beam.

Guy, Sir Mordaunt and Hugh reclined on deck. They gazed up at the azure sky, their arms across their faces, shielding their eyes from the blazing sun. Knights and squires crowded the decks to avoid the stink of piss and animal dung below.

'He has no sea legs, that one,' said Sir Nicholas that evening, as the men drank wine together. He was sweating profusely. He pointed at one of the older knights who clung onto the rail of the ship. 'He's been sick as a dog since we left shore. Shat himself, too, from the state of his braies.'

The other men laughed heartily.

''Tis no wonder, for think of the perils we face!' said Dodd, a runt of a squire dressed in a black leather jerkin. His tiny darting eyes reminded Hugh of a rat. 'I heard tales of giant sharks that would take a bite out of your leg with their razor-sharp teeth.' He gestured out at the expanse of water around them. 'Even if we survive the voyage upon the treacherous sea, what of the monsters on land that would eat us? Tigers, lions, bears and huge serpents that can squeeze the breath from your belly or poison you with their venom!'

Guy snorted. 'You'd have us skulking in our beds like frightened maidens. We must embrace the adventures before us, savour our moments of glory knowing we undertake the noblest quest and that God smiles down at us.'

'You are full of the fire and enthusiasm of young men,' said Sir Reyner. He waved a mailed finger in the air. 'Hunger, exhaustion and danger are more likely to be our constant companions. Those infidels would murder us in our sleep or stab us in the back. Turn-cloaks and sneaks the lot of them. Worse are those beautiful temptresses that would lure us into their beds only to slit our throats when they've had their wicked way with us.'

The Abbot of Dover furrowed his brows. He flexed his bare arms, which were as sinewy as trees. Used to preaching the holy war, he was a veteran of the Second Crusade. 'You men drink too much. This is a quest ordained by the Pope himself, requiring piety, abstinence and the purest dedication. We are tasked with the defence of God's country from those who would defile it with their heresies.'

'Do you take us for Templars or Hospitallers?' said Sir Walter, with a gap-toothed smile. 'Surely God would not begrudge us a few earthly pleasures when we readily shed our young blood in his cause!'

The abbot turned his head away and swaggered across the deck to speak to the captain.

'A knight endures hardship, deprivation and the highest risk,' said Sir Walter. 'Then it signifies that we should be entitled to our fair share of the pleasures of the senses. You young squires are green in the ways of the world. Once you've bedded a few beautiful girls, you'll see that things aren't so bad.'

'Indeed, they have canny tricks those eastern women!' said Sir Manard. He smiled and revealed a mouthful of crooked teeth. 'They'll have you squirming with pleasure.'

'Pay no heed to old foxy, here.' Sir Mordaunt gestured at Sir Manard. 'By his accounts, his prick is as long as his sword. He earned his nickname from a remarkably prolific stallion in my stables. He has a particular talent of telling facetious stories about his permanent and oversized erection. And don't let him get started on his fruity nocturnal visions!'

The other knights fell about laughing.

'We all turn to dust in the end,' retorted Sir Manard. He turned a delicate shade of crimson. 'I'll not sniff at a sundry conquest! I'd sooner die in battle or in a woman's arms than die in agony with the spotted fever.'

'I have pledged myself to Lady Eleanor and there you have it,' whispered Hugh to Guy beside him. 'I want nothing of dancing girls.'

Guy shrugged. 'Have it your way, cousin. But you deny yourself for nothing.'

They let the matter drop and silence fell upon them as they watched the sun set below a sun-bleached sky.

11.

A Way Out

Sometime later that night, Eleanor woke gasping and spluttering, choking on the metallic taste of blood. As she took in more air to her lungs, she revived. She tried to open her eyes, but one of them was swollen shut. Instinctively, she brought her hand up and touched it and she winced at the pain. It came away sticky with blood. Heart pounding, she looked for her husband. Rolf lay face down on the bed beside her. He was snoring and drool leaked from the side of his mouth. He reeked of wine and sweat.

She paused for a minute, absorbing the reality of what had just happened. Rolf had tried to kill her! For a moment, she had thought her life was over. Still breathing fast, she examined her belly for any signs of injury and was relieved to find none. But her arm and hip, which had taken the full impact of her husband's fist, throbbed horribly.

She had to get as far away from her husband as possible. But where would she go? There was no time to think. Her only hope was to escape while Rolf was dead to the world and she made an attempt to get up. There would be no opportunity during daylight hours, with her mother-in-law and Rolf monitoring every move she made. Her bruised body protested vehemently. Engaging what felt like every muscle and sinew, she raised herself slowly and painfully to her feet. The next moment she stubbed her toe sharply on Rolf's iron keys, which hung from a loop on his discarded belt.

A way out of the castle! She could hardly breathe in her excitement.

She glanced back at her husband and looked for signs of consciousness. Fortunately for her, he had consumed a bellyful of wine and was dead to the world. She had to pick up the keys without waking him. She inched forward and wrapped them carefully in her nightgown to prevent them from knocking together and causing a clamour. To disturb Rolf or any of the servants would be suicide. Everything depended on her making it out unnoticed down the stone spiral staircase to the ground floor.

Every step brought fresh agony, but she forced herself on like a swimmer in icy water. Blood still dripped from her nose. She staunched the flow with a kerchief from her dressing-table. Kneeling painfully beside the chest, she found a long dark cloak that she pulled around her shoulders and some slippers for her feet.

As she tiptoed to the door, her heart raced. The door let out a shrill shriek of protest as it swung open. Aghast, she glanced back at her husband sprawled on the bed, but he made no sign of stirring. She listened carefully before she set off down the passageway. The castle was quiet now. Presumably all its occupants were sleeping off the wine after the feast. She crept out into the torchlit passage, hardly daring to breathe as she passed Beatrice's apartments. Thankfully, no lights issued from within; apparently her mother-in-law and her handmaidens slept soundly. The torches in the corridor burned low, which meant there were only a few hours before dawn. She had to make haste. With a tight stomach and a hip that throbbed dreadfully, she hobbled along the corridor. Every so often, she cast a glance over her shoulder, fearful of being followed. Despite her bruised and battered body, she made quick progress to the staircase. Counting on the fact that it would be less heavily guarded, she had chosen to descend the one used by the servants. Down on the narrow stone steps she slowed her pace. All would be lost if she missed her footing.

The landing was deserted save for a man-at-arms slumped asleep at his post at the bottom of the stairs. Terrified lest he should awake and raise the alarm, she stepped carefully over him. Fortunately, he didn't stir.

His saggy cheeks were flushed. Evidently, he, like Rolf, had drunk his fill of wine. Along the ground-floor corridor she picked up her pace again, desperate to find the passageway that would take her out of the keep.

With the torchlight throwing eerie, dancing shadows on the walls, she hurried along the passageway that led through the kitchens, past a grain store and across an expanse of cellars stocked with barrels of wine and salted meat. She was so weary now. Her arm, hip and face ached and she longed to lie down. But she pressed on through the dingy interminable passageway.

At length, she reached a point beyond which there were no flaming torches to light the way. The darkness pressed against her one good eye, threatening to suck her into nothingness. For a moment she was thrown – she could go no further. Then, thankfully, initiative seized her and she grabbed a flaming torch from its holder. Hope and light returned, and the shadows retreated before her.

It was damp and musty in the narrow passageway. She made slow progress, praying that she was going the right way. Water dripped unpleasantly from the ceiling and cobwebs brushed her face and hands.

Finally, she found herself in front of some steep steps and a heavy door. The door was locked. She fumbled with Rolf's keys and tried each one in turn. Surely one had to fit the lock! But they refused to turn. With panic rising to her throat, she tried one key after another. Then, at last, she found one that fit.

The wooden door was reinforced with steel and

evidently wasn't used much for it creaked loudly as it swung open. Breathlessly, she stepped out into the moonlight and found herself in the orchard, among the gnarled apple trees, heavy with ripening fruit. On the other side of the moat, she had emerged from a seemingly innocuous gardener's shed. Her heart gave a leap of joy. The night air was raw. With a shiver, she drew her woollen cloak more closely about her. The massive grey ramparts of Dover Castle, across the moat, towered over her.

Seized by an impulse, she pulled off her wedding ring and threw it into the moat. It made a tiny splash, like a frog jumping into the water. The gesture had a wonderful sense of finality. She had left Rolf for good.

At that instant, she heard a sound somewhere high above her. Someone was moving on the ramparts overhead. Rooted to the spot, she held her breath. After a moment, the sentry moved on and she let out a sigh of relief. But where to now?

She knew of no place to go and the thought terrified her. Out of the blue, the priest's prayers for the fallen women taken in by the nuns at St Mary's Priory sprang to her mind. Would the sisters of St Mary's offer her sanctuary? It was her best hope.

The Priory of St Mary was on the hill on the other side of Dover. To reach it, she had to walk around the town walls, following the path that ran alongside the sprawling huddles of stinking hovels. It was safer than entering the town, where the night watch might see her.

As fast as she could manage, she limped along the cliff path down to the town, taking care not to veer too close to the sheer drop. All her body pained her, particularly her hip. Not only was she dog-tired from lack of sleep, she wasn't in the habit of walking any distance as the only exercise she took nowadays was up on the rampart walk. The rocky scree path was hard on the soles of her feet compared to the rushes and heavy rugs that carpeted the castle floors and the silk slippers she had grabbed in her hurry to escape offered little protection against the sharp stone.

A thought occurred to her and she kicked her slippers off beside the cliff edge. Perhaps Rolf would assume that she had thrown herself off the cliff into the sea that pounded on the rocks below. And she hurried down the path wincing at the pain of the sharp rocks on her bare feet.

The tattered fringes of the dwellings outside the town walls were quiet, save for the yelps and growls of a pack of dogs scavenging around for scraps. In the moonlight, their green eyes flashed at her menacingly, and they bared their teeth. They looked hungry. With a couple of well-aimed rocks, they scuttled off into the undergrowth with a whimper.

Each stab of pain in her hip made her gasp as she hurried along. The bruises on her face still throbbed. Tears seeped from her swollen eye and made the wounds on her face sting. Even her belly felt swollen and tender, despite having escaped her husband's wrath. But the thought of the baby growing inside encouraged her on until she found reserves of strength within herself that she never knew existed.

After an hour's walk, she left the last of the lowly shacks behind her. The path grew steep as she made her ascent up the cliff. Dread building in the pit of her stomach, she considered the awful possibility that the nuns might turn her away. What would she do then?

The imposing walls of the Priory of St Mary came into view. She hoped that the priory would prove more hospitable than the castle she had just flown. The path was treacherous, a narrow pass of sheer, craggy rock with loose scree, and she found it difficult to keep her footing. The last few hundred yards of the heathery slope up to the wrought-iron gates felt like the hardest steps she had ever taken. As it was crucial that she look as desperate and impoverished as possible so no one could possibly recognise her as being a noble lady, she knelt in the dirt, caking her face and arms and travelling cloak in fresh mud, her feet were already filthy and bleeding.

The priory was in darkness and there was no sign of life or movement within the walls. Listening intently, there was nothing save for the rustle of tiny nocturnal creatures in the undergrowth and the hoot of an owl far away in the valley. With a great effort, she conquered her fear and knocked gently on the wooden door. For a long time, there was no answer. At a loss, she glanced back towards the east, to Dover

Castle on the crest of the cliff, where the first bright shafts of dawn were breaking through. Then she knocked again, rapping on the door with all her might.

12.

The Lionheart

After a couple of weeks of hard riding, Hugh longed for the rest afforded by a voyage at sea. Covered in blisters and aching all over, he struggled to walk, let alone fight, after a full day in the saddle. Somehow, he had never envisioned that travelling would be so strenuous; all he had thought about was the glory and romance of going on crusade.

The Angevin territory extended further than he could have ever imagined. The terrain ranged from dense forests, which rolled across the valleys and hills, packed with game and resonant with birdsong, and sprawling vineyards to impressive winding rivers that teemed with perch and trout. Now and again, they followed the old Roman roads and made use of crumbling ancient bridges. At other times they travelled across country through forests and farmland. Frequently, it was a difficult task to find a safe path across gushing streams and their horses struggled to find their footing among the slippery rocks and foaming cataracts.

Armed to the hilt and a great number as they were, the knights and squires made a formidable show of strength and had been largely welcomed by those they encountered. That was not to say it was easy to converse with the locals. The dialects in France were profuse and differed dramatically over relatively short distances. The emaciated peasants, bent double as they toiled in the fields, barely spoke. They merely straightened and stared at the crusaders like simpletons.

Sir Mordaunt, Guy and Hugh could at least communicate in French with the highborn. The crusaders travelled from manor to manor where lords offered them shelter for the night, fresh milk to drink, meaty stews to warm their bellies and fodder for their horses. At other times the company had to make camp on the edge of the forest and were obliged to hunt for game or fish the rivers for their supper.

'Behold Chinon Castle!' exclaimed Guy one sunny afternoon. His vivid blue eyes glistened with excitement.

Hugh looked up at a spectacular castle with sheer grey walls set on the top of a craggy precipice overlooking the river Vienne.

'It occupies an enviable position for a castle with

natural rock defences on three sides and a deep ditch on the fourth,' said Sir Mordaunt. 'See how the castle is divided along its length into three enclosures, each separated by a deep dry moat. The westmost enclosure was built by the late king, I believe.' Henry II had ruled England for thirty-five years – far longer than Hugh's brief life. Though his eldest son, Richard, had barely ruled for six months, it already seemed to Hugh that the old king's reign was now of a bygone age.

Knights and squires thronged around Chinon Castle, all bearing their respective coats of arms on their shields and surcoats. A church campaign to preach the crusade had recruited knights from all the far-flung corners of the Angevin Kingdom. Many of them were seasoned fighters and veterans of famous battles, but others were green like himself and had never fought in earnest. There was an infectious air of excitement and anticipation in the ranks. These men had come together to make common cause with their king. Chinon Castle was already filled to capacity, so the visiting knights and squires had to raise their tents in the deep ditches between the enclosures.

After they had set up camp, Sir Mordaunt drew Hugh aside. 'Tomorrow evening, King Richard has planned a knighting ceremony ahead of our departure for the crusade. In the absence of your father, I have put you forward for the honour.'

'Thank you, Uncle,' said Hugh with a rush of pleasure. 'I have been waiting for this moment my entire life. To be knighted by the king himself . . . Surely there can be no greater honour!'

'No need to be awestruck. I think your moment has come. The herald informed us that you fought valiantly in the tournament and therefore I think you have quite proven yourself. But today you must prepare for the ceremony with your devotions. I have ordered that the squires prepare your cold bath.'

'Very good, my lord. Thank you.'

That afternoon, three enthusiastic squires filled the bathtub with buckets of water from the river. They stripped to their small clothes and dunked Hugh repeatedly under the cold water. The churls derived too much pleasure from his torture as he gasped for air and coughed and spluttered water from his mouth and nose.

Hugh donned his best clothes ready for his night's vigil in St George's Chapel. It was almost dark inside the chapel when he crossed the threshold, save for the distant glimmer of candles at the altar. The air was heavily scented with incense. All that could be heard was the low murmur of prayer. Some thirty squires knelt and prayed for God's guidance and protection in their new endeavour. He took his place and knelt beside them. One by one, the priest called the squires to present themselves for confession, penance and absolution. His turn came and he knelt before the priest, head bowed and eyes fixed on the flagstone floor.

'You come before God to be shriven before you are

sworn a knight,' said the grey-haired priest in Latin. His breath reeked of onions.

'I do, Father,' he said. 'I hope that God might find me worthy. That I might offer him service in his battle against the devil.'

'Have you looked within to find the sins in your heart?'

'I have, Father. I have been overwhelmed by the sins of anger, and a reluctance to fulfil my duty as my father's son.'

'Be reassured that God is magnanimous, dear boy. He forgives you your trespasses. All he asks is that you do your best to serve him.' The priest anointed him and drew the sign of the cross on his forehead with holy water.

Hugh rose and re-joined the other squires at their vigil. As he knelt, he cast his thoughts back to the years of preparation that had preceded this moment. For seven long years he had served as a page, where his duties had consisted of feeding the falcons, serving at high table and helping in the kitchen. His stomach cringed at the memory of the cruel and violent 'correction' he had received from his older brother at such a tender age. Then came his years as a squire at Eleanor's father's castle in Normandy, where he had learned to wield a sword. He could not help but smile at the memory of the happy hours he had spent in Eleanor's company, when they had shared their love of chivalric romances. And there were the war games he had played with Guy, sparring with wooden swords. Somehow, it still didn't feel quite real that they were off on crusade together.

His heart ached at the sudden recollection of the happiest moments of his life spent in his mother's bower where she would read and sing to him. A shadow crept over his heart and eclipsed these happy memories. The cruelty of his father and brother and their attempts to humiliate him, their jeers and jests at his expense, left a bitter taste in his mouth. But now, all that hardly mattered and he forced such thoughts from his mind. All these moments of his life had merely propelled him to where he was now and prepared him for his destiny. And here he knelt in the sight of God, prepared to be dubbed a knight and serve his king and God.

As the hours passed, he offered prayers for his mother. In his mind's eye, she gazed down on him from Heaven, love shining in her eyes.

But then, with an unpleasant sinking of his heart, his thoughts turned to poor Eleanor in Dover Castle. Ever since he had seen her at the tournament, he had feared for her safety. With a shiver he remembered the terror that had lurked in her beautiful eyes. Rolf was a brute. Raw rage washed over him at the thought of the knave laying his hands upon her and his breath caught in his throat. Then the sweet, agonising ache of longing for Eleanor threatened to tear his heart in two.

~

At dawn, he struggled up from his knees. His long vigil was finally over. His legs had gone to sleep and he had to rub them vigorously to get the blood back into them. It was difficult to keep his eyes open and he let out a huge yawn.

'Dear boy,' said Sir Mordaunt, when he returned to the tent. 'Get yourself some sleep else you shall be exhausted later and fit for nothing. I cannot understand these ridiculous night-long vigils – an hour or two of prayers would be sufficient preparation in my opinion.'

Assenting happily, Hugh snuggled down in the tent. As soon as his head hit the feather pillow, he drifted off to sleep.

The sun was at high heaven when he next awoke.

'Ah there you are,' said Sir Mordaunt. 'Refreshed after your sleep, I hope?'

'Thank you.' Hugh yawned and stretched to the tips of his fingers. Blinking in the sun's glare, he looked around for something to eat.

'Have some bread and cheese.' Guy offered him a plate of food. 'I saved you this from lunch. I knew you'd be hungry. There will be the feast tonight, of course, when the dubbing is over.'

Hugh sank his teeth into the fresh bread and savoured the flavour of the pungent cheese.

'You'd better get your armour on,' said Sir Mordaunt. 'The ceremony will begin shortly.'

He pulled on his armour. It was almost a second skin now he'd become accustomed to the weight of the chain mail and he felt strangely naked when he wasn't wearing it. He polished his sword and helmet until they gleamed.

'How I envy you,' said Guy. 'You are about to be knighted by Richard the Lionheart, the greatest soldier and strategist the world has ever known!'

'Make haste,' said Sir Mordaunt, when he emerged from the tent. 'The other squires are filing into the chapel.'

Hugh hurried down the nave and joined the other squires kneeling in front of the altar. In the presence of a relic of the True Cross, he gave a deep bow. As he knelt, his knees creaked dreadfully.

The coats of arms and banners of all the greater barons of the Angevin Kingdom hung from the high-vaulted roof of the nave, illuminated by at least fifty candles that flickered in the sudden draught as the great ironbound door swung open and the king and his retinue marched up the aisle. A heady mixture of men's sweat, leather and incense hung in the air. Trumpeters sounded a fanfare. Every seat in the chapel was taken. The crusaders sprang to their feet, their heads turned and gazed upon their king, whose athletic physique towered over most of the company.

'King Richard must be at least six feet tall!' said the squire beside him.

Known as 'the Lionheart', the king was a handsome man with a lean bronzed face, red-gold hair and bright blue eyes. He made a magnificent figure in his mail with a cloak of satin and ermine.

Hugh shivered in anticipation of what was to come. Surely nothing could beat this moment. To be dubbed by the greatest warrior king on earth . . . the Lionheart. To think that he had envied William for his knighting ceremony that had taken place at the Temple in London. The late King Henry must have been old and dreary in comparison to his son! Wait until he told his father and brother about this; William would be green with envy.

At a sign from the priest, the squires knelt and bent their heads low in supplication.

'We come together to knight these squires,' said the priest. 'It is a chance for them to repent and do wondrous deeds. These brave men offer themselves and their wealth for recovery of the land where truth itself was born from the earth in order to bring about our salvation! They make the journey to the Holy Land with a humble and contrite heart to serve God in the right faith. They offer their lives to protect Christians overseas and bring others to Christ.'

'There can be no nobler cause,' thundered the king in a deep voice that filled the chapel.

The herald announced each squire in turn as the king dubbed them on the shoulder with his heavy sword. On tenterhooks, Hugh listened out for his name.

At long last he heard the herald call out his name and saw the king approach. He waited for the touch of the king's sword with bated breath, his eyes dropped to the slate floor in deference. Finally, the sword touched his shoulder and an intoxicating energy coursed through his body. His spirits soared. Finally, he was a knight!

'Arise, Sir Hugh de Eynsford,' said the king.

Hugh pulled himself to his feet. Standing tall, his pride oozed from every pore.

～

That night at the king's banquet, he joined the greater barons and knights at the high table with Sir Mordaunt and his cousin. The Great Hall was so vast it stopped his breath with its high-vaulted ceiling and tall slender arches and pillars. The coats of arms of all the houses taking part in the crusade hung from the rafters. Sweet incense and the mouth-watering smell of roasting meats permeated the air. Damask cloths covered the tables, which were laid out with great pitchers of wine, silver goblets, plates and spoons.

The hall resounded with a deafening fanfare of trumpets that heralded the king's arrival. A moment's hush descended. At a signal from the herald everybody rose to their feet, bowing low to their king.

'Pray be seated brave knights and squires and ladies,' said the king in a voice rich with intensity.

'Finally, you are in your proper place,' said Sir Mordaunt. A full-beam smile lit up his bronzed face. 'Your dear mother would have been so proud.'

'To knighthood!' toasted Guy, his face flushed from the good wine.

'To knighthood!' said Hugh. Sweet excitement brimmed up within him. No longer would he serve the other knights. He was a knight of the realm, a warrior of God who commanded respect.

He glanced over at King Richard, surrounded by a captivated audience. All the knights and ladies vied for his favour. The grand ladies dressed in the finest furs adorned with glistening jewels couldn't get enough of him it seemed. King Richard was prime meat as he was not yet married. There could be no greater prize than being Queen of the Angevin empire.

'It fills me with pride to be led by such a splendid warrior king,' said Hugh.

'Mark you,' said Sir Mordaunt in an undertone. He placed his goblet down on the table with a sharp clack. 'It is by no means an easy task being a soldier in the king's army. King Richard demands the highest standards of discipline. Trouble amongst the men is ruthlessly suppressed. If a knight is killed, the murderer will be bound to the victim and flung into the sea. If one knight stabs another, they will lose a hand. If a man hits another without drawing blood, they will be thrice dunked in the sea. Any heard uttering blasphemous language will be fined an ounce of silver for each transgression.'

But nothing could tarnish this moment for Hugh. 'I have you to thank for all of this, Guy. If it had not been for you, I would have wasted away in my father's castle. And here we are, excellently feasted with roasted venison and rabbit stew alongside pheasant

and quail. I have never sampled such delicious food!'
Hugh mopped up the rich gravy with bread fresh
from the oven.

Only one thing was wanting: dear Eleanor. Thoughts
of her occupied the fortress of his mind like a dogged
invader.

13.

An Empty Belly

In the weeks that followed her arrival at the priory, Eleanor did nothing but sleep. With no natural light in the windowless chamber in which she lay, she soon lost track of night and day. There were only the insistent bells that summoned the nuns to their prayers. Their loud clanging infiltrated her muddled dreams and pierced through the unreality. The din brought her back to the here and now: to her cot in the austere infirmary, to the all-pervading smell of sickness.

One morning, she opened her eyes to find a sharp-eyed nun with a hooked nose and a commanding air looking down on her. 'Who are you?' She poked Eleanor's arm with a bony finger. 'You have stolen these fine clothes, haven't you, you thieving whore! Confess!'

'No, if you please,' begged Eleanor. 'I was given them by my mistress.'

'Again, I ask you. Who are you?'

'No one of consequence,' said Eleanor. 'My name is Matilda. I was the servant of a Norman noble-woman.'

'And yet you are plump and well fed.' The nun's voice cut like broken glass. 'And there is no ring upon your finger. You are a kept woman, or perhaps a concubine!' And she landed a slap on Eleanor's cheek.

'No!' Eleanor sobbed and winced with pain. 'Nothing like that! I accompanied my mistress from Normandy to wed. She dismissed me from service because of the scandal of my condition.' Tears flowed down her cheeks and she sobbed. 'He . . . he promised to marry me but when he discovered I was with child, he beat me!' Her heart pounded and she laboured for breath, terrified lest the nun should turn her out into the street and Rolf should find her.

The infirmarian rushed to Eleanor's bedside. 'Please leave her alone,' she begged. 'Can't you see how she has suffered! Do you deny this woman succour in her hour of need?'

'Get up, you wretch,' said the nun, somewhat appeased. 'Your fever has gone. It is high time you joined the other women and earned your keep.'

An elderly nun, shrunk and wrinkled with age, helped Eleanor out of her cot. Eleanor's legs shook with weakness as she shuffled along behind the woman. The small dormitory resounded with groans, moans, cries of pain and wracking coughs. It reeked of vomit, foul body odour and fetid bodies. The old nun was astonishingly spritely for her age and Eleanor struggled to keep up with her as they emerged into grey stone cloisters. She had a sudden impression of being back at Dover Castle. Dread built in her belly and she gave herself a little pinch to remind herself that she was free of that prison.

They ascended two flights of stairs and entered another dormitory of twelve beds. The smell of damp and old sweat pervaded the chamber. All the beds were occupied save one, a narrow cot in the corner of the room, and she clambered gratefully into it. Eleven gaunt, pale faces stared back at her. All the women had the tell-tale swollen bellies of pregnancy. The aged nun left the room without a word.

Eleven pairs of eyes scrutinised her. They appeared to be a motley bunch. For the most part, the women were young, like her, but there were a few older women too. She was dismayed to observe that they all had an undernourished, pinched look about them, as though they had never eaten a good meal in their lives.

The woman who lay in the cot on her left had a cap of close-curling black hair and a little anxious heart-shaped face. Years of fearful, unhappy thoughts had left their mark and worry was etched in her features.

The woman to her right had a thatch of fair hair with a hint of gold. She had merry eyes and her mouth was large, and when she smiled, as she did now, it was very large indeed.

'Welcome to the Priory of St Mary.' She smiled as though it were all a good joke. 'I am Sophie.' She put out a red, calloused hand.

Eleanor shook it, warming to Sophie immediately. 'My name is Matilda.'

'Well, Matilda, this is Margery.' Sophie gestured to the woman on her left.

Just then the great iron door at the end of the dormitory opened. A harsh-faced nun with tiny black eyes and thin, pursed lips poked her head around the door. 'I heard voices! It is the hour of sleep, as you all well know. Let there be silence!'

With that she snuffed out the large church candle in the chamber. The room was dark save for two small twinkling candles. The door closed behind her with a bang.

Silence descended on the dormitory. Eleanor was transported back to her childhood where she had had no choice but to obey her elders.

Try as she might, she couldn't get to sleep. She lay awake in the darkness for hours and listened to the other women breathing. Loud snores emanated from the far side of the room and made it very difficult to drift off. She prayed that she would find kindness and friendship within these walls. Just then the baby fluttered in her belly. It was a delightful sensation, a reminder that she was not alone.

~

Early the next morning, a loud bell reverberated about the priory. Eleanor woke with a crash, feeling sick from lack of sleep. It was horribly cold in the chamber. She shivered and drew the thin coverlet up to her neck. The women around her dressed themselves in long plain brown kirtles and fastened white aprons around their waists. Just like the nuns, they covered their hair with white wimples. Should she follow their example?

'Well, don't just lie there, sweetie,' said Sophie. 'Get dressed. You'll find your kirtle at the foot of your bed.' She yawned and pointed at a heap of clothes.

The robes that Eleanor had thrown on in her escape from Dover Castle were like silk compared to the rough-spun sacking fabric of the kirtle supplied by the priory.

Her dismay must have been visible in her face, for Sophie said, 'I think the nuns oblige us to wear such abrasive robes as a penance. I've heard of religious zealots wearing hair, holly shirts, and even hedgehog skins!'

It was the first time she had ever dressed herself – not that there was much to do. There were no strings or ribbons to draw tight, no buttons to fasten or brooches to pin. As far as she could tell, the garment in front of her only had a single seam. As she lifted the cloth over her head, she caught the ripe odour of another woman's unwashed body. Her stomach turned; the kirtle wasn't even clean! The robe hung loose and shapeless on her body with plenty of room for an expanding belly. Wistfully, she thought of her splendid gowns back at Dover Castle that she would never again have the opportunity to wear. If only the nuns had permitted her to keep the nightgown in which she had arrived. The sacking dress was like a uniform, for all the women in the dormitory wore the same. She secured a grubby wimple over her long tresses. But where were the slippers or shoes for her feet? Surely the nuns didn't expect them to go about barefoot. Many times, she had seen the poor in the markets, shuffling around with bare calloused feet caked in dirt and often bleeding. She glanced down at her own delicate feet and hoped they wouldn't meet a similar fate.

The women moved towards the door of the chamber. She shot an enquiring glance at Sophie.

'We must make haste for Prime in the chapel,' said Sophie, in answer to her silent enquiry.

She tagged along behind the procession of pregnant women. The uneven rock floor was jagged and cold under her bare feet. They walked, single file, through the dimly lit passages. If only there was some natural light. With all her heart, she longed for sunshine to warm her skin. It had to be weeks since she had inhaled fresh air. The prospect of an underground existence filled her with claustrophobia.

Presently, they turned into a large hall that was completely bare save for an ornate rood screen on one wall, which depicted pious souls prostrate in the presence of God. Following the other women's example, she knelt before the screen, her head bowed. A low murmur of chanting came from behind the screen.

Her knees ached with the discomfort of having to kneel for so long. Of course, she had been accustomed to kneeling in prayer in her previous life – only then her knees had enjoyed the luxury of a soft cushion. The service was excruciatingly long when kneeling on bare rock. When at long last the priest gave his closing blessing, she found it inordinately hard to struggle to her feet. Apparently, she was not alone; there was a collective chorus of moans from the women around her as they dragged their aching bodies up from the floor.

The women processed through the door and she followed. Hunger gnawed at her empty stomach. 'Where to now?' she asked Sophie, who was just in front of her. Sophie put a finger to her lips and inclined her head towards the nun.

Eventually they entered another chamber, this time with windows and furnished with a long refectory table and twelve low wooden stools. One of the women among them, a tall woman with a horse-face and droopy eyes and a huge belly that hung low, served out potage into small earthenware bowls with a wooden ladle.

There was no cutlery on the table, not even a spoon. The women slurped their broth noisily from their bowls. Never had she seen such sloppy, uncouth manners. But she saw no alternative and put the bowl to her lips and followed their example. Naturally, she had expected the potage to be hot, but it was barely lukewarm. There were odd lumps floating around in it, bits of chicken claw or muscle perhaps.

'Even a sprinkle of salt would have rendered the dish more palatable,' she whispered to Sophie who sat on the stool beside her.

Sophie nodded. 'The cook reserves her talent for the higher ranks of nuns. The prioress would never sup such miserable slop.'

'Is there any bread?' She cast a hopeful glance down the table.

Sophie shook her head. 'We count ourselves lucky if they spare us some.'

One of the women collected the empty bowls and they rose from the table. A hush hung over them like an oppressive curtain. Dared she break the silence and speak?

They filed out of the hall after a chilly-mannered nun known as Sister Agnes who presided over the buttery, along the cloister until they came to a halt in front of an old oak door. The nun produced a key from her girdle and unlocked the padlock. The door swung open. Its rusty hinges protested shrilly. They found themselves in a huge walled kitchen garden. How wonderful it was to breathe fresh air once more and feel a breeze on her skin, even if an unseasonable chill had arrived in the last week. The plantation stretched as far as the eye could see. There was row upon row of garlic and onion plants, and carrots.

'If the nunnery cultivates such a crop, why are we reduced to eating grubby vegetable water?' Eleanor mouthed to Sophie.

'They would not want to waste such luxuries on us,' said Sophie in a low voice. She pointed to the animal enclosures from which emanated the grunts of sows, the lowing of cattle, the clucking of hens and even the far-off neighs of stabled horses. 'We're never offered fresh milk to drink or eggs or bacon to eat either.'

A grizzled old man with sparse tufts of woolly hair approached, a stern expression carved on his weather-beaten face. With a brusque nod, he indicated they should follow him. The women acquiesced without a word. He brought them to a patch of bare earth and gestured they should dig. Eleanor gasped. She hadn't anticipated that the nuns would oblige her to labour in the fields like a peasant. Such work was surely not suitable for pregnant women.

Suitable or not, the women around her churned up the rocky earth with their spades. She followed their example as best she could. It was backbreaking work. In her entire life she had never done any physical labour and before long she had to stop and rest her aching muscles. Even the women habituated to the work struggled with the task and had to rest period-ically and rub their overburdened backs.

'The nuns are using us as slaves,' Eleanor said to Sophie, who was beside her. 'If only I could have a sip of water or wine. My throat feels parched. The effort of digging has sapped the last of the energy from my exhausted body.'

Sophie rubbed her back and scowled. 'The nuns regard hard work as a necessary penance. They work us to the bone!'

At that instant Eleanor noticed that Sister Agnes was glaring at her. Summoning the last of her strength, she turned back to her digging. She longed to strike up a conversation with Sophie or one of the other women but the nuns clearly prohibited all talk.

It transpired that the women's labour was not over. The next task the man allotted to them was to plant lily bulbs in the freshly dug earth. The constant bending down was intolerable with her protruding belly, so she got down on all fours to plant, even though this position was gruelling for her knees.

Eventually all the bulbs were planted and they moved on to plucking cherries off the trees in the orchard. At least it was not necessary to bend down to accomplish this. The cherries were fat and ripe and looked inviting. She longed to taste one and glanced at the other women to see if anyone else dared consume any, but not one of the women took so much as a bite.

'These cherries are not for the likes of us,' said Sophie with a rueful smile. 'They are destined for the prioress's table or for the noblewomen who shelter within the priory walls.'

'I had heard tales of hardship in nunneries, but I had not anticipated this!' All the women she had known to sojourn in nunneries had been noble, sent to a nunnery for safety while their husbands or fathers fought in the wars. Her mother always used to say women were particularly vulnerable during times of conflict when the menfolk of the house were fighting in the crusades overseas. She had recounted terrible tales of rape and pillaging that had occurred when enemy militias ravaged through the lands. Even women in nunneries were sometimes not safe, she had said. And she had relayed horrific stories of men storming religious houses and taking pious women by force, abducting them and defiling them. But she had reassured Eleanor that such cases were rare. Fortunately, few men risked consigning their souls to the devil for violating God's wives.

This, she supposed, was the reason the church built the priory like a fortress, with thick, towering and windowless walls – to keep out the pillaging hordes. Beatrice had once told her that many noblewomen spent time in this priory and enjoyed the hospitality of the nuns. Apparently, their fathers and husbands had paid handsomely for the privilege. Eleanor dearly hoped there were none under this roof who might recognise her as Baron Rolf's wife.

Before long, the tree was bare of fruit and the women filed back into the priory. She hurried after them. As they entered a large kitchen, they paused and wiped their muddy feet on a coarse mat. There were two huge fires in the kitchen. On one a whole hog roasted on a spit, and on the other a cauldron bubbled away merrily. It was delightfully warm in the kitchen. Her frozen extremities began to thaw, especially her bare feet that had never been exposed to the elements. The smell of roasting meat made her mouth water.

After they had washed their hands in a bowl of freezing water with some soap, the women scrubbed muddy carrots. Then the cook had them chopping onions and garlic, which made her poor swollen eye weep profusely. Her stomach gave another lurch of hunger at the torture of preparing food.

When the vegetables were prepared, they dried their hands on their aprons and filed out of the kitchen. She was bursting with questions that she longed to put to Sophie and the other women. She gently pulled at Margery's sleeve to get her attention. Margery started in alarm and put her finger to her lips. Chastened, Eleanor kept silent.

They returned to the long hall where they had broken their fast hours earlier that morning. Eleanor entertained delightful thoughts about savouring delicious food. The woman who sat beside her was stick-thin and her rounded belly protruded grotesquely. Two of the women struggled under the weight of a cauldron brought from the kitchen. The contents smelled good. When they ladled out the potage into the bowls, she was disappointed to discover that it was as thin and watery as their earlier meal. Evidently, the nuns had ordered the cook to water down the soup to make it go further. Nevertheless, she was grateful for it, as inadequate as it was. Above all it was such a relief to be able to sit down and rest her weary limbs.

Nones, or afternoon prayer, followed lunch. The women filed into the chapel once more. Some of them waddled like ducks under the weight of their enormous bellies. There was a chorus of groans as the women eased themselves into seated positions on the cold hard floor. On the other side of the rood screen, she was sure there were pews. As far as she knew, in parish churches the priest didn't expect anyone to sit on the floor. She made a great effort to move her aching body.

They stood to sing a psalm, and then lowered themselves onto the floor again for the priest's sermon. They couldn't see him as he stood behind the rood screen, but she pictured him as being a tall, imposing man, because his voice was strong and boomed around the chapel.

'Have a care,' said the priest. 'For evil are the ways of the world. Remember the story of Joan of Gundrunlane, the nun who failed to give God his proper dues and omitted to give thanks to him before she ate a lettuce, so consumed by greed was she.'

Beside her Sophie raised a languid eyebrow. Eleanor suppressed a snigger.

'She received the devil onto her as a result,' said the priest. 'And when a holy man demanded that the devil come forth out of her body, the devil replied that the fault was not his. "Why do you blame me?"

spoke the devil. "I was sat upon the lettuce and she failed to make the sign of God and so ate me with it!"'

'They mean to preach us to death!' murmured Sophie under her breath.

'Indeed,' said the priest. 'It is better to remember the example of the saintly nun Cecily, who, when the pittance was distributed among the other nuns, was inadvertently neglected. However, you will see that this did not happen by chance: no, it was the will of God that she might rise to revel in his glory. She did not moan and whine about her deprivation, no. She bore it like a stoic. Indeed, she relished the neglect. The Father Abbot saw how she gave thanks to God by her saintly attitude and offered her an invisible pittance. Presently, the humble and pious Cecily tasted the most indescribable sweetness in her mouth. This feeling descended through her throat and all over her body. Never had she experienced anything so exquisite in her life. Moreover, it was not merely a physical sensation but a spiritual sweetness too. Thereafter, she declined a pittance for the rest of her days.'

'The nuns are lucky to get a pittance.' Sophie spoke in hushed tones. 'We'd never be allowed any special delicacy. We would be lucky if we got to eat some bread! By the priest's reasoning, we have the opportunity to achieve sainthood every day.'

Eleanor nodded. 'The meals here are pitiful, but I have yet to encounter any sweet physical or spiritual sensation. The priest would blame us for not being grateful enough for what the nuns have given us. Frankly, I doubt whether the physical and spiritual sweetness the priest describes would be enough to nourish the growing children in our bellies.'

A growing sense of gloom took hold of Eleanor. Had she been wrong to flee the castle as she had done? But Rolf had tried to kill both her and her unborn child. It had been all that she had been able to do to shield the life in her belly with her arms and legs. She looked down at the yellowing-brown bruises on her wrists, testaments to her struggle. No, she could not have stayed. There was little point in eating well if the man who had sworn to love and protect her murdered her and her unborn child.

The priest dismissed the congregation with one final 'Praise be to God!' and the service was over.

None of the women on the floor moved for a moment. If they felt anything like her, they would be too exhausted to move.

Sister Agnes towered suddenly over them and glared down like a vengeful demon. 'Get up, you common sluts!' The nun's rotund face and nose were flushed red, as though she had indulged in more than her fair share of wine. Her eyes were angry slits and they darted about the chamber. 'Stop flaunting your debaucheries!'

The women scrambled hastily to their feet and followed the nun to the buttery. With not so much as another ounce of energy to spare, Eleanor walked like the living dead. After a life of servants waiting upon her hand and foot, nothing could have prepared her for a life of toil. To be expending such physical energy without enough sustenance when she was with child was too much. It was no surprise her body wanted to give up.

In the buttery, Sister Agnes allotted her the task of churning the cream to make butter. She poured the cream off the milk into a wooden pail and set about stirring it with a wooden spoon. Her legs ached as she stood. She stirred for half an hour without stopping when a painful spasm seized her hand. She stopped stirring and dropped the spoon into the pail and earned herself a scolding from Sister Agnes. It was a revelation to discover the labour that went into producing the butter she had spread on her bread every day for most of her life. Never had she considered its provenance, never had she thought of it as being the result of another's toil.

When at long last she saw the first yellow flecks in the mixture that heralded the appearance of butter, she experienced a novel sense of achievement despite her exhaustion and the cramps in her hand. The experience was short-lived, for Sister Agnes then compelled the women to scrub the buttery floor. There was no bending down with a protruding belly, so they were back down on all fours and scrubbed the floor with brushes and soapy water.

She reflected once more that she had enjoyed a privileged life. Here she was no better than a slave living a life of drudgery. But what choice did she have? She knew of no other places of refuge for a battered wife and an expectant mother. With no influential friends in Dover to turn to for help, there was no alternative. Her parents were too far away and Rolf's spies would have intercepted any letters she wrote to them before their dispatch from the castle. Except for a few jewels, she had no money. Her rich dowry had gone straight into Rolf's coffers and was no doubt financing his military campaigns. Even if she had had the forethought to grab the few jewels she had possessed before she escaped, they would have given her away because of their value. Therefore, she'd had no option other than to present herself as a destitute, battered woman and seek refuge at the priory. But surely this was not how it would end for her? A hopeless life of exhaustion and servitude could not be her destiny!

When the floor was finally clean, they filed through the cloistered walk back to the lavatorium to wash their hands before supper and Evening Prayer. After that, they climbed the stone stairs to the dormitory, where they were left to their own devices for a time, free from the eagle eye of their gaoler, Sister Agnes.

'I declare I'm quite spent after today,' complained a tattered creature with a scrawny face and wisps of mousey-brown hair that escaped from under her wimple. She lay back in her cot.

'I couldn't lift another finger,' said one of the older women, with a grey haggard face and deep-set eyes.

'Sister Agnes was driving us hard today, and there's no mistake,' said Sophie. 'No rest for the wicked!'

Eleanor's heart warmed at Sophie's merry smile.

'Sister Agnes is in a black mood, mark you.' A scrawny waif with a huge belly and a mop of tangled black hair let out a loud yawn. The girl was no more than sixteen by Eleanor's reckoning.

'There's been no bread for weeks,' said a girl with terrible pustules on her face. 'You'd think they were trying to starve us!'

'There's plenty of food for them of rank,' said another woman with a harsh laugh. Her jet-black brows puckered over tiny fierce eyes. She looked close to giving birth, for her bump strained under her sack-cloth kirtle. That day she had earned a sharp scolding from Sister Agnes for being slower than the others. 'If that woman shrieks at me one more time . . . screaming at a woman nine-month gone!'

'To be sure, she is a wicked, cruel nun,' said Sophie. 'To bully you thus, Hilda, when it is a matter of days before you give birth!'

'I don't know how you manage,' said Eleanor.

'Yes, welcome to Hell!' Sophie gave her a wry smile. 'Who beat you black and blue?'

'My fiancé,' said Eleanor. 'He promised to marry me, and this is how he treated me! Then, my mistress threw me out onto the street and I had nowhere to go save here. All my family are in Normandy.'

'Men . . .' said Sophie. 'They'll always let you down

in the end. All us women here are a testament to that. They'll have their wicked way with you and leave you high and dry as it suits them. However much they profess to love you, there will always be a reason why they cannot be with you! When my sweetheart got me with child, I became an inconvenience. And what's worse . . . despite all that, I still love him. More fool me!'

'I had thought the nuns would give me charity,' said Eleanor. 'But this feels more like servitude. Is it always like this here?'

'This and worse,' said Sophie. 'The dogs in this house are better treated than us! They want to beat the devil out of us with hard work, or so it seems.'

'There ain't many of us that will get out alive,' said the girl with the pustule-covered face.

This grim thought weighed heavily on the women and they fell silent.

The girl seemed aware of the gloom that had settled over the company because of her words, and by way of diversion introduced herself to Eleanor. 'I am Anne.' She gave Eleanor a crooked-toothed smile.

'And this is Hilda.' Sophie pointed to the woman with the impossibly large belly. 'She's due to give birth any day. And our youngest . . .' She pointed to the scrawny waif. 'Is Sarah.'

The women smiled encouragingly at Eleanor, and an unaccustomed warmth spread in her heart.

'What about that naughty nun who ate the lettuce!' said Sophie, with a twinkle in her eye.

'Aye, it's a perilous life for God's wives.' Hilda smirked.

'Did I tell you the one about the Abbess of Chaulmont?' asked Sophie.

'No, tell us,' they chorused, eager for a tale.

'Well, I have it on good authority,' said Sophie, 'that the said abbess once got up in the dead of night to reprimand one in her order who had brought a man to her bed – a monk from the neighbouring order, no less.'

There was a mock tutting of outrage from some of the women at this, and light danced in their eyes. Eleanor found that she was smiling, caught up with the merriment.

'Well,' Sophie confided, 'the naughty nun happened to look at the abbess when she came into her cell to reprimand her. And do you know what she saw?'

'No, tell us. What did she see?' they chorused.

'She saw that the abbess sported a pair of man's breeches atop her head. She had mistakenly grabbed them instead of her wimple in her hurry to apprehend the errant nun. They only belonged to her lover, a priest who had been sharing her cell!'

A ripple of amusement went around the room. Titters and sniggers gave way to wholehearted belly laughs as the tensions of the day evaporated in giggles. Eleanor's sides ached. She couldn't remember having laughed like this for a long time. A few of the women, their huge bellies pressing on their bladders, had to rush to relieve themselves in the privy.

The Song and the Sword

The door crashed open and an acid voice cut through the mirth with the precision of an executioner's axe severing head from body. 'What is this devil's work? No good can come of hilarity!' Sister Agnes's eyes were aflame with righteous indignation. She stood stormy-faced, her hands on her hips, on the threshold of the chamber.

This interjection provoked another round of helpless laughter from some of the women.

'Your past ill lives have caught up with you,' said the nun. 'I would have thought you women would have many regrets at finding yourselves in such a predicament by your wanton behaviour.' Sister Agnes seemed hellbent on extinguishing every happy thought from the room. 'Perhaps a day or two in solitary cells will cure you of this impudence!'

A hush descended on the women. Malevolent faces glared up at Sister Agnes. Why did she have to spoil their fun? Why begrudge them some joy when the nuns worked them to the bone?

'I will see to it that there will be no ration of bread with your potage at supper this evening. Perhaps that will help you mend your ways!' And with that Sister Agnes swept from the chamber.

'What a bitch!' said Sophie, her face flushed crimson.

Eleanor nodded. 'I had expected to encounter generosity of spirit at the priory, but so far, all the nuns I have met have been unpleasant characters.' It was an irony, because she had expected, in her later years, to found a religious house and be an abbess herself. It was customary that upon a noblewoman's marriage their husband gift his wife some land with which to build a religious house. His wife would then spend time there during her husband's lifetime or retire there after his death. Needless to say, Rolf had provided her with no such bequest. And she was hardly going to demand her due.

What fate awaited her now? She did not relish life here under this ascetic order that seemed to believe that hardship equated to sanctity. The bells rang out from the tower and broke her chain of thought.

The women rose stiffly, hoisting themselves out of bed. They filed out of the chamber, down the stairs and through the cloister to the chapel for Evening Prayer.

For the third time that day, Eleanor eased down onto the unyielding stone floor. Then she followed the example of the other women and knelt before the rood screen.

A low, ghostly chant came from the other side of the screen. She bowed her head and prayed for a miracle.

Mercifully, Evening Prayer was shorter than Nones, the afternoon service. Eleanor steeled herself for the last push of the day: supper. She had never felt so exhausted.

'We are segregated from the nuns because they fear our *wanton devilry*,' said Sophie. 'Apparently, this risk is heightened when the nuns are eating as it is believed that they might inadvertently ingest some of our *fiend-ishness*.' She rolled her eyes.

The meal was as measly as the others they had eaten. It was the same paltry potage. There was no sign of any bread, though she doubted that there would have been any in the first place. The women ate hurriedly, as though fearful that someone might appropriate what little they had in their bowls.

When they got up from the table, Eleanor's belly still ached with hunger. Despite her best efforts, she couldn't help torturing herself with memories of the lavish meals she had enjoyed in the recent past at Dover Castle. When she had arrived at the convent, she had been plump and healthy, but the meals at the priory were fast undoing all that good work. After just a few weeks of eating such a meagre diet she was growing horribly thin. How emaciated would she be after months of eating such fare? Surely she hadn't escaped her husband's violence only to starve to death at the Priory of St Mary?

14.

Messina, Sicily

In mid-September, Hugh had his first glimpse of the coastal city of Messina, flanked on either side by the Sicilian mountains. Mercifully it had only been one day and night's voyage from Salerno on the mainland. Thus far, he had found the sea voyages very wearing, and he had soon lost patience with the never-ending expanse of water. The thought that there would be leagues upon leagues more of it to come before they arrived in the Holy Land filled him with misery. Long hours of inactivity on the cramped ship left him pacing restlessly across the deck like a prisoner with no prospect of escape. Had it not been for Guy's company, he didn't know how he would have borne the tedium. Always hungry, there was nothing but unappealing dry provisions on board to satisfy his appetite. The filth and stench of his own body sickened him.

The sea was like a temperamental mistress: sometimes fair and yielding and other times savage and cruel in her anger. Only the week before, a storm had hit them off the coast of Amalfi. The wind had howled around the ship like a wild beast, shaking the vessel until it rattled. More than once, he had thought their moment had come and their quest would be over before it had even started. But the wind had eventually blown itself out and the waters had become calm again.

Plagued as he was by saddle sores, he much preferred overland travel. There was plenty to look at: the expanse of forest, great cathedrals and churches, the snow-capped mountains, the meandering rivers, Roman ruins and formidable castles and picturesque villages perched on the summits of mountains. The crusaders had visited so many abbeys during the course of their journey he was hard pressed to recollect any one distinctly. While they stayed under the roofs of the religious houses, the company were required to abide by the strict rules of the house and remain chaste and spend long hours in prayer. The company had travelled by way of Tours, Lyon, Valence and Marseille, visiting each of the abbeys in turn. Then, by boat, they had docked at Genoa, making stops at various places along the coast including Pisa, Portofino and Naples. These sojourns in the religious houses had come as a welcome respite from the endless sea.

Overall, the journey had passed peacefully, no one daring to challenge such a formidable army as theirs – save in Montelimar, where the inhabitants took against the crusaders. The king's response had been decisive: he had his men assault the town and take the lord prisoner. It had taken the earnest entreaties of his nobles to afford him liberty.

Best of all was when the crusaders were permitted to roam the taverns and inns of the towns and cities they visited. Free of the abbot's disapproving glares, they passed the time a good deal more pleasantly. Hugh had become accustomed to drinking ever increasing quantities of wine and had even started to laugh at the men's bawdy jokes. And there was nothing he liked better than a game of dice.

The ship dropped its anchor in the waters outside the city of Messina. Grateful to disembark, Hugh crowded onto a rowing boat bound for the shore. He shielded his eyes with a hand, blocking out the sun's glare, and cast his gaze up at the hilltop city. The skyline was dominated by the dome of the cathedral, which was partly obscured by wooden scaffolding. Below the cathedral sprawled a city of white stone; above it towered the massive grey ramparts of a castle. Hundreds of ships must have been docked in the harbour.

'Look at the fearsome stone gargoyles that guard the gates of the city,' said Guy. 'With their protuberant eyes and grotesque mouths.'

But the gates themselves had been thrown open and they received a magnificent reception.

'It appears that all the inhabitants have come out to welcome us,' said Hugh. 'From withered old men leaning on their staffs through to the squalling babes in arms.'

People lined the streets in droves, welcoming them with shouts and cheers. As he processed through the city with his fellow crusaders, he was conscious of their curious stares.

'It is far hotter here on land than it was out at sea,' said Guy.

Hugh nodded. Under his chain mail, he perspired profusely. 'Back home in England, the leaves would be starting to turn burnt yellows, oranges and reds by now, but here in Sicily it is still summer.'

Stalls outside shops overspilled onto the street. Clucking hens pecked at the bars of their cages. Other cages burst with squealing piglets or boasted flame-coloured exotic birds with an abundance of elegant plumes. Colourful arrangements of olives glistened in baskets.

'It is the fruit I long to eat most of all,' said Guy.

Hugh's mouth watered at the sight of dark red grapes, giant round melons ripening in the sun, figs, dates and even early season oranges. Inside the shops, he glimpsed cured meats and smoked fish hanging from hooks on the ceilings.

Straight-backed servants wove through the crowd, balancing amphoras of wine precariously upon their heads. Dark-skinned women in long simple robes offered him blood-red poppies and Sicilian purple saffron crocuses to buy. Other shops displayed carpets woven with vivid red and golden thread hanging from their doorways and silver and gold ornaments for the table flashed in the sun.

'Look how the traders stop to gape at us in wonder,' said Hugh.

Occasionally he got a tantalising whiff of cooking: mouth-watering smells of onions, garlic and spices frying in olive oil. Big-bellied men nodded to him in easy greeting, looking eminently satisfied with their lot in life. People in the city were for the most part dark-haired and olive-skinned.

Sir Mordaunt puffed up behind them. 'The city is a cultural melting pot . . . Jews, Muslims, Greeks and Christians live harmoniously in each other's pockets.'

'Some of these women are truly beautiful,' said Guy. 'Look at their long shiny hair and their dark alluring eyes!'

Other women were clad from head to toe in black cloth with only slits for their eyes. They sidled past the crusaders in fear, as though if they wished hard enough to be invisible, they would succeed. Heavily bearded and moustached men were dressed in long simple garments to keep the sun's incessant glare off their skin and trap the cool air. They sat in the tea shops playing at backgammon or walked about hand in hand. Their dark eyes looked on with suspicion at the sight of the pale-skinned crusaders and they whispered among themselves in some eastern tongue.

'Under the sun's glare, I'm baking in my chain mail,'

said Hugh. 'I envy these people their loose-fitted cotton robes and their leather-thonged sandals.'

For all the opulence of the city, there were thin hungry people in Messina too. The fetid stink of beggars, with their stumps and festering fly-covered sores, lingered in the air.

'Look . . .' said Guy. A turbaned snake charmer was entertaining the crowd.

They pushed through the throng and jostled for the best position to watch open-mouthed as the dark-skinned man lured his long, coiled serpent out of a basket with an eerie tune played upon a pipe.

Finally, they left the crowd behind and made their ascent up a steep stone staircase to a church. Inside, it was almost pitch-black and wonderfully cool after the glare of the sun. The air was suffused with sweet incense that went some way to offset the stink of their sweat. Up at the altar was the distant glimmer of candles glinting on ornaments of gold and silver. The knights knelt at their devotions while the priest murmured over them in Latin.

After their prayers, the crusaders were led into a large hall with an arched ceiling and thick colonnades and with traces of ancient frescos on the walls. Long trestle tables gleamed with silverware. King Tancred of Sicily had laid on a feast for them.

Trumpets gave a fanfare and King Tancred took his seat at the helm, overseeing proceedings. A squat, ugly balding man with a wiry black beard and tiny black eyes, he made up for this natural disadvantage with a splendid cloak of flowered silk that hung about his shoulders and jewelled rings glistened on every one of his fingers. Tancred rose and welcomed King Richard who towered over him.

Eagerly, Hugh took his seat at the high table beside his cousin and uncle with the rest of the nobles. A squire knelt before him with a bowl of water and he washed the salt and dirt off his hands. Servants served them fresh shellfish and a capon stew accompanied by a full-bodied sweet wine. He munched greedily and sucked the rich juices off his fingers. 'These Sicilians know how to cook!'

Guy nodded. 'These must be the sweetest, juiciest figs I have ever tasted!'

'King Richard and King Tancred are to go into council directly,' said Sir Mordaunt in a low voice after they had eaten their fill. 'They have many matters of importance to discuss including the restitution of King Richard's sister Joan and her dowry.'

Hugh nodded. It was common knowledge that King Tancred had imprisoned the king's sister.

'All knights and squires are to raise their tents outside the gates of the city. After that, the king has given us leave to explore the town at our leisure.'

After the meal Guy and Hugh went to check on their horses. The squires had brought their destriers from the ships and had tethered them outside the city walls where the camp would be made for the night. A flurry of rearing and whinnying beat up from the horses as they were rubbed down and curried by the squires and then fed handfuls of fresh sweet hay. Hugh's destrier seemed no worse for all the travelling but he could tell the animal was itching to be put out to pasture.

Satisfied the squires were taking good care of the horses, they pitched their tent and pulled off their hauberks. Then they set off together to explore the steep, cobbled alleys of the parched city. The very air shimmered. The sun's glare on the bone-dry white stone buildings and their terracotta roofs was blinding and Hugh was forced to shield his eyes with his hand. The afternoon sun scorched, and he was uncomfortably aware of his perspiration pooling in the small of his back beneath his leather gambeson.

The crowds had dispersed without a trace. The inhabitants must have retreated from the afternoon sun to the sanctuary of their homes. All the houses were shuttered and the city appeared silent and deserted. It felt eerie that there was no one around, save a few dusty cats sitting on walls, who peered down on them with suspicion, and a pack of mangy dogs scavenging in the dirt. There were only a few twisted trees in the city, but this was hardly surprising. After all, what vegetation could thrive in such an arid climate? Hugh's mouth was dry and he longed for some wine to moisten his cracked lips. By now, he was familiar with the southern custom of siesta in the heat of the day. If only he was at liberty to take refuge within the cool, thick-stoned walls of a house and catch some hours of sweet sleep on a feather bed. But here he was a stranger and all doors were closed to him.

'My father says the Greeks make up most of the population of this city,' said Guy. They paused, admiring a view of the turquoise sea below heaving onto the white sand.

Hugh nodded and mopped his brow. 'It is a beautiful city, but it is too hot, dry and dusty for me.'

'Behold in the distance, Mount Etna towers over us.' Guy pointed directly behind them at a huge mountain that loomed dark on the horizon. 'When she is angered, she is said to spew rivers of fire and choking dust and fumes.'

Hugh shook his head. 'Who would choose to build a settlement in her wake? A foolish man, surely.'

'You speak true, cousin. This is a hot and inhospitable country, but we have many more leagues of parched territory to cover before we get to the Holy Land. The abbot says the road ahead is an exposed desert track where we will roast under the sun's harsh glare.'

Even the prospect of the desert journey made Hugh feel parched. 'Perhaps among all the shuttered houses and shops we might come across a tavern where we may quench our thirst.' And then he saw it, a small establishment squashed between two large houses. 'Look a tavern open for custom.'

They bent their eager heads under the stone archway of the entrance and found themselves in the gloomy interior of a stuffy one-roomed tavern crowded with trestle tables and benches. Knights of their company sat in a pool of candlelight.

'Pray take a seat, young sirs,' said a burly knight in full battle dress. 'Join us in a cup of wine.' His lank hair covered a pockmarked face and a crushed nose. With a meaty hand, he gestured towards the wooden bench.

Hugh recognised him. He travelled under the banner of De Cleres.

'By all means,' said Guy. He lowered himself onto the bench. 'I am Sir Guy, and this is my cousin, Sir Hugh de Eynsford.'

Hugh envied Guy's ability to speak easily with any man he encountered, highborn or lowborn, whereas he was plagued by a shyness he could never quite shake off except for when he was in his cups. The tavern keeper poured out a goblet of wine and handed it to him. Thanking the man, he took a seat opposite Guy and gulped down a long draught of the sweet refreshing wine.

'Well met, sirs,' said the knight. He brought his goblet down on the table with a splash of crimson wine. 'I am Sir Ferrant, and this is my squire, Gerbod. We joined the king's company in Marseille. I am familiar with your corner of England. Indeed, my father is in talks with Baron Rolf as he intends to marry my sister.'

'But Rolf is already married,' blurted out Hugh, before he could stop himself.

'Lamentably his wife died recently,' said Sir Ferrant. 'And now he looks for a new wife.'

Hugh stared at the knight, uncertain if he had heard him clearly. A great shudder ran through him, and his heart began a slow thumping beat that shook the bones in his chest. Dead? Not dead! Please, God . . . you cannot take Eleanor from me too! He turned to Guy for support. Guy looked uncomfortable.

Enraged, Hugh pushed himself upright, his hackles rising, and he spilled his goblet of wine. 'You knew Eleanor was dead and you didn't tell me!' he shouted. His voice veered higher. His hands flew to Guy's throat. 'I cannot believe that you held back such news!' Then, just as quickly, he let his hands drop. He fell silent and took a few rasping breaths, his hand braced against the wall to stop himself from falling.

Guy leapt up and put a conciliatory arm around his shoulder. 'Cousin, forgive me. We only found out by chance this morning. It seems she died two months ago, soon after we left England. We knew you loved her. Father thought it was better that you did not know. We did not want you to hear such sad tidings so soon after you had lost your mother.'

'Sit down and have a drink,' said Sir Ferrant. 'You have had a nasty shock.'

Hugh sat down with a thump and could not suppress a choking noise in his throat. The grim news hit him like a sword in the gut. His world folded in on itself. His mind was tumbling, then hurtling headlong down a rabbit hole of despair.

A part of him could appreciate that his cousin and uncle had meant no harm in withholding the news from him even though he still shook with anger. 'Dearest Eleanor! I cannot bring myself to believe it. Dead. How?'

'Complications of childbirth, it seems,' said Sir Ferrant.

'That bastard Rolf killed Eleanor. I am sure of it.' Hugh's voice broke as he uttered her name and something cracked deep within him. 'She might be still alive if only I had gone back for her after the tournament.'

'Dear cousin, come and drown your sorrows with a cup of wine.' Guy refilled his goblet and passed it to him.

Hugh sank into a desolate silence. Absentmindedly he emptied his goblet and downed the next one when a serving wench refilled it. His insides seethed with churned up emotion. Just like that, the future he had always dreamed of was obliterated. He let out a bellow of anguish and slammed his fist down on the table. Nothing would ever bring him joy again.

Beside him, Guy held his peace. His cousin knew better than to engage him in conversation at that moment. Long moments passed and they remained in silence, drinking steadily. Numb, Hugh had no sense of the passing time.

Presently, a comely girl with a head of glossy dark brown ringlets and olive skin approached and set a jug down on the table. She was dressed in a jade kirtle that accentuated all her curves and brought out the colour of her emerald-hazel eyes.

'Look cousin, this sweet girl means to comfort you,' said Guy. 'Let her help you.'

Despondent, Hugh pushed the girl away. 'I will not betray Eleanor's memory.'

At that moment, Sir Walter ambled up to their table and sank his weight onto the bench beside them. 'You are a devil to find, you two!' He mopped the sweat from his brow. 'Been here a while, too, from the look of you.'

Conscious he was horribly drunk, Hugh struggled to focus his eyes on the knight. He didn't trust himself to speak. What was there to say now, in any case?

Sir Walter seemed satisfied without a reply. 'This Tancred is a short and ugly fellow,' he blundered on rather too loudly. 'No wonder he is known as the Monkey King! The fool brings dishonour on his people. They should blame him, not us, for their unhappiness.'

'He may be an ugly midget,' said Guy. 'But he's a good soldier and it would be foolish to underestimate him.'

'Good?' Sir Walter crashed his cup down on the table. 'A man who holds a woman ransom has no honour in my eyes. I do not wonder that the king is angry.'

'It isn't any woman either,' said Sir Manard, who had puffed in, red-faced, behind Sir Walter. He pulled a low stool up to the table. 'It is the king's sister, and she is entitled to land and wealth of her own.'

'He has reneged on his promises to offer funding

and men for the crusade,' said Sir Walter. 'We would ensure that he honour his word.' Sir Walter unsheathed his sword with a dramatic flourish.

'But he refuses to pay?' said Guy.

Sir Walter returned his sword to its sheath and took a long swig of wine. He wiped his mouth on his sleeve. 'He has no choice. He cannot hope to defy the Lionheart. King Richard and the French King Philip will hold him to his word, mark you.'

Hugh hardly listened to what they said. None of it mattered to him anymore. He drained his cup. Under the table he clenched and unclenched his fist on his lap. He took deep jagged breaths. Grief and rage leapt and hissed like flames in his heart. Adamant he would make Rolf pay for what he had done to Eleanor, he heaved himself to his feet and took a few staggering steps towards the door. But all the wine he had consumed had got the better of him and the room swam under him.

15.

A Pittance

The bells for Prime shook Eleanor awake, and she felt strangely tearful. Nevertheless, she soldiered on and forced her body out of bed, steeling herself for the day of physical exertion ahead. She had no wish to end her days here at the priory, a broken woman. At all costs, she simply had to make it through this hardship for the sake of the new life that fluttered in her belly.

With a shiver, she drew her filthy woollen dress close about her. It was unseasonably cold for mid-September. Gazing up at the ceiling, she noticed a small icicle had formed high up in a damp, cracked corner. Had she been at the castle she would have been wearing furs in such temperatures. Instead, the women didn't have so much as a cloak between them and their breath hung in the air like smoke.

They huddled together like animals for warmth in the unheated chapel for Prime that morning. She hardly noticed the smell of unwashed bodies these days.

'Just how long is the priest going to go on for?' said Sophie with a groan. 'I'm in no mood for a lecture. My knees throb from kneeling on the flagstone floor!'

'Pride itself is the biggest sin . . .' the priest was saying. 'For with it we have no hope of absorbing God's teaching and passing through into the Kingdom of God. There is vanity too. I see too many silks and scarlet colours in the gowns of the women before me. If you women do not mend your ways, you will become the devil's playthings, saucy temptresses leading good honest men astray.'

'Certainly, no one could accuse the women on this side of the rood screen of dressing provocatively!' murmured Sophie under her breath.

Eleanor glanced down at her own miserable rough-spun garments and ran the tip of her finger along the abrasive fabric of her dress, the hem of which was caked in mud and dirt.

'It is my sworn duty,' said the priest, 'to ensure that the devil does not establish his kingdom here in the Priory of St Mary, a place that is consecrated to God.

'It must not be forgotten that the love of man brings great sadness, but the love of Christ gladdens the heart. The path to the Kingdom of God is verily through self-discipline, hard work, coarse garments, a hard bed and the bearing of evil. Pray tend to self-denial and eschew self-indulgence!'

'This must signify that we're well on our way to the Kingdom of God,' mouthed Sophie and she favoured Eleanor with her winning smile. 'After all, we are working ourselves to the bone, wear coarse garments, sleep in uncomfortable beds and bear the tyranny of Sister Agnes!'

Eleanor grinned.

At last, the priest concluded the service. The women struggled to their feet and hurried off to break their fast in the refectory. Eleanor was ravenous and gulped down her potage. But the gnawing hunger that now haunted her day and night was not sated.

Sister Agnes sent them out into the great meadow that morning to clear the ditches in the mizzle and a knife-edged wind. Very soon Eleanor's woollen gown was saturated. It clung to her skin and provided no protection against the biting chill. The skin on her fingers was red-raw and her knuckles bled. She prayed her baby in her belly was warm, protected from the harsh nip of the arctic blast.

After they cleared the ditches, they returned to the warmth of the kitchen, where a leg of beef turned on a spit. The fat of the meat blistered anyone who stood too close. Steam came off her damp gown and her skin stung with the sudden warmth. What she would have given to linger in the kitchen to warm up properly and dry out her gown! However, Sister Agnes had other plans for them.

Directly, she found herself on her hands and knees collecting the old reeds and food debris off the refectory floor from the feast the night before. The refectory was icy, now the fires had gone out. Hungry as she was, she was sore tempted to eat remnants of meat, bread and gristle that had fallen from the table. The women carried the debris outside to the pigsty where it would be fodder for the animals. Then they brought armfuls of reeds from the storeroom to lay on the refectory floor.

Bowls of steaming potage greeted them for luncheon. Eleanor thawed her frozen fingers around the bowl as she supped it slowly. She forced herself to savour the unappetising liquid for as long as she could. Perhaps, in this way, she could fool her body into thinking it had consumed ample food. At any rate, she felt a little warmer.

Some energetic churning in the buttery warmed her up that afternoon, but her sodden rough-spun garments stuck to her and irritated her skin. She prayed that Sister Agnes would permit them to change into dry clothes soon. As though in answer to her prayer, Sister Agnes scolded them to change their garments as if they had gotten soaking wet of their own volition.

'Sister Agnes is probably worried that the prioress will chide her for driving her flock in soaking wet garments,' said Sophie with a bitter smile.

More comfortable in a dry woollen dress, Eleanor knelt in the chapel for Nones. Were it not for all the kneeling, she would have enjoyed her time in the chapel. It was a welcome break from labouring, a short rest for her overworked body.

'I want to talk to you of love . . .' intoned the priest. This was a new and unfamiliar voice coming from behind the screen. It was clear and passionate.

'There are many forms of love, all of which are of different value. Firstly, you will all, I hope, be acquainted with the supportive love derived from friendship. More powerful than this is the love that can exist between a man and a woman.'

She loved Hugh and he loved her, but such thoughts were futile now; they could never be together.

'More powerful than that still,' said the priest, 'is the love between a mother and her children.'

She derived a rush of comfort from the thought of the baby growing in her womb.

'For the mother who loves,' said the priest. 'Is ready to die for her child or to spill her own blood to cure her child of disease.

'Higher than that is the love of the body for the soul, but the love that Christ bears to His dear spouse, the soul, is the greatest love of them all! Let me tell you a tale of love so that you may know more of this great thing. There was once a noble lady who lived alone in her castle. Her husband had long since died and she lived quite undefended by any man. She was under attack from all sides as her neighbours, greedy barons, wanted to appropriate her lands and wealth for themselves. But all was not lost, as there was a great king who desired to help her. He sent messengers carrying missives of support, valuable trinkets, and food to sustain her. But, alas, the lady remained resolute, as she could not find it within her heart to love him. The love within his heart was undiminished by this rejection and he continued to send her food to keep her from starving, but still she refused to let him into her heart. The great king, however, was full of love and insisted that the great lady was in danger, and she risked dying a shameful death. He foretold that he would receive a mortal wound on her behalf and perish rather than she come to any harm. And so, it passed. He perished from the thrust of a sword. Do you suppose that the lady found it within her heart to love him now that he had died for her? Verily, she was not worthy of his love!

'Thus, is the love of Christ. There is no more thoughtful or attentive lover. There is no man with greater wealth, greater power, greater understanding or greater wisdom.'

Eleanor longed to give herself up to such love, a love that would nourish and protect her, no matter what happened.

'Compare with this heavenly bliss the woeful state of mortal marriage,' said the priest. 'The children screaming . . . the supper burning . . . the animals chasing around the furniture . . . the husband chiding and beating his wife. Such love as exists between a man and a woman will eventually be lost through lack of love or physical infirmity – for a mortal husband must always wither and die. Truly, there can be no comparison.'

Her hair stood on end at the memory of her own unhappy marriage.

'Today, I call you to your confession,' said the priest. 'It is vital that you share your innermost thoughts and desires in the confessional. For, although you are not worthy, Christ will forgive all. What is crucial is for you to be honest and meek about your sins. Confession without honesty is verily an embrace with the devil himself. The act of lying is to make your tongue a cradle for the devil's child and to nurture it as surely as a doting mother would nurture her baby. I bid every soul present to come to confession!'

She was seized with the desire to unburden her horrid truth onto a loving other, but surely this was impossible. A feeling of great dread settled upon her and bile rose to her throat. Fearful of vomiting in the chapel, she scrambled to her feet and murmured her excuses to Sister Agnes who shot her a stormy look and reluctantly permitted her to leave the chapel.

At a run, she made for the kitchen gardens, desperate to fill her lungs with fresh air.

The garden was icy, although the mizzle had abated. There had been no snow as yet this year, but a layer of frost made everything glisten. She retched and brought up her meagre lunch and bile. Exhausted from the effort, she sank down onto the frozen ground.

Perhaps it would be better if she froze to death outside in the deserted garden. It was impossible for her to commune with Christ through confessional. If she imparted the truth, she would imperil herself and her unborn child.

She could not be truthful any more than the compulsive liar could stop lying. A paralysing terror seized her, as though a devil sat upon her shoulder – a devil who claimed her very soul.

Just when she thought herself lost forever to the depths of Hell, one of the cooks emerged from the kitchen. Wrapped up in a woollen cloak, the woman made a rotund figure. She had a rosy-cheeked face and merry blue eyes that twinkled.

'My, my!' she exclaimed when she caught sight of Eleanor slumped on the ground. 'You will catch your death of cold out here.' She helped her up with a plump arm. 'You must come into the warm and heat yourself up in front of the fire. You are quite blue with cold.'

Indeed, she was cold to the bone and her teeth chattered. She warmed immediately to the kind soul who offered her hospitality. Once inside, the cook threw off her cloak, having no need of it in the cosy kitchen, and wrapped it around Eleanor's shoulders. She took Eleanor's hands and pressed them between both her own. Eleanor appreciated the maternal gesture.

'To think you might have died out there, if I had not come upon you,' said the woman. 'And you so close to having your baby! Here . . . I'll get you a hot, spicy ale. That will warm you up something proper.'

Eleanor sank down onto a stool in front of the fire, grateful for its warmth. Cup in hand, she sipped the ale. The liquid travelled down her throat to her belly and then seeped through her blood.

'Here . . .' The woman turned to the cauldron and ladled out some meaty-looking stew into a bowl. 'To think they put you on such measly rations when you women have growing bairns in your bodies. And they work you so hard. It is plain wickedness, if you ask me.'

Gratefully Eleanor took a mouthful of the hot tender meat. For a moment, she savoured the taste and texture of the flesh in her mouth before she chewed it and swallowed it down.

The woman refilled the bowl as soon as Eleanor had emptied it. 'The sisters won't notice. They are plump and well fed.'

With a full belly, Eleanor's spirits rallied. It was the most comfortable she had been in weeks. How much better things seemed when she wasn't starving!

'There you are!' Sister Agnes burst into the kitchen with a crash. 'Get up, woman, there is work to be done!'

The cook stood in front of Eleanor, like a mother protecting her child from hungry wolves.

'I found her half-starved, collapsed in the kitchen gardens. Near frozen to death, she was!'

'Do you presume to tell me how I should run my

house, Albreda?' Sister Agnes had a dangerous glint in her eyes.

'Of course not. I beg your pardon.' The cook was cut down to size. It seemed to Eleanor she had shrunk at least three inches. 'I do not question your authority, Sister.' She bobbed a curtsy for effect. 'But this woman is ill and needs someone to take care of her, anyone can see that.'

Eleanor's heart went out to this kind, dear woman who dared stand up to Sister Agnes.

'You fatten up the wretch with the meat for the holy feast!' said the nun. 'That is more than a slut such as she deserves.' She turned to Eleanor. 'Make haste, woman! Hard work will go some way to redeem your sins in the eyes of the Lord.'

~

The following day, Eleanor woke unusually refreshed. After Prime and the usual breakfast of potage and a few crusts, the women were set to work in the kitchen garden. She must have been singing while she dug that morning for Sister Agnes admonished her.

'And what, pray, do you sing about?' The nun's face twitched with anger.

Her head dropped, she awaited Sister Agnes's punishment. But it never came, because a man's voice broke in.

'Hark, what an angelic voice!' The man wore the long robes of a priest. He had a tangled grey beard and intelligent blue eyes. 'To whom does it belong?'

'It was she, Precentor,' said Sister Agnes. She pushed Eleanor forward roughly.

Eleanor bowed and lowered her eyes meekly.

'You have truly been gifted by the Lord! My dear, you must join with the ancren and make part of the choir.'

In the presence of the precentor, Sister Agnes had become meek and mild, a changed woman. 'If it pleases you.' She gave a long bow. 'I will send her to practice.'

'We start presently,' said the priest.

Eleanor wiped the worst of the dirt off her hands on her apron and followed the priest through the cloister and into the priory, which was fragrant with the smell of incense. The choir sat in parallel pews adjacent to the altar. The priest gestured she should take position by the hermits who came to the priory to sing and worship. Beside her stood a woman dressed as humbly as herself, in a rough woollen gown. The woman turned and smiled at her, a good-tempered sparkle in her hazel eyes.

A dozen women, mostly nuns, made up the choir. Several nuns accompanied them on lutes. On this side of the rood screen, the music was resonant and unchecked by stone. Eleanor cast an admiring glance about the room and took in the high carved wooden ceiling and the beautiful frescos that adorned the walls, which depicted the coming of Christ, the Last Supper and the Crucifixion. Finally, she turned towards the altar and allowed herself a moment, gazing up at the tall gilded crucifix, full of awe at the beautiful depiction of Christ's great suffering.

The musical score that she shared with the woman beside her was a manuscript of great beauty. The first psalm they sang was unfamiliar. It appeared to be a song arranged with the nuns in mind for it extolled the merits of being a wife of Christ as opposed to the poverty and suffering of being a mortal man's wife. She picked it up as they went along.

A maiden did once ask me to recommend a mortal love to her,
And forsooth, I did reply a mortal love will wither and die.
For a man is a whimsical creature, what pleasures him one day may offend him the next.
His eye may stray to other fair maidens in his vicinity,
His heart will err and shatter your own irreparably into tiny fragments
And even if he keeps faith with you, and he possesses a healthy physique,
He may be taken from you by some terrible malady
And at the end he will inevitably wither and die.
Choose instead to be a heavenly bride,
Christ's generosity knows no bounds,
He will continue to love you when you age,
And the bloom of your maidenhood fades.

His love will never falter.
Long after the mortal man has withered away
And his corpse is eaten by maggots,
Christ will still love you.

Every note she sang invigorated her. Following the precentor's lead, she lingered on the long vowels and savoured the sounds and the dynamics. In song, all boundaries were gone and she was at one with the other women. It was a glorious, joyous moment. What could be better than this? Delicious shivers travelled up her spine. Inside her womb, her baby had woken, and kicked against her rhythmically, sharing in this wonderful moment.

Choir practice was over in the blink of an eye. Soon, the other nuns closed their scores and filed out of the priory and into the cloister. Sister Agnes scowled at her. Hurriedly, she took her leave of the precentor and the choir and hastened to join the other women.

The women gave her curious looks as she joined them in the buttery. But there was no opportunity for talk as Sister Agnes monitored them closely, birch in hand to punish them for sloppy work. She found that she had new reserves of energy. As she churned the cream of the milk into butter, she couldn't suppress a smile. Even Sister Agnes screaming, 'Wipe that lascivious smile off your face, slut!' at her couldn't snuff out the new flame that kindled in her heart. To her astonishment, she found the work was no longer a chore. Indeed, it was with the greatest satisfaction that she saw the yellow flecks in the pail multiply and turn into thick, yellow butter.

In the last few hours, singing with the choir, she had been acquainted with a hitherto unknown sense of contentment – joy, even. It thrilled her to think she would sing again with the choir on the morrow. Perhaps coming to the priory had not been a mistake after all.

It felt as though hardly any time had passed before the bell signalled that it was time for the midday meal. She followed the other women into the refectory. Not once had she thought about her hunger that morning.

～

That afternoon, the bell that summoned all for Nones rang out all too quickly. As per usual, she went to follow Sophie and the other women into the chapel. But Sister Agnes pulled her aside. 'From now on you shall join the ancren in the choir in the priory.'

The other women stared at Eleanor in astonishment. A few of their faces were distorted by envy as they perceived she was enjoying preferential treatment.

Nones on the other side of the rood screen was far more enjoyable. While the pregnant women knelt on the flagstone floor, on this side of the screen the nuns sat in pews and knelt on comfortable cushions to pray. The choir even enjoyed the respite of misericords to rest their weary legs. This was something that she, with her swollen belly and aching legs, particularly relished. The prioress and all the other grades and offices of nun down to the apple-cheeked novices sat in their allotted pews.

The priest who presided over the ceremony that afternoon wore a long black habit decorated with the insignia of Canterbury Cathedral. A shrivelled old man, he had a thin wisp of grey hair at the temples. The service began with the psalm they had practised that morning. It filled her with great joy to sing God's praises together with so many others. It was one thing to practise with the choir but to sing in a service was another thing altogether. There was nothing like it. When the singing ended, she was bereft.

The elderly priest pushed himself to his feet. She had expected him to have a decrepit, ailing voice to match his body, but it had retained the power of a much younger man. It was a voice she recognised from the other services she had attended.

'It is important to remember the laws of Christ and the rules of appropriate behaviour. At all costs, a nun must eschew the sin of pride. There are also the sins of avarice, sloth, lust, covetousness, greed and wrath. A nun must always adopt appropriate clothing. A woollen dress in a dark colour, neither too warm nor too cold, should be sufficient.'

He surveyed the congregation with narrowed eyes. 'I see ermine and silk among the congregation today. Shame on you who wear it!'

There were some red faces in the pews as the nuns

who sported such luxuries bowed their heads in shame.

'As to what a nun should eat, Brides of Christ should eat neither too little, nor too much.'

Disapproving faces turned and looked at a plump nun with dimpled cheeks in the third row. The poor woman blushed a deep shade of scarlet.

'Then there is the question of visitors. In his last visitation the bishop observed that many of the nuns were receiving visitors. Men, no less!'

This provoked some gasps of outrage from some prim-looking nuns in the front row.

'I am mortified to hear from the prioress that there are some nuns who persist in receiving male guests at the priory. This must stop! How are we to preserve the sanctity of this priory with such wanton behaviour? Such wickedness and flouting of the rules can only end in devilry!'

The priest paused for a moment, looking round the chapel to verify that all the nuns had their heads bowed in reverence. Apparently satisfied, he concluded his sermon.

The service ended with a resounding anthem. Once more Eleanor's spirits soared to the heavens as the music and song filled the chapel. To sing in a choir was truly paradise on earth!

After the service, she joined the other women in the priory kitchens. The kitchens were a hive of activity. Sophie and the other women prepared vegetables for the feast of St Cecily that evening. A pair of capons that roasted on the spit smelled excellent. Eleanor joined Sophie and chopped a mountain of carrots for a potage. The delicious smell of frying onions and garlic wafted across the kitchen from a huge cauldron that hung over the other fire. It tantalised her to smell such appetising food and disheartened her that she would not have so much as a mouthful of it. A watery potage awaited the pregnant women tonight, just as it did every night.

One of the cooks at the other end of the kitchen opened the bread oven and brought forth a freshly baked loaf. It smelled mouth-wateringly good. All the women turned and watched the cook place it on a rack to cool.

Sister Agnes's eagle eye missed nothing. 'Back to your work, you slovenly lot!' Her voice cracked like a whip.

She didn't like to think about what she would have done for a slice of freshly baked, hot-buttered bread at that moment. It was torture to be so close to good food without any of it passing one's lips. Hunger ravaged her belly. The other women felt the same she was sure. Their eyes darted around the kitchen. They were like a pack of starving wolves looking for titbits. How terrible it was to know such hunger. To eat in moderation was one thing, but it was quite another not to have enough to eat day after day.

A few minutes later, new smells enticed her nostrils. The cook had opened a box of pittances or sweetmeats and was arranging them on a platter. A gift to the nuns from some wealthy benefactor, apparently. The sticky sweetmeats looked delicious. It was all she could do to hold herself back from popping one in her mouth. However, Anne proved unable to resist the temptation.

'Thief!' Sister Agnes's voice scaled terrifying new heights. 'We have a thief in our midst on Saint Cecily's day of all days!'

Anne nearly choked on her sweetmeat. Poor soul, it was a pity she didn't even get to enjoy it.

Sister Agnes seized Anne by the ear. 'Let none of you thieving sluts try and pinch any of them either.' With that, she marched Anne out of the kitchen.

16.

The Attack on Messina

An insistent clang of bells woke Hugh from groggy dreams. It had been the third morning running that he had no memory of having gone to bed. Yet again he felt wretched. Drenched in sweat after the heat of the night, he had a tormenting thirst and blinding headache. Once again, hope died in his heart as the realisation dawned that Eleanor was dead. Curled up on his side, he was as a man who had been pierced through the heart with a poisoned arrow. But there was no time for him to wallow in his grief because Guy shook him by the shoulder.

'Wake up, wake up! The camp is alive with news of an attack on crusaders last night!'

With the greatest reluctance, Hugh scrambled to

his feet and flung on his clothes. Guy and Sir Mordaunt stood outside the tent waiting for him. The sun's rays were as daggers to his eyes and he brought up his arm, shielding them from the great light.

'Several members of our party were set upon by Greek scoundrels wielding long knives in the early hours,' said Sir Mordaunt.

'They are dead?' Hugh's head and heart pounded.

'Unhappily. They were taken by surprise.' Sir Mordaunt threw his hands up in a gesture of despair. 'The streets of Messina run red with the blood of Christian soldiers.'

'What will come of it?'

'The king is reported to be furious and promises their lives will be avenged!'

'Then it is war?'

'Undoubtably. He has called all the barons in for council.'

Hugh's addled mind drifted back to Rolf. His blood fit to boil, he clenched his fists and dug his fingers deep into the palms of his hands. It would be good to shed some blood – to rid himself of the terrible rage that coursed through his veins. If only he did not feel so abysmal. His head was splitting.

Guy handed him a wine skin.

With a step back, he recoiled at the thought of consuming more of the evil liquid.

'Have some, cousin,' pressed Guy. 'You'll see . . . you'll feel better.'

He gagged at the smell of the wine, but all the same, he took a great swig.

A huge grey cloud obscured the sun. He squinted up and his eyes watered against the light. It wasn't like any cloud he had seen before. It was more like a smog. It constricted his throat and he laboured to breathe.

'The mountain yonder spewed it out this morning,' said Guy. 'Without a breath of wind to chase it away, it just hangs there.'

'A harbinger of doom,' said Hugh. He felt at the very brink of despair, as if he were living in a nightmare made true.

Guy gazed at him with pity in his eyes. 'Come to the tent. Father will explain the battle plan.'

They found Sir Mordaunt and his right-hand man pouring over a crudely drawn map.

'We will make our attack from the east,' said Sir Mordaunt. He traced their route with a fat finger. 'The scouts have returned from reconnaissance and we know that King Tancred's main forces are installed here . . . here . . . and here. We anticipate Tancred will send out his cavalry from the north gate and we shall be there to meet them. If we succeed in overpowering them, we shall assail the castle walls with the siege towers. The trebuchets will target these walls here . . . and here. And King Philip of France's army will make their charge at the main gate.'

'Victory is ours,' said Guy, his eyes aflame. 'Our forces will prevail.'

The Song and the Sword

'Do not be so certain.' His father waggled his finger. 'There is no forgone conclusion. Tancred defends his city and castle and his men are strong, skilled and war-hardened. We have a tough fight ahead of us. Reportedly, he inspires such slavish devotion in his men that they would go to their deaths if he bid them.'

Glad to have found something to take his mind off his lost Eleanor, Hugh went in search of food and drink to cheer his wounded heart. After a plate of bread and cheese, he felt a little stronger and returned to his tent and prepared for the battle. He donned his chain mail and sharpened his long sword to a razor-sharp edge. This was the moment he had been waiting for all his life. At last, he had the chance to prove himself.

The hours passed but the day dragged on. Every man in the camp made ready for war. He watched with detached interest as the carpenters hammered and nailed furiously as they assembled the siege towers and the trebuchets.

'Will King Tancred not know something is afoot?' asked Hugh. 'I mean, with all this activity.'

'Perhaps,' said Sir Mordaunt. 'Likely he has been prewarned of our attack. Word could have got out of King Richard's attack on the monastery of La Bagnara this afternoon. The defenders soon ceded to him when they appraised the size and substance of their foe. Apparently, the monks emerged with their hands raised in defeat. They saw the sense in living out their days rather than dying prematurely, no doubt. King

Richard and King Philip, who has recently arrived in Messina, have installed their soldiers in La Bagnara and are using it as a base for their operations. It has been confirmed that tonight, we make our assault on Messina. Both of you . . . go and sleep while you can.'

Hugh and Guy embarked on the short walk back to their tent.

'There are all the hallmarks of an approaching storm,' said Hugh. He shifted about in his uncomfortable steel hauberk. 'Can't you feel the heaviness in the air? See how the insects are congregating.'

They watched as hundreds of tiny flying ants spiralled in a curious column high into the sky, where a flock of opportunistic swallows circled.

'Without question, the rains are itching to come,' said Guy. 'Not before this infernal heat has squeezed and wrung us dry.' He mopped his brow under his helmet with the edge of his surcoat.

'And yet there is no wind. And that ominous cloud still hangs over us and spoils the very air that we breathe.'

'Finally, we are going to war, Hugh.' Guy's blue eyes glinted in the sun. 'Think of it! This is real war, not play!'

'It cannot come fast enough for me. I have had my fill of this endless waiting.'

∼

The Song and the Sword

War started in the pitch black of the small hours of the next morning. The grey cloud from the mountain had consumed the stars and the moon. The camp watched in silence and waited for their orders. At long last, the westerly wind began to stir away the noxious cloud. By the light of the crescent moon that emerged, Hugh could just make out the shadows of the men who soundlessly scaled the rough-hewn walls of the city's first defence. As they crept through the city, they set alight fields, barns, houses and trees. The crusaders took the inhabitants by surprise and slew any man they came across. To further weaken resistance, the king sent a party to set fire to King Tancred's crops and burn down their store houses and in the distance for miles around Hugh saw little fires spring up.

Before long, the watchmen at the ramparts of the city heard the rumours and blew their horns, sounding the alarm. Shortly afterwards bells pealed from the towers of the churches, rousing the citizens of the city and alerting them to the danger that threatened their walls.

Blood-curdling screams pierced the darkness, high-pitched shrieks of women and children among them, and sickened Hugh to the stomach. A terrifying tumult ensued. A wave of horror and doubt assaulted him as he witnessed the wild joy of destruction. It was one thing to kill a soldier in the heat of battle, but to kill women and children . . . well, that was quite another matter.

Now the surprise attack had been sprung, the crusaders whipped up a clamour with the shrill and urgent tones of their horns and trumpets and the insistent thunderclap of their big drums. The noise thrilled him and overturned his feelings of revulsion. His battle lust was awakened.

As more of the city caught alight, the sky above was as bright as day, the air thick with smoke and fear. Soon the castle at the heart of the city was besieged and encircled by a ring of flames. In the chaos that followed, the raiders threw open the city gates to the crusaders.

All around Hugh, knights tightened girths, prepared their saddles and reassured their horses, while others stared uneasily at the burning city. All the bravado of the preceding weeks was forgotten, and in the torchlight, their faces were grim and some even looked afraid.

A great rumble rocked the earth beneath his feet. A thunderclap louder than he had ever heard shook him to the core. The horses whickered and reared and the knights struggled to soothe their steeds.

Guy pulled at Hugh's sleeve. 'Behold the mountain yonder!'

In the darkness, fire spattered like blood out of the crater of the far-off mountain. Hungry tributaries of red flame and magma rushed down its slopes and hissed like some fearsome big cat when they met a source of water.

Doom hung over their venture. All the same, each

knight faced it silently and without quailing. With a great effort Hugh mastered the fear that bubbled up in his belly.

More time passed and then Sir Mordaunt raised his hand. He rode along the line of his horsemen. Heart racing, Hugh sprang upon his horse and the rest of the company did the same. A single trumpet rang out somewhere off ahead and, with a thunder of hooves, the host moved swiftly across the plain and drew their swords as they approached the city and converged upon its open gates.

As expected, a sortie of horsemen surged up boldly out of the gates. With fierce battle cries they brandished swords and spears.

The ordered mass of crusaders held together and charged as one with a great shout. Against such a force as theirs the defenders surely had little hope of holding them back for long. A horn resounded behind Hugh and rallied the host into the attack. Against all odds Tancred's cavalry fought back fiercely with skill and bravery, preferring to slay as many of the invading knights and choosing death over the shame of ceding to their foe. The plain filled with the ring of swords and the clash of steel. Hugh couldn't help admiring the defenders' valour as he held up his sword, which shimmered in the moonlight and slashed and felled the enemy from their horses.

As they approached the city's walls, an intense rain of whistling arrows felled the men riding alongside him. It was a race against time to get to the wall and out of bowshot, and he thrust forward faster. By some fluke of fate, he remained unscathed.

Once through the gates, they hastened to the fortress and galloped up the narrow streets to the summit of the hill. Flames licked the ruins of the shops and houses around them.

Ahead teams of French soldiers strained as they propelled a huge battering ram. It comprised a massive trunk of oak reinforced with a lethal iron tip and housed in a wooden hut roofed with animal skins for protection. It lurched and bumped along the uneven cobbles on wooden wheels. Faster and faster, it went towards the ironbound gate of the castle and swung with a tremendous thwack that shook the very walls, and the ground thrummed beneath Hugh's feet. Though the wood splintered, the huge door held and the attackers withdrew and renewed their storm. The ram thundered repeatedly into the door until it caved in with a terrific creak and stout planks and beams toppled down, crushing the foot soldiers beneath it.

On the east flank of the fortress, French trebuchets hurled heavy rocks more than three hundred yards, bringing sections of the curtain wall crashing down. The French knights poured through the breaches into the castle.

On the west flank, a crusader company drove a great siege tower clattering up to the wall. The small dark figures of the archers let off a volley of arrows from the battlement above and they threw great vats of boiling oil over the ramparts. The men cowered under a roof sewn of animal skins. One knight was not so lucky: the stricken and agonised cry of a man doused with boiling oil pierced the night air and Hugh could not repress a shudder.

'To me, to me!' cried Sir Mordaunt. 'We must take out those archers on the battlements! To the siege towers!'

Hugh and the other knights of his party jumped off their horses and made for the siege tower. His heart thumping, Hugh climbed nimbly to the top and was one of the first to breach the castle's curtain walls. Fortunately, he dodged the arrows that whistled past his face. Once over the battlement, he launched into single combat, slicing and chopping the waiting sentries with his heavy long sword. Steel rang upon steel up on the narrow ramparts. By turns Hugh lunged, cut and hacked. A tough labour of a fight still awaited the crusaders up on the battlement, for the Sicilians were war-hardened and ferocious even in despair, greatly outnumbered though they were. With growing weariness, Hugh wondered if they were pitted against a too-powerful enemy and had overestimated their advantage. Sir Mordaunt was right: these men wouldn't blanch at dying for their king and kin. Many knights of his company lay slain about him and the battlements were strewn with bodies.

A great wave of recklessness propelled Hugh into action. He hardly cared if he lived or died. He sprung up the steps to one of the towers and thrust forward with his sword so that the men on the battlements fell back to avoid its evil point. Once at the top, two men fell to his lunges and shrieked as they plunged over the side of the sheer battlements.

Abruptly the tables turned, and he was no longer the pursuer but the quarry, forced to run for his life. His foe, two of Tancred's elite royal guard, highly trained knights with their scimitars flashing in the moonlight, appeared from nowhere and were fast on his heels. Their swords sliced through the steel, flesh and bone of the crusader beside him as easily as water. A pang of fear shot through Hugh.

There began a great fight between them. They hacked and cleaved until their chain mail was dented and split and blood ran down the walls of the battlements like spilled red wine. Wrath descended before Hugh's eyes like a mist and battle lust coursed in his blood. At last! He did not know how it happened, but he brought his sword down on one of the knights in such a crushing blow the blade sliced through helm and bone and cleaved the man's head in two.

The other knight cried out in fury and pressed forward, bent on avenging his friend. Blades clashed together. Hugh found himself cornered against a wall with the point of the Sicilian blade nearing his throat. He took a great ragged breath, fearful that death might snatch him from the world any moment. His fear was answered by a powerful rage that emanated from

deep within his belly. With one great lurch, he sprang
clear and retaliated swiftly and pushed back brutally
with his sword, sending the man toppling over the
parapet, the sword still in his gut. A split second later,
another foe appeared and made at him. The two of
them sprang to each other's throats like wolves.
Diving low, Hugh got him round the waist in a wrestler's grip. They writhed on the ground and struggled
in their chain mail, until Hugh managed to stick the
point of his knife under the man's hauberk. And he
pushed hard and deep until the blade met soft flesh
and the man went limp in his arms.

In the courtyard below, Sir Mordaunt yelled. A
quick glance down told Hugh his uncle was in peril.
With his back to the wall and six foes closing in on
him, Sir Mordaunt was fighting for his life. Heart
pounding, Hugh raced along the length of the battlement until he found a stairway down to the courtyard
and rushed to his uncle's assistance.

At that instant, drums rolled and a horn blew three
times and bells pealed from every church in the city.
Grim-faced defenders flung down their weapons and
gave themselves up to their captors. The crusaders
cheered as they watched King Tancred emerge from
the keep waving a flag of surrender flanked by King
Richard of England and King Philip of France.

~

Later, Hugh heard that King Tancred had surrendered swiftly, eager to prevent further bloodshed. But that did not prevent the looting that went on for many hours after the battle was done.

'The kingdom of Sicily has the reputation of being richer than England,' said Sir Mordaunt the next day as they watched knights drag cartloads of plunder into the camp in the blistering noon sun.

Hugh was astonished by the hoard. There were hundreds of caskets of Spanish gold, quantities of finely wrought jewels beyond reckoning, signet rings, jewelled daggers, silver church vessels, carved ivories, the richest furs, silks and damasks, fine wines and spices. The mood at camp was high-spirited and the crusaders whistled at the loot.

'They drool at the sight of gold,' he whispered to Sir Mordaunt. He could not suppress his disgust. Even the abbot's eyes lit up with unwholesome greed. 'The real premise for this crusade is acquisition of treasure. How naive I have been. I've joined a band of thieving marauders endorsed by the king. Where is God's purpose in all this senseless slaughter and pillaging?'

Sir Mordaunt nodded. A hint of sadness lurked in his eyes. 'I fear you speak the truth.'

~

That evening Hugh gulped down pitcher after pitcher of wine and beer in a tavern that stank of sweat and leather. As he pushed his exhausted body to the very precipice of life, he drank as though he was a fathomless well. It was all the same to him, he neither cared whether he lived or died; better to leave this terrible world in the throes of pleasure. He was not the only one who was drinking like a fish. Other men had that same insatiable thirst that could not be quenched.

'You did well out there, young sir.' Sir Walter slapped him hard on the back.

'It was my first kill,' said Hugh, and the blood rose to his face.

'Thrice well done then, you,' said Sir Walter. 'I saw you fighting valiantly. Must have slain at least eight of those infidels. You are a talented young knight. You'll be the champion of a tourney, I'll be bound. All the pretty ladies will give you their scarves to tie about your lance.'

'I am grateful for your generous words,' said Hugh. 'But I do not think that the act of killing is a memory I will ever look back on with pride.'

'We impaled some infidels out there!' said Sir Manard. 'We'll hunt down every one of them like vermin and slit their throats and spill their guts until the streets are a river of their blood!'

Hugh's cheeks grew hot. 'The men of Messina were not all infidels! Last night I spiked Christians with my sword!'

'Hugh's right,' said Sir Mordaunt. 'Curb your tongue, Sir Manard. We are not barbarians. We are God's army!'

Sir Manard shrugged and staggered over to the counter for another jug of wine.

'No sport comes close to drinking with one's brothers after a kill, does it?' Sir Walter flung an arm around Hugh's shoulder.

'Indeed. To many more victories!' Hugh toasted his goblet to the knight's.

'And to more gold!' said Sir Walter.

'We'll have a king's ransom in treasure before this campaign is over!' said Sir Manard. 'Enough to buy ourselves a castle back home and fill it with some whores!'

Presently, Guy hobbled into the tavern. His cousin had taken an arrow in his thigh when he had scaled the castle wall.

'It is nothing but a flesh wound,' said Guy, and dismissed it with a wave.

But the gash looked deep and Guy limped and winced with pain as he moved. Hugh's fears were allayed when Guy drank as much as the best of them and seemed to be his usual cheerful self.

Hours later, in a drunken fog, Hugh turned his attention to the profusion of attractive women in the tavern with their olive complexions and their dark brown tresses that glistened in the candlelight.

'Look, cousin,' said Guy. 'What delicious wenches are on offer! I've acquired a taste for these women. They are so unlike the chaste, pious ladies back in England.'

Hugh had to agree. These women dressed

provocatively. Their dark eyes laughed and promised such pleasure. Rather them than Lady Bethany any day!

~

After drinking all night long, another sun-drenched morning dawned with a clamour of church bells. In the light of day, as the wine wore off, he saw these women for the whores they were. As loyal and softly spoken as alley cats, they reeked of sin, ripe with the sweat of soldiers. His association with them made him feel cheap and dirty. Aghast, he realised he had betrayed dear Eleanor's memory. All his old shame and self-hatred flooded back.

Unwanted memories of the battle filled his mind. War had left him with a bitter aftertaste. The screams of the women and children still rang in his ears. There was blood on his own hands. The smell of other men's blood was all over him. Ten men he had slain, ten men with mothers, sisters and perhaps children. The horrible foulness of it all weighed heavily upon him.

17.
Child Bed

Eleanor did not see Anne again until several days later, as Sister Agnes sent her off to solitary confinement to think about her 'wicked' behaviour. Poor Anne emerged a pale, pathetic-looking creature with puffy red eyes.

Midway through breakfast, Anne cried out in agony and clutched her back. The other women started in alarm and rushed to her side, panic in their pinched faces. Anne cried out again, bent double in pain.

'She must be in labour,' said Sophie.

Eleanor didn't doubt it. As ripe as a melon, Anne's belly was enormous, incongruous with her stick-thin arms and legs. At fifteen, Anne was the youngest of the women there apart from Eleanor. Fear was painted on her wretched face.

'I want my mama,' she wept. She clung to the table for dear life.

Sophie took her in strong sinewy arms. 'There, there, Anne. All will be well. You are about to have your baby.'

Beads of perspiration gathered at Anne's temples despite the inhospitable chill in the refectory. The girl's pustule-covered face contorted in pain as she experienced another contraction and she roared like a milking cow.

'Let me examine you,' said Sophie. 'I helped my mother bring four of my siblings into the world.' She turned to the other women. 'Get some hot water from the kitchen.'

A couple of women hurried to the kitchen to retrieve the water and the others gathered round.

'Get down on your hands and knees,' said Sophie.

Anne complied and evidently got some relief from her new position.

Eleanor looked away as Sophie lifted Anne's gown and checked how close she was to giving birth.

'It won't be long,' said Sophie. She emerged red-faced from under Anne's woollen kirtle.

They all watched in horrified silence. The other women probably feared their forthcoming experience of giving birth as much as Eleanor did.

Sophie directed Anne to pant like a dog. Anne looked like a woman possessed. Her mousy-brown hair was sodden, plastered to her face and neck. She let out a great howl of pain. Her blood-curdling shriek resounded around the refectory. The noise she made reminded Eleanor of the wolves baying at the moon back in the forests of Normandy.

She expected pain giving birth. After all, carnal relations with her husband had been agony. The thought of a baby coming out of the same orifice felt inconceivable even though it was the most natural thing in the world.

At that moment, the door of the refectory swung open. The veiled figure of Sister Agnes towered in the doorway like a terrible portent of death. She took in the scene before her. 'This is not some pageant side-show. Off with you all, get back to your work!'

All the women save Sophie moved away from Anne and scuttled out of the chamber. Sophie alone remained at Anne's side. Anne continued to howl.

'You will remain to help the woman.' Sister Agnes regarded Anne with an expression of distaste. 'I will alert the infirmarian, in case her skills are needed.'

Eleanor made her way to choir practice aware of a lump in her throat. A trickling sense of foreboding spread across her stomach. She had not yet given any thought to what would happen when her baby was born. Terrified as she was at the prospect of giving birth, she had banished all worries about what would happen after her baby was born from her mind to concentrate on survival. But Anne's experience forced her to think about the inevitable.

The Song and the Sword

Choir practice that morning came as a welcome distraction from her fears about the future. Their voices drowned out Anne's loud screams, which she suspected reverberated throughout the priory complex. Perhaps the poor creature would have been better off in the infirmary in a bed where she could rest. Perchance some herb might have been found to numb the pain. She failed to suppress a shudder at the memory of being in the infirmary surrounded by the diseased and dying. To be among the sick, delirious with their raging fevers and the stink of their rotten, putrid flesh, was no place for a new baby and its mother.

With a concerted effort, she forced such frightful thoughts from her mind and plunged herself into her beloved singing. The choir sang a celebratory psalm that heralded God's omnipotence and forgiveness.

By the time choir practice was over, peace had returned to the priory. Not knowing whether this was an ominous sign or not, she swallowed uncomfortably. The other women headed for the buttery and she hurried to join them.

As usual, Sister Agnes monitored the women's work closely. The nun's face was taut and she was quick to admonish them for sloppy work. Eleanor longed to ask for news of Anne, but she dared not so much as to exchange a glance with any of them as Sister Agnes looked particularly deadly that morning.

When at last they had completed their tasks, they filed out of the buttery and through the cloister to the refectory. There was no sign of Anne or Sophie, but the floor was damp and bore the moist traces of having been recently mopped. The women ate in silence. With some potage and bread in her belly, Eleanor felt a little better.

～

In the afternoon, a crestfallen Sophie joined her as she dug carrots in the field. Eleanor didn't have to ask what had happened; it was written all over her friend's face.

'How is Anne?' she said urgently, anxious lest the reappearance of Sister Agnes bring their conversation to an abrupt end.

Sophie stopped digging and straightened and massaged her lower back. The late afternoon sun was gentle on her friend's face, but there was sadness in her eyes. 'It was awful.' Her voice was pumped full of emotion. 'There was nothing the infirmarian could do. Anne lost so much blood and the child was still-born and Anne died shortly afterwards.'

'How terrible!' Eleanor squeezed her friend's work-branded hand.

'There will be more of us before long, you'll see.'

'Will they mark Anne's passing?'

Sophie turned her head towards her sharply. 'I doubt it. Lives such as ours aren't worth a penny to them. They'll put her body in a pauper's grave.'

It was all so desperately bleak. Not only were their

chances of surviving childbirth slim, but what had they to look forward to afterwards.

'There are no children at the priory,' said Eleanor. She didn't know why she broached the subject. All she knew was that she didn't want to think about Anne's death.

'No, none.' Sophie shook her head. 'Children are regarded as a distraction from a life of contemplation. The babies who are born here from women such as ourselves, who have taken refuge within the priory, are found adoptive parents or face being sent to the orphanage. Girls from the age of thirteen may enter the priory and the boys may, of course, go to the monastery.'

Thus, in a trice, she had the answer to the question she had not even dared contemplate. If she wanted to stay at the priory, she would have to give up her baby. She kicked herself for not having thought about the future before and realised she had been blind to the truth. Momentarily, she was struck dumb with shock, tears pricked her eyes and then she gave voice to the unthinkable. 'I cannot give up my baby.'

Sophie gave her a strange look. 'Then what will you do? How will you survive?'

'I know not.' Eleanor's eyes brimmed with tears. 'I have no family or friends to turn to.'

At that moment Sister Agnes returned, her face as black as a thunderous sky, and her arrival put pay to further conversation.

When the bells rang for Nones, Eleanor made her

way to the chapel to take her seat with the choir. However, a severe-looking nun with a cadaverous face barred her way.

'There have been complaints from many of the nuns.' The nun spoke in an unpleasant rasping voice. Her blue eyes were full of ice. 'There are some who consider it unclean that a woman in your condition should be singing in the Lord's house.'

The nun's words stung as surely as any slap. Tears brimmed in her eyes and she shot the precentor an appealing look. He raised and dropped his shoulders, his face suddenly sad. The hermit she usually stood beside at practice smiled back at her in sympathy.

Blinded by tears, she retreated to the door. Head bowed and eyes fixed on the floor, she joined the other mothers-to-be in their section of the chapel. She was conscious of the other women's stares. There was a murmur of enquiry from the group, but Sister Agnes put a stop to that with an indiscriminate flick of her birch at the women in her vicinity. Sophie shifted over, making room for her. She saw Eleanor's tears and reached out and squeezed her hand. Try as she might, Eleanor couldn't stop herself from weeping. Being part of the choir meant everything to her, and now the nuns had deprived her of her solace.

When the choir began the anthem she had practised earlier that morning, she could only sob the words. The nuns had silenced her and she had lost her voice and all her agency. This meant a return to the choked-up passivity she had endured at Dover Castle and the scourge of submission that ate away at her very soul.

Later, in the buttery, the other women softened towards her. If she had won back the friendship of the women once more, perhaps it was a small consolation for the loss of her beloved choir. They worked in silence, as Sister Agnes would not permit any 'idle prattling'.

Supper that evening was an unexpectedly jovial affair. Sister Agnes was absent and the nun who filled in for her was a meek mouse of a woman with an apologetic, anxious-looking face. Sophie once more came into her own with her bawdy jokes and caricatures of Sister Agnes and the cadaverous-looking nun who had prevented Eleanor from taking her place in the choir. Eleanor laughed heartily, even though she felt she ought not to. Had not the priest decried any kind of hilarity at the expense of another? And yet the laughter that came from deep in her belly did something to soothe the wound the nun had inflicted on her with her words.

They even indulged in some singing after the meal. They sang of chivalrous knights and the rescue of damsels in distress. How delightful it was to sing again. The nuns couldn't take that pleasure away. Eventually the nun keeping watch over them suggested nervously that it was time for Evensong, and indeed the bells rang out summoning them to chapel.

That night, she fell asleep as soon as her head hit the pillow, exhausted by the emotion of the day, but her heart gladdened by the women's camaraderie.

18.

News from England

Earlier that same day, a messenger arrived with a dispatch from England for Sir Mordaunt. Guy and Hugh watched anxiously as he broke the seal.

His uncle's tired face crumpled as he read the news and an uneasy chill crept over Hugh.

'What ails you, Father?' Guy reached over and slipped his arm under his father's.

'Alas, bad tidings.' Sir Mordaunt spoke in little more than a whisper.

Guy pulled his father down into a chair.

'Rolf has taken advantage of the king's absence to seize our castles,' said Sir Mordaunt in a strangled voice. 'His men have burned our villages and crops and put our best men to death.'

There was a moment of shocked silence.

Hugh's head pounded still from all the wine he had consumed the night before but now the pain in his head seared as though some barbarian had taken an axe to his skull. 'My father?'

'Dead. And your brother also.'

Hugh was incredulous. *His father dead*. The thought was inconceivable. Surely no one could have crushed his old battle-axe of a father.

'And Mother?' Guy spoke in a cracked, frightened voice.

'Rolf has taken your mother and your sister hostage.' Shock plastered his uncle's face a delicate shade of grey.

Hugh left Sir Mordaunt and Guy to console each other and went for a walk around what was left of the city of Messina. He scarcely believed what he had just heard. A bleak panorama of devastation greeted him. The crusaders had torched the majority of the white houses and shops of the city and blackened ruins were all that remained. By and large, most of the fires had been extinguished, but the ground was still hot underfoot in places and warmth seeped up through his boots and scorched the soles of his feet. Here and there, a tendril of smoke rose up into the hot air from red-hot cinders that still smouldered. The air was acrid with smoke mixed with the smell of charred flesh. It left a bitter taste in his mouth and it seared his lungs to breathe.

The survivors, large-eyed and pale, picked about

the wreckage of their homes and looked for items that could be salvaged. The crusaders had already plundered anything of value. A mournful silence had descended on the city, broken only by women who tore the day apart with their wails, hunched over blackened bundles that looked horribly like the remains of children, and the screeches of scavenging hawks circling overhead.

It suddenly occurred to him that this might be all that was left of his home too: a few charred ruins where his father's castle had once stood, his father's people burned in their beds, their women raped and dishonoured. The thought was too ghastly. All the servants and squires in the castle, people he had always taken for granted, even his friend Bardolf, all obliterated, his father and brother dead.

Unbidden, an image of his father's severe face and granite hair came into his mind's eye. For his entire life his father had been critical and cold towards him. His brother had hated him too. Much as he despised them both for the way they had treated him, this was no victory. He shook with rage. Somewhere deep within him, he had nurtured a hope that he might eventually prove his father wrong and win his respect by some great deed in battle. Rolf had extinguished that hope. Furthermore, Rolf had not only taken Eleanor from him, he had murdered his kin.

To his surprise his eyes remained dry. He let out a bitter laugh at the irony that he had been finally cured of sentimentality by his father's demise.

The Song and the Sword

From the corner of his eye, he caught a glimpse of the corpse of a battered and abused woman. Gripped by lurching revulsion, he retched violently. His vomit was burgundy like the grape. There was nothing in him but that evil wine. At that instant, the numbness gave way to a creeping terror. Loath to appear a coward, he moved as quickly as he could through the charred streets without breaking into a run, desperate to escape the confines of the city. If he were out on the hillside, away from all its horrors, he might feel better. He needed space and peace to think and make sense of what had happened.

As he emerged onto the rocky hillside, he revived a little. Nothing grew here but small thickets of coarse wiry grass and gnarled olive trees. Beneath a large overhanging rock, he found a lonely spot sheltered from the scorching sun where he could think without fear of being disturbed. There was not one cloud in the sky above him, not one breath of friendly wind, only the sun's glare that beat down on him. It was quiet, save for the occasional squawks of crows and ravens that circled overhead in search of a corpse to feed upon.

Despite the blistering heat, ice trickled through his bones to the pit of his stomach. The events of the last couple of days had thrown him into disarray and he struggled desperately to make sense of any of it. More than anything, he wished he had never come to Messina and that he had never gone on crusade. *Fool*. He had convinced himself that being a knight would be the answer to his prayers, but things had turned out worse than ever.

His exhausted mind wandered and, for a brief happy moment, he indulged a fantasy of being with Eleanor and of holding her in his arms. But cold reality sliced through his reverie like sharp steel through a carcass. What was done was done. He couldn't turn back time. He seethed at the memory of Rolf's demeaning glance at the banquet and the man's excruciating superiority.

He sat motionless on the hillside until the sun set in magnificent crimson over the turquoise sea. How could God's creation be so beautiful and yet be a place of such cruelty and suffering?

The insistent long notes of the horn from camp summoned him to supper. Suddenly aware of the hunger in his belly, he scrambled to his feet. Unaccountably old and weary, he skidded and slipped down the scree-covered hillside to the colourful mass of tents of the crusader encampment below.

'I cannot but think that I am at fault,' he said, when he encountered Guy on his way to get their rations.

'What on earth do you have to be sorry for, dear cousin?' Guy put an arm about his shoulders.

'If only I had been at home to help defend my father's castle and land against Rolf and his marauding knights! Instead, I am stuck in this accursed place and have lost everyone I have ever loved. Rolf has murdered Eleanor, killed my family and taken my ancestral home. The most infuriating thing is that I am powerless to do anything about it, since I have given my word to the king himself that I will fight in the crusade.'

Guy furrowed his handsome brow. 'You could have done nothing to prevent what has happened any more than I could have done.'

Hugh tried to say something to this accusing voice in himself. To tell it that it was not his fault and he didn't deserve it. But the voice continued to accuse him. 'The way I see it. It was my fault my father's castle fell. If I and the other knights had stayed at home, we might have had a chance of defending it. I persuaded my father to send me and the other knights and squires on the crusade. By my own pride and ambition, I left my family undefended.'

'You cannot blame yourself.' Guy's voice shook. 'This is the devil Rolf's work! He is the scum of the earth!'

Hugh nodded. 'You speak true, cousin. Does the king know what he has done? Surely the Lionheart will respond resolutely to such aggression from one of his favoured barons.'

'In all probability he already knows. But my father will raise the issue at the council tomorrow.'

Hugh was struck by how pale and sweaty his cousin looked. Guy was uncharacteristically quiet and he assumed it must be the news from home. Neither of them was in the mood for drinking with others that evening and they retired to their beds early.

That night, thunderbolts cracked across the sky and

flashes of lightning illuminated the tent. The rain came down in torrents. Hugh slept fitfully and counted his blessings that their tent held under the deluge.

～

The following evening, Hugh took the air in the cloistered rooftop gardens of the castle of Messina. A private place, hidden from the hustle of the city, it was an environment reserved for prayer. Moorish inspired archways and cloisters enclosed the sacred gardens in which spectacular fountains gushed into ponds. Curious species of exotic-looking plants, including laurel and myrtle shrubs, grew in its borders.

His mind was a whirlwind of thoughts. He paced the gardens like a restless lion, trying to get a measure of his situation. The deaths of his mother, Eleanor, his father and brother ran over and over in his mind. Driven to distraction, it was too much to bear. The blood in his veins boiled with fury and a white-hot desire for revenge.

The garden was silent save for the tinkling of running water. Momentarily distracted, he watched fascinated as a pair of small birds washed in a pool of water. Large perch and carp circled in the ponds, dark shadows in the greenish water. The fragrant scent of purple primrose permeated his nostrils and he inhaled the perfume deep into his lungs. The sunset took his breath away: layers of red and gold over the azure sea. Far below him on the beach, white horses chased each other over the pristine white sand. A gentle breeze teased his face and tousled his hair.

Presently, his uncle entered the garden, accompanied by Sir Walter and Guy. Sir Mordaunt appeared a broken man after his audience with the king. The ravages of despair were in evidence in his knotted brow and tight white lips.

'The king refuses to release me from service,' said his uncle. He braced his weight on the edge of the breast-high wall and shook his head.

Hugh shifted his weight from foot to foot. 'I would have thought he would have been more understanding given his sister's predicament.'

'King Richard himself isn't above carrying off his subject's wives, daughters and kinswomen at sword point,' said Sir Walter. 'And, when he's sated his animal urges, handing them down to his soldiers.'

A cold shiver travelled down Hugh's spine.

Sir Mordaunt raised his fingers to his lips. 'Silence fool! Such talk is sedition. Pray leave us. I wish to speak to my nephew and son alone.'

Sir Walter had the grace to look abashed. With a creak of leather, he swaggered out of the garden.

'Allow me to go in your stead,' said Hugh as soon as Sir Walter had gone. 'I yearn to go back to England. All I can think of is to avenge Eleanor and my family.'

'I will go with you,' said Guy.

'There are some eighty knights who have sworn fealty to me,' said his uncle. 'The king cannot risk losing such a number from his retinue. And, as you are my deputy, Guy, he will not release you either. However, he has conceded to allow me to send one of my men back home in my stead. I trust no man more than you, dear nephew.'

'Of course,' said Hugh. 'I was planning to return to England in any case to recover my land.'

'Pray take the ransom to the Bishop of Rochester,' said Sir Mordaunt. 'I know him and trust him. He will negotiate your aunt's and cousin's release on my behalf, pay the ransom on their heads and see them safely installed in a convent, where I can be sure they will be out of harm's way.'

Hugh agreed, willing to do anything to ease his uncle's suffering. 'Of course, dear uncle, I am determined to repay the kindness that you have shown me in any way I can.'

His uncle flashed him a grateful smile and there were tears in his eyes. 'Truly, I am indebted to you.' He took in a couple of rasping breaths. Then he did his best to summon his composure. 'Here is my share of the plunder from our recent endeavour.' Sir Mordaunt handed Hugh several heavy, bulging bags of gold coins. 'It should be more than enough to pay the ransom. Travel with the messengers and clerics. I fear you will be obliged to make the journey overland as the shipping lanes of the Mediterranean are closed for winter. It is imperative you set sail for Salerno before the winter storms arrive.'

Hugh gulped and nodded. He struggled to believe that he was about to abandon the holy crusade and return to England. 'With all that has come to pass, my heart is not in the crusade. It has not turned out to be as honourable a venture as I had imagined. I want no part of the raiding and looting I saw at Messina. What's more, I have had my fill of this dusty, unforgiving country, missing with all my heart the verdant pastures and forests of home. Besides, it is high time that I face my responsibility. I am the lord of Eynsford now, and I have a duty of care to my people. I am determined to demand restitution for what has been stolen from me and avenge my family and Eleanor.'

Nevertheless, a terrible, crushing sadness weighed heavily upon him. Even the realisation that he was now at liberty to break off the engagement with the odious Lady Bethany did not afford him the comfort it might have done. Alongside the sadness lurked a niggling fear. After all, he would be setting forth for home alone. Ahead of him was a perilous journey and he would be carrying a precious cargo. He might be set upon by thieves or become the prey of outlaws and brigands. Perhaps he might end his days beaten and left for dead, bleeding in a ditch somewhere far from home. He shook his head in shame at contemplating such cowardly thoughts.

'There can be no more honourable quest than to rescue a lady and her maiden daughter.' Hugh swallowed his fears. 'And, once I have discharged my duty, I will be free to get my revenge on Rolf.'

'There will be men in England who will join you willingly,' said Sir Mordaunt. 'Rolf has offended many in his military campaigns. Seek them out, if they are still alive. Not all were slaughtered. Many others, I think, could be enticed to defect from his allegiance.'

Hugh nodded solemnly.

'It makes me mad to think of that brute touching my wife and daughter,' said Sir Mordaunt. He drove his fist into the palm of his other hand.

Hugh found it impossible to put his fury into words and simply stared out to sea. The grey volcanic stone of the wall in front of him was abrasive beneath his fingertips. He raged at Rolf who had ripped his beloved Eleanor from him, and he vowed to get his revenge. At the sound of a low horn somewhere in the city behind him, he turned abruptly towards the landward side of the island and caught sight of a skein of black smoke floating up from the huge crater of Mount Etna.

19.

A Terrifying Prospect

The cold bite of winter receded and the sun came out, thawing the frozen soil. As the weeks passed, Eleanor's belly had grown so large she waddled as she went about her daily chores. Sister Agnes might chide her for her languorous pace, but she no longer paid the nun any heed.

One chilly morning in mid-March, she was digging in the priory's physic garden when she was alarmed to find that liquid flooded down her leg.

'What is wrong with me?' she cried. And she looked down at the shameful puddle in the mud.

'It is the baby coming,' said Sophie. 'Sister Agnes, would you give me permission to accompany Matilda to the infirmary? Her labour has started.'

Sister Agnes opened her mouth to argue – then closed it again. She pursed her lips and gave a curt nod. Evidently, she had no wish to be involved in the messy, distasteful business of childbirth.

Eleanor clutched her friend's arm. 'Thank you so much for being with me. I don't know how I would have borne it if I had to face this alone.'

They barely managed to walk through the cloister to the infirmary before a contraction brought her to her knees. She was unable to repress cries of agony. Sophie put her arm about her shoulders and helped her the last few yards to the infirmary.

A lean-looking nun greeted them and ushered them into a small lime-washed cell furnished simply with a cot and a crucifix with an arrow slit that served as a window. She left the room without a word.

'How about you lie down on the mattress, Matilda?' said Sophie. 'You'll be needing all your strength soon, so try to rest.'

She sank her weary body gratefully onto the straw mattress. It was infinitely preferable to the damp earth or the cold flagstone floor. She was so exhausted, but her mind was wide awake and refused to allow her to sleep.

'I cannot help feeling frightened,' she fretted. 'How will I take care of this child? I cannot think of being parted from my baby. But how will we get by in this man's world. To what low will I need to stoop to keep us both alive.'

'Dear Matilda, do not worry about that now.' Sophie

clasped her hand. 'Everything will be alright, you'll see. Just get some rest now. I'll be here when you wake. I shan't leave you.'

Eleanor squeezed her friend's calloused hand. It was warm and comforting. She allowed her eyelids to close.

A contraction awoke her sometime later. The pain was urgent and insistent, and fear overcame her once more. 'Once the baby is born, we shall have to leave here, but where shall we live? I have nowhere to go, no family.'

'Hush now, rest,' said Sophie, who was by her side in an instant. She dabbed at Eleanor's cheek with the edge of her apron and cradled Eleanor's hand in hers. Immediately, Eleanor drew courage from her friend's presence.

It felt as though she had only been asleep an instant when the next contraction disentangled her from deep dreams. This time the pain was more intense and she struggled to bear it. Her body had a mind of its own, it seemed, and she no longer exercised any control over it.

'Try to pant,' said Sophie. 'It will help with the contractions.'

Two hours passed swiftly. There was now no time to rest between contractions, and she had barely closed her eyes when another was upon her.

In the epicentre of the next contraction, she disengaged from her surroundings. She was no longer in the austere cell. Instead, she found herself in a red cavern, as hot and fiery as any furnace. In the throes of agony, she lost her reason and shrieked and moaned like a wounded animal. She thought the pain would never subside and when it did, she became aware of Sophie's anxious face watching over her and of Margery, who struggled in with a steaming cauldron of hot water from the kitchen.

'I am so sorry,' she gasped. And she clasped Sophie's outstretched hand.

'Nonsense,' said Sophie. 'You are doing well. All is as it should be.'

Nothing had prepared her for the searing pain of labour. What was going on in her body was a mystery to her and she exerted no control over it. Just when she thought she could endure no more, the contractions returned with renewed vigour and she wailed and thrashed. The periods of respite became shorter and she feared she would writhe forever in the grip of pain's fiery flames. Only occasionally did the fog of agony clear and did she become aware of a gentle hand on her back or an encouraging voice in her ear. The pain was all-consuming. All concept of time was lost to her. Then she experienced a sudden moment of clarity where she became aware of Sophie's urgent tones. 'When I say push, you must push.'

'But I am broken,' she gasped, utterly vulnerable in Sophie's arms. 'I cannot go on. I go to meet my maker.'

On her hands and knees – she had no notion of how she had gotten into such a position – she reared like a frighted horse at the sudden rush of pain, but a firm hand held her down and a voice ordered her to push.

The pain was excruciating. Screams filled the room. It was her own voice. Yet it felt separate, an entity of its own. More pushes, more screams. She pushed with all her might and concentrated all her energy into the pushes so that the pain might relent. She thrashed about on the straw mattress and put her hand down in warm liquid. When she brought it up, she screamed, for blood dripped from her fingers. Looking down at the mattress beneath her she saw in horror that it seeped with blood. It was like the sordid scene of a frenzied stabbing. Her head swam and she thought she would be sick.

'You have to push!' cried Sophie.

'The baby is coming!' shouted a voice.

'One more push!' said another.

'Here it is!' Sophie lifted a tiny bloodstained body from the mattress.

There was a moment of silence as Sophie bent over the tiny body and frantically massaged the baby's back.

Eleanor's heart thumped like a battle drum. Why was the baby not crying? Prolonged sticky minutes passed and still there was no cry. An eternity. This had to be the worst moment of her life. It was unbearable. What little hope was left in her heart was snuffed out.

Then at long last, the cry of a child! A joyous sound. It was alive!

'It's a girl!'

Eleanor couldn't move. She doubted she had an ounce of energy left in her exhausted body. It even hurt to smile. And then Sophie very gently placed the baby in her arms, against her naked breast. A flash of recognition travelled between her and the baby, as though they had always known one another. The baby gazed up at her through half-open eyelids. She was perfect, serene and happy. Her tiny lips sought out Eleanor's nipple of their own accord but found her mother's chin instead and suckled it. Weak as she was, Eleanor laughed out loud with joy. Guiding the baby to find her nipple, she watched transfixed as the baby sucked ravenously although her milk had not yet come. Of all the happy moments of her life, none had come close to this one. She could have lain there for hours doing nothing but contemplate her baby. However, she was weak and her arms and legs ached with exhaustion. Every movement she attempted was excruciatingly difficult and slow as though her limbs were weighed down with heavy iron chains. To her distress, she could barely lift her arm to stroke her baby. And she was horribly tired, so desperately tired. Helpless, she drifted in and out of a groggy sleep.

'Here, you must eat something,' said Sophie. She spooned something warm and substantial into Eleanor's mouth.

Her taste buds leapt at the flavour of meat and she swallowed it down gratefully. Then there was a plate of bread and cheese. She had not realised how hungry she was until she sank her teeth into the warm crust and tangy cheese. It had to be the best she had ever tasted.

'You are weak and have lost a lot of blood,' said Sophie. She kissed her gently on the forehead. 'But we shall nurse you better and your baby is healthy.' She beamed down at her and her baby.

Eleanor felt moved with love towards her. 'What dear a friend you are! How I love you!' All self-consciousness was gone in that moment of perfection.

Sophie, who was usually so tough and strong, blinked back at her, tears and love in her eyes.

Sophie cleared up around her, and helped her into a fresh, warm gown with a convenient slit at the front to facilitate breastfeeding. Then she left her alone to sleep.

Alone with her baby, Eleanor experienced waves of intense love for her child. Nothing in the world would induce her to forsake her beautiful baby. In that perfect moment, she named her daughter Mary.

∼

The first few days of her daughter's life passed like a dream. Awake for short periods to feed, the baby drifted in and out of sleep. She followed her lead; she needed as much sleep as she could get to recover her strength. The kindly cook, Albreda, brought her food on the least pretext: meals of chicken and beef and delicious sweetmeats and cheeses. And she ate better than she had ever eaten in the priory.

Baby Mary had an insatiable appetite. She nursed greedily at the nipple and gained weight rapidly. She was a happy, sleepy and contented soul. It was indescribably wonderful to have a child of her own.

The other women came to visit them. Sister Agnes spared them begrudgingly in the spirit of 'Christian generosity'. Bright and wide-eyed to see the baby, they seemed relieved that a child had been born into the world safely. After Anne's death, many of them had come to doubt whether a healthy delivery was possible. Eleanor had never experienced such warmth and love as she had from these women. There were no snide comments, nor signs of envy, just joy at the birth of a healthy baby. Each one of them expressed regret that they had no gift for the child, but she reassured them that they brought the greatest gift of all: a loving reception for her baby girl.

～

By the end of the week, Eleanor had recovered enough to get up and move around again. Never could she recall feeling so content, and yet an insidious anxiety lurked in the back of her mind.

'How long will the nuns permit me to stay in the priory?' she asked Sophie, when she next visited.

Sophie put her mind at rest. 'Well, I've been thinking about what you said. The tavern where I work in

The Song and the Sword

Dover is always looking for great singers. Perchance they will find you paid work and board. When you leave the priory, you must go at once to the Three Kings tavern in the "Minories" and ask for Ancel. He will help you, if he can.'

Eleanor let out a great sigh of relief. Hope for a future at long last and somewhere to go. She couldn't find words to express her gratitude to her friend, but somehow it didn't seem to matter. Understanding and love passed between them unhindered.

∿

Thus, ten days later, Eleanor departed the Priory of St Mary with all her possessions and her baby wrapped in swaddling clothes. The priory had been her home these past six months and she would never forget the experiences she had had here, but she was eager to be free of the place. A kindly nun brought beautiful clothes for her: a gown and matching cloak of excellent quality trimmed with ermine. It had been relinquished by a nun who had been shamed into parting with it after one of the priests' sermons. She accepted them gladly. They were very welcome as the spring air still had a harsh nip.

The nun pressed a coin purse into her hand as they embraced.

'God be with you and your child,' said the nun. 'Do not forget that he watches over you and his love is everlasting.'

'I cannot thank you enough,' said Eleanor.

Sophie put an arm around her. 'I shall see you in Dover, all being well.'

Eleanor held her friend close. 'I wish you all the best for the birth of your baby. Thank you for everything you have done for us.'

And it was with a heavy heart that Eleanor relinquished Sophie's embrace and set forth into the unknown.

20.

In Search of Lost Love

By the beginning of April, Hugh had made it as far as Normandy, bow-legged after weeks on horse-back. Thankfully, the journey from Sicily had been uneventful. In the company of an order of monks who eschewed the spoken word, he had managed to avoid the stray war bands who wandered the countryside and the wild men that lurked in the forests, intent on robbing passers-by. And he had been happy enough to accept the simple, silent life of a monk on his journey. What need had he of the joys of life? He had to fulfil his quest. Nothing else mattered.

In any case, he had no inclination to talk to anyone. For the first few weeks, his days had been filled with an interminable greyness. Hopelessness weighed heavy on his heart. It left him so weary he wanted to do little else but sleep.

As autumn ceded to winter, a gruelling freeze had fallen upon the travellers. The harsh, biting cold and driving sleet and snow had seared his exposed skin and compounded the pain of loss. The stark winter landscape around him mirrored the bleak emptiness in his heart.

In the fullness of time, the spring sun melted the snow and the mountain streams became gushing torrents that cascaded down the mountains of the Alps. New buds of life broke through the soil and burst forth from the boughs of trees. His mood lifted. The overwhelming desire to do nothing but sleep relinquished its grip on him.

One day, he crossed a five-arched bridge that spanned a wide gushing river and he had the curious sensation of having been there before. Sure enough, he saw a sign overgrown with brambles pointing in the direction of Eleanor's ancestral home. A sudden chill seized him between the shoulders as though someone in the future walked over his grave and his heart yearned to return to the place where once he had known such happiness. And his thoughts came to rest on Eleanor's smooth chestnut hair and her shadowy, hazel-green eyes.

He spurred his weary horse on and took the path down into a peaceful valley where he came upon a spring bubbling up from beneath mossy stones. From here, there was a view of the headland where Eleanor's father's castle stood, surrounded by dense forest, accessible only via a narrow causeway that led to it from the mainland.

A light sea breeze tousled Hugh's hair as his horse galloped over the causeway. Once on the headland, he took the forest path that wound up to the gates of the castle, high on the rocks above the pounding sea. He unsheathed his blade and knocked three times on the gate with the pommel of his sword. While he waited to be admitted, his thoughts returned to five years before, when he had first arrived at the castle ready to squire for Eleanor's father and learn honour, courage, gentleness and self-discipline that would one day prepare him to be a knight.

The old guard at the gatehouse recognised him at once and drew back the gates with a great creak of steel, and he rode through into the inner courtyard and into the ornamental gardens. A light evening wind whispered behind him and brought with it a familiar scent. It had been here among the blossom-festooned hawthorn bushes that he had first heard Eleanor's haunting voice as she sang songs of courtly love while she and her ladies wove garlands of sweet pea in their laps. When the afternoon sun had caught her chestnut hair, it had glistened a rich copper and the large eyes that had looked up at him had been hazel-green and full of eager lights with the slight hint of shadows. Vividly, he remembered that long look they had exchanged before the steward had led him away. From that moment, something within him had woken as if from a deep bewitched sleep and his heart had started to ache with longing.

Swallows, newly returned from warmer climes, swooped among the gables and eaves of the stables and brought to mind his second meeting with Eleanor. He had come across her fiddling with the buckle on her palfrey's saddle. She struggled to unfasten it and he had put out a hand to help her and their fingers had touched. Instantly they had both looked up into each other's eyes. Having looked, he hadn't wanted to tear his eyes away and neither, it seemed, had she. At that moment, it had seemed that nothing moved or sounded around them and even the swallows had stopped calling overhead. When at last they pulled their eyes apart, Eleanor unfastened the buckle and he saw that her fingers trembled.

He approached the ironbound door of the main keep and pushed it open. Along the passageway to the Great Hall he passed the library. A fleeting glimpse of weighty tomes on the shelves through the gap in the heavy tapestries sparked memories of the happy rainy afternoons Eleanor and he had spent reading each other thrilling tales of chivalric adventure.

The torches in their wall-sconces burned tall and steadfast. At the far end of the Great Hall, Eleanor's father sat in his great seat spread with finely dressed furs. In the year and a half since Hugh had last seen him, the baron seemed to have grown old. A deep line, like a knife scar, had developed between his brows and his eyes were full of sorrow. Staring absently into space, he pulled at his greying beard. Then Hugh came up the hall and knelt at his feet. Weary, narrowed eyes gazed down at him through the smoke of the fire in the huge stone hearth.

'Hugh . . .' said the baron. 'Is it really you? You are a man grown!' As he spoke a faint murmur seemed to hang in the emptiness under the high-arched roof. He fell silent and, in the flickering light of the fire, it seemed to Hugh that he listened to some voice deep within himself.

Despite the fire that blazed in the hearth, Hugh felt cold to the bone. Once this Great Hall had resounded with laughter and animated chatter, but now a desolate stillness had fallen upon the empty, lonely space and it brought to mind a mausoleum.

'You must understand . . .' The baron spoke in a halting voice. 'I am tormented by memories of my heartbroken daughter whom I left in Dover to die little by little. If I had only permitted her to marry you, Hugh, you would have both come to live in our family home. Such wrong I did her, I am ashamed to admit before anybody, let alone the sky and God. The strategic alliance was foremost in my mind and I paid no heed to her happiness. Now you will understand why I long to die because Hell is Heaven compared to the thoughts that torture me in my waking hours and in my dreams.'

The anger that Hugh had once felt towards this man, who had prevented him from marrying the woman he loved, died in his breast and he was moved with pity for a father's suffering.

'Dear Hugh,' said the baron. He took Hugh's hand in his. 'I have done you the gravest disservice. My vision was clouded by greed. For what is wealth without love? Stubborn, I refused to see the truth and I saw what I wanted to see in Rolf. I told myself Eleanor would grow to love him as I had grown to love her mother. Damn my stupid pride! But you were always the better man. Once you give of your heart it will not lightly return to you! Pray forgive me!' At this he got down painfully. 'On bended knee, I beg your forgiveness. Pity an old foolish man.'

'Do not be too hard on yourself.' Hugh helped the baron back into his seat. 'Rolf deceived many – my father being one. You will have heard of his and my brother's passing at the raid of Eynsford Castle.'

'It grieved me to hear such tidings.' The baron shook his grey head. 'Such a tragic loss of life! These days there are many lords who come to believe that military power is all that counts, and that might is the same thing as right.'

'Lately I have returned from the crusade in order to avenge the deaths of Eleanor and my father and brother. And, if God wills, take back my ancestral home.'

'You have all my support, for such a quest,' said the baron. 'Forgive me. I have been a terrible host. You must be famished after your journey. Pray sit and sup with me at the table.'

With the wave of a jewelled hand, he summoned his manservant to his side. 'Pray summon Lady Anneis and bring us supper and wine.'

The Song and the Sword

Presently, Eleanor's mother appeared in the doorway dressed in a long sombre gown. She clapped her hand over her mouth, stifling a little cry when she recognised Hugh. 'Dear Hugh, how wonderful to see you!'

Hugh was shocked by the change in her. Once beautiful, like a sun-ripened fruit, she was shrivelled and now withered on the vine, and she was all bones in his arms.

'Please forgive me for weeping like this.' Her voice trembled. 'It brought to mind how happy Eleanor was when you were living here. You know she loved you?' She shot her husband a reproachful look.

Hugh nodded. 'And I her.'

'You know that wicked Rolf did not even get word to us about poor Eleanor's funeral,' wept Lady Anneis. 'My darling daughter was buried before I even got to say goodbye, her body laid to rest in St Mary's Church in Dover.'

'Hugh has returned from crusade to avenge her death,' said her husband. 'And avenge the murder of his father and brother. He means to reclaim his ancestral home.'

'Rest assured we will do anything we can to help,' said Lady Anneis. Her eyes shone in the torchlight. 'That man is a devil!'

At that moment, a serving squire brought in a charger of venison and they sat down to a hearty meal and drank wine from silver goblets. Hugh ate until he grew full and his eyelids drooped with tiredness.

The steward made up his former room.

For a long time that night, he lay awake and watched the moonlight through a gap in the drapes. After so many nights on straw mattresses in abbeys or on rudimentary beds in shepherds' huts or huddled on the ground when he could not find shelter, it was a luxury to lie on a goose feather mattress – yet he could not get a wink of sleep.

Perhaps it was the familiar surroundings, but he simply couldn't bring himself to believe that Eleanor was dead. He could almost smell the lingering scent of rosewater that had always trailed after her. So, this was what it meant to be haunted. The very chamber seemed to ring with her infectious laughter. The rippling sound of her slender fingers as they plucked the strings of the harp seemed to echo through the castle.

His mind's eye filled with memories. One was of galloping wildly alongside each other on the beach, the waves crashing beside them. Another of walking hand in hand deeper and deeper into the forest as they followed the way of the deer, the wind hushed behind them. Until eventually the trees fell back, and they came to the bank of a lake, its rushes stirring in the wind and lake birds crying overhead. Here on the banks of the lake they had exchanged a lock of hair and an exquisite kiss.

It had been the easiest thing in the world to be near Eleanor. Silence was comfortable between them. They had no need of words to convey their meaning. Love came in through their eyes and moved effortlessly between them. But all this was lost to him, and it seemed that his life was already over before he had even started. And he wept as though his heart would break.

When sleep claimed him, he had strange, muddled dreams, of a great and terrible hope that culminated in a tantalising reunion with Eleanor who returned to him with the shadow of a smile – only for her to slip through his fingers and disappear again out of sight and leave him to yearn for her and to search endlessly to find her again.

At sunrise, he stared up at the canopy of the bed where a maiden with flowing auburn hair and dressed in a glistening gold damask gown lay with her eyes closed in a barge that floated along a turquoise silk-worked river. When he had lived here as a squire this had always made him dream of Eleanor and so it did now.

At long last, he dragged himself away. He rose and dressed and went to breakfast in the Great Hall as had been his habit when he had lived at the castle.

Baron Adelard and Lady Anneis were already sitting at the table.

'I trust you slept well?' asked Lady Anneis. 'Are you sure we cannot press you to stay with us a little longer?'

'Thank you for your hospitality,' said Hugh. 'But I am keen to continue with my quest.' He broke off a hunk of bread and buttered it with his knife.

'My man will find you a new suit of chain mail and

a fresh shield and sword,' said the baron. And he beckoned to his manservant who brought bags filled with jewels and gold and settled them on the table beside Hugh.

Hugh was about to protest, but the baron waved away his objections. 'What need have I for it now? Allow me to make this gesture – anything I can do to mend the hurt I did my daughter. Eleanor would have wanted you to have it. Besides, you will need supplies for your venture to restore your ancestral home.'

Thus, his heart aching with the bitterest longing, Hugh rode off in a new suit of chain mail that glistened in the early morning sun, his saddle bags weighed down by bags of coin and jewels of incalculable value. Eleanor's parents bid him farewell from the great gate.

21.

The Three Kings

The iron-studded door of St Mary's Priory closed with a crash behind Eleanor and her baby. It was a crisp, bright April morning and she gathered her fur-trimmed gown about her to keep out the cold. Anxious to have a roof over their heads by evening, she set off at a stout pace down the steep mountain path.

On the horizon, she could make out the outskirts of Dover, an untidy mass of huts and hovels that lay outside the town's walls. A morning mist hung over the rooftops like a blanket of smoke. It was wonderful to be out in the open on the bare shoulder of the cliff, away from the high walls of the priory that had confined her for so long.

The sound of dogs barking and raised voices

greeted her as she approached the shanty dwellings. The narrow pathways of the settlement heaved with the poorest of the poor going about their daily business of survival. Children with swollen bellies stared up at her with imploring eyes. She longed to help, but she had no more than a few pennies to her name. If she did not manage to find work as a singer, she might be reliant on the charity of others, like these poor wretches. The thought tied her stomach in knots.

The wattle-and-daub settlements became more sophisticated as she neared Dover's walls and reflected the relative wealth of those who lived closer to the town. A huge iron gateway, with a drawbridge and moat, loomed ahead. She joined the queue of people and carts. They were mostly hawkers come to pedal their goods, and farmers with livestock, vegetables and grains to sell, bound for the town market.

As she finally reached the head of the queue, she declared her business to a dusty-looking official in a pointed Phrygian cap. The man waved her through without a second glance.

She held her baby and possessions close as she threaded her way through the heaving mass of people in the streets. Sophie had recommended that she secrete the purse the nun had given her into the inside of her gown, away from prying fingers and she was glad. In a crowd such as this, a pickpocket would make light work of robbing her. Sophie had given her some landmarks to guide her to the tavern. At the main square, she was to take the second street to the right of the church. She tried to repress a shiver when she caught a glimpse of the imposing fortress and keep of Dover Castle in the distance, perched on the pinnacle of the cliffs overlooking the town.

Hot and flustered from the effort of making her way through the jam-packed mass of bodies, she had never seen such a hurly-burly of people. It was daunting after being secluded in the priory for so long. The crowd consisted of people from all walks of society: from artisans trying to make a living selling their work to grocers bearing panniers laden with fruit and vegetables. The noise and smells overwhelmed her, particularly the stink of the fishmongers determined to sell their latest catch who hollered at the tops of their voices. Porters tottered around with tall ceramic jars on their heads, transporting wine and other liquids. Stout housewives pushed past her laden with baskets of produce. The air was alive with the grunts of pigs and the lowing of cattle herded by farmers through the streets towards the market.

She made slow progress through the throng. Peddlers and beggars accosted her from each flank. The former tried to sell her their wares and desperation lurked beneath their smiles. And the latter implored her for alms, and tugged at her heartstrings with their sorrowful, hungry eyes.

As per Sophie's directions, she took the second street to the right of the church in the main square and entered a part of the town filled with seedy-looking inns and alehouses. She pulled her veil over her head to conceal her hair and hurried past the noisy revellers who swigged down great flagons of wine and ale. She had no intention of being accosted by a brute who had consumed a bellyful. This looked to be an unsavoury quarter of the town, the haunt of the worst sort of man: grubby sailors, mercenaries, thieves and men for hire. Greedy eyes devoured her. One man even waggled his tongue at her as she scuttled past.

At long last she found herself before the Three Kings tavern. It had once been a fine building. Skilfully carved female figures and animals playing instruments decorated the spring stones of the gables over the entrance, supported by the crowned heads of three kings. But the paint and stucco had peeled off the walls and the building was as shabby and dilapidated as the others in this part of the town.

A stringy, toothless old crone with a shock of unnatural red hair greeted her with suspicion at the door, but she soon thawed and was polite enough when she explained her errand and that Sophie had sent her.

'Dear, sweet Sophie,' said the woman. She brightened up. 'How is she? She must be ever so close to having her baby?'

'Any day now,' said Eleanor.

'We do miss her something rotten. Any friend of Sophie is welcome here. I will get the master directly.' And with that she disappeared off into the depths of the tavern.

Moments later, a thickset, middle-aged man with

merry eyes and an egg-bald head pumped Eleanor's hand. 'A singer, you say? I am always looking for great singers. Come in, come in! Let me introduce myself. I am Ancel.'

Eleanor followed him into the tavern, a deceptively large hall, with wood pillars at intervals supporting the roof. The smell of stale food and fermented grapes hung in the air. It was furnished with long benches set against trestle tables as well as smaller round tables with stools, all facing an impressive stage at the far end. Ancel gestured that she should take a seat on a bench.

'Some ale perhaps to quench your thirst?' He smiled at her with yellow teeth.

Eleanor nodded. She was parched.

Ancel clicked his fingers and a servant girl appeared, and he sent her off to get them drinks.

'And you were with Sophie. How is she? I would not have sent her away but for the big belly being bad for business.' He caught sight of the little bundle in Eleanor's arms. 'You have a baby. A boy?'

'A girl.' Eleanor hoped her baby would not be 'bad for business'.

'Perhaps you will sing for me when you've had your fill of ale.' He beamed at her.

'Gladly.' Eleanor drained the remaining liquid from her goblet and put her sleeping daughter down carefully on the chair beside her and stood up. She felt suddenly self-conscious standing up like this in front of strangers. So much was riding on her ability to sing.

From among her repertoire, she sang one of the songs she had sung at Dover Castle with the other ladies. It was a song celebrating the age of chivalry, about a knight rescuing a damsel in distress. While she started off shyly, she soon became emboldened by the looks of approbation from her small audience. When she finished Ancel and the red-headed crone rewarded her with a hearty round of applause.

'Truly remarkable,' said Ancel. 'You'll set the house on fire. You have a beautiful voice. We would be delighted if you would come and sing in our tavern. I can offer you payment of four pennies per week plus bed and board. How does that sound?'

'You are too kind.' Eleanor perked up considerably at this reception.

'You will start tonight after our players have performed their play.' He gestured to the woman who had greeted her at the door. 'Katherine will show you up to your room at the top of the tavern. It is very humble, you understand, but it should do for you and your child.'

Katherine favoured Eleanor with a toothless grin and indicated that she should follow her outside and up a wooden staircase on the outside of the building, accessible through a doorway cordoned off with a rope. The steps creaked as they ascended right to the top of the building. She showed Eleanor into a small room with a low wooden bed, and a window with wooden shutters that looked out onto a courtyard.

Relief washed over Eleanor as she stretched out on

the narrow bed. Thank God they had a roof over their heads and food to eat. And she would even receive payment. It was possible for her to make a living after all.

Baby Mary woke soon after and demanded milk. She nursed her for an hour and was just beginning to think of supper for herself when the mouth-watering smell of roasting meat wafted up from the kitchen downstairs.

Presently, Katherine knocked on the door. 'Would you like to come down for supper? The household usually dines at five – early because of the evening performance.'

Eleanor followed her down the stairs and into a warm kitchen full of cheer. Katherine ushered her to join the company of men seated around a large oak table where Ancel sat at the helm.

'Welcome, Matilda!' said Ancel, with his ready smile. 'Don't be shy. Pray sit with us.'

'Ancel tells me we have a treat in store tonight,' said a young man with a thin, merry face and flyaway red hair. 'I am Arthur. Pleased to meet you.'

Katherine brought a cauldron of steaming vegetables to the table. She ladled out the stew into bowls and added pieces of roast chicken.

Eleanor tucked into her dinner. Not since her days at the castle had she eaten such substantial fare.

'They did not feed you at the priory, I'll wager,' chuckled her new employer.

'Nothing like this.' Eleanor smiled back.

'We'll dig out a gown for you for the performance this evening and liven up your face and hair. I'm sure you'll scrub up a treat!'

Eleanor blushed. Although at Dover Castle she had dressed up every day, painted, coiffed, and decked out with lavish jewellery, the prospect felt awkward now, somehow inappropriate after her stint at the priory.

Once Eleanor emptied her bowl, Katherine offered her a second helping, but Eleanor was delighted to find that she had the novel sensation of being full and could not bring herself to eat another morsel. How much better things seemed when one had a full stomach. She helped Katherine clear away and wash the dishes.

'It is good to have some help around here again,' said Katherine. 'Usually Sophie helps me, but she has not been here for months.'

After they had cleared away the dishes, Katherine applied herself to the task of preparing Eleanor for the performance that evening. 'Come to my chamber. I will look out a gown for you.' And, once they were in her room, she bent down and rummaged in a trunk of costumes.

After a while, she straightened again and produced a rather crumpled gown. Made of silk and with fur trim, it had once been fine, but the moths had made a meal of it in places and it had seen better days.

'We could dress this up with some costume jewellery.' She held the dress up to Eleanor. 'It should fit you – you have such a slender figure.'

The gown looked far better on and it fitted her remarkably well.

'Perhaps this golden girdle would accentuate your waist,' said Katherine. She was enjoying herself now.

'Now for your hair.' And she removed Eleanor's veil.

She loosened Eleanor's braids, and brushed out her locks, which had grown thick and lush with the pregnancy. 'What beautiful hair you have. A glorious mane!'

Katherine coiled half the hair and pinned it up in a bun on the crown of Eleanor's head, and left long tendrils of wavy hair cascading down her back and shoulders. She stood back and admired her handiwork. Then she hobbled to some drawers in a dresser on the far side of her room and returned with greasepaint – blocks of heavy colour.

Eleanor sat down before a sheet of brushed steel, which reflected a slightly warped version of her face back at her. It had been so long since she had worn any make-up that it was a rather peculiar feeling to see a stranger emerge in the steel. Katherine accentuated her eyes with heavy charcoal and stained her lips scarlet. It was a less subtle look than she had carried off at the castle. Indeed, Eleanor's mother would have been shocked for she looked like some foreign courtesan with her huge shadowed eyes and bright lips, but it was perfect for the stage. Katherine finished off the look with some rouge on Eleanor's pale cheeks.

'You look like a princess,' she said.

She had to agree that Katherine had completely transformed her.

'You will be our star performer. We haven't had a good singer in years. Talented singers are scarce.'

Eleanor retired to her chamber to feed Baby Mary. After a good three quarters of an hour, by which time she could hear signs of activity in the tavern below, the baby fell asleep in the corner of the bed beside the wall.

There was a tentative knock at the door. Katherine asked if she was ready to come down. 'I'll keep an eye on the baby. I've brought my spinning with me.' And she settled into the chair beside the bed.

Eleanor gave her an appreciative smile and descended the stairs to the kitchen, heart in her mouth at the prospect of performing.

A gasp of admiration from the players greeted her when she entered the kitchen.

'What a rare beauty you are!' said one with a whistle.

'You'll quite eclipse us with your loveliness,' said another. 'She's certainly outdone you, Leonard.'

Eleanor was sure she blushed to the roots of her hair. She sat down hurriedly beside Arthur. A glance around the table told her she was not the only one who had transformed.

Leonard's cap of fair hair had been coiffed into golden curls. Now he donned a woman's kirtle. And his eyes were lined with charcoal and his lips smeared with scarlet paint. If it had not been for his square jaw, heavy brow and ungainly legs he would have been every bit as glamorous as her. Leonard adopted effeminate airs and a high-pitched, rasping voice.

He stroked Eleanor's hair. 'Gorgeous, quite gorgeous, darling!'

At the thought of how such behaviour would have appalled Sister Agnes, she couldn't suppress a giggle.

Across the table, Simon, a handsome man of powerful build with a mop of dark brown corkscrew curls and sparkling blue eyes, sat proud in shiny chain mail. Under his arm he gripped a steel helmet with a feather protruding from its pinnacle. He swept a mock bow in her direction. Then, he took her hand in his and lavished a kiss upon it. Mortified, she withdrew her hand quickly and blushed again, which gave rise to good-humoured chuckles from the other players.

The villain of the piece, Henry, boasted a lavish fur-trimmed mantle with a black helmet and breast-plate. Katherine had worked her magic on his eyes with charcoal and reddened his lips with paint, which gave him the aspect of a fearsome savage. He deepened his voice appropriately. Now in full character, he looked at her from head to foot, as though he undressed her with his eyes.

In addition to the main players, Richard and Joseph, who played the front and back end of a dragon respectively, appeared to be the fools of the company. The highborn of Normandy regarded mummery as too bawdy an attraction for young women so she had little experience of it. True, Rolf had invited mummers to perform at the castle, but they had been subject to strict censorship while they performed in front of the ladies of the court, as there was no wish to promote lewd and unseemly behaviour among the noble-women.

Within a short time, the musicians arrived. Ancel introduced them to her before they began setting up in the pit below the stage in the main room of the tavern. Though the night was young, already their faces were flushed red with wine. They beamed at her. Two of them were lute players, and there was also a flute player and a drummer. They all wore light green tunics with matching hose and pointed mid-calf boots with brightly coloured turnover tops and small round caps with stalks.

Two serving wenches with bosoms that almost spilled out of figure-hugging gowns and an abun-dance of dark curls hanging negligently about their shoulders, bustled into the crowded kitchen. Laden with empty jugs and bowls, they then replenished the jugs and ladled steaming stew into the bowls and swept back out into the tavern.

The patrons were arriving. They were a noisy, uncouth lot. She heard raised voices above the din. Foul-mouthed and blasphemous, they sounded as though they had consumed a belly full of wine. A sickening feeling crept over her at the thought of performing in front of these people.

The Song and the Sword

'Don't worry, darling, I'll protect you from the throng,' said Simon. His chain mail flashed in the lamplight.

She shot him a weak smile and hoped she looked braver than she felt and crossed and then uncrossed her legs.

The musicians went out into the tavern and took their places beside the stage.

'The minstrels will be providing the entertainment before the mummery starts,' said Ancel. 'You'll sing in the interval before the third act. The audience will have warmed up by then. They'll love you. Don't you worry, dear. Just sing your heart out.'

But she couldn't help trembling. She sat silent and nursed her goblet of wine in her hands. Never had she performed in front of so many people. The prospect of all those eyes boring into her was terrifying. The kitchen door was ajar and she stole a glance into the tavern. It was full to the rafters. A powerful stench of sweat assaulted her. The raucous audience looked to be a bawdy lot. They swigged down wine and ale and noisily slurped their bowls of stew. There was a lot of jostling, backslapping and resounding laughter. She prayed the rabble would remain good-spirited. The damage such a crowd might wreak when roused did not bear thinking about. She was reassured to see that Ancel employed some muscle to keep the peace. Two great hulks of men stood beside the door and two more occupied positions by the stage. They towered over the horde, surveying the crowd for troublemakers.

She became fearful that the frightful din might wake Baby Mary sleeping on the floor above. At the priory, Mary had been a drowsy infant, even sleeping through the regular tolling of the bells. The thought of her baby crying alone in this strange house was unbearable.

As if in answer to her fears, Ancel whispered, 'Don't you worry about your baby. Katherine's a grandmother to eighteen children. Loves bairns, she does.'

She forced herself to smile.

In the kitchen, the players ran through a few scenes. Simon was on his feet with a clank of his sword. With a flourish of his arms, he delivered a tumultuous soliloquy. The others applauded appreciatively.

In no time at all, a gong resounded around the tavern and announced the start of the performance. An eager silence descended upon the audience. To a flurry of applause, the players climbed the steps to the stage. The audience rewarded Leonard's pretty manners with catcalls and wolf-whistles. He lapped it all up and walked tall and proud. Her hair stood on end as she imagined the way the men might stare and pass lewd judgement on her without troubling to lower their voices. The prospect repulsed her, but she had no other way of earning her bread and butter.

Engrossed by the antics of the players on stage, she forgot her anxiety momentarily. The players flounced and preened as they imitated King Henry's courtiers. She caught herself grinning at the absurdity, particularly the king who swaggered and belched and strutted about the stage like a peacock. All the while, the token maiden, played by Leonard, fluttered her eyelashes and cooed at him.

The story, a classic tale of chivalry, drew her in. A gold-hungry dragon paced about the stage and breathed real fire, in a canny deception that had the audience gasping in admiration. The evil dragon abducted the fair maiden. The audience loved it. They stamped on the floor with their boots and brought their goblets crashing down on the tables and produced a terrifying uproar. Eventually it was time for the interval. The players climbed down from the stage. They bowed graciously to their adoring audience who made an awful racket, shouting, cheering, applauding and hammering their fists on the table.

As directed by Ancel, who gave her one last encouraging smile, she screwed up her courage and made her way through the throng to the stage in a state of great agitation. She felt as though at any moment she might collapse in a hopeless heap on the floor. The blood rushed in her ears and made such a clamour she wondered that the people around her did not hear it. And she barely heard the none-too-polite comments and whistles bandied about around her.

At last, she was at the foot of the stairs and she made her ascent to the stage. In trepidation, she looked out across the sea of upturned faces. The crowd was silent in anticipation. A lute played the opening bars of her song, and she opened her mouth to sing. Her voice faltered at the first few notes, but she willed herself on and soon got into her stride. The audience stared at her transfixed, captivated by her voice. She sang one of the romantic songs she had sung at Rolf's castle. Her voice, confident of the harmonies, fairly rippled through the score. Given free rein before an adoring audience, her voice reached sweet heights it had never attained before. As she came to the end of the song, she noticed she had moved many in the crowd to tears.

'We have a true angel in our midst!' exclaimed one man. His eyes sparkled with fervour.

Cheers, applause and stamping resounded around the tavern. The crowd was hungry for more. They refused to be satisfied with just one song.

The lute took up the bars of the next song. It was a song about a woebegone woman whose husband fought in a distant war overseas. Pain surged in her breast as she sang and she thought of her dear Hugh, lost to her forever, and she poured all her longing for him into her song. Yet again, she commanded the audience. Awed as mortals before their God, the audience was cowed by her voice. She held all those men in the palm of her hand. It intoxicated her to feel so strong. Never had she possessed such power and glory. As she came to the diminuendo of the final verse, the audience roared. They were on their feet and they cheered, applauded and stamped.

To finish, she sang about a young virgin approaching her wedding day. And as she sang, she reconnected with the girl she had been but a year ago, and the hopes she had entertained for her own marriage, and how the reality of her marriage had dashed her hopes. Tears welled in her eyes and blinded her so the audience was a blur.

The crowd went berserk. The walls of the tavern shook. She had never heard such a noise. It took the combined efforts of Ancel and the ostlers he employed to keep the riff raff in check and escort Eleanor from the stage to the safety of the kitchen. Hands reached out to touch her, to stroke her hair. 'One more! One more!' chanted the crowd.

'What a success you are, my dear!' said Ancel. His eyes were bright. 'I could not have hoped for better. People will come from afar to hear you sing. Well done! You look done in. Go and rest.'

Gladly, she disappeared up the wooden staircase to her chamber still stunned by the excitement of the evening. Baby Mary slept peacefully on the bed, a look of contentment on her tiny face. Katherine looked up from her spinning.

'Not a peep from her,' whispered Katherine. 'She's been as good as gold. I gather you have been rather a success! I've never heard the crowd get so excited!'

All of a sudden, Eleanor felt so weary and exhausted. Katherine took herself off to bed after she helped her out of her gown. She yawned as she washed the paint off her face and then she stretched out gratefully on the mattress beside Mary.

For a long time, she lay awake in the darkness with

an arm over her eyes and ran over recent events in her mind, hardly believing what had happened. What an overwhelming response to her singing. She could not have hoped for better!

~

The next morning, Mary woke at dawn and demanded a feed. Still half asleep, she brought the baby to her breast. Downstairs there was no sound of any other member of the household stirring. What a luxury it was to languish in her warm bed and drift in and out of sleep. The women back at the nunnery would have been up for Prime already. And it was likely that Sister Agnes would have them hard at work on their knees scrubbing a floor by now.

It was mid-morning before she heard sounds of life downstairs. She wrapped the baby in swaddling clothes, pulled her cloak about her shoulders and went down to the kitchen. A bleary-eyed Katherine shuffled about in a pair of old sheepskin slippers.

'Good morning, love,' said the old woman. 'I am afraid you'll find that we keep late hours here on account of the evening performances. Ancel generally starts to cool things down around midnight. He aims to have all the stragglers out by half past one.'

The kitchen door into the tavern was ajar. The servant girls cleared the debris from the night before. Laden with dirty crockery, they brought it to the sink. Then they cleaned the dishes with sand and bracken and a final rinse of clean water. These women had their work cut out. The tavern was in a shocking state. It stank of stale food and wine and ale and food debris was ground into the rushes on the floor, and there were puddles of spilled wine and ale on the tables.

Katherine offered Eleanor bread and butter with a plum compote. She wolfed it down gladly.

After breakfast, she helped Katherine with the dishes and then went up to her chamber and dressed for the day. She pulled on the woollen gown she had worn in her escape from the fortress months before, thankful the nuns had let her have it back when she had left the priory.

She threw open the shutters and gazed out of her window, from which she had a view of the stark walls of Dover Castle keep. She cringed to think her dreaded husband was so close and the tavern was within view of the keep. She counted on the fact he would never venture here. It was a downtrodden, squalid part of town frequented by opportunists, criminals and army deserters seeking refuge from the gallows. Of course, she did not doubt he would have his spies here in the quarter, listening for unguarded, suspicious conversation. It was common knowledge among the nobles that outlaws used brothels and sordid taverns to conduct their meetings. In this quarter, brothels and dingy taverns were two-a-penny. Therefore, Rolf would have spies everywhere – and she shuddered at the thought.

Had Rolf sought her out after her escape from the

castle? Cut off from the outside world, she had heard nothing of the baron while she was at the priory. Perhaps her disappearance had suited him. After all, he had been itching to kill her. Probably, he had supplanted her with his newest mistress. Or perhaps his mother, Lady Beatrice, had arranged a new marriage of advantage, one that would extend his lands or bolster the gold in his coffers.

Thoughts of her mother-in-law made her stomach tighten. What would Beatrice say if she saw where she was now and how she earned her living?

At noon, Katherine knocked on the door of her chamber and called her for lunch. She sat down with Katherine and Ancel to a plate of fresh eggs on hot buttered toast.

'The players live in digs in the vicinity, but sup with us in the evenings,' said Ancel. 'I trust you slept well?'

'Better than I have for a long time,' said Eleanor. It was comfortable to be in Ancel's and Katherine's company. They had good hearts and meant well.

'You really were a roaring success last night,' said Ancel. 'We've already had many requests for more of your singing. People asked after you at the market this morning. It is good to keep the crowd hungry for more. You must rest this afternoon. You have a performance again tonight and we must not frustrate your adoring public.'

Baby Mary woke with a soft cry and looked up at her with watery-blue eyes. She was hungry again. There was nothing for it. She had to feed her. And she took leave of Ancel and Katherine and went upstairs to her chamber.

In her room, she lay out on the bed and propped herself up on some pillows to nurse Mary. It was so gratifying to see her baby feeding and thriving against all the odds. There had been times at the priory when conditions had been so hard she had doubted they would make it through the winter. A cold shudder crept down her spine as she remembered Anne, who had not been so lucky.

She must have drifted off to sleep for a gentle tap at the door woke her. Baby Mary had relinquished her nipple and fallen asleep again.

'Come in,' she said quietly, so as not to wake the baby.

Katherine poked her head around the door. 'Would you like some supper?'

She swaddled her sleeping baby, adjusted her gown and smoothed down her hair, which had become dishevelled after her nap. She would not miss supper for the world. Delicious smells of roasting meat drifted up from the kitchen.

The players were gathered around the table and they beamed at her in welcome.

'What a debut!' said Leonard, a greyish shadow upon his jaw.

'Truly incredible!' said Simon. His eyes were bright, and his corkscrew curls bobbed.

'Come, come . . .' Ancel seemed determined to father her. He reassured her with his patronage.

Having been cloistered away in the priory for so long, she felt like a mouse in the company of men.

'Katherine,' said Ancel. 'Fill up Matilda's plate. We must build up her stamina. Matilda, this is Marcus – he's the head of our merry band of players.'

She smiled briefly at Marcus and tucked into the roast beef set before her, relishing every tender morsel – at the priory she had been so long deprived of meat.

'News from the keep,' said Marcus. He rested his sinewy arms on the table. The oldest player of the company, he had a long white beard flecked with grey. His sharp blue eyes darted from face to face. 'Baron Rolf is bolstering recruits to put down a rebellion in the north.'

At the mention of Rolf's name, she looked up. The hairs on the back of her neck stood to attention and she shivered involuntarily.

'I always said that he would not crush the northern barons for long,' said Ancel.

'He has been as mad as a fiend ever since his wife died.' Simon shook his head.

She sat up very straight and listened keenly.

'Killed off more like!' Ancel gesticulated wildly. 'He's always picked off anyone who has opposed him. There have been countless executions of late.'

Her stomach turned as she recalled the greyish-green, fly-infested heads Rolf had mounted on spikes at the gates of the citadel. Their sightless, bulbous eyes still haunted her.

'He has grown fearful of losing his grip,' said

Marcus. 'In recent weeks, three whorehouses in the quarter have been subject to raids. Rolf is determined to flush out the outlaws.'

Fear colonised the pit of her stomach and her heart raced. Even here she was not safe from Rolf. His spies were everywhere, perhaps even in this very room. There was no one she could trust.

'We live in dark times and no mistake,' said Ancel. 'Pray do not let us frighten poor Matilda. She has gone quite white.'

Concerned eyes turned to Eleanor and she flushed. She felt like a fraud, and she hastily drank down a draught of wine from her goblet.

'You were quite something last night,' said Simon. He refilled her goblet and touched her lightly on the arm. He smiled softly. His sky-blue eyes met her own for an instant, and something flashed between them.

An unexpected tenderness lurched in her heart. Feeling her colour rise, she took another great swig of wine. Never had she felt so giddy and unstable.

Making a concerted effort to pull herself together, she got to her feet and helped Katherine with the dishes as the servant girls were busy in the tavern.

'You are good,' said Katherine. 'It's been hard these past months without Sophie. I am not as strong as I once was.'

Eleanor spooned sticky honey cake out into dishes. She licked the spoon. It was so long since she had tasted anything so sweet.

Simon caught her eye as she passed him his bowl

of cake and provoked that same delightful feeling in her heart. But she loved Hugh. How was it possible to love Simon too? What she felt for Simon was something altogether different, more visceral. In her relatively short life, she had never quite experienced the spark she felt now. Anyway, Hugh was lost to her forever and married to Lady Bethany. The thought was like a dagger in her heart.

After she had cleared the supper dishes, she went up to feed the baby. Mary suckled greedily. When she had her fill, she slipped off the nipple and fell into a milky sleep.

Presently, Katherine appeared, a selection of gowns draped over her arms. They settled upon a gown of salmon-coloured silk for that evening, still fine despite its age. Eleanor had not worn such a soft gown for months and she ran her finger over the fabric appreciatively. Fortunately, she had lost her swollen belly almost immediately after the birth. Baby Mary was so insatiably hungry she had fairly sucked the fat and nutrients from her mother's body. Katherine had to pinch and tuck the silk dress in at the waist. Thankfully, though, she was getting good food here. How wonderful it was to dress in a beautiful silk gown once more. However, a stab of guilt checked her joy when she remembered the priest's warning about the sins of pride and vanity.

As Katherine helped her pin her curls up on her head in a fetching manner, she experienced an exquisite twinge of desire for Simon.

Katherine made quick work of Eleanor's make-up. Her shaky, arthritic hands still had artistic flair. The ladies-in-waiting at Dover Castle would have been envious of her creation.

Eleanor made her final adjustments to her gossamer veil, which was as light as air, and admired her reflection in the slightly distorted steel mirror.

'You're as pretty as Venus herself!' said Katherine.

Eleanor thanked her and hurried downstairs, leaving Katherine in charge of the sleeping baby.

In the kitchen, the players strutted about in their costumes and practised their lines. There was a gasp of awe as she crossed the threshold. And she blushed with shy pleasure.

The players returned to their rehearsal. Amidst the noise and general chaos, Simon caught her eye and gestured she should come to his side. She complied without hesitation; every moment with Simon was as intoxicating as nectar.

Simon took her hands in his and gazed into her eyes. A ripple of warmth went from her heart to her groin.

Outside in the tavern, the patrons were arriving in droves. The musicians played a gentle lilting melody. The crowd jostled and argued over the best seats in the house. The tavern teemed with people.

'They are here to see you, you know,' said Simon. 'And who would blame them?' He squeezed her hand.

A jolt of pleasure went through her body at his touch.

'Come, come,' said Ancel. He clapped his hands for

silence in the kitchen. 'The play must commence – the audience is champing at the bit.'

Simon relinquished her hand. Losing his gentle touch left her bereft.

Ancel was right. The audience were on tenterhooks in anticipation of the spectacle.

'We've never known the performance to be so well attended,' whispered Simon.

His breath was warm on her neck and ear and it smelled faintly of wine and spices. How she longed to be alone with him! To be so close to him yet denied the pleasure of his touch was a delicious torture. The next moment, he had followed the players out into the tavern and left her quite cold and alone.

From the curtained doorway of the kitchen she watched the play unfold. Henry came onstage first and delivered an ironic soliloquy in a deadpan manner, with not so much as a smirk on his face. The audience fell about in stitches and spluttered out their wine and ale in mirth. Next the lovers, of which Simon was one, took to the stage. Leonard, dressed up as a fabulous Grecian goddess, pawed at him. Unfamiliar stirrings of jealousy tugged at her heart. What fool-ishness was she reduced to now: fawning over Simon. Had not the priest sermonised for long hours on the flaws of mortal love? Impulsively, she pushed all such thoughts from her mind. God's love was everlasting, and he would not begrudge the innocently stoked love between a man and a woman. Just then a recol-lection stabbed her: she was married.

The Song and the Sword

Jerked from her thoughts, Ancel's hands pushed her onstage to sing. The familiar lump returned to her throat and she suppressed an urge to flee. The fear was as bad as it had been the night before – she was sure she would faint.

With deep breaths and taking extreme care on the steps up to the stage, at last she stood before the audience who gazed up at her with eager faces. The lute took up the opening bars of the song. She opened her mouth to sing. Yet again her first notes faltered. And then, of its own accord, her voice sang out clear, pure and resonant. Her voice had the audience enthralled and they listened as though in rapture.

As she sang out the familiar lines of the song, she implored God for His love and glory, knowing that she was unworthy. Strong and powerful, her voice seemed to originate from some hidden depth in her half-starved frame. She came to the end of the first song and the audience rose and applauded, cheered, stamped their feet and banged their cups on the table. They implored her for more. The noise deafened and frightened her, yet it excited her too. Every hair on her body stood on end and shivers travelled up her spine. She did not want the moment to end, but it felt so unreal, so fragile, that it might vanish at any instant.

Then she took up the second song. Never had she known she could wield such a seductive power over others. Her audience and she were as one, caught up in her words, and in the delicate quiet notes that caressed their ears as well as the glorious loud notes that made them shiver. To sing with the choir at the priory had been so special, a veritable communion with Christ, but to sing for an adoring audience – now this was something else. At the close of the song, the audience went wild. She had a sudden mad urge to throw herself out into the crowd so they could bear her aloft in their arms. Hands reached up to touch her. Ancel and his two ostlers escorted her off the stage to safety.

She felt curiously light. Beyond the noise and hubbub of the tavern, Simon waited in the shadows. As she passed, he took her hand and bestowed upon it a reverent kiss. Such wonderful sensations spread across her body and she was rooted to the spot.

The next moment, Katherine crashed down the stairs with a shrieking baby in her arms. Evidently, the din had woken poor Mary, and she was anxious for her mother.

Reluctantly, she turned away from Simon and her admiring audience. Climbing the staircase, she cooed at her baby, at once back to the humdrum and ordinary, filled with disbelief at what had happened.

22.

Back to Eynsford

A mid-May sun beat down on Hugh as he was conveyed by rowing boat from his ship to the port of Dover. His blood grew hot at the sight of the stark grey curtain walls of Dover Castle, the seat of his enemy that loomed ominous on the cliff and cast a menacing shadow over the sprawling rooftops of the town.

The boat docked at the quay, and he wasted no time in exchanging his warhorse for a fresh young courser. Eager to leave Dover behind, he wound his way impatiently through the thronged narrow streets with their overhanging houses towards the gate of the town. His priority was to deliver the ransom to the Bishop of Rochester to secure the release of Guy's mother and sister. From there he planned to return to Eynsford.

At last, he left behind the detritus of the town with its shanty dwellings and leper colonies, and he breathed in deep the scent of apple and cherry orchards and of the heather that basked in the late spring sunshine. Keen to steer clear of the main traffic, he spurred his horse on the climbing path up to the clifftop coastal road.

A westward sea wind tore at his surcoat and tousled his hair. The cliff path was so narrow he was forced to dismount and coax his reluctant horse along. On his left rose a sheer face of craggy rock and on his right was a vertiginous drop of chalk and the boom of the white-crested waves below. Above him, gulls wailed and soared across the clear blue sky.

Before long, the path grew wider and veered inland through the forest. Gratefully, he swung up into his saddle and spurred his horse on to a gallop. After what he judged to be a two-hour ride, he slowed his pace and stopped to water his horse in a ford.

At a faint noise in the undergrowth, his horse tossed his head and pricked his ears. From out of a patch of darkness beneath the boughs of an oak tree rode a shabby-looking knight errant on a raven warhorse. His filthy surcoat hung in tatters over his tarnished chain mail and he brandished a rusty-looking blade.

'Yield and I will let you pass,' said the knight. 'This looks to be a fine steed and will be of use to me. And your armour must be worth something. Likewise, whatever weighs down your saddle bags.'

'You make free with my possessions.' Hugh wheeled his horse round and drew his sword. 'Come and take them, if you will!'

They came together with an almighty crash of steel. Taking great two-handed swinging blows, they hacked at each other and drew blood where their searching blades abraded their flesh through their chain mail. Hugh breathed heavily through the slit in his helm. With a great surge of fury, he raised his blade above his head and brought it swishing down through the knight's helm and cleaved metal and bone and split the man's head, bringing his lifeless form crashing down from his horse onto the ground.

Having staunched his wounds as best he could, he urged his horse forward into the forest ways, praying he would not be set upon by any more knights errant or bandits. He pushed the horse hard and broke his journey only to camp in the forest and catch a few hours of sleep. The following day, he made good progress and found himself at the cathedral by lunch-time.

After a wait of some two hours, the bishop granted him an audience. A small hunched monk showed him into the bishop's chamber: a large hall with a painted vaulted ceiling.

'Well met, Sir Hugh,' said the bishop. A sharp-eyed man with scant pewter hair, he wore a purple woollen ceremonial robe. He gestured that Hugh should take a seat. 'I have been expecting you. Sir Mordaunt wrote to me and explained your mission.'

'Very good, my lord bishop.' Hugh bowed reverently and took a seat.

'You have brought the ransom I trust?'

Hugh lifted the heavy velvet coin purses onto the table.

The bishop opened the bags and sifted through the gold coins with a jewelled hand. He rapped at the table with his crosier and immediately a tall monk with an aged stoop shuffled to his side.

'See that this gold is counted carefully,' said the bishop. 'The lives of a noblewoman and her daughter hang in the balance. We will take our cut of ten per cent as agreed with Sir Mordaunt.'

The man leaned over and lifted the purses. He carried them over to the sloped desk at the far side of the chamber. There, he turned his back on them and counted the coins.

The bishop turned to Hugh. 'You can rest assured that I will broker the swift release of these women. I will travel to Dover on the morrow and see to the matter myself.'

'Thank you, my lord.'

The bishop beckoned Hugh closer. 'What I have to say is for your ears alone.'

Hugh moved obediently closer and inclined his head so the bishop did not have to raise his voice above a whisper.

'I need not press upon you the high stakes of the matter of which I speak, I think.'

Hugh nodded.

'You are, of course, aware that Rolf has seized the lands of your father and uncle.' The bishop shot Hugh a sympathetic look. 'Your father and brother were murdered and many of your father's knights were slaughtered but some still live to tell the tale. These men have been meeting in secret these past three months in a tavern in Dover. I have advised them of your return. They are keen to meet with you. You will find them at the Mermayd next Wednesday evening. Just ask for Sir Roger.'

Hugh's spirits rose at the news that his late father's most loyal knight had survived the raid. He could not wish for a tougher or more useful ally. 'I cannot thank you enough.' He rose and bowed.

'Sir Mordaunt has been a lifelong friend. I am glad to do whatever I can for his kin.' The bishop turned to his master of coin. 'Is everything accounted for?'

The monk turned and nodded.

'Very good,' said the bishop. And he dismissed Hugh with a wave of his jewelled hand.

~

After another day's hard riding, Hugh passed meadows with rows of stooped peasants swinging their scythes over the long grass. He was beginning to recognise his surroundings. These were the woods of his youth. And he breathed in deep the comforting smell of damp wood and bracken. For as long as he could remember, his family had hunted here among the ancient oak trees accompanied by a pack of excited hounds.

Somewhere ahead, a great cawing and flutter of wings beat up in the undergrowth. He bent his head, avoiding the low boughs in a thicket of trees, and raised it to a sight that took his breath away. Crows pecked at the putrid bodies of three men that swung by their necks from a crude gibbet. Disturbed, the birds screeched and took flight with a beating of wings. The men were fully clothed in the simple, threadbare garb of peasants and rudimentary boots hung on their limp feet. The bodies were in a state of advancing decay and the birds had made a meal of their faces and hands. The stench was unbearable. Shaken to the core, he just about recognised them as his father's tenant farmers – a father and his two teenage sons.

With a slash of his sword, he brought the bodies crashing down. Sweating under his surcoat and mail and barely able to suppress the violent heaving of his stomach, he dug them a grave in the earth with his bare hands and covered their corpses in bracken. Afterwards he took care to wash the dirt off his hands in the meandering stream that was close at hand.

By and by, the shadows had lengthened and he looked for a place to sup and sleep. After the ugly sight he couldn't bring himself to go to Eynsford

Castle. Not tonight, he told himself. Presently, he came across a dilapidated-looking inn on the edge of a small hamlet. He dismounted and tethered his horse and, stowing his precious cargo from his saddlebags under his arm, stooped under the lintel. He found himself in a small, smoky room that smelled strongly of fried onions. It was crowded with labourers and a few lazy hounds stretched out in front of the bright fire in the hearth. The men looked up curiously from their mugs of beer and broke off their conversations and stared as he strode to the bar and took up a low stool by the window.

'Will you be wanting anything to eat or drink?' asked a ruddy-cheeked woman with an ample bosom.

'A bowl of stew and a mug of ale, if you please.'

The woman set down a bowl of steaming stew before him.

'This last year I have been abroad. And I heard rumours on my travels, but pray tell me what came to pass at Eynsford Castle?' He sampled a mouthful of the stew that he found to be substantial, despite a dearth of meat.

'Right enough, it was a shameful thing.' The old woman shook her head. She let out a little shiver as she filled his tankard with ale.

A wasp hovered in through the open window and fussed around his bowl of stew and mug of ale. He brushed it away with the palm of his hand.

'Raiders came in the early hours and stormed the castle.' The woman massaged her hands. 'They say the lord and his first-born had been feasting and drinking and had passed out with their heads on the table. Blood-curdling yells, such a clamour and tumult there was apparently. They were hard at it throughout the night as the Eynsford men did not give up without a fight.'

A murmur of interest stirred up among the people around them.

'A bloodbath by all accounts,' said an old man who had come to stand beside him. He waggled a calloused finger and there was a glint in his eye. 'The lord had his throat cut from ear to ear and his son suffered the same fate! The raiders ravished the women of the house at the point of a sword!'

At this Hugh's fingers clenched under the bar and his blood ran hot and rose like a wellspring.

'The likes of us left starving after they burnt the crops,' said a grubby-looking young man. He let out a sharp laugh in the back of his throat and broke into a bitter, gap-toothed smile.

'What's more, the new lord won't stand for any dissent, neither.' The landlady settled the jug down on the table with a crash. 'He had old Arthur and his two young sons strung up on the gibbet yonder as a warning to us all. Evil times we live in, make no mistake.'

The wasp returned. It crawled along the rim of Hugh's mug of ale and then it blundered down into the liquid. It let out a frantic droning as it made a last-ditch attempt to get airborne before it drowned. He scooped it up with his finger and threw it out of the window and onto the grass. He drained his beer and asked the innkeeper for a bed for the night. The landlady showed him up to a private garret furnished simply with a straw mattress on a pallet. He took off his chain mail and climbed between the rough linen sheets and was soon asleep.

A crowing cock woke him at dawn from deep troubled dreams. Weary as he was after his long journey, he drifted back to sleep and he didn't wake up until the sun was at high heaven. He threw on some clothes and broke his fast on bread, cheese and ale. Half an hour later, he was back on his horse. A short ride brought him to Bardolf's mother's tumbledown cottage on the edge of the forest. For a moment, heart sore, he lingered outside unwilling to find out anything more that would add to his grief.

A small hunched woman opened the door cautiously and shuffled out in slippers to see who was outside. Grey grief had prematurely aged her weather-beaten face. However, the sides of her wrinkled mouth went up into the warm smile he had known since infancy. 'Hugh! Returned so soon from crusade! Please come in and have a cup of ale.'

'I came as soon as I had word.' Hugh stooped under the low lintel.

'Perhaps you are hungry,' she said. 'Here, help yourself to bread and cheese.'

Thanking her, he sat down. 'Pray tell me how is Bardolf?' He spoke tentatively, hardly daring to hope that his friend had survived the raid.

'Rolf's men slew my own son before my eyes!' Her eyes filled with tears. 'Though I kneeled in the dirt, my hands clasped together, pleading for his mercy. What harm did he do them! They even cut off the head of that old blind dog of his.'

Another stab of pain pierced Hugh's heart. 'I am so very sorry.' A trickle of blood from the cut on his eyebrow, which had opened up again, trailed down his nose. And he brushed it away with a mailed sleeve.

'Let me see to that.' There was a mother's concern in her eyes. And she went to the kitchen for some salve and dressed the cut on his brow. 'There, that's better.'

Her grey eyes looked for a moment directly and deeply into his own. 'Not knowing whether you would make it back, I rescued one of your mother's favourite samplers from the inferno. She stitched it when you were but a babe in arms.' She put a hand on his shoulder. 'It isn't much I'm afraid, but it is something for you to remember her by.'

A solitary tear welled in his eye, but he forced himself to smile. 'Thank you, that was so thoughtful of you.' He packed the precious sampler back in his bag and felt around for a bag of gold. And he brought out a handful of gold and pressed it into her reluctant hand.

'Thank you kindly, but I have no need of it.'

'At least allow me to help chop up some wood for the fire.'

She smiled at that and brought him an axe, then he

went into the courtyard garden and chopped wood for a fire.

In the end, he could only prevail upon her to take a single gold coin. With sadness in his heart, he embraced her gently. He wished her well and took his leave.

Before long he rode hard up the scorched hillside to Eynsford Castle. The heart went out of him at the sight of the blackened tree stumps and charred thickets of heather that littered the slope.

At the crest of the hill, he had his first glimpse of the shell of the castle that for so many years had been his home. With a sharp intake of breath, he reined in his horse and stood for a moment and took it all in. The devastation had to be seen to be believed. What was left of his home stood half in ruins and ivy scaled its charred towers. Despite the months that had elapsed since the raid, an acrid stench still lingered in the air. Only one part of the building appeared to remain habitable and still lived in, for from the windows on the upper floor gleamed a faint shaft of light.

Heart in his throat, he dismounted. He tethered his horse to an alder tree, and crept forward through the scorched undergrowth. The branches around him disintegrated into ash as he brushed past them. He moved as though in a dream. The blood pounding in his ears almost deafened him. A sudden baying of hounds in the castle's forecourt took him off guard. Rooted to the spot, he had to stifle a cry.

Ahead, the great ironbound door of the keep was charred beyond recognition. It hung off its hinges by an iron thread and was propped ajar with a huge rock. In the thickening dusk he could just make out a young boy in a tattered smock who sat at the foot of the broken stone staircase holding a lamp. Once that staircase had been fine and its walls had hung with intricate tapestries. Now the lamp-flame danced on the walls and he saw they were shabby and smoke-stained with dark patches of encroaching damp.

The hounds paced the forecourt. They had their hackles up and sensed something hidden in the undergrowth. There was nothing for him here. Barely daring to breathe for the slow drum of his heart, he melted soundlessly back into the trees. His hands shook as he untethered his horse. Springing into the saddle, he spurred his horse on. With a thunder of hooves, he galloped off into the darkness of the night. Hot fury pulsed in his veins and hunger for revenge gnawed at his belly.

23.

Betrayal

On the stroke of five earlier that same evening, the players arrived at the Three Kings for supper. In the six weeks Eleanor had spent at the tavern she had attempted to act nonchalantly around Simon, but her eyes sought his out all the same. He beamed at her in response and something in her belly leapt for joy. Warmth spread across her body and she was unable to repress a smile.

The players took their places around the table. Simon took the stool on her right and she flushed with pleasure.

Ancel cleared his throat importantly, and a hush descended on the company. All eyes were on him.

'Now it is a matter of weeks before the Corpus

Christi pageant. And we have costumes to prepare and lines to learn.'

The eyes around the table became bright and animated.

'You will sing at the pageant, I hope?' Ancel smiled at her.

'We always have a stage,' said Simon. 'We'll have an hour's slot in which to perform, and everyone will attend.'

'Yes, please do,' said Henry.

All eyes were upon her. While she did not have the heart to refuse them, to perform in front of her husband, even in the guise of a humble singer, would be foolhardy beyond measure. Rolf or one of the other knights or ladies would be sure to recognise her.

Katherine favoured her with her wide toothless smile. 'We have some fine gowns especially for the occasion.'

'But of course,' she assured them. For the time being, she could think of no pretext to refuse, but she would have to come up with a plan to avoid such a performance.

'This year we will perform *The Last Judgement*,' said Leonard in a falsetto. 'And we even have our own hell-mouth.' He batted his eyelashes.

'Yes indeed,' said Ancel. 'It will be the highlight of the pageant!'

'Sophie always loves the pageant,' said Katherine. 'I hope she'll be back in time.'

'That's more than likely,' said Ancel. 'She wouldn't miss it for the world.'

Eleanor wondered what it would be like when Sophie returned. God willing, Sophie and her child would survive the birth. But her friend planned to give up her child. How Sophie could do such a thing, she could not understand. She could not have given up Baby Mary for all the gold in the land.

'Some of the songs you sang last night would go down a treat at the pageant,' said Leonard. 'They had grown men in tears.'

'We have a lot to discuss tonight,' said Ancel. 'As the Wine Merchants' guild are making ready for the pageant, a number of the freemen will be taking part in our performance.'

The company let out a chorus of groans.

Leonard curled his lip. 'I have no wish to share the stage with some jumped-up town officials and market traders!'

'Marcus . . .' said Ancel. 'You will be God.'

The bearded giant bowed in recognition of the honour. Doubtless he was perfect for the part. At six foot two, he towered over the average man and sported a long greyish-white beard.

'Arthur, you will be Judas,' said Ancel. 'Judas is always a redhead.'

Arthur shrugged and rolled his eyes to the ceiling.

'Henry, you will be Pilate. That is, if your belly hasn't grown too big for the costume!' A series of guffaws beat up from the players around the table. 'And Simon, you will be the Devil.'

'He is always a devil!' said Leonard in his usual falsetto.

'Aye, he's none too good, I'll warrant,' said Ancel.

Simon was no devil in her eyes, far from it.

'The rest will be the judged,' said Ancel. 'The public will have a treat in store.'

Katherine ladled the chicken stew out into bowls and the company tucked in.

The baby stirred and displayed signs of hunger, so Eleanor was obliged to abandon her stool beside Simon and go upstairs to nurse her.

When Mary had been fed, she drifted off to sleep again and Eleanor was free to dress for the performance that evening.

Katherine brought a fine gown of red velvet to her room.

'We'll try it on for size tonight, because you'll be wearing it for the pageant. If any adjustments are needed, I'll have plenty of time to make the necessary alterations. Ancel wants you dressed up like a fine lady.'

She helped Eleanor into the gown. She had not worn anything so regal since her days at Dover Castle. It felt odd looking at herself dressed as a noblewoman, as though she were an imposter.

The dress fitted her exceptionally well and only needed a little stitching on the hem where the seam had come unravelled. Katherine fixed the hem on the spot.

The Song and the Sword

'You're a veritable lady,' she said through a mouthful of pins. 'One would think you were noble-born, the way you carry yourself!' She helped Eleanor with her hair and face paint. 'Go downstairs and enjoy yourself. I'll look after Mary. I've brought my spinning to keep me busy.'

Downstairs, the kitchen was frenetic. The players were running through their lines and the serving girls rushed in and out, laden with jugs of ale and wine and bowls of steaming stew. She took up the stool beside Simon.

'What a fine lady you are!' Simon kissed her hand.

Warm ripples of pleasure travelled from her hand to her heart.

'Come, come! It's time!' Ancel clapped his hands. 'The musicians are ready.'

The players filed out into the tavern and ascended the stage. She watched from behind the curtain. The tavern heaved with people swilling down flagons of wine and ale.

Before long Simon returned to the kitchen. Playing the part of the king, he would not be needed on stage again until the final act. He took her hand and sat down beside her. They were alone at long last.

'It seems fitting that I should be dressed as a king and you as such a fine lady.' He spoke quietly and flashed her a soft smile.

She sat utterly still, transfixed by his gaze. How wonderful it was to be close to him, as though all the cares in the world had fallen from her shoulders.

He leaned towards her and brushed his fingers against her cheek tenderly, which set off a lurch of longing within her belly. He moved his face closer and brushed his lips against hers. She had never known such rapture.

The next moment a serving girl burst into the kitchen, a platter strewn with remnants of stew in her hands. She startled Eleanor, who drew back from Simon abruptly.

Simon stood up, took Eleanor's hand and said, 'Come, follow me!'

She could not resist. She would do anything to be near Simon. He drew her into the tavern and around the back of the crowd to a curtained area she had not noticed before. Behind the curtain was a small narrow cot covered with a stained blanket. She recoiled at once as she realised its purpose. But Simon held her close. His proximity was reassuring. It made her forget her surroundings. She trusted and loved him with every ounce of her being. He leaned over her and kissed her. Never had anyone kissed her like this before. Rolf had never wasted any time with preliminaries. She had the sensation of diving into Simon and he into her as if they were one. How tender he was. Helpless to his touch, she melted in his arms.

He lowered her onto the cot and they were as one, united in indescribable pleasure. This could not be wrong. God had created such wonders! They moved together rhythmically and raced to an end that neither of them wanted to come. And then it came, and she had to bite her lip to prevent herself from crying out in glory, an agony of pleasure.

She lay panting, her limbs entangled with his.

A loud round of applause and cheering resounded around the tavern. Simon sprang to his feet, his face flushed.

'You have to sing, hurry!' he whispered.

Soundlessly, he dressed. He smoothed her skirts and hair and pushed her out into the crowd.

The audience were on their feet and they took cover among them and made for the kitchen. She found herself in front of Ancel who gestured to her. She looked behind her for Simon, but he had vanished.

'Where were you?' Ancel's face was flushed.

She mumbled something about the privy, and then felt a pang of shame at how easily lying had come to her.

Ancel bundled her onto the stage where she stood before her audience. The lute began the introduction and she opened her mouth to sing. This time the notes came effortlessly. Glorious once more before her adoring audience, she sang from her soul. She poured her yearning for Simon's love into the romantic songs she sung.

The audience were in uproar and clamoured for more. Hands reached out to touch her, to stroke her hair. Ancel came with his henchmen and escorted her to the safety of the kitchen.

'I've never seen anything like it, upon my word!'

Ancel's eyes were ablaze. 'They fairly worship you, my dear.'

'Truly wonderful!' said Marcus. 'You have an enchanting voice.'

One of the servant girls brought a hat filled to the brim with silver coins into the kitchen and handed it to Ancel.

'All for you, my dear girl. You are truly extraordinary!' Ancel mopped his bald head in sweaty excitement. 'Up you go, my dear. Get some rest. We will need more of the same from you tomorrow!'

Her head in the clouds, she climbed the staircase. What an evening! Never had she been happier. All the hardship was over – she had met the man of her dreams. She could make a living from her singing and she had her baby girl. Who could ask for more?

Mary was sleeping soundly when she tiptoed into the room. She thanked Katherine, kissing her impulsively on the cheek, which provoked a titter from the old woman.

'Well, I never did. You sweet girl.' Katherine giggled and hobbled off to bed.

Eleanor tore off her gown and cleaned the paint from her face. Her mind was aflutter. There were so many things to think of now. She and her baby had a future. She had someone to love, someone to look after her.

The baby awoke shortly after and cried out for milk. She climbed into bed beside her and nursed her until she drifted off to sleep.

The Song and the Sword

Eleanor's body quivered at the sweet memory of Simon's touch. What delights they had shared. If only he were with her now. How she longed to be close to him. Her thoughts danced off into a glorious future. A future she had never dared hope for. A life filled with a wealth of love and music. She would start anew with Simon. All that had passed between her and Rolf would be a distant memory. A sudden moment of disquiet seized her when her love for Hugh tore at her heart unbidden. But Hugh would be married now, and she should forget him, and she pushed her feelings for him away. This was different. With Simon, her baby would have a father. Never had she imagined that she would again feel so intensely for another – that a man's touch would kindle such a flame of love in her heart. She did not sleep for hours, so sweet were her thoughts and feelings that she never wanted sleep to bring them to an end.

∽

Towards dawn, sleep claimed her. And she slept deeply until Katherine materialised, mid-morning, with boiled eggs and bread on a tray.

'You look exhausted, sweet girl,' she said. 'Eat up and then get back to sleep, else I declare you will have dark circles under your eyes!'

She did as she was bid and slept deeply until noon when Katherine brought up another tray, this time with soup and bread.

307

'You'll never guess who's downstairs!' Katherine's blue eyes were bright with excitement. 'Sophie is back!'

Eleanor's heart leapt for joy. 'How wonderful! Is she well? What about the baby?'

'A bonny little boy,' said Katherine. 'The nuns have found him a loving family. Eat up your lunch, dear, and come down and see her.'

Eleanor wolfed down her soup and bread, dressed quickly in her old woollen kirtle and dashed downstairs with her baby, so excited to see her dear friend Sophie and to fill her in on what had happened.

Sophie made a gaunt, frail figure in the kitchen. She had lost her pregnancy belly, but the flesh around her middle hung loose.

'Sophie!' Eleanor embraced her friend with fervour. 'So good to see you.'

'Aye . . .' Sophie looked slightly grey about the gills. 'It is good to be home!'

'We'll have to feed you up proper,' said Katherine. 'Make no mistake, we'll restore you to your bonny self in no time. Simon will be so glad to see you. He's been that worried!'

'Simon?' Eleanor gulped.

'Yes, dear. He's Sophie's sweetheart.' Katherine beamed at her protégé.

Eleanor felt as though the ground had given way beneath her, and she was hurtling into an abyss. 'But the baby?' She pointed at Sophie's empty belly.

A shadow passed across Sophie's weary face.

'Simon has a wife and children in London. He could not marry me. I could never have kept my baby.'

This fresh news struck Eleanor like the sweating sickness. Her head swam and she sank to her knees overwhelmed by dizziness and nausea.

'Goodness gracious, dear!' said Katherine. 'Are you quite well? We must have her rested for the performance tonight. Sophie, help me get her up the stairs.'

Eleanor let the two women bundle her upstairs and they installed her in bed with the baby who slept peacefully beside her.

Alone in her chamber, she was distraught. How could she have dared assume that something would go right for her? What a fool she was! She had let herself become consumed by lust and vanity. Alas, she had not heeded the priest's wise counsel about the frail, imperfect nature of human love. She had thought of nothing but her own needs, her own longings. She had assumed that Simon felt the same, yet he not only had a sweetheart, but a wife and children too!

Filled with guilt, she thought of her friend Sophie whom she had unwittingly betrayed. Sophie had brought her everything: she had given her the wherewithal to keep her child and be a mother. Poor, malnourished Sophie downstairs. Her dear friend who had been obliged to sacrifice her own baby. And how had she repaid her? It was too awful.

She cried herself to exhaustion. Weak and empty, she forced herself to stop. She could not do this. To collapse was not an option. She owed it to Ancel and Katherine, and the rest of the company – not to mention Baby Mary and Sophie. She had to pull herself together.

Fear consumed her at the prospect of the performance that evening. She glanced at her reflection in the brushed-steel mirror. What a sorry picture she made. What a foolish, self-indulgent slut she was! She splashed her face with the water Katherine had brought her that morning. It was freezing cold, but it did her some good. As best she could, she disguised her puffy eyes with paint. She needed to shake herself out of this maudlin mood and she decided that her best course of action might be to busy herself with the baby's laundry in the washhouse that adjoined the kitchen.

'Are you sure you're feeling better, love?' Katherine looked worried.

'You are too good to me.' Eleanor felt thoroughly ashamed. She set about washing the baby's clothes.

'Sophie's gone up to rest,' said Katherine. 'Poor thing. The nuns have quite starved her. She is a shadow of her former self. What an ordeal she has been through. Those men don't know the half of it!'

'Indeed, they don't!'

'Let me finish those, dear,' insisted Katherine. 'You are still quite pale. You must get your rest. Ancel will be furious if he sees you exhausting yourself with the washing when you have to sing tonight.'

Reluctantly, Eleanor went upstairs to bed. She

would have preferred hard work to the thoughts that plagued her. Mary was fretful and would not be soothed. Evidently, her tiny stomach pained her. Poor little mite. She berated herself for having indulged for so long in her own fancies and woe when the little one suffered so. Thus, she paced about the chamber, and jiggled the baby on her shoulder, but still Mary was inconsolable. And Sophie was next door resting. She was anxious that the baby might disturb her friend. Softly, she sang a lullaby her nurse had sung to her years ago when she was an infant. The song soon had the desired effect and Mary fell fast asleep. Exhausted, she took the opportunity to close her own tired eyes.

~

Sophie tapped gently on the door to call her down for supper. She sat up, groggy and disorientated, and then everything dawned on her in a wave of horror. The prospect of seeing Simon at the kitchen table filled her with dread. There was no way she could avoid facing him. No one must guess what had happened. No, she would not have Simon come between her and her friend. With a damp cloth, she rubbed at the smudges of paint on her face and applied a fresh layer of make-up. She was passable, she thought, regarding herself in the mirror. True, her eyes were rather puffy, but she would say that she might be sickening for a cold if anyone remarked on her appearance.

Sounds of merry laughter and the smell of meat stew wafted up from the kitchen as she descended the staircase with Mary in her arms. Her stomach felt uncomfortably tight and the blood pounded in her ears. Sophie was in mid-flow, recounting the story of the errant nun who had inadvertently ingested the devil when she forgot to make the sign of God before eating a lettuce.

'And when the priest commanded the devil to come out of the woman, the devil replied that it was not his fault that he was sitting upon the lettuce at the time!'

There was a splutter of laughter from Leonard as she entered the kitchen. Katherine made room for her to join the others around the table and handed her a generous portion of mutton stew in a bowl. She ate quickly, her head down, preoccupied with avoiding Simon's eye. She did her best to keep her joy at the safe return of Sophie foremost in her mind rather than the profound disappointment that had cleaved her heart as surely as any butcher's knife. Katherine poured her a goblet of wine and the alcohol did something to dull her senses, and for that she was grateful.

'They tell me you are a roaring success!' said Sophie. 'I always knew your voice was special. A gift from God, that's what the nuns and priests called it.'

A gift from God it was, and she would do well to remember it. How carried away she had been on a tide of pride and vanity. Silently, she begged God's forgiveness.

She helped the other women clear away the plates and dish out the plum pudding in honour of Sophie's return. Sophie ate hungrily. She was glad that her friend would soon recover her flesh and be merry once more.

Simon had taken the seat beside Sophie. He gazed at her adoringly. Then he took Sophie's hand in his and bestowed a kiss upon it. Eleanor, who, despite her best efforts, had not missed this gesture, experienced an agonising stab of jealousy. On the pretext of getting ready for the performance, she took leave of the company and hurried upstairs with the baby.

In the privacy of her chamber she shed yet more tears. She had no right to be jealous. She had no claim on Simon. She was merely a foolish woman who should have known better than to stray from her marriage vow. Worse, she had betrayed her love for Hugh. Although she spoke sternly to herself, it did no good, for her tears still came steadily.

She stepped carefully into the velvet gown she had worn the night before. It would do nicely to complement the romance on the stage that night, which was of a gallant knight rescuing a damsel in distress. No one, it seemed, would rescue her. She was reliant on her own wits and the generosity of friends.

There was a gentle knock and Sophie poked her head round the door. 'I hardly recognise you. You are quite the lady. Born to it, I'd have said.'

She smiled but experienced a pang of guilt that she was not being honest with her friend.

'Let me help you with your hair,' said Sophie. 'Why, it has grown lush with all the good food you've eaten here.'

'I must thank you so much for helping us.' Words were inadequate to express the gratitude she felt towards her friend.

'Not at all,' said Sophie. 'I am glad you have been such a success. It is excellent for Ancel that your singing has drawn in such a crowd. His coffers are quite overflowing with coins, and he is full of thanks to me for recommending you! Now let's have a look at your hair.' She stood back and admired her hand-iwork. 'You look beautiful!'

Eleanor painted her face, copying the techniques she had watched her ladies-in-waiting use back at the castle.

Sophie stood beside her, riveted. 'Anybody would think you were quite the expert. Would you work your wonders on my ugly mug?'

'You have a beautiful face!' protested Eleanor. She restored some colour to Sophie's washed-out cheeks with some rouge.

Presently, Katherine arrived to watch Baby Mary, armed with her spindle and some saffron thread. Eleanor and Sophie went downstairs and joined the players rehearsing in the kitchen.

'They are a talented troupe, aren't they?' Sophie whispered so as not to distract them from their lines. 'My sweetheart Simon is the best of all, isn't he?'

Eleanor could only nod.

As she waited to perform, the familiar dread crept up her spine. Her heart ached horribly. She felt terror at the prospect of the exposure on stage when she was feeling so raw.

'Don't worry. You are a wonderful singer!' Sophie squeezed her hand.

Her friend's kindness induced fresh pangs of guilt that only intensified the fear growing in her gut. She looked out into the main tavern beyond the curtained archway where the audience slurped down their stew. Belching loudly and wiping their mouths on their sleeves, they slugged down great draughts of ale or wine. She had no wish to face them.

The players took up their positions on the stage. Simon played the hero of the piece, the gallant knight, to Leonard's damsel in distress. A murmur of amusement rippled around the room. But she was so anxious that her head swam and she did not catch a word of the dialogue.

The first half of the performance was over in the blink of an eye. She found herself pushed through the throng towards the stage. Greedy hands reached out to her as she passed. She shrank from their grasp. These people did not know her – they could not imagine how unworthy she was.

Finally, she stood face to face with her audience. Desperately, she prayed to God to intercede and help her to not disappoint the eager folk who had come to hear her sing. She felt like an empty vessel. Her mind was horribly blank as the lute player plucked the first notes of the song. As she opened her mouth, she felt cold despair, not knowing how to start.

Yet again, God did not fail her. Miraculously, sweet notes fell from her tongue. She had only to open her mouth and music flooded out like a cascade of water melting from mountain snow in spring. The audience were on their feet again when she had finished her first song and applauded with all their might. That they loved her was clear. She could not disappoint those who waited for her song.

She began to sing. The second song released her from the dread that had held her in its icy grip. Free as a bird she soared across the heavens. God had chosen her to sing, to bring the people joy, and she had only to sing from her heart. Opening her heart, she sang of her own longing, her disappointment, and the glory of omnipotent God.

Many in the audience wept. Indeed, she tasted the salty tears that trickled down her cheeks. Ordinarily, such a public display of her emotion would have shamed her, but now she found she did not care. As she came to the last stanza of the song, the audience was in tumult, and cheered, stamped and clamoured for more, but Ancel and his ostlers emerged from the wings and escorted Eleanor back to the privacy of the kitchen.

Sophie stood in the doorway of the kitchen with tears in her eyes. 'How beautifully you sing, Matilda!'

Overwrought with emotion, Eleanor retired to bed on the pretext of feeding the baby. She had made it through the performance, and for that she was grateful. The baby was fast asleep and Katherine had dozed off, too, her head bent over her spinning. She roused the old woman with a gentle shake, and she awoke and yawned and took herself off to sleep in her chamber.

Eleanor flopped down beside the sleeping baby. A torrent of tears came unimpeded; she had nothing left to be strong for. Wracked with pangs of heart-breaking sorrow, she sobbed into her pillow. If only Hugh were here to hold her, to take care of her and make everything better. Distraught and weary as she was, she did not sleep for hours. She heard the church bell strike the hours of one, two and three, before she passed out with exhaustion on her tear-drenched pillow.

Shortly before the church bell chimed six, Mary squealed and demanded milk. Eleanor woke, with a groggy awareness of feeling frozen. Her throat was raw. While the baby was suckling, Eleanor grew by turns sweaty and hot and then shivered with cold.

When she did not appear in the kitchen for breakfast, Katherine brought up a plate of eggs and bacon on a tray.

'Matilda, are you ill?'

Eleanor could only moan feverishly. Her throat was on fire.

For the next couple of days, the world became a haze of confusing red shadows. A host of ghostly figures congregated round her bed and clamoured for her attention. She shrank from them and begged them to leave her in peace. Occasionally, she had some respite from the redness and became aware of a white light that blinded. In these moments Sophie was at her bedside and caressed her cheek and mopped her brow with a cold kerchief. Eleanor implored her friend to protect her from the demons that tried to tempt her and drag her into the hell-mouth. But the redness returned and Sophie vanished. And she was subsumed by a terrible heat. She had a glimpse of Rolf's face, twisted in an expression of perverse depravity, his eyes as red as a demon's. Then awful screams filled the room and she shook with fright. Presently, she discerned the screams were her own and were mixed with the desperate cries of a hungry baby. And then she was aware of an insatiable, clammy creature that suckled at her breast.

24.

The Mermayd

Hugh arrived in Dover late on Wednesday afternoon. It was market day and the streets heaved with people. He pushed through the crowd until, at long last, he found himself at the steps of the great church of St Mary. Beneath the watchful eyes of the grotesque gargoyles maintaining a vigil over the doorway, he removed his helm and stepped across the threshold into the gloom of the church within. Tiny flickering lamps lit the interior of the building and threw dancing shadows on the frescoed walls and columns. The church was awash with pilgrims, come from all corners of the kingdom, who knelt before the altar in submission to their God. Limping cripples and the sick were among them, their bodies shaking with hacking coughs, come for a miracle from the Lord. He gave them a wide berth. Monks, nuns and ancren chanted their prayers, their heads bent in supplication. He knelt before the suffering Christ at the altar. He gave thanks for God's protection and his grace and begged for guidance in his quest for revenge.

At last, he rose to his feet and moved from tomb to tomb, struggling to decipher the engravings on the slabs in the scant candlelight. His breathing was laboured and his heart heavy in his chest. With an excruciating stab of pain, he read Eleanor's name on a slab of grey marble. The thought that just below the slab, deep in the earth, lay his beloved's body choked him with a tide of grief that caught him by the throat. Eleanor was really gone and here was her final resting place. Head bowed, he wept freely and sank down onto his knees on the flagstone floor. He grieved for what he had lost and begged Eleanor's forgiveness.

The church bells tolled the hour of six and he scrambled to his feet. With one last genuflection, he said his final goodbyes to Eleanor. The time was ripe, and he was finally ready to wreak his revenge. Having put his grief aside, a thrill of anticipation surged within him at the prospect of the meeting. Finally, he was ready to avenge his loved ones and to defend his people. Never had he felt such a gratifying sense of purpose, not even when he had trained to be a knight.

The Mermayd was empty save for the landlord, a short stocky man with a bald head, and a prominent hooked nose. He looked up from the jug he was cleaning and eyed Hugh shrewdly.

'I was told to ask for Sir Roger,' said Hugh.

'He does drink here of an occasion. Who shall I say is asking for him?'

'My name is Sir Hugh de Eynsford, but he might also know me as Hugh nephew of Sir Mordaunt.'

'Very good, m'lord. I'll see to it immediately. Perhaps a drink while you are waiting?'

'A cup of wine.' Tantalising smells wafted into the bar from the kitchen. 'And a bowl of stew if it's ready, thank you.'

'Certainly, sir.' The landlord poured him a goblet of wine. He ladled out a bowl of stew, put it in front of Hugh and then disappeared into the back room.

Hugh bolted down his stew.

Presently, the man returned. 'If you'll follow me, they are all upstairs in council.'

Hugh followed up two flights of creaky wooden stairs to an attic. As he crossed the threshold, he experienced a pang of fear. Perhaps he had put too much trust in the bishop. What if the man had sent him into a trap? But when he entered the room, stooping under the low rafters, he recognised at least six knights who had fought for his father among the motley-looking group of men sat around the oval table. Their faces had a hard, hungry look.

Sir Roger, he recognised at once. The knight had aged a great deal in the months since he had last seen him and carried an ugly gash across his cheek. There was a clang of steel and the squeak of leather as the men rose to their feet to welcome him.

'You've returned a man.' Sir Roger slapped Hugh on the shoulder. 'Wet your whiskers in battle too, I've heard.'

Hugh was relieved to detect no trace of the mocking tone Sir Roger had once used to address him.

'He fought alongside Richard the Lionheart no less!'

The other men shot him looks of admiration.

'I'll do the introductions, shall I?' said Sir Roger. He set his goblet down on the table.

'This handsome fool is Osbert Le Maliale, the bastard son of Sir Mordaunt.' He pointed at an ugly knight with a mouth packed with buck teeth. 'He's a good fighter, mind – takes after his father.'

Osbert favoured Hugh with a broad toothy smile and proffered him a beefy red hand to shake. The poor wretch bore no resemblance to Sir Mordaunt save for a shock of unruly blond hair. He was nothing like Guy either. Who would have supposed that both men shared a father?

'You may remember my son Robert.' Sir Roger gestured to a strapping lad who was now as tall as his father. The resemblance was uncanny. Robert had the same shaggy head of brown curls and fierce black eyes. They even had the same hooked nose. 'Mark you, he's a knight now.' Sir Roger regarded his son with pride. 'Dubbed him myself three weeks gone. He more than proved his prowess with the sword when Rolf's men attacked.'

At the sound of the name the atmosphere in the room became strained.

'That blackguard!' Robert's eyes were full of venom.

'These four knights are all that remains of Sir Mordaunt's household.' Sir Roger pointed to four men who looked to be in their twenties. They were kitted out in chain mail but were without insignia on their surcoats. Long swords hung from their belts.

Sir Roger moved along the table. 'This is Geoffrey Le Blunt and his son John.' He gestured at two swarthy men who both sported a tangled mass of black hair.

'They were both on an errand in London when Rolf's men attacked their manor and stole all their worldly goods. Geoffrey's wife and daughter were raped and murdered.'

'I am bent on revenge, Sir Hugh.' Le Blunt's voice was gruff and rasping. 'I will see that Rolf pays for what he has done. Even if it kills me.'

At that, the men beat a rhythmic tattoo on the tables with their mugs of ale. Before the noise had fully died away, Sir Roger gestured to a vacant stool and poured a mug for Hugh from a large pitcher.

There was a desperate, ruthless look about the men around the table. They resembled outlaws more than knights.

'Rolf is vulnerable when he leaves Dover Castle.' Sir Roger paused to belch and wipe his mouth on his sleeve. 'Inside its walls we have no hope of touching him. We have no siege towers, trebuchets or battering rams. He outnumbers us twentyfold, so our best weapon is surprise. We'll have no hope of winning the castle with a mere thirty-five men, but we may yet get the upper hand in a raid.'

'He'll be surrounded by his guard.' Osbert swilled his wine around in his goblet. 'It will be difficult.'

'That it will,' said Sir Roger. 'But I do not fear the challenge.'

'We can hurt him by destroying his crops and burning the town.' Le Blunt speared an apple with the point of his dagger.

'What of the women?' said Osbert. 'I'll not imperil my father's wife or my half-sister.'

'The bishop has already whisked them away,' said Sir Roger. 'He sent word this morning that they were leaving Dover.'

Hugh breathed a sigh of relief. At least his errand had been fulfilled and his aunt and cousin were safe. Now he could concentrate on wreaking his revenge.

25.

The Corpus Christi Pageant

Two weeks later, Eleanor's fever finally left her. The worlds of flame and light receded, to be replaced with the everyday surroundings of her room. Her throat still felt raw and she could only croak hoarsely. Sophie and Katherine continued to bring her food and drink and take care of Mary, as they had done throughout her illness. At first, she had little appetite and could stomach nothing more than a few spoonsful of broth but, bit by bit, her appetite returned and her strength with it. Her voice, though, remained stubbornly elusive and she counted her blessings that she would not be prevailed upon to sing in the pageant.

She watched as Sophie put fresh clothes on the baby. Her friend's face was forlorn as she worked. In a rush of sadness, it dawned upon her how much Sophie must miss her own baby, whom she had carried for nine months only to give away. It struck her how kind it was of her friend to help with Baby Mary when it must remind her of such agonies.

'You are too good to me and Mary,' Eleanor rasped, barely managing a whisper.

'Hush now. You must rest so that your voice is restored, my dear.' Sophie gave her a weary smile.

Try as she might, Eleanor could not shake off painful feelings of guilt about what she had done. As the days passed, her longing for Simon began to diminish yet she still felt rotten about how she had betrayed her friend. She was also sick with worry that her foolish actions might have led to her becoming pregnant, rendering Baby Mary's and her own situation yet more precarious. Her monthly blood had not yet returned after having her baby, and so she had no idea whether she was with child. She could not stop weeping at the thought and was obliged to hide her tears from Katherine and Sophie. If only she had someone to confide in.

When Katherine came in with her breakfast, she sat up in bed and asked if she could help with the preparations.

'How wonderful that you are feeling better.' Katherine beamed. 'There is plenty to be done. Sophie has no gift for embroidery, so it has all fallen upon my shoulders. I shall be glad of the help. I'll bring in my work and we can get started.'

The Song and the Sword

Katherine returned with a heap of costumes in her arms and a box of thread, ribbon and lace. 'There are roses to be embroidered for the bodices of these dresses.' She passed her some thread and a needle.

It was wonderful to be doing something useful. She was fed up of languishing in bed, but she still felt too weak and dizzy to get up. Embroidery with Katherine was so much more pleasant than it had been with the ladies at Dover Castle.

'Mark you,' said Katherine through a mouthful of pins. 'It will be a fabulous pageant this year. We've been putting on a performance ever since I can remember. Corpus Christi has always been my favourite. The pageants are a celebration for people to look forward to.'

Eleanor understood the common people's excitement for pageants and feast days. Without these celebrations, life would be nothing but hard work.

'There was, of course, the tourney last year.' Katherine had a wistful look in her eye. 'What a splendid joust and mêlée! We put on a play for that too. The crowd loved it, particularly Leonard and Simon's act – they did their usual farce. There's nothing like a tourney for colour . . . all those splendid banners and brightly coloured tents. The knights looked so dashing . . . their chain mail flashing in the sun. All the ladies looked so beautiful sat up on the canopied platform in their red velvet gowns and hoods, particularly Rolf's new bride. Dressed in such finery she was. As pretty as a picture. But such a sad girl all the same. Well, I suppose she was forced to marry that brute. Such a shame that she died.'

Eleanor felt her colour rise and was stricken for a moment.

'Silly me, wittering on when you are not well.' Katherine studied Eleanor's face. 'Would you like a cup of wine or ale?'

'No, no,' said Eleanor hurriedly. 'It gives me pleasure to hear you talking. You are a remarkable seamstress. Your needlework is so intricate. Where did you learn such skill?'

Katherine beamed a toothless grin. 'When I was young, I worked in the royal household as an assistant to the seamstress. They let me take those gowns you wear in the performances as a parting gift.'

Eleanor had wondered how the tavern had come into the possession of such fine gowns.

'You embroider finely yourself – with the skill of a lady.' Katherine cut some cloth with a knife.

'You are too kind.' Eleanor hastily changed the subject. 'You must have made some wonderful gowns for the queen.'

'Indeed. Queen Eleanor was a beauty. We made her gowns of rare quality, inlayed with diamonds and studded with pearls!'

'They must have been quite something.' Nostalgia lurched in Eleanor's belly as she remembered the feel of her silk gowns and ermine cloak on her skin and the way her jewels used to glisten in the sun. 'Did you ever meet the queen?'

'Good gracious, no! The likes of me would never have been allowed to meet her. But all the servants who attended to her person said she was a gracious queen. I caught glimpses of her from afar, of course. I was anxious to admire my handiwork. It was a pleasure to make her gowns. She still kept her figure trim, even after all those children.'

'How did you come to leave the royal service?'

'Ancel begged me to come and look after the children when my daughter died in childbirth.' Katherine sighed, and pushed a tendril of hair back into her bun. 'I could never refuse him. He was always good to me and my daughter. Besides, I am happier with my kin than those highborn lords and ladies. Ancel has always treated me well.'

'I am sorry to hear about your daughter.' Eleanor nursed her baby who had woken and started to whimper.

'Yes, it was a cruel blow. She left so many children without a mother.' A shadow fell across the old woman's face and her eyes filled with tears. 'But 'tis the way of nature, the women who survive childbirth are lucky. Infants who survive childhood illness are lucky too. I am glad to say that most of my grand-children grew into adulthood. My granddaughters are settled and have families of their own now. My grand-sons are fine strapping lads. Now, if you don't mind sewing this ribbon along the seam of this dress, I'll go and see to our lunch.'

Katherine returned at noon with a bowl of pottage

and two slices of bread fresh from the oven upon a tray.

'Eat up my dear and get your strength back.' She put the tray on Eleanor's lap. 'You gave us a scare with that fever, my love. This afternoon perhaps you'd like to make a sling for baby. God willing, you will be well enough to come to the pageant tomorrow and see the splendour for yourself. She'll be more than happy wrapped in cloth and tied to your body. My granddaughter always carries her little one in a sling.'

'Thank you, I will, if you can spare the fabric?'

'Think nothing of it. I am just glad that you are feeling better.'

~

The following day, Eleanor hoisted herself out of bed. Her muscles were weak after languishing in bed for so many weeks. The headiness of the influenza still weighed upon her, but she was determined to pull her weight and help with the preparations. To her delight, she found a smear of blood on her small clothes and heaved a sigh of silent relief. She was not pregnant after all.

She breakfasted on bread and cheese and then nursed Mary. After she had dressed in her humble woollen kirtle, she went to the window and surveyed the busy courtyard below. It was a hive of frenetic activity. The Wine Merchants' guild had stationed their wheeled stage, upon which the players were to perform, in front of the tavern. She took the baby outside to steal a peek before the performance. The stage comprised a painted screen in two halves. The left side represented the cloudy celestial Realm of God and depicted the Golden Gates through which the saved souls must pass to join the angels and archangels in Heaven. The right side represented the Mouth of Hell, surrounded by a host of demons and devils; an opening led into a pitchy cavern from which issued ribbons of yellow and orange fabric to create the appearance of fire and through which the Damned would pass.

In the kitchen, the members of the troupe were in their costumes and practising their lines. On one side of the room stood God, dressed in white leather hose and coat that reached the floor. He had washed and combed his hair and had added chalk to his beard to make it white. Surrounding him were the angels, the musicians who wore diadems, their skin painted gold and sporting white feather wings. The Souls of the Saved stood beside them dressed entirely in white and with garlands of summer flowers around their necks.

On the other side of the kitchen, Simon made the final adjustments to his devil's mask. It was painted with a very wide mouth, bright red staring eyes, a large nose and a red beard. His wooden clogs were carved skilfully into cloven feet, and from his rear end hung a forked tail. Goat hair covered his cloak and hose. She shivered. He looked every bit the fiend.

In his left hand, he brandished a trident with three curved points.

Beside him stood the lesser devils, their faces blackened with soot and their eyelids and lips stained blood-red. Dressed from head to toe in black buckram, they held drums and horns. The Damned were also dressed in black, their faces and hair blackened by coal dust.

'Matilda!' said Ancel. 'I'm so glad that you are well enough to enjoy the pageant. Katherine has told me how much you helped with the costumes. Don't the devils look splendid?'

'I wish I could have done more.' Eleanor spoke in a croaky whisper.

'Oh, dear me, no,' said Ancel. 'Rest your voice, if you please.'

'I hope you are feeling better.' Simon's voice came from behind his devil's mask.

Eleanor froze. For days she had worried she might go to pieces if she was obliged to speak to him, but she replied without thinking. 'Much better, thank you.'

'How wonderful to see you up and about!' Sophie took her arm. 'We'll have such a wonderful day together at the pageant, you'll see.'

Presently, the Worshipful Company of Wine Merchants arrived en masse. The servant girls scurried in and out of the kitchen laden with great jugs of ale ahead of the pageant. Katherine and Sophie passed round a platter of sweetmeats.

Eleanor took a bite of a sweetmeat. It was delicious.

The Song and the Sword

After much deliberation, the freemen of the guild tethered the horses to the stage. The Heavenly Host, the Saved, and the devils and the Damned clambered on board. The stage rolled slowly into motion and bumped and lurched over potholes in the street. Everyone else followed on foot.

Eleanor carried the baby in a sling made from a large piece of buckram and walked beside Sophie. She had wrapped herself in a long, hooded woollen cloak that she gathered about her both to keep out the cold and to help herself blend in with the other women in the crowd. She wanted to be as inconspicuous as possible.

The whole world was out that bright crisp morning of Corpus Christi. The bells in all the churches rang out in celebration of the festivities. Designated an obligatory holiday for all, everyone had to attend the pageant. They made slow progress through the narrow, winding streets. There was such a press of the crowd that she grew quite fearful of Baby Mary being crushed. People greeted each other enthusiastically and hollered at their friends from one side of the street to the other. Still weary and fragile after her illness, she was overwhelmed by all the noise. They processed towards the main square, where the town officials had erected scaffolding that created a canopied platform to accommodate Baron Rolf and his entourage.

The crowd jostled for the best position from which to see the spectacle. Four of the leading guilds of the town, the Fishmongers, the Mercers, the Grocers, and the Wine Merchants, had prepared pageant stages and each depicted a religious play.

The freemen of the town were in attendance; the insignia on their robes marked out their various trades and distinguished them from their apprentices and the peasants who had arrived in droves from the countryside.

When at last the square was bursting with people, a fanfare of trumpets heralded the arrival of the baron. Her heart took a leap of fear as she saw Rolf in a golden cloak, high up on his mount. A maiden dressed as the legendary Queen Guinevere led the baron's horse and a host of lords and ladies of the court accompanied him. The ladies looked splendid, dressed in red velvet tunics with white hoods; every lady led a lord by his horse's bridle. The lords, in their heraldic surcoats, sat upon elaborate saddles decorated with silk tassels, colourful fringes and the crests of their respective houses. They bore polished spears, swords and axes. Helmeted soldiers bearing arms flanked the procession of noblemen and women on each side. Evidently Rolf was taking no chances; civil unrest frequently reared its ugly head on such occasions.

At last, the baron and the rest of the nobility took their seats. She scanned the faces in the crowd and looked for people she knew. Her stomach somersaulted at the sight of Beatrice. In an attitude of superiority, her mother-in-law's lips were pursed. Cecily occupied the seat beside her and looked as beautiful as ever. It was odd to think that Eleanor's rightful place was in their midst, high on their platform, sitting in comfort. Instead, she stood on the edge of the heaving crowd among the lowest orders of the town. She knew where she would rather be: anonymous, and at her friend Sophie's side.

She stole a glance at Sophie – dear Sophie, who was so good and brave. She never wished to be parted from her and was thankful her mistake did not mean their friendship was all over. Much as she struggled with being untruthful to her friend, she knew that the truth would only bring Sophie pain.

Trumpeters heralded the start of the pageant. The first stage, depicting *The Miracle of the Fishes and the Feeding of the Five Thousand*, rolled into a prominent position. The crowd craned their necks for a view of the play. Young children were borne aloft on their fathers' shoulders to better enjoy the spectacle. A choir that she could not see began to sing the Psalm of Souls and everyone joined in. To sing along with the crowd, rasping though her voice still was, brought a shiver of excitement to her spine. A tinderbox of anticipation hung in the air.

When the first play had finished, the second stage rolled into view. It featured a company of actors dressed in gaudy oranges and yellows. A huge flabby man played Pontius Pilate. He was surrounded by the Pharisees and Judas – with his usual shock of red hair. The actors had to bellow so their voices would carry across the square. The audience booed and hissed at the performers. Few people here were used to attending any kind of entertainment. They were too poor to have a life beyond toil.

The Grocers wheeled a third stage into position that depicted *The Last Supper*, with a long table at which sat Jesus and all his disciples – including another carrot-headed Judas. With garlands of white lilies round his neck, Jesus knelt and washed each of their feet in turn.

Finally, the Wine Merchants' stage trundled into position for the final play of the day: *The Last Judgement*. The souls queued up before God and the Devil for judgement. The rippling notes of a harp and a lute welcomed the Saved through Heaven's gates and the angels offered them delicious sweetmeats. The Mouth of Hell was a different story. The Devil made a deafening din clanging together a pair of brass cymbals. The audience gasped as real flames and smoke issued from the pitch-black cavern. Her heartbeat quickened momentarily, but a glance at Sophie's face reassured her it was all part of the performance. The devils moved in and out of the Mouth of Hell and shouted 'Ho, ho!' and cackled wickedly, to the delight of the crowd who booed them vehemently. The Devil claimed the Souls of the Damned and he dragged them into the Mouth of Hell by their hair.

All at once, she perceived a change in the atmosphere, after which everything happened very fast. A little shiver went through the crowd like a wind through the leaves of a tree. Hooded figures sprang up from among the crowd. Like the Damned in the pageant, their faces were blackened and unrecognisable. From their mouths issued a series of blood-curdling battle shrieks. They brandished daggers, swords and axes. To her horror, the wicked fiends set about stabbing men, women and children indiscriminately, apparently motivated by the sheer joy of destruction. They cut people down and sliced them up with their swords even as they attempted to flee.

She looked up to the canopied platform, where there were even hooded figures among the lords and ladies. By some ruse, the attackers had infiltrated the ranks of the nobles. The ladies screamed in alarm and attempted to flee. The men who bore arms engaged the hooded figures in combat. The crash of steel on steel reverberated around the square.

Rolf's soldiers rushed to their lord's defence and cut down the attackers with their long swords. The soldiers' horses reared and screamed.

Terrible, ear-splitting shrieks resounded across the square. The crowd stampeded in all directions. They had no option but to move with the others to avoid being trampled underfoot. The throng took on a deadly, crushing identity of its own.

Cold fear overcame her. She had lost control over her own body. Instead, she moved with the momentum of the crowd around her, knowing that to miss her footing would mean certain death.

'Sophie!' she called out in dismay as a surge in the crowd sent her friend lurching away.

'Make for the tavern!' was the last thing she heard Sophie shout before her friend disappeared in a sea of faces.

It was increasingly difficult to stay upright. Many of the older people had fallen, too frail to stand their ground. She struggled to keep her footing as she stumbled over their bodies. She put her arms out in front of her, defending the helpless baby who was strapped to her breast. The crowd veered to the left and then to the right. She stumbled, but exerted all her effort to keep on her feet. She must not fall. The weight of hysterical people around her pressed in, a frenzied tangle of limbs. People pushed hard and struggled violently. The very air stank of desperate fear, of disaster. It was every man and woman for themselves, and her heart beat frantically. Weak after her illness, she would not be able to take much more of the crush. Never had she felt so tired. Panic rose in her throat like vomit. Gasping, she struggled to draw breath. Only the thought of her poor baby strapped to her breast made her soldier on and fight to survive.

Then, just when she thought they would surely be crushed to death, she and the people around her burst out of the square. They emerged in a side street, away from the hysterical bulk of the crowd.

Momentarily she experienced a wave of relief at being free of the horde. But then she realised she did not recognise a single person around her. Desperate for a glimpse of Sophie, she scanned the crowd, but her friend was nowhere to be seen.

Just then she noticed that flames and smoke issued from the surrounding buildings. In horror, she realised the raiders were going from building to building, torching the entire town. With all her heart, she wanted to wait and find Sophie, but a mass of people rushed from the square and threatened to engulf them in the crowd once more. She set off at a run through the smoke to avoid the horde of screaming people and shielded her baby as best she could from the flying sparks that rained down on them from the burning buildings.

The hooded men appeared to be everywhere. Great hulks of men, they smashed, looted, and stabbed their way through the town. Galvanised into defending their town, armed freemen engaged in hand-to-hand combat with the attackers. They hacked and swung at the foe with lances, swords, daggers and whatever they could lay their hands on. There was a terrible confusion of steel and blood.

Eleanor darted this way and that through the twisted alleyways. By some miracle, she managed to elude the attackers and avoid the collapsing timbers of the burning houses that crashed down all around her. Eventually she found herself in front of the tavern. Her heart froze. The buildings on either side burned fiercely. She estimated she barely had minutes to recover her worldly goods before the tavern caught alight and the rafters and thatch became a mass of flame.

Hitching up her skirts, she hurried up the staircase.

Any delay could mean asphyxiation for her and her child. She rushed into her chamber and grabbed her coin purse. When she dashed back, the foot of the staircase had caught alight. There was no other way out. Precious seconds passed and she choked and gasped for breath, dizzy with smoke. This had been a stupid, stupid mistake for which they would pay with their lives. She should have escaped while she had the chance. Clammy horror crept over her at the realisation they would both die for the sake of a handful of coins. With no way out, her shoulders fell as she resigned to her fate. All her struggles had been in vain, for here it would end. And their fate was to burn alive!

The resourceful part of her rose up with her remaining strength and refused to surrender. She simply had to find a way of getting down. It was a matter of thinking fast, but her mind was sluggish and swam with the smoke. There was still a chance they could make it out alive and she had to take it. The stinging smoke blinded her, but she took a desperate leap down the burning staircase, doing her best to shield the infant strapped to her breast from the flames. The heat was intolerable, the smoke caught in her throat and she couldn't breathe. They were going to die! Down the steps she charged, slipping and bumping along the burning wooden stairs to the ground. At the bottom she landed with a thump and lay stunned for a moment, gasping for breath. She let out a shrill shriek as she realised her clothes were on fire and she rolled on the ground and put out the flames that licked the bottom of her gown. Thank God her baby was unharmed!

When she turned back to the tavern, she saw with a thumping heart they had got out just in time because now the thatched roof was on fire. A light sea breeze served to stoke the flames. She watched in despair as her livelihood and home went up in smoke.

Bent double, she paused, catching her breath. Her heart pounded. The pressing question now was how would they escape with their lives? She had no intention of allowing herself to be stabbed or raped, or indeed burned alive. Alone, with no one to turn to, she had to fend for herself and her child. The smoke threated to overwhelm her and she had to come up with a plan soon. She glanced down at the baby in the sling. Mary was alert, as though aware of the enormity of what was going on around them. And, thanks be to God, she was not even crying. Where might they find refuge? She could think of only one place: the priory. They would have to find a way out of the town. She knew of one gate, but the main square was impassable. They would have to escape via the harbour gate on the other side of the town – if only she could find it.

Thus, instead of running back towards the square, she took the streets in the opposite direction and found herself in an unfamiliar part of town. From the look of the warehouses, she supposed it must be the merchants' quarter – only, now, the great warehouses

were alive with flames. The ground shook with terrifying explosions as barrels of pitch and oil caught
alight. The heat was incredible, and it scorched her
face and singed her hair. Every breath burned her
lungs. But still she pressed on, through the mass of
people running for their lives.

The flames appeared to reach at least ten feet into
the sky. The fire was so hungry even the few buildings
the attackers had failed to torch had now caught alight.
The wooden buildings would be as dry as tinder, for
it had not rained for weeks. Thick grey smoke above
the town obscured the sky and sun, and Eleanor had
the impression of being in a huge furnace.

She ran blindly. Thick smoke made her eyes smart
and water and she could not open them more than a
slit. The smoke choked and burned her lungs and she
was continually brushing off the sparks that flew off
the burning buildings. Vainly, she followed the main
flow of people who seemed to be rushing in one
direction, as she had no idea where to go. She only
knew that the wrong decision could spell death for
her and her daughter.

At last she found herself on the quayside. Staying
close to the water, she looked for somewhere to hide
or for a gate out of the town. People sprinted past her
in all directions, fleeing for their lives. She was obliged
to step over the bodies of the unfortunate souls who
had either perished at the hands of the attackers or
been asphyxiated by the smoke.

Suddenly a great monster of a man blocked her

path. Blacked out like the devil, his face was a twisted mask of cruelty. An aura of horrible foulness hung about him. He licked his lips. His filthy tunic was splattered with blood. Wielding a crimson axe, he leered at her with an evil grin. Her blood ran cold and an icy shiver crept down her spine. She tried to sidle past him on the left. But he put out an arm as big as a tree trunk and refused to let her. He meant to kill them. And she knew a sudden rush of panic. But he dropped the bloodstained axe and pushed her back onto the ground with a meaty hand. She stumbled backwards flat on her back. Still strapped to her breast, Mary howled. The man undid his braies. By the light of the flames, Eleanor saw that his manhood stood erect. She shuffled hastily backwards on her elbows. But she was cornered; there was a wall at her back. The man roared like a wild animal and clawed at her skirts. She kicked at him with all her might and aimed for his overhanging gut. But it was no good; he still bore down on her. She scrabbled around in the dust until her fingers closed around a wooden stick. She hit the man as hard as she could across the face, but still he was unstoppable. And she was so weak. He clouted her across the face with a mailed fist. She tasted blood in her mouth. It was like Rolf all over again. There was nothing she could do. He was going to force himself upon her. She sobbed and shrieked and her baby howled.

26.

Revenge

On the morning of the day of the pageant, Hugh, Sir Roger and his son entered the town of Dover in the guise of traders peddling wagons of vegetables. They hung woollen cloaks and hoods over their chain mail and swords. It was easy to mingle with the peasants entering the town to celebrate Corpus Christi. The watchmen at the gate didn't give them so much as a second glance and simply waved them through.

Hugh pushed through the heaving streets behind Sir Roger and his son and headed towards the main square. All around him, the sound of animated chatter and the babble of laughter hung in the air in antici-pation of the festivities. Even the cripples leaning on their crutches looked upon him with cheerful expressions. Pigeons fluttered above the crowd and strutted across the rooftops. An assortment of stray dogs skulked in doorways waiting for scraps. Though it was still morning, men drank deep from skins of wine and ale. A group of men ahead of them burst into a raucous and bawdy song.

But Hugh was in no mood for singing. He kept close to Sir Roger and his son Robert. He had no intention of losing sight of them in the crowd. His companions strode purposefully ahead, overtaking the aged who hobbled along with the aid of sticks and the gaggles of eager children who hung round their mothers' skirts. They wove in and out of the solemn processions of pilgrims, monks, nuns and sandaled friars dressed in the habits of their respective religious orders from far and wide. Many of the pilgrims were barefoot; some even sported spiky chains about their bloodied ankles while others held huge crosses aloft, adorned with an effigy of the weeping Son of God.

At length they fell into step behind a large wooden stage on wheels that bounced and pitched in the potholes on the street. The stage was so wide and the street so narrow there was no space to overtake it. A fat flabby man dressed in a Roman toga waved at the crowd from his throne on the stage. Beside him knelt a man with a shaggy head of ginger curls drawing jeers and catcalls from the crowd.

At last Hugh and his companions emerged into the crowded square. The June sun beamed down on them

345

benevolently as though it approved of their mission. Ahead, Sir Roger pushed through the jostling crowd to get a place near the front. He used his weight to carve out a path in the dense throng. There were a few indignant gasps and some pushed and shoved but, for the most part, people yielded to him and let him past. Hugh followed behind and apologised on Sir Roger's behalf where the knight had caused offence.

They found themselves at the front of the crowd where a line of Rolf's soldiers stood protecting the canopied platform where the lords and ladies sat. Hugh waited with bated breath. Finally, they were in position, on the cusp of their attack.

Up on the platform a stream of chattering lords and ladies took their seats. The last time Hugh had been here was the day of the tournament – the very day he had been too cowardly to rescue Eleanor. A sudden wrenching ache took him in his throat.

Rolf and his new wife arrived last of all, heralded by a fanfare of trumpets. Rolf's chain mail glistened in the sun. Hugh felt his stomach turn.

Would they be able to carry off their attack? The platform was protected by at least thirty men-at-arms and they themselves were just three. It was a daring plan and, even if they succeeded, they would be unlikely to escape with their lives. However, this was their chance; there would be no better oppor-tunity to get close enough to Rolf; his litter was too well protected when he travelled; his castle was impregnable. Behind them, a force of some forty men, mostly undisciplined lowborn and dispossessed peasants, mingled in the crowd ready to cause mayhem. They had not been short of volunteers. Notorious for his cruelty and greed, the baron was unpopular even among his vassals.

A second fanfare of trumpets kicked off the pageant. Hugh watched in fascination as the first stage rolled into position. It was the play of *The Miracle of the Fishes*. A choir beside the platform burst into song. Children on their fathers' shoulders watched spellbound. The audience cheered as the players threw small packages of sweetmeats to outstretched arms in the crowd. Like pigeons, people scrambled on the cobbles and grabbed at them. Little scuffles broke out among the crowd. Deftly, Hugh caught a package in his left hand. He unwrapped the cloth and sank his teeth into a small sweet square of honey cake.

With a clatter of hooves, a pair of carthorses heaved the second stage into position. It was the stage they had followed into the square. He recognised the huge flabby Pontius Pilate and the red-haired Judas. The players hollered at each other so that their voices would carry across the square. The audience loved it. They booed and hissed eagerly at the performers. The performers were not subtle as they bandied about knock-about humour with Roman soldiers riding on hobbyhorses. The performance ended with the crowd shouting down Pontius Pilate with cheers, laughter and applause.

A long refectory table occupied the third stage. Hugh recognised the blue-eyed and golden-haired Jesus and the inevitable redheaded Judas among the disciples. The play depicted the Last Supper. The Son of God knelt and washed each of the disciples' feet then fed them wafers and offered them sips of wine from his goblet.

The last of the performances was fittingly *The Last Judgement*. Hugh shot a look at Rolf. The baron held his body taut and his lip curled like a dog about to snarl. He had no idea what was coming to him.

On the stage, the souls queued up before God and the Devil for judgement. The soft ripple of a harp welcomed the Saved through Heaven's gates and the angels offered them delicious-looking sweetmeats.

Suddenly a deafening din of clashing brass cymbals roused Hugh from his reverie. The Devil dressed in black buckram with hideous red eyes and lips danced frenzied about the stage with cloven feet. Hugh let out a gasp of alarm, as did the people around him, as real flames and smoke issued from the cavern on the other side of the stage. He had never expected such ingenious effects. The devils moved in and out of the Mouth of Hell and shouted 'Ho, ho!' in monstrous voices. They cackled wickedly and cracked their whips across the stage. The crowd booed them, relishing every moment of the entertainment. The Devil claimed the Souls of the Damned and he dragged them into the Mouth of Hell by their hair.

This was their cue. At once, Sir Roger, Robert and

he bent down as if to secure the buckles of their boots and hastily smeared charcoal all over their faces. It had been Osbert's idea to blacken their faces for the attack in part to disguise their identities and in part to drive fear into the hearts of their enemies. Screaming war cries at the top of their lungs, they unsheathed their swords and charged at the line of soldiers in front of them.

Caught by surprise, the soldiers folded and crumpled under the thrusts of their swords. In the chaos and confusion, the three of them broke through the ranks.

Hugh had been tasked with cutting Rolf off from the protection of his men-at-arms. With one lithe leap, he vaulted onto the platform to the horror of the ladies whose high-pitched screams assaulted his ears. The thrilling thought that finally he was getting revenge upon the baron set his hair on end and made the blood course through his veins. He held his long sword in a two-handed grip ready to attack. He plunged the blade into the first guardsman who challenged him and twisted it in his gut so his entrails overspilled on the cobbles. He sliced off the arm of the second man who confronted him with a swish of his sword and splattered the man's blood over his surcoat. He buried his dagger deep into the fat belly of the third. He dived and ducked, dodging the swings of the other guards' swords.

Having eliminated opposition in his vicinity and won some breathing space, he sought out Sir Roger among the confused mass of lords and ladies bent on escape. Sir Roger had been tasked with assassinating Rolf while he sat sipping wine with his new young wife. He wanted to kill Rolf himself, but they had drawn lots and it had been Sir Roger who won that honour.

He caught sight of Sir Roger engaged in single combat with Rolf. Sir Roger's years of experience were pitted against the ruthless younger man who had yet to be defeated in any tourney. Their swords crossed and steel clanked against steel. To start with, it looked as though Sir Roger had the advantage. He bore down on Rolf with his superior weight. He cut and sliced with his sword, but Rolf succeeded in deflecting his blows.

To Hugh's dismay, the older man showed signs of tiring and slowed his attack. It was the younger Rolf, with greater reserves of energy who pressed his advantage now. Rolf brought Sir Roger crashing down onto the floor with a side slice at the knee joint. The older man howled in pain and thrust his sword into Rolf. But it did no more damage than glance across the baron's chain mail. On the ground, Sir Roger flailed around and sliced with his sword, but Rolf was as agile as a cat and dodged his blows easily. Then, with a bone shattering crash, Rolf brought his long sword down on Sir Roger's head and cleaved his skull in two. The old man's blood splattered over Rolf's shrieking wife who cowered behind a chair.

Hugh's heart missed a beat. Sir Roger was dead.

He cast around and saw Robert cut down as he ran towards his father. He lay twitching on the ground until a guardsman sliced off his head with a swish of his sword.

It was up to him to assassinate Rolf and he ran towards the baron. But all at once he perceived it was now the soldiers who had the upper hand. They had recovered their discipline and a wall of swords greeted him. The soldiers pushed him back and he had to leap off the platform into the stampeding crowd to escape their onslaught.

Chaos and horror awaited him in the crowd. The stage portraying the Final Judgement had been ripped to shreds by the mob. The Devil fled the scene and ran as fast as he could in his clumsy cloven feet fashioned from wooden clogs. It might have been an amusing sight, if it had not been for the ghastly situation. The lesser devils lashed a path through the crowd with their whips. The Damned followed suit. Fresh blood splattered God's white gown and beard. Pontius Pilate slipped on the blood-strewn cobbles in his sandals and toga. Crimson to the roots of his hair, he panted and sweated like a pig. The Pharisees ran for their lives, their curly black wigs askew. A mountain of a man with a blackened face and mailed fists pummelled Judas bloody.

The Fishmongers' wheeled stage had been knocked on its side. The barrels upon it had overturned and people scrambled in the gutter for free fish. Red-faced fishmongers bellowed at them to stop.

The world appeared to be falling into shards. Minutes before there had been joy and mirth in that square, but now it reeked of fear. He could taste it, bitter in his mouth. More terrible sights met his eyes. Men, women, children and livestock stampeded in all directions. They screamed and howled as they attempted to flee their attackers and find some way out of the square. They were as hysterical as trapped animals. The air rang with unearthly shrieks and the hollers of desperate people calling for their lost friends, relatives and children.

Men with blackened faces hacked down people in their path. They cut them to pieces, no matter whether they were the elderly, women or children. A creeping chill travelled down Hugh's spine. An ill-disciplined horde, the attackers were full of the joy of wanton destruction and bent on doing the devil's work. The square was a river of blood and studded with corpses. Men rutted like beasts over the crumpled forms of screaming women. It was the Mouth of Hell itself. As he approached, he saw cold fear in people's eyes when they caught sight of his blackened face.

Five or so soldiers followed him into the crowd and set about him with their long swords. He leapt onto a wheeled stage that stood abandoned and put his back against the gates of Heaven. He parried deftly, steel scraping against steel. He gave as good as he got, thrust for thrust. To start off with he appeared to be at an advantage. He poked the murderous point of his sword into the gaps in their mail. With a quick lunge, he severed a soldier's sword arm. He turned to a soldier at his right flank and dealt him a blow with the hilt of his sword that sent the man reeling onto his back. But new swordsmen came to relieve their brothers. Alone, Hugh was hard-pressed to keep them at bay. They surrounded him now and they were determined to bring him down. Worse, a crossbow bolt sailed past him and narrowly missed his face. Realising the futility of his position, Hugh took advantage of one unguarded flank and jumped down and sprinted off towards the mass of townspeople. He ran as fast as his legs would carry him to the sanctuary of the crowd.

But the crowd did not afford sanctuary; it brought new perils. Stricken people veered from this way to that, desperate to escape with their lives. People shied away from him and shrank at the sight of his blackened face. Women blanched and screamed in terror. Men bellowed with fury in his face. They probably thought he would butcher them alive and take their daughters and wives at knifepoint, like the brutes he and Sir Roger had let loose on their town.

He lamented their folly. How could they have thought that such an ill-disciplined group of men would behave with honour. His association with the marauders who murdered, raped, burned and looted their way through the town brought shame upon him. He had joined the conspirators to depose Rolf, not to terrorise the common people. He was a knight with honour, not a barbarian savage. But he remained a devil in the world's eyes until he found some water and washed the charcoal off his face.

Some people were not so frightened of him. A stout man with a big belly tried to stab him in the neck. His lips parted in a snarl. 'I'll spit you like a chicken.'

But Hugh was quicker. He seized the man's arm and twisted until he was forced to drop the knife. He struggled and kicked at Hugh with stumpy legs, but Hugh smote him across the face with a mailed fist and he yelped and spat out blood and some splintered teeth.

Out of nowhere, a man with crazed wide eyes and a face puckered with scar tissue charged towards him. Saliva foamed white around his mouth. Hugh pushed him back with a chain-mailed arm. The man fell back on the ground and lay there convulsing and twitching.

'For shame, to attack a cripple!' screamed a bedraggled-looking crone leaning on a cane. 'Never have I seen such villainy!'

'I meant him no harm!' cried Hugh. 'I don't want to hurt anyone!'

But the people around him crossed themselves and chanted prayers under their breath.

'Have mercy on us!' gasped a middle-aged woman who shrank back at his blackened face.

The sickening smell of blood and ripe unwashed bodies filled his nostrils. The square was awash with blood. He nearly slipped on the bloodied cobbles and thought he would be crushed for sure under the stampeding crowd but, somehow, he managed to stay on his feet.

Used to fighting knights and soldiers, he had no taste for fighting civilians. But still they either shrank from him or came at him from every direction. Men charged. The impact of their heavy bodies winded him. Even the women lashed out. Some scratched at his face with sharp talons. Others thundered their fists on his back in a volley of blows and screamed in his ear. A stooped, grizzled old man dealt Hugh an eye-watering blow on the head with a wooden staff that sent him reeling. 'You butcher!' the old man spat through a gap-toothed smile. 'Foul fiend! I'll beat you to a bloody pulp!'

Luckily Hugh's chain-mail hood offered him some protection, but his surcoat hung in shreds. The aged prodded and poked at him with sticks. Children pelted him with stones, apples and any other missiles they could lay their hands on. Even emaciated beggars put out their legs and tripped him. 'Fie, fie, fiend of darkness!' one of them screamed, his eyes brimming with malice.

Hugh flexed his sword and swung it around in wide sweeping circles. Covered in goose prickles, his hair stood on end. While he was not going to attack these people, he was not going to let them attack and kill him either. He had to make a show of his strength. Most people backed away after that, not willing to lose an arm or their lives in a fruitless attack. But just when he thought he had escaped the worst, he felt a sharp pain in his foot and looked down at a knife imbedded in his boot. A ragged barefoot urchin shot

355

him a passing look of malicious glee and disappeared into the crowd. With an agonising stab of pain, he pulled the bloody knife out of his foot and limped off.

Try as he might, he could not get out of the square. He was trapped. There was a bottleneck of people trying to escape the chaos at its every exit. When at liberty to do so, he rubbed at his face frantically with his surcoat, desperate to get rid of the black. Sooner or later, he would die for sure out here in this hostile throng. The people around him glared and pure hatred pulsed in their eyes. If they succeeded in getting him to the ground, they would trample the breath from his body. No one seemed to perceive that he was not on the attack and was just fending off their aggression. He couldn't blame them; it was he who had unleashed this horror upon them. Sir Roger and Robert were dead, but he found that he felt nothing. What of Osbert and Geoffrey Le Blunt and his son? He sincerely hoped they were not on the rampage through the town murdering and looting. The plan had been to assassinate Rolf and burn his crops, nothing more.

It was then that he noticed columns of black smoke rising from burning buildings around the square. The town was an inferno. He had been so busy avoiding blows he had not even realised that smoke now stung his eyes and hurt his lungs. What hell had they unleashed on the citizens of this town! He would forever rue the day he had joined with the conspirators. His insides squirmed as he thought that at this very moment Rolf was probably hurrying back to shelter behind the curtain walls of his castle while the townspeople faced the full onslaught of the attack.

A shower of molten sparks billowed onto the crowd. There were screams of horror as people brushed frantically at the cinders on their hair and clothes. Some cried out in pain as their skin burned red raw. Panic spread like wildfire and they ran for their lives.

The glorious June day had turned as grey as his heart. The choking smoke that rose from the burning buildings obscured the sun and blue sky. A moment of claustrophobia had him by the throat. Was this how it was going to end? Would his fate be to be burned alive or trampled by an angry mob?

Finally, he burst out of the square entangled in a horde of agitated people who scattered in different directions. The streets beyond the square were wedged solid with people too. He was desperate to find water and wash the charcoal off his face. It felt shameful, abhorrent to be marked out as a raider. He wanted to rid himself of the stain from his face and soul.

Flames issued from the buildings around him. The air was thick with stinging smoke. It was hard to make anything out through the interminable grey, and he stumbled on the dead who lay twisted in the street. The cobbles were a slippery mess as though someone had sluiced them with blood.

Desperate to escape the crowds, he limped off the main streets and into an unsavoury alleyway lined with sprawling hovels. His foot pained him. For as far as the eye could see, the reed-thatched roofs were a mass of flame. If only he could find some water, he might rest easy. Try as he might, every bucket and pail he came across lay empty and discarded. The townspeople seemed to have abandoned any attempts to douse the flames. His stomach sank.

Eventually he came across an abandoned cloister of a religious house. In its cobbled courtyard, he found a shallow well and a wooden bucket. He pulled the bucket up and splashed his face with water and washed the dirt off. With fingers and nails, he scrubbed at his skin, trying to remove all trace of the charcoal until his face was red raw. Determined to rid himself of the evil mask, he wanted the vile stain of association with those fiends cleansed from his heart and soul. When he had finished, he leaned breathless against a stone wall. Water dripped from his face onto his clothes. Finally, he took a long refreshing draught of water.

The air grew dense with acrid smoke and his every breath seared his lungs. All the buildings around him burned fiercely. The crackling and popping of the flames was punctuated by the occasional crash of timber or masonry and the bangs of far-off explosions.

Sparks rained down on him. He had to stay alert and staunch the hungry little fires that kept erupting on his clothing and in his hair. All he could smell was the pervasive bitter smoke. He retched at the odour of singed clothing and hair. He simply could not stay here. It was only a matter of time before burning timber or masonry came tumbling down upon his head and killed him. That was if the choking smoke did not finish him off first.

As fast as he could, he limped towards the harbour, his sleeve over his mouth and nose, attempting to keep out the fire's toxic fumes. As they had in the square, people sprinted off in all directions, hysterical with fear. Fortunately, this time people did not turn against him.

Presently, Hugh found himself in the mercantile centre of the town where flames already ravaged the vast warehouses. He jumped in alarm at a loud explosion as the combustible goods inside the warehouses caught fire.

He thought he could taste the faint salty tang of the sea upon his lips, but he could not be sure. The thick smoke had drowned everything in choking grey. If he could at least get to the harbour, he might find a light, refreshing breeze from the sea.

At last, he made it to the quayside. Eyes streaming, his heart pounded in his chest. He struggled for breath. Bent double, he leaned against a wall and coughed his heart out and gasped. Then he retched again and vomited. Afterwards he felt a little better. The air smelled fishy, but at least he had some breathing space.

Exhausted, he sank down onto a shallow step beside the quay and leaned his back against a crumbling stone wall. A sea breeze blew gently on his sore face. The tide was coming in. To his left, blurred forms moved in the distance. Ear-splitting shrieks carried on the wind from the town behind him, but he paid them no heed. He hung his head in disbelief.

What on earth had happened? He had difficulty believing what he had just witnessed with his own eyes. It was unreal, like a deeply disturbing dream. How had their plans miscarried so irrevocably? He seethed to think how close he had got to Rolf and yet still he had failed to kill him. He hammered at the wall behind him with his clenched fist until it hurt. And to think of all the men Sir Roger and Geoffrey Le Blunt had rounded up: knaves and blackguards every one of them. They were butchers and assassins. The atrocities they had committed were unspeakable and unforgivable. They had no equal in their villainy. His blood boiled at the memory of the carnage they had wrought, and he gnashed his teeth.

But what now? He looked down at his blood-smeared surcoat. Black with smoke, it had been ripped to shreds. Bespattered in gore, his cloak hung in tatters. The scratches on his face stung where those awful women had gored him with their nails. His stabbed foot throbbed horribly. It was a ragged wound that needed cleansing. If only he had some wine to pour on it. He put a trembling hand through his hair and found that chunks were missing. Deep in shock, he felt shaky and sick. Under his chain mail, he dripped with perspiration.

He wanted no part of this spoiled world of violence and hatred, where every man was out for himself. He had had his bellyful of it. He'd lost his appetite for revenge. There was no pleasure in it – he saw that now – nothing but shame and regret. In so little time he had lost so much, more than he could bear. But, worse still, he had stumbled into this world of violence, fire and hatred. He would rather experience profound sadness than this hellish nothingness.

Sick to his soul, he pulled his knees to his chest and hugged them close. The bitter taste of bile that lurked in the back of his throat brought back the darkness. It was the horrendous gloom that had visited him previously. Once again, it held him in its vice-like grip. The world was grey with smoke and misery, and he felt just as grey and bitter inside. He looked up imploringly towards the weary heavens obscured by thick black smoke. An onerous nothingness choked him half to death. Shut in on himself, he felt half dead already. There was nothing but agonising pain that filled the world. And he felt dreadfully lonely. He lashed at himself with his own contempt and bit his lip until it bled. If his life was so futile, he might as well abandon it now. He would rather die upon his own sword than at the hand of another. But at the instant he drew his sword to do the deed, a crippling curtain of sadness washed over him. A terrible aching took his throat and tore his heart in two. He was alive again and in white blinding pain.

Tears ran down his face but this time he did not berate himself for his display of emotion. The troubling darkness was lifting and he felt a rush of hope. The premature death of his father had robbed him of the opportunity to prove to his father that he was worthy. Suddenly he saw with sharp clarity, as though the scales had fallen from his eyes. And it dawned on him that he had been worthy all along. This was what the people who had truly loved him had always told him. Conjuring up his loved ones in his mind's eye brought them nearer to him and eased his pain. It was the depth of his feeling and his solicitude for the other that defined him. His pain was not weakness. Rather, it was strength.

He had lost the people who helped him to be the best man he could: his mother and Eleanor. While they were gone and he felt the pain of their absence keenly, he could still be the brave, honourable and worthy man he had always aspired to be. Winning battles with a sword was only half the story: they alone did not make a man either honourable or Godly. It was by his actions that God would judge him and how other men would remember him.

Whatever he could do to remedy the situation, he would do. He had to make amends and be the sensitive loving son in whom his mother had taken so much pride and the young man that Eleanor had loved. His path was clear now; he knew what he had to do. He had a cause to champion. The people of Dover needed his aid. Ultimately, he saw there was light and power in caring for another and that light banished the darkness.

～

The Song and the Sword

He wiped his tears away on the back of his sleeve and pulled himself to his feet. Far off, he could hear a woman's shrill cry of distress. As fast as his injured foot would permit him, he ran towards the sound. Down an insalubrious alley, a man rutted in the shadows over a limp form.

'No, I implore you!' cried a woman. Somewhere close by, a baby wailed.

But the man just lashed at the woman's face with his fist.

Hugh's mouth went dry. His blood boiled and his pulse quickened. There was no question. He had to act. He unsheathed his sword swiftly and lunged forward.

The man was caught unawares and staggered back into the dust. He recovered quickly and drew a long sword from a sheath at his waist. An ugly man with a black-jowled face, he had scant wispy black hair upon his head. Built like the gladiators of old, he had huge arms, his chest was like a barrel and he had the blunt hands of a wrestler. From beneath his blackened face, his eyes flashed with malice. He shot Hugh a gap-toothed smile – a queer, sick smile.

They sized each other up for an instant. Then the man lunged at Hugh with his long sword. The blades kissed with a clang of steel. The man had a strong wrist. He bore down upon Hugh with all his weight. But Hugh was nimble. He dodged from this way to that and matched the man thrust for thrust, parrying skilfully.

And then Hugh had the upper hand. The point of his sword was at the man's neck. The man sneered up at him and his lip curled in a snarl. Should Hugh show mercy and let this man go? He was a monster, but who was Hugh to play God. Suddenly, the decision was out of his hands. The man was on the point of stabbing him in the thigh and so he drove his sword point deep into the man's fleshy neck until a fountain of blood spurted out. The man twitched and gurgled his last few breaths.

Cowed like an animal, the woman huddled in a doorway shaking in fear.

'Perhaps I could escort you to the docks or to the safety of your family?' said Hugh gently.

His eyes were suddenly drawn to the woman. She had the most beautiful hazel eyes. With a thundering heart, he was sure he recognised her. It could not possibly be Eleanor! Eleanor was dead. Or was she?

'Eleanor!' He ran towards her. 'Eleanor is that you?'

27.

Reunited

The knight was calling her name – her *real* name! Eleanor's heart pounded. Who could possibly know her here?

'Eleanor!' called the knight, this time more urgently. The voice sounded familiar.

Then she recognised him and took in a sharp intake of breath. 'Hugh! How wonderful!' It felt indescribably good to see him again. He made a fine figure of a man, gallant and handsome in his chain mail.

'Is it really you?' He seized her hand and pulled her to her feet. 'You are alive. All these months I thought you dead!'

'I had to escape Rolf's violence. He would have

killed me and my baby given half a chance!' Eleanor looked down at the baby in her arms.

'What a monster!' He clenched his free fist in a flash of anger. He glanced down at Mary. 'So, this is your daughter.' A pair of big blue eyes smiled up at him from a smoke-blackened face. He reached out and caressed her head gently with his fingertips.

'Yes. This is Mary. My daughter.'

'She is as beautiful as her mother.' He gazed at her, a shy smile on his lips.

She blushed with pleasure.

'I praise God that you are alive.' He pulled her close. 'Ever since the night of the tournament, I have been berating myself for not going back to rescue you. However in the world did you get away from Rolf?'

'Rolf had me closely guarded night and day. I only got away by the skin of my teeth . . . in the dead of night . . . through the siege supply passage.'

'That was clever of you. Do you remember how we used to play hide and seek in the supply passages of your father's castle?'

They shared a conspiratorial smile at the memory. He squeezed her hand.

'And what did you do then?'

'I sought sanctuary at the Priory of St Mary. The precentor invited me to sing in the choir with the nuns and ancren.'

'I always said you had the voice of an angel.' He smiled again.

It was such a warm smile. How she had missed that smile!

'My voice proved to be a gift from God for I found work singing at a tavern in Dover. My father told me that you were betrothed to Lady Bethany. Did you get wed?'

'No.' He shook his head vigorously. 'I had no wish to marry her! When my mother died, I jumped at the chance to join Guy and his father on the crusade. When I learnt of your death and then my father's and brother's deaths in Messina, I was bent on revenge and desperate to return to England. Thank God, dearest love, for it brought me back to you!' Hugh kissed her hand. 'You have no notion of how long I have dreamed of being with you. At last God has answered my prayers!' He drew her closer, until her head rested upon his shoulder. 'I have always loved you, and only you.'

Her heart was in her throat. She had waited all her life to hear those words.

'And I love you!' She yielded to his insistent arms. They nestled close. Mary gave a little wriggle of delight, safe between them.

'I fear to let you go, lest you evaporate like an apparition.' He tightened his grip on her and drew her hard against him.

He bent and kissed her parted lips. It was an exquisite moment. She had never felt so safe or so happy.

He relinquished their kiss. 'We must away to safety. I have a boat. I will take us to one of your father's ships where we may get passage overseas. Have no fear. I have money. I still have my share of the spoils from the battle of Messina. We will get married and find a manor to live somewhere in Normandy.'

'That would be truly wonderful!' Tears of happiness ran down her cheeks.

~

He helped her into the small rowing boat. Never had anything ever felt so right in her life. As if by magic, a wonderful future had enfolded in front of them. Good things were finally going to happen. The sun beamed down on them.

'To think that out of such horrors we found each other again!' He pulled at the oars. 'God does work in mysterious ways!' He smiled and his eyes were merry. His beautiful warm smile filled her with joy.

'The world is good again.'

When at length they reached the ship, Hugh helped her climb up the rope ladder. On deck, the captain waited for payment. Hugh handed him a gold coin that bought them a cabin of their own for the journey.

Hugh left Eleanor and Mary in the cabin to wash the smoke off their hands and faces. How wonderful it was to be clean again. Shortly afterwards, he returned with an armful of fresh clothes and a hair-brush. Among the clothes was a kirtle made from salmon-coloured linen. It was fine enough to befit a lady. And it fitted her perfectly. Her heart danced to wear such beautiful clothes again. She brushed out her tangled hair until it shone. She changed little Mary into a pretty red dress too. The baby waved her arms around in delight. Hugh looked so handsome in a comely tunic of leather and a pair of fresh braies.

They went to find the ship's cook in the galley. She was starving, having not eaten since that morning. The cook served them a plate of salt herrings and a huge hunk of bread and they washed down their meal with goblets of good Gascon wine. Never had food tasted so delicious or the wine so sweet.

That evening, they strolled about the deck, hand in hand. Then they stopped and leaned on the rail and watched the sun sink slowly on the horizon. The ship had brooked no delay in departing for Normandy. They had left their old lives behind forever. The feel of his arms about her shoulders was sheer heaven, their gentle strength a sanctuary.

28.

Epilogue – Two Years Later

The last yellow petal of the day's sun sank low on the crimson horizon as Hugh sat on the veranda and sipped wine from his goblet. With a certain sense of satisfaction, he looked out over his vineyard where deep red grapes festooned row upon row of twisted vines.

Beside him, Eleanor sang to the baby cradled in her arms. Her lilting melody soothed their child and he gazed up at his mother mesmerised, his blue eyes unblinking, until his eyelids began to droop. Attentive, Mary stood at her mother's side and caressed the baby's head with a tiny hand. At two years old, she was the image of her mother, with the same shadowy hazel eyes and mane of chestnut hair.

Eleanor shifted her weight in the chair. It would

not be long until the child in her belly joined their brood. In the last light of the day her long hair glistened and her face radiated happiness.

Above Hugh's head, swifts flittered in and out of the rafters with twigs and leaves in preparation for nightfall. In the distance, on the crest of a hill, dark shapes moved. Presently, he discerned three riders kicking up a cloud of dust. He rose to get a better view and squinted into the dying sun. As the figures approached, he saw that at least two of them wore chain mail and bore the surcoats of crusaders.

As a precaution he ushered Eleanor and the children inside. He drew his sword from its leather sheath and tightened his belt, ready to defend his family.

The thud of hooves grew louder as the riders drew near. His heart gave a leap of joy when he recognised the banner of the Order of Our Lady that flapped from their standard. Sir Mordaunt and Guy were among them, their tousled blond hair unmistakable. A dark-haired and olive-skinned maiden mounted on a white palfrey accompanied them. Hugh quieted the baying hounds as best he could.

'Eleanor, come out, for it is Sir Mordaunt and Guy!'

Eleanor emerged from the house, the baby asleep in her arms and Mary clutching at her skirts.

'Hugh!' Guy reined in his white destrier and dismounted with a leap. There was a great gash across his forehead. His skin had grown dark and his hair was even blonder. 'It is so good to see you!'

They slapped each other on the back and hugged.

'It is wonderful to see you! How did you find us?'

'We made a stop at Baron Adelard's castle and he told us that you and Eleanor lived here.'

By now Sir Mordaunt had come to join them. As blond and dark as his son, he dismounted, hurried forward and pumped Hugh's hand. 'It pleases me greatly to find you settled! We thought Eleanor was dead!' He bowed and kissed Eleanor's hand. 'May I congratulate you both on your beautiful family!'

Eleanor smiled broadly.

'And who is this pretty child,' said Sir Mordaunt. 'She is the image of her beautiful mother!'

'This is Mary,' said Eleanor. 'And our youngest is Richard.'

'What a fine boy! He has his father's eyes.'

'Join us in a cup of wine,' said Hugh, 'for this reunion warrants a celebration!'

'Gladly,' said Guy. 'Before I do, I must introduce you to my bride, Rosa.' He helped his wife dismount. She was a slender, comely lady. Her hair gleamed and her eyes sparkled in the fading light.

'Welcome, Rosa.' Hugh smiled at Guy. 'My heart is glad that you too have found love and happiness. You must have had so many adventures. I cannot wait to hear all about them. Pray sit and tell us.' He lit several candles with a taper and settled them on the table and poured wine into goblets. 'Please make yourselves comfortable.'

With a creak of leather, Sir Mordaunt lowered himself into a chair. He took a sip of wine from the goblet Hugh offered him and took up the tale. 'After you left for England the king hatched a deal with King Tancred to free his sister and restore her dower. We remained in Messina until the spring when we set sail for Acre. Three days into our voyage, a storm scattered the fleet. When we landed in Crete, we discovered that some twenty-five ships had been lost, including the one carrying the king's fiancée. Later, it emerged that the self-proclaimed emperor of Cyprus had seized the ships and plundered the cargo.

'Stirred by the sound of trumpet and drum, we hacked our way through Cyprus. Awed by our might, the people of Cyprus fell deferentially to their knees.' He turned to Hugh. 'The last whimper of resistance snuffed out, we amassed a colossal fortune, of which we owe to you a share for the service you rendered our family.'

'I did what any man would have done,' said Hugh.

Sir Mordaunt shook his head. 'Don't sell yourself short! Without your part, I would have lost all that is dear to me and no amount of treasure could have restored it.'

'It was in Cyprus that I met my lovely bride,' said Guy. 'At the king's wedding no less!' He took Rosa's hand in his and they looked upon each other, and love blazed in their eyes.

'In July,' said Sir Mordaunt, 'we arrived in Acre to join a beleaguered crusader army who had besieged the city for two years. We found them reduced to eating horse entrails to stave off starvation. The skills of the Saracen archers were no match for our siege engines. Within a month, we breached the walls and the garrison capitulated.'

'What was Acre like?' asked Hugh.

'Unbelievably hot and humid,' said Guy. 'We sweltered under the date palms and sweated like pigs in our mail. Huge cockroaches scuttled through the crowded narrow streets and the city emitted a stench that could only be mitigated by a thick mist of perfume. The markets were a marvel to behold and sold a thousand spices and the sweetest figs, pomegranates and dates I have ever tasted. Knight Templars, merchants, assassins, beggars and slave traders thronged the streets. And thousands of whores. Sir Manard wiled away days of ease and nights of pleasure on plump cushions until he finally breathed his last in a brothel on the bosom of his favourite wench.'

Hugh laughed. 'He got what he always wanted, then.'

A shadow passed over Sir Mordaunt's face. 'There a shameful thing came to pass, for which I shall suffer pangs of conscience until the end of my days. When Saladin neglected to pay the ransom on his garrison, the king had all the men bar the commanders slaughtered – some two thousand soldiers. It pains me to say that many crusaders took great pleasure from the senseless bloodbath.'

'What was he like, the king?' asked Hugh.

'Our king was the beating heart of the crusaders,' said Guy. 'Before long, King Philip skulked home to

France with his tail between his legs. King Richard snatched the prize of Joppa for Christendom and inflicted heavy losses on Saladin's host.'

For a moment a flicker of battle-lust and thirst for adventure snuck into Hugh's heart, but one look at Eleanor and their children left him in no doubt that his proper place was by her side.

'You should have seen the crusader castles,' said Guy. 'Impenetrable fortresses with sheer walls and crammed with thousands of knights and squires from all over Christendom.'

'The time came for us to march to Jerusalem,' said Sir Mordaunt. 'Our road took us through an arid landscape riddled with venomous snakes and scorpions. The sun beat down on us without mercy and the vultures swooped overhead and screeched and waited for the next man to drop dead. Mounted Saracen archers lurked in the hills, like lethal stinging flies, and waited to converge close on us and pick us off only to take off on their swift-footed mounts when we tried to engage them. And many a time they lured us into ambushes where we lost hundreds of men.'

'Twice King Richard led us to Jerusalem,' said Guy. 'But Saracen sorties of wild men brandishing scimitars defended the city. Among the horde were fanatics who threw themselves upon our swords as though their lives meant nothing to them. Though we smote them down in droves, their sheer number made it impossible for our vanguard to win any ground. Weary of the incessant skirmishes, the king made a truce with

Saladin that gave us Acre and allowed us access to the sites of Christian pilgrimage.'

'And how did you find your way home?' asked Hugh.

'Before long,' said Guy, 'the king got wind of his brother John's attempts to seize the Angevin throne and connive with his enemy King Philip. He deemed the time ripe to return home. We sailed by way of the Adriatic Sea to avoid French hostility. A wild storm lashed at our fleet and a violent wind shredded our sail and we were thrown overboard. Thankfully, we caught hold of floating debris and the sailors hauled us back on deck. A week later, we made our way to harbour and continued our journey overland. Later we learned that the king was captured in Vienna and held ransom by Duke Leopold.'

'There is talk,' said Hugh, 'that, at his mother's behest, the money has been raised for the ransom.'

'This is good news,' said Sir Mordaunt. 'His duplicitous brother cannot be trusted to act on his behalf.'

'Now we must topple Baron Rolf!' said Guy.

Hugh stood up. 'There will be time enough for that by and by. This is a moment for celebration! Thank the heavens you both made it safely home. Now allow me to pour you another cup of wine!'

Guy's eyes flickered with amusement in his bronzed face. 'Gladly!'

And they all roared with laughter. Long into the night, the wine flowed, and the air rang with the joyful sounds of their merrymaking.

We hope you enjoyed reading

THE **SONG** AND THE
SWORD

Please leave a review wherever
you buy books online.

For more information about the
author check out her website:

www.IsabelleChevallot.com

🐦 @IChevallot

To join the mailing list for details
of events and new releases email:

IsabelleChevallot@icloud.com

Lightning Source UK Ltd.
Milton Keynes UK
UKHW011830150922
408931UK00004B/447